THE DISCOVERERS

Paul King

BANTAM BOOKS
NEW YORK • TORONTO • LONDON • SYDNEY • AUCKLAND

THE DISCOVERERS

A Bantam Book / July 1994

ISBN 0-553-29831-3

Published simultaneously in the United States and Canada

Bantam Books are published by Bantam Books, a division of Bantam
Doubleday Dell Publishing Group, Inc. Its trademark, consisting of the
words "Bantam Books" and the portrayal of a rooster, is Registered in
U.S. Patent and Trademark Office and in other countries. Marca Regis-
trada. Bantam Books, 1540 Broadway, New York, New York 10036.

PRINTED IN THE UNITED STATES OF AMERICA

RAD   0 9 8 7 6 5 4 3 2 1

CHAPTER 1

CONSTANTINOPLE, 1453

The huge cannon boomed with a thunder so loud that all who heard it quaked in fear. A flash of light and a cloud of smoke poured from the mouth of the cannon as a two-hundred-pound stone shot hurtled, black against the sky, toward the walls that surrounded the city. The heavy ball struck with terrible effect, knocking holes in the defenses, turning the mortice into powder, and shattering sections of the palisade, sending jagged wooden shards flying in every direction to strike down hapless victims.

"Ayiieee! We are all going to be killed! We must surrender! We must surrender! I don't want to die!" one of the Genoese defenders shouted. He stood and began to run along the top of the wall, screaming in terror, his nerves finally shattered by weeks of battle.

"Stop him! Someone stop that man!" Captain-General Giovanni Giustiniani shouted, pointing at the berserk soldier. Giustiniani was the commander of the Genoese element of the Christian defenders of Constantinople. "Someone pull him down!"

Giustiniani's warning came too late. With a whistling rush of wind, a Muslim longbowman's arrow made a hundred-yard flight to bury itself in the terrified defender's chest. Grabbing the arrow, the victim tried to pull it out, but he only succeeded in breaking it. He held the shaft in his hand and looked, as if surprised, at the blood that began pouring from the broken shaft still lodged in his chest. He stood there for a moment longer, then pitched forward, falling outside the wall.

An Islamic warrior, brandishing his curved scimitar and using the cover of heavy cannonading, dashed toward the wall to sever the head of the fallen Christian soldier. He started back toward his own lines, making the loud, distinctive ululation of victory. He was almost to safety when the arrow of a Christian crossbowman found its mark and sent him sprawling facedown in the sunbaked, blood-soaked dirt. The slain Christian's severed head rolled like a ball from the fallen Muslim's hand.

For two months now the mighty Islamic army of Mohammed II had been laying siege against the badly outnumbered defenders of Constantinople. Never before had such powerful engines of war been used in battle. Every day the Turks bombarded the city with frightful effect. Every night, as the Christians worked desperately to repair the walls damaged by the day's heavy cannonade, bonfires burned brightly in the Turkish camp. The Sultan's warriors were using the firelight to build new firing platforms even closer to the palisade so that they might move their cannons and ballistae inexorably forward.

Then, on the fifty-third day of the siege, the Sultan rode through the sprawling camp of his huge army to announce that the final great attack against Constantinople would take place very soon. He promised his soldiers of the Faith that after the fall of the city, in accordance with the customs of Islam, they would be allowed three days of unrestricted sacking and pillaging.

"All treasure found in the city will be fairly distributed among my faithful warriors," the Sultan declared.

The proclamation was met with a shout of jubilation: "There is no God but Allah, and Mohammed is His Prophet!"

That night the Sultan's army was in a state of high

excitement, shouting and singing to the music of pipes and ouds. Then, at midnight, their celebration abruptly ceased, and all the fires were extinguished. The Sultan had commanded that the soldiers prepare themselves for the battle to come with one full day of rest and atonement.

The next day, for the first time since the siege began, stillness reigned outside the walls. The great cannons were silent; there were no shouts of challenge and no barrages of flying arrows. Some inside the walled city even expressed hope that the Turks had conceded and were now getting ready to withdraw.

But most knew better. Most understood that the moment of truth had finally arrived. That night the soldiers kept particular watch and strengthened the defenses against the final onslaught. However, as only the engineers and a few guards were needed for this task, Captain-General Giustiniani released the rest of his men long enough to join with the people of Constantinople in one last great outpouring of piety.

Almost as if in open defiance of the Prophet, who according to legend hated the sound of bells, the chimes of every church in Constantinople began to peal. Against this resonating background the faithful Christians began their procession through the city's streets, bearing upon their shoulders the icons and relics of their religion. They passed along the length of the wall, pausing to invoke the blessings of all the saints upon those spots where the Turkish bombards had done the most damage. Those in the procession, Greeks and Italians, Orthodox and Catholic, sang hymns and repeated the kyrie eleison as they paraded through the city, winding up in the Church of Holy Wisdom.

Among the Italian defenders of Constantinople were Venetians and Genoese. These two city-states, both maritime powers, had put aside their age-old enmity long enough to come to the aid of Christendom's easternmost citadel. And though many of the Italians were truly motivated by the holiness of their mission, it was not insignificant that the fall of Constantinople would give the Muslims undisputed control of the eastern Mediterranean

and the Black Sea—a disaster that would cut off the trade
that had made Venice and Genoa wealthy.

After the procession of the defenders through the city,
Emperor Constantine arrived at the church, along with his
courtiers, senators, and archons, all arranged according to
their rank and position.

The Venetian Council of Twelve was there, as were
the Venetian nobles. They, like the Emperor and his court,
were dressed in ceremonial silks and velvets. Giovanni
Giustiniani, the captain-general of the Genoese forces,
came with his officers. The military men were fresh from
the ramparts, and many wore the gleaming armor of
soldiers and sailors of high rank.

The crowd of worshipers was swelled by huge numbers of Constantinople's ordinary citizens, those from the
middleclass down to servants and slaves. Their homespun
clothes were mingled with the colorful garb of the highborn.

It had been five months since many of the more pious
Greeks had attended mass, because they believed that in
the union of the Eastern and Western churches the liturgy
had been defiled by the Latins and renegades. On this
evening, however, the only people absent were those defending the city wall. Priests who had previously maintained that the union of the Orthodox Church with Rome
was a mortal sin now came to the altar to administer communion alongside their Catholic brothers. The cardinal
was there with bishops who had not previously acknowledged his authority. Everyone made confession or took
communion, without regard as to whether the bread was
leavened or unleavened, not caring whether it was admin-
istered by Orthodox or Latin. The images of Christ and
His saints looked down upon the worshipers as the priests
in their splendid vestments moved through the solemn
rhythm of the liturgy.

All present confessed their sins in a murmuring
chorus. Some said the words in Latin:

> "*Comfietor Deo omnipotenti, beatae Mariae
> semper Virgini, beato Michaeli Archangelo, beato*

Joanni Baptistae, sanctis Apostolis Petro et Paulo, omnibus sanctis, et tibi, pater, quia peccavi nimis cogitatione, verbo et opere: mea culpa, mea culpa, mea maxima culpa. Ideo precor beatam Mariam semper Virginem, beatum Michaelem Archangelum, beatum Joannem Baptistam, sanctos Apostolos Petrum et Paulu, omnes Sanctos, et te, pater, orare pro me ad Dominum Deum nostrum."

Others spoke in Greek.

Everyone heard the same words, regardless of language:

"I confess to almighty God, to blessed Mary ever virgin, to blessed Michael the archangel, to blessed John the Baptist, to the holy apostles Peter and Paul, to all the saints, and to you, Father, that I have sinned exceedingly in thought, word, and deed, through my fault, through my fault, through my most grievous fault. Therefore I beseech blessed Mary ever virgin, blessed Michael the archangel, blessed John the Baptist, the holy apostles Peter and Paul, all the saints, and you, Father, to pray to the Lord our God for me."

One of those making confession in Latin was a young Genoese, Giovanni Ruggi. A sailor rather than a soldier, Giovanni was one of the many who had been taken from their ships two months earlier and put on the palisade to strengthen the defenses.

Standing beside Giovanni and making her confession in Greek was Iole Zarous, the daughter of the merchant in whose house Giovanni was being quartered. Soon after his arrival Giovanni and Iole had become lovers, this despite the enmity often found between Greeks and Genoese and despite Iole's father having spoken out against it. But with Constantinople in its last hours, Zarous seemed less inclined to interfere with his daughter's happiness, however brief it might be, and he had made no protest tonight as he watched his daughter and the young foreign defender leave his house and join the procession to walk hand in hand to the church.

Now, standing in the nave of the church during communion, Giovanni and Iole shared a tiny crumb of the sacred Body of Christ and declared to each other, in this holy assembly, that their love was eternal. Giovanni took something from his pocket and held it out to Iole. It flashed in the light of the thousand candles, glowing as if it were made of candlelight itself.

"Let this be a pledge of my love for you," he said, fastening the clasp around her neck.

"Oh! It is a chain of gold!" Iole said, holding it up between her thumb and forefinger to examine its beauty. She looked at Giovanni with eyes sparkling with joy and wonder. "But no, Giovanni, how can I accept such a marvelous gift? It must have cost a fortune!" She reached around to the clasp to remove it.

"Had I seven fortunes, I would give them all to you," Giovanni replied, putting his hands on hers to stop her from removing the chain. "Please, you must keep it. Don't you like it?"

"I have never seen anything so beautiful."

"Then you will not take it off?"

Iole smiled up at him. "It will stay around my neck until the day I die," she promised solemnly.

"Citizens, behold!" someone shouted. "The Emperor speaks!"

Emperor Constantine moved down to the transept crossing, and as the people began to gather around him, he addressed them:

"My friends," he said, his voice trembling despite his attempt at composure, "you have heard the roar of the huge cannon that the Turks have employed against us. You have seen the damage their mighty engines of war have inflicted upon our walls. You are aware of the vast army lying just outside our gates. And yet, despite all that, the Turks will not prevail, for we have God and our Savior.

"My loyal Greek countrymen, you know that a man should always be ready to die for his faith or for his country or for his family or for his sovereign. But I say to you now that you must be prepared to die for all four causes. For is there a man among you who doubts the perfidy of the infidel Sultan who has brought on this war to destroy the true faith and to install his false prophet in the seat of Christ?

"And you Italians, gathered here in this great and noble cause, know you now that one hundred, nay, *five* hundred years hence, men will write stories and women will sing songs of your faith and your courage.

"To all I say: Let our spirits be high. Be brave and steadfast. For with the help of God, we *will* be victorious!"

"Soldiers, sailors, warriors for Christ!" Giovanni Giustiniani shouted. "We will never surrender to the Turks!"

The cheers of the military were joined by those of the citizens. The sounds of defiance still echoing from the mosaic ceilings of the enormous domed church, the great carved doors were thrown open, and the worshipers began to leave, returning to their homes or duty stations.

As Giovanni Ruggi and Iole Zarous walked through the night, their way was guided by golden patches of candlelight spilling through windows. Overhead, the vaulting darkness was filled with brilliant stars, some so large and bright that it seemed as if Giovanni could reach up and pluck one down. Countless others, not as brilliant, dusted the blackness with what seemed to be luminous powder.

"Why must you go back to the wall?" Iole asked. It was not the first time she had posed the question.

"You know why," Giovanni answered. "To defend against the infidel."

"Infidel or heretic, what does it matter? Some in our city say better a Sultan's turban than a Pope's miter," Iole said.

"Surely you can't believe there is no difference between the Holy Father in Rome and the Sultan!"

"The Sultan threatens our religion less than the Pope," Iole insisted. "In the cities already under his control the Greek priests are free to serve the Christians and without defiling the liturgy. Only the bells are forbidden. The Turks never molest the poor people so long as they pay their tributes. And it is said that the tributes paid to the Sultan are less than the taxes imposed by the Emperor."

Giovanni stiffened. "Iole, why do you talk so? That is the talk of a defeatist."

"It is the talk of reason," Iole insisted. "If the Emperor and the Latins have their way, the city will be sacked and our people slaughtered."

"What would you have us do? Throw open the gates to the invaders?"

"Yes! It is known that the Koran says a people who surrender shall be shown mercy."

"Mercy? I would rather die at my post than throw myself upon the mercy of the Turks!"

Iole began to weep. "But, Giovanni, that is exactly what will happen. You *will* die at your post, and so will thousands of others—not only the soldiers who defend us, but the citizens of the city as well. And for what? To defend the Emperor and the Pope?"

Trumpets sounded, calling the defenders back to the wall. Giovanni turned to Iole and put his hands on her shoulders. "Beloved, I must go now."

"You go to die," Iole said.

"If so, I have the Church's promise that I will be taken directly into heaven. And with the life I've led, that sounds like a good bargain," Giovanni said, smiling and trying to make light of it.

"I am serious," Iole said. "If you go to the wall now, you will die. Come with me. Wait in my house with me. When the city falls, we will throw open the doors and invite in the Muslims. They will not harm us."

"No! Hide from them! Do not let them in!" Giovanni pleaded. "They will be drunk with bloodlust. Do you really think they will follow the teachings of the Koran? Those who surrender to them will be surrendering their lives."

The trumpets sounded a second call, and Giovanni, feeling like an animal caught in a trap, looked toward the wall. "I must go," he said. "But promise me—please, promise me!—you won't surrender yourself to the Turks. You'll hide until they are gone."

"If you insist," Iole said. "But if you are killed, my fate will not matter to me. I would not want to live."

"I won't be killed," Giovanni said. He pulled her to

him and smelled the scent of flowers in her hair. "I promise you, I will not be killed. A soldier knows such things."

"I love you," Iole said.

"I will come for you, my darling," Giovanni vowed. "Win or lose, after the battle, I will come for you. I will take you with me. Promise me you'll wait for me."

. "I will be there for you."

"You, sailor! Did you not hear the trumpets?" a passing officer shouted.

"I'm coming!" Giovanni replied.

He broke the embrace, walking away to join the others. But Iole reached for him and he reached back. Their hands joined a moment longer; then they slipped apart until only their fingertips touched. Even through that tiny connection Giovanni could feel the love, and the anguish, of his beautiful Iole.

"Now, sailor!" the officer ordered. "Your comrades need you."

"I will come for you, Iole!" Giovanni shouted the promise over his shoulder. "Wait for me!"

"I love you, Giovanni! I love you!" Iole called.

Giovanni started running toward the wall. When he reached the end of the street he turned for one last look back and saw Iole still standing in the patch of light, her hand still extended toward him as if she could draw him back to her.

A double line of walls surrounded the city. Those who were to defend the outer palisade would take their places, then have the sally ports of the inner wall locked behind them—ensuring that they would fight until they fell. It was being said of those on the outer wall that they were now without sin. Giovanni Ruggi was one of those who took his position there.

Suddenly the Turkish camp, which had been quiet for so long, exploded with a horrifying noise. For as far as Giovanni could see in either direction around the wall, raging Turks were rushing in with their attack, screaming battle cries, while drums, trumpets, and flutes added to the din.

All over Constantinople church bells began to peal in

a prearranged signal that the attack had come, though such was the noise of the fighting that the signal was scarcely needed. The defenders on the walls prepared to meet the enemy, while inside the city, old people, women, and children crowded the churches.

Giovanni fitted a bolt into his crossbow and watched as the mass of shrieking humanity surged toward the wall. Spotting one particularly large fellow brandishing a scimitar over his head and shouting encouragement to those around him, the Genoese raised the bow to his shoulders, took aim, then shot. He followed the flight of his bolt and saw it plunge into the big man's neck. The man dropped his scimitar and put his hands up to the wound, clutching at the bolt, trying to pull it out. Blood spilled between his fingers, and then he pitched forward.

"Fight for Christendom!" an officer near Giovanni shouted, but his rallying cry was cut off by an arrow that had been loosed by a longbowman from within the ranks of the attackers.

Giovanni shot again, but he let out a curse of frustration when he saw this bolt harmlessly hit the ground.

Leading the Turkish attack were the bashi-bazouks, the Sultan's irregular troops. There were thousands of them, including many from Christian Europe, such as Slavs, Hungarians, Germans, and even a few Italians and Greeks. These men of no scruples were willing to fight against their fellow Christians for the money the Sultan paid them.

Behind the bashi-bazouks were the janissaries, the Sultan's most elite forces and his own personal guard. Their purpose in this attack was to keep the mercenary bashi-bazouks from retreating.

The bashi-bazouks were handicapped by their numbers. There were so many of them that they got in each other's way, and as they bunched up against the bottom of the wall, they were easily killed by stones, bolts from crossbows, and Greek fire.

"Giovanni, the ladder!" someone shouted, and Giovanni looked over to see a red-bearded man just reaching the top of a scaling ladder. Grabbing a lance, Giovanni thrust it into the man's chest; then he and two of his comrades took hold of the shaft and pushed hard, propelling the ladder backward and disposing of three other attackers with it.

"Swordsmen! We need swordsmen here!" Giovanni shouted, and a handful of men brandishing sabers answered his call, rushing along the top of the wall, stepping over the bodies already littering the walkways. They hacked and stabbed at the scaling attackers as each new threat was presented.

The fierce fighting continued for two hours before the bashi-bazouks were allowed to withdraw. At first the defenders actually thought they had been victorious, and a few even started to cheer.

"Hold your cheers," Giovanni said, wiping the sweat from his face and pointing toward the hill across from the Civil Gate of Saint Romanus. His comrades, seeing what Giovanni was seeing, groaned; a few began to weep.

A second attack was suddenly launched, this one by the Anatolian guards—a much larger army, better uniformed, better disciplined, and better armed than the bashi-bazouks had been. Cannons boomed, and the walls trembled and shattered under the assault. A large hole was opened, and the Anatolians began to pour through.

"To the defense!" someone shouted, and Giovanni jumped down from his position on the palisade and joined the other Christians who had gathered at the breach in the wall. The Anatolians coming through were slaughtered by the score and eventually beaten back.

When the Anatolian attack was defeated, the Sultan brought forth his own guard, the janissaries. If these most elite regiments of his army were also beaten back, the siege would fail, and the Turks would have no choice but to withdraw.

The beautifully uniformed janissaries moved in, pelted by arrows, stones, javelins, and shot. Despite the hail of missiles launched toward them, their ranks remained unbroken. Wave after wave of the powerful soldiers rushed up to the walls, tearing at the stones with their bare hands and hacking at the beams that supported them.

The battle continued for over an hour, with the janissaries unable to make any headway. By now the Christians had been fighting for over four hours without so much as a moment's respite. Giovanni felt his muscles aching and his breath coming in ragged gasps, but he knew he couldn't rest; if he did, it would be the end.

He saw one of the Turks raise a firearm, and he reached for a bolt to load his crossbow, only to discover that his quiver was empty. A half-full quiver was on the body of a soldier beside him, so he dropped to one knee to take out one of the missiles. As he loaded his crossbow, the Turk discharged his gun. There was a flash of light, a puff of smoke, and a loud bang, and then the ball whizzed by Giovanni's ear. He heard it hit something—or someone—just behind him. At that same moment he was able to raise his crossbow and shoot. When he saw his bolt plunge deep into the Turk's chest, he let out a small cry of victory.

"Friend, I am shot," he heard someone say, and when Giovanni turned to see who had spoken to him, he gasped in alarm.

Captain-General Giustiniani was standing just behind him, weaving back and forth. The Turk's ball had struck the Genoese commander. Giovanni groaned in anguished frustration. If his quiver had not been empty—if he had been a second faster in getting off his shot—this would not have happened.

"We need help here!" Giovanni shouted. "Call for a surgeon! The commander has been hurt!"

Giustiniani sank slowly to the ground, then pulled his hand away from the wound and looked at the blood pooled in his palm. He coughed, and more blood oozed from his mouth. He looked up at Giovanni and smiled sadly.

"I fear there is little a surgeon can do for me now, my brave fellow," he said. "I am done for."

"It is my fault. I should have shot the Turk more quickly," Giovanni said, despairing.

Giustiniani started to laugh, and again he spewed out

blood. "Do not berate yourself. You killed him. I can die happy now, knowing that my slayer has already died."

One of Giustiniani's bodyguards knelt beside his commander, examined him for a second, then looked up. "He cannot stay here. We must get him away from the field of battle."

"How are we to do so?" another asked. "The inner gate is locked. We're trapped on the outer wall."

"No, we aren't."

"You know a way we can get out of here?"

The soldier grinned broadly and held up a key. "A good soldier is always prepared. Let's get him out of here."

Giovanni watched as they carried the wounded commander toward the locked gate. After they opened it, they made no effort to close it again, and a few other defenders decided to leave, then others still, until suddenly a mad rush of Genoese soldiers was pouring through the gate and fleeing the battle, running through the streets of the city toward the harbor.

"Wait!" Giovanni shouted to them. "Wait, stand here with me! Victory is nearly ours! We only need to beat them back one more time!"

Giovanni reached for one of the soldiers, intending to grab him and hold him fast, but no sooner did he get his hand on the soldier's arm than there was a sudden burst of color and light before his eyes as something crashed into the back of his head. He went down.

The sun was three disks above the horizon when Giovanni regained consciousness. There was an ache in the back of his head and the smell of death in his nostrils, and he tried to decide if he was dead or alive. When he reached the conclusion that he was still alive, he opened his eyes and saw that he was lying on the ground between the two palisades, surrounded by bodies of attackers and defenders alike. For a moment he wondered how he had survived, and then he realized that he must have been taken for dead.

He heard a man scream, then a loud cackling laugh.

"God is good! Praise be to Allah!" someone shouted, and the shout came not from outside the walls as they had for the last six weeks, but from inside. Giovanni knew then that Muslims were inside Constantinople. The battle was over and the Turks had won.

He heard a couple of thumping sounds nearby and, very cautiously, he turned to see what it was. A Turk *tsaush* dressed in a green cloak and white turban was walking through the bodies, like Satan's acolyte, swinging a scimitar and lopping off the heads of the Christians, whether they were dead or wounded. Other than an occasional twitch from the wounded, the Turk assassin, who was calmly eating an apple as he made his gruesome rounds, was the only one moving in this place of the dead.

Slowly, quietly, Giovanni felt around on the ground beside him, looking for his crossbow. He found it, then found a bolt that he fit into the slot. He pulled the string back, engaged the trigger, then sat up and took aim.

The *tsaush*, who had just severed another head, sensed the movement behind him and turned toward Giovanni. The Turk was holding the bloody scimitar in one hand and the severed head, by its hair, in the other. The apple was clamped by his teeth. When he saw the crossbow aimed at him, his eyes opened wide in terror and he tried to shout, but the apple restricted the sound, and it came out no louder than a surprised gurgle.

Giovanni loosed the bolt, and it whirred across the space between them in an instant, burying itself in one of the Turk's eyes, spilling blood and brain matter down his cheek and onto the apple still clamped in his mouth. Silently, the Turk fell flat on his back, his arms flung out to each side, the bloody scimitar going one way and the just-severed head the other.

Quickly, Giovanni went over to him and stripped him of his cloak and turban. A moment later he was dressed as the Turk had been, and, so disguised, walked through the gate, still open from when the Genoese had taken Giustiniani from the field.

Giovanni cautiously moved through the streets of Constantinople. The victorious Turks were availing themselves of the three days of unrestrained looting, butchery, and rape the Sultan had promised them. The streets were awash with blood and lined on both sides with headless bodies. His ears were filled with the lamentations and wails of hapless citizens.

Down an alley he heard a young girl scream. When he looked in that direction, he saw that two of the Sultan's soldiers had grabbed her, while a third was ripping off her clothes. When one of the soldiers saw him he shouted out,

"Brother, come and enjoy her with us!"

Giovanni waved them off.

"What is wrong with him?" one of the soldiers asked.

"Perhaps, like our Sultan, he prefers beautiful young boys."

One of the rapists laughed. "My choice is beautiful young *girls*. Like this one. God is good!"

Giovanni hurried on through the streets, leaving the young girl to her fate. He knew there was nothing he could do for her. Besides, he had to find Iole. Even now the Italian ships in the harbor were filling with evacuees, and Giovanni planned to be on board one of them—but not until he had Iole with him.

A pall of smoke hung over the city from burning houses, many of which had been torched by the fleeing Italians, partly to deny the Turks the fruits of their victory and partly lashing out in a blind rage at the Greeks they had come to help but had grown to despise.

The Turks were not to be denied, however. Even now, wagons so full with plunder they were overflowing hauled away Constantinople's treasures as the victorious warriors systematically went through the city, quarter by quarter and house by house.

Giovanni's luck held; he continued unrecognized as wagon after wagon lumbered by and as he encountered roving bands of looters. He moved with a singularity of purpose, heading for the Zarous house, which was on a side street very near the Hippodrome.

At first Giovanni was afraid that no one had escaped the rape and plunder, but when he reached the Zarouses' street, he began to feel more hopeful. Their street was amazingly free of Turks; in fact, he had not seen a single one since leaving the hippodrome. Only Italians were evident.

His heart skipped a beat, and he almost shouted for joy; he wasn't too late!

Then the Zarous house came into view, and he stopped short, stunned. It had already been looted. Furniture had been thrown through the windows, and the spitted, mutilated bodies of the family and their servants lay in the street.

"But no! How can this be?" he said aloud. Then, with a cry of rage and pain, he saw Iole. Her beautiful hair was full of blood and her throat was cut. Flies were crawling through the wound, in and out of her mouth, and across her half-open, unseeing eyes.

"Iole!" he screamed, and there was more anguish in the word than in all the cries and all the words he had ever uttered until that very moment.

"Who are you?" a man beside him asked in Venetian-accented Italian. The man who spoke had an ugly scar, like a flash of purple lightning, across his right cheek. He was wearing a thick gold chain—the very chain Giovanni had given Iole.

Suddenly Giovanni realized the horrible truth. It was not Turks who had done this—it was Italians! Italians who even now were stuffing their clothes with valuables.

"*Bastards!*" Giovanni shrieked, rushing toward them. He was armed only with anger and courage, for though he had taken the cloak and turban of the *tsaush*, he had not taken the scimitar.

The leader of the looters had time only to raise his sword, but not time enough to bring the blade around. As a result he could only use the heavy hilt, but that was enough, given Giovanni's already weakened condition, to knock Giovanni out. He went down and the leader raised his sword. He was about to administer the death blow when a troop of the Sultan's janissaries came charging down the street.

Spotting them, the leader of the Venetians lowered

his sword, grabbed a golden candlestick and a silver goblet, then shouted to the others, "Let's get out of here!"

The janissaries, seeing a figure they believed to be one of their own lying in the courtyard, passed Giovanni by, giving chase instead to the Venetians.

It was dark when Giovanni came to again. Slowly, painfully, he got to his hands and knees, where he stayed until his head was somewhat clearer, then stood up. He nearly passed out again and had to grab the gatepost to support himself.

From the loud shouts, the praising of Allah, and the occasional screams, Giovanni knew that the looting was continuing. He heard the clatter of iron-shod hooves on cobblestones and raised his head to see three mounted warriors galloping by.

One of them was swinging a severed head shouting, "Behold the head of the Emperor! Know before Allah that I, Mehdi Jamshidi, have done this deed! Behold, the head of Emperor Constantine!"

Giovanni took one last look at the Zarous family, lying dead in their courtyard, master and servant together, the class gap that had separated them for a lifetime now closed by death. Pulling himself up, clutching the Turkish cloak about him, he started for the waterfront.

Dying shrieks and triumphant yells rose from all about him, from house and street, as he worked his way toward the harbor. Looters dashed by displaying their treasure, too intoxicated by their victory to even notice him. In many cases the Turks had already begun battling among themselves, killing each other in fights over women. Meanwhile, dervishes were working themselves up into a religious frenzy, killing and mutilating the Greek slaves who refused to acknowledge the Prophet. The headless bodies had grown drastically in number since earlier that day, and they were now stacked up in piles on both sides of the street.

The wounded cried for Allah to be merciful. Only Allah's name was invoked because only Muslims were

wounded. Christians were dead. When not crying to Allah,
the wounded cried for water. They were being attended by
a few of their own surgeons and by several old Greek nuns,
who because of their age and lack of beauty had not caught
their captors' eyes. Giovanni took in such details as, in
staggering lurches and limping steps, he continued to work
his way through the city toward the docks.

Finally he reached his goal, and he stood on a pier,
looking out at the Bosporus. The water was dotted with the
heads of desperate swimmers paddling from Christian ship
to Christian ship, begging to be taken aboard. Some few
were being rescued; many others were being beaten off
with oars and swords.

"They won't be able to get away," a Greek businessman, standing on the edge of the pier, said. In a hand
stained with blood he was clutching a small leather pouch
of coins.

"What did you say?" Giovanni asked. He had since
shed the Turkish cloak and now stood on the dock as what
he was: a wounded, defeated Genoese sailor.

The Greek turned and looked at Giovanni. Perhaps at
one time he would have been filled with admiration for
Giovanni and other Italians like him for coming to the aid
of Constantinople. Perhaps more recently, maybe even as
recently as that day, the Greek would have hated Giovanni
and the others for abandoning the people they had come to
defend. But Giovanni saw nothing in the Greek's face—
not admiration, not hate, not fear, not even sorrow. It was
as if the cataclysmic events of the last several days had
never happened, and the Greek was merely making an
observation, like commenting on the weather.

"I said they won't be able to get away," the man repeated. He pointed to the opening of the harbor. "The
Turks have stretched a boom across the mouth. They figure
it will hold the ships trapped in the harbor until they are
through sacking the city." He held up his pouch of money,
jingling the coins inside. "I am told the ships will take only
those passengers who can pay their way. Well, I can pay
my way—but what is the use? They won't escape."

One of the Venetian galleys started across the harbor

just then, heading for the mouth of the bay, leaving a long, rolling wake behind it. Its speed came from the sixty-six men on the long sweeps who, responding to the coxswain's drum, were rowing at twenty-six beats a minute. The galley hit the boom, then, with a shudder, bounced back. Two of the crewmen leapt forward with axes, however, and within minutes the boom had been chopped in two. The harbor was open.

The Genoese ships abruptly weighed anchor to get under way, and Giovanni recognized his own vessel among them. Diving into the water, he began swimming toward it. He managed to grab hold of a dangling rope as the ship passed by and started to climb up. One of the sailors, spotting him, ran toward him with a long pole, intending to shove him off.

But another recognized him and called out, "No, wait! It is Giovanni Ruggi! He is one of our own! Let him come aboard!"

Willing hands then reached down to grab hold of the exhausted Giovanni, who gratefully accepted their help. Once aboard, he looked over toward the canopy that was spread over the high poop and saw that someone was lying on a pallet underneath, being attended by a half-dozen solemn-faced men. He walked toward the wounded man and saw that it was Captain-General Giustiniani. Giustiniani, recognizing Giovanni, smiled sadly.

"You are the young man who killed the man who killed me, aren't you?" he said.

Giovanni came to attention, bowing his head slightly. "But you aren't dead," he said. "And I pray for your survival."

Giustiniani coughed up a clot of blood. The surgeons wiped his mouth and fanned the flames of the incense burner, then held the incense under his nose.

"Get that damned thing away," Giustiniani ordered, waving his hand weakly.

"But Your Excellency, you must give the healing vapors an opportunity to work," one of the surgeons insisted.

"Don't be an idiot," Giustiniani growled. He looked at Giovanni again. "You, sailor, what is your name?"

"Giovanni Ruggi."

"I am glad you escaped, Giovanni Ruggi. You were the bravest and best of all my men."

"Thank you, Your Excellency," Giovanni said, keeping his head bowed.

"Please leave now," one of the surgeons ordered. "He is much too badly hurt to be talking to you."

"Damn the Sultan," one of the other surgeons said. "I will pray every night for the rest of my life for God to strike him dead."

Giovanni returned to the rail and looked back at the flames and the carnage of the murdered city as it slipped behind them. Let the others damn the Sultan and pray for his death; what the Sultan and his soldiers did were acts of war. But the scarred Venetian wearing Iole's stolen golden chain had committed murder, and he was the one whose death Giovanni craved.

"I will find you," Giovanni vowed through clenched teeth, staring at what was left of Constantinople and seeing the face of his enemy. "I will find you, and I will kill you."

CHAPTER 2

VENICE

Aldo Cavalli stood at the window of the warehouse of the House of Cavalli, looking out across St. Mark's Canal. Sitting on a high stool behind the young man, bent over the record books and wearing a pair of leather-rimmed eyeglasses low on his nose, Leonardo Ippolito, the *fattóre* of the House of Cavalli, was reviewing the figures Aldo had entered into the ledger. He was the third generation of Ippolitos who had kept books for the House of Cavalli.

Aldo's interest was not in the numbers. He found ledgers, bookkeeping—in fact, the banking business in general—very boring. He would much rather have been outside, and as Ippolito checked on Aldo's figures, the youth watched the billowing, luminous clouds scudding across the blue July sky. The clouds were huge, making even the most imposing buildings in Venice look small. They cast bluish shadows over the rippling surface of the water, across the graceful curves of the gondolas, and upon the furled sails and gilded prows of the merchant galleys.

"Messer Aldo?" the manager said.

Aldo was so lost in his thoughts that he did not hear Ippolito call him. *Out there is where I should be*, he thought as he watched one of the galleys slipping by, the oars dipping and lifting as it passed the customs house at the end of the point, heading out to sea. *I should be one of the* balestrièri della poppa. Bowman of the quarterdeck was a position traditionally occupied by young Venetian noblemen when it came time for them to spread their wings. Aldo Cavalli was fifteen now, certainly old enough to spread *his* wings. And he was the son of Sandro Cavalli, head of the Ca' di Cavalli. That certainly qualified him as a nobleman, for the House of Cavalli was one of the biggest and most successful trading houses in all of Venice.

Unfortunately, the fall of Constantinople had disrupted shipping schedules, creating fierce competition for the reduced number of places for young noblemen as crossbowmen on the great galleys. Though the House of Cavalli was still doing a brisk business, Aldo knew that his father preferred not to send him out with one of his own ships. As the owner's son, Aldo would get preferential treatment and be protected from hardships. Sandro felt that such a shielded education would be no education at all.

"Messer Aldo," Leonardo Ippolito called again.

Aldo turned. "I'm sorry, Ser Ippolito. Did you speak?"

Ippolito chuckled. "I was merely going to congratulate you on the accuracy of your numbers. You did an excellent job in balancing the books. Your father will be very proud of you."

"Yes, I suppose so," Aldo replied, almost as an aside. Realizing how condescending his response must have sounded, he apologized. "I'm sorry, Ser Ippolito. It's just that my mind is elsewhere."

Ippolito nodded. "I know where your mind is, Messer Aldo. It is on the quarterdeck of that galley. You don't fool me any more than you fool your father."

"My mind is there, and I should be, too," Aldo insisted. "Why does my father make me stay here? Doesn't he realize that I am old enough and big enough and strong enough to take my rightful place on one of the galleys?"

"In due time, Messer Aldo," Ippolito replied. "That

will come in due time. Don't forget, your father was a man of adventure himself. He knows much about such things."

"If he knows, then why does he punish me so?"

"Messer Aldo, forgive me, but you are not being fair. I would hardly call learning to administer a large and successful business like the House of Cavalli punishment," Ippolito said dryly. "Especially now. The fall of Constantinople has delivered most other Venetian businesses into extremely severe circumstances, but due to your father's wise management and clever diversification, your family's business is riding out the storm." He pointed back to the ledger. "But that isn't something I need tell you. I am sure you have reached the same conclusion as a result of your own bookkeeping."

"Yes, yes, I know the business is doing well," Aldo said. "And I know that it's due to my father's management. Still, that doesn't make me any less anxious for a bit of adventure."

"I predict that the day will come when you will have as much adventure as you could want," Ippolito said. "In the meantime, you would do well to learn all the intricacies of the trading business."

"Is there more for me to do today?" Aldo asked.

Ippolito smiled. "No more today. You need some time for yourself. Too many numbers can make you blind."

"Even if I go blind, I will never wear anything like those," Aldo teased, pointing.

"What is wrong with my spectacles?" Ippolito replied, holding them up to admire them. "Why, we Venetians make the best eyeglasses in the world. They form a major part of every ship's cargo."

"I know. Have I not made all the entries?" Aldo stretched, then scratched. "If my father comes—"

"I will tell him you have finished all your work," Ippolito promised.

"Thank you, Ser Ippolito," Aldo said with a grin. He put on his hat, so floppy that the back of it was almost as long as his shoulder-length hair, and left the counting room as quickly as he could.

Outside the warehouse Aldo paused for a moment,

adjusting to the brightness of the day. He was a tall, graceful youth, still too young for the robe, but elegantly dressed nevertheless in bright green hose and a fashionably tight tunic that showed off his broad shoulders and narrow waist. Because he was under twenty-five, he was required to wear the *calar stola*, the strip of blue cloth hanging from his shoulder, but like most self-respecting youths he kept it rolled up and thrown over his arm. His belt had but a few inexpensive jewels and cost well below the twenty-five-ducat legal limit for his age group. The Cavallis were not a showy family.

Standing outside the warehouse, Aldo smelled the lure of salt water, and he meandered toward the waterfront. His route took him through a run-down district, one that stank of fish and rotting vegetables nearly enough to make him gag. Here also were the dark, dank warrens full of cheap taverns and cheap whores that catered to sailors from ships of the many nations that called on Venice.

Pulling out a linen handkerchief, Aldo held it to his nose to blot out the smell.

"Here, lad, you won't be needing a handkerchief," one snaggletoothed old harridan called out from a crooked doorway. "If it's something pretty you're wanting to smell, put your nose in here!" She put her hands on her breasts, then cackled loudly, joined in her laughter by a bunch of other whores and drunkards.

Once Aldo reached the waterfront itself he was out of the worst part of town, and the clean sea air swept away the stench so that he could put his handkerchief away. A forest of masts representing ships from all over the world crowded the docks. As he walked by the ships he heard the musical intonations of the languages of many nations, and though he could only speak a few of them, they were so much a part of his heritage that all had a pleasant familiarity to him.

He passed a number of small *trattoria* serving not only seafood, but the foods of many of the nations that had sent the ships. Such a touch of home represented something familiar for the visiting sailor while providing a touch of exotic cuisine for the curious *cittadini* of Venice.

From the waterfront Aldo wandered over to St. Mark's Piazza. There a crowd of listeners was gathered around a speaker. Aldo had no idea whether it was a political speech or a story being spun, but whichever it was, the orator was having no trouble holding the interest of his listeners. Curious, Aldo decided to walk over and see what was going on.

The speaker was a big, powerful-looking man, impressive in his brightly shining breastplate, a sword dangling at his side and a thick gold chain around his neck. On one side of his face was an ugly, jagged purple scar, and as he talked, he had a habit of laying a finger along the scar, as if exploring its limits.

"Who is he?" Aldo asked the man standing beside him.

"Why, don't you know?" the man replied. "That is Captain Filippo Strozzi. He was at Constantinople. He is telling of its last hours, before the final assault by the Turks." He then put his finger to his lips. "Shh, don't speak now. I wish to listen."

Aldo noticed a ship's officer, a Portuguese from the looks of him, standing in the crowd. The Portuguese stood with his arms folded across his chest and his legs slightly spread, listening intently. He made an impressive sight, and Aldo subconsciously mimicked the officer's stance as he, too, turned his attention to Captain Strozzi.

"There were eighty thousand of the heathens," Strozzi was saying. "Eighty thousand camped outside the walls, banging on their infernal drums, playing their pipes, and calling to Allah. And on the outer wall we were less than four hundred Venetians—four hundred of the bravest men of Venice, against eighty thousand infidels, and we were facing them all alone."

"But that can't be true," someone said. "What of the Genoese? What of the Greeks?"

"Bah!" Strozzi scoffed, dismissing the question with a curt wave of his hand. "Were Genoese there? Were Greeks? Perhaps. But this is a story about bravery and honor, which leaves no place for anyone except"—he held up a finger and shouted the last word—"*Venetians!*"

It had the desired effect, for those who were gathered to listen to his tale cheered.

"I spoke to all the lads who were in my command," Strozzi continued, pulling out his sword and holding it over his head. " 'Be brave!' I exhorted them. 'Be steadfast! With God on our side, we cannot lose!' Even then there were many who would have broken and run if I had not reminded them of their duty.

"The Turks engaged their bombard against the walls. They have bombards unlike anything you have ever seen," he went on. "The cannons are as big as trees, and they fire shot that weigh as much as two men. *Boom! Boom! Boom!*" he suddenly shouted, waving his hands about. His imitation of the bombard was so unexpected that a few of the women in the crowd could not help but let out cries of surprise.

"With every shot more and more of the palisade began to crumble. It became obvious that soon there would be nothing left of the wall and no one left to defend the city, save the brave Venetians whom I commanded.

"Then, the cannonading stopped."

Strozzi paused and held his finger up to play upon the silence.

"I could hear the heavy breathing of my men," he continued in a quieter voice, "and the sobs they could not choke back. I knew then that if my men were to take heart, they would have to be inspired by my own brave action. I vowed then that I would be the leader they could follow. I moved forward to face the enemy."

Strozzi pointedly advanced two steps, then brought his sword around so that the point was facing forward. The listeners in the front ranks fell back.

"I waited," he said. Again, he played upon the silence.

"And then they came!" He cupped his mouth and gave a loud ululation, *"Al-la-la-la-la-la-la-la-la,"* all the while fixing his listeners with a fierce gaze.

"Imagine, if you will, that call coming from the lips of eighty thousand of Satan's own warriors!

"Al-la-la-la-la-la-la-la-la-la-la!" he wailed again, repeating the otherworldly sound as loudly as he could.

"They rushed toward us, a solid wave of Turks, screaming, brandishing their mighty curved swords, loosing arrows, hurling lances, shooting firearms! I slashed to the left . . . I slashed to the right . . . I thrust straight ahead!" Strozzi illustrated every move with a corresponding move of his sword.

"For twelve hours without letup we continued to fight. My blade ran red with blood—the blood of forty, fifty, sixty heathen souls!"

Strozzi continued to demonstrate, slashing, thrusting, hacking at the air, though from the fire in his gaze it was easy to see that, in his mind's eye, he was watching his blade cut into human flesh.

Suddenly Strozzi quit his demonstration and just stood there for several moments. Finally he said in a mournful voice, "And then, surrounded by my dead comrades and by hundreds of heathen bodies, I realized that the battle was over. We had lost. Constantinople would be given over to the infidel."

Captain Strozzi hung his head for a long moment, and Aldo was surprised to hear weeping from many among the crowd.

Finally Strozzi looked up and began to speak again. "We left the city that very day," he said very softly. "The Genoese slunk out like the craven cowards they are. I, on the other hand, fought my way out, turning the very waters of the Bosporous red with the blood of the heathens I killed when they tried to board my ship. And now I stand before you today, your humble servant."

Strozzi pulled his blade down and back, then made an elegant, sweeping bow. His story was roundly applauded by all who listened, including Aldo Cavalli.

Aldo had known of the Venetian force going to the relief of Constantinople. The idea of going away to war, particularly a war in which right was so clearly established and in which one could not help but have God's blessings, had been particularly appealing to him. In fact, the prospect had been so exciting that he nearly ran away to join with the Christian warriors. He was discovered and stopped at the last minute by one of the galley captains, who knew Aldo's father. He wished now with all his being that he had gone, for if he had, he could have been standing there not just listening to the brave captain, but sharing in the glory of his defense of Christian Constantinople.

After wandering around the city for the remainder of the afternoon, Aldo hired a gondola to take him home. Because the gondolier recognized him, Aldo did not even have to give his destination. He sat back in his seat as the craft slipped silently down the canal, passing under arched bridges and before the vaulting facades of the elegant homes and buildings fronting the glistening Grand Canal.

The sprawling Cavalli *palazzo*, with steps and statuary that came right down to the water, was one of the architectural marvels pointed out by gondoliers to travelers visiting Venice for her beauty. Splendid from the water, the *palazzo* was even more impressive from the land side, with its gilded marble tiers rising from lush, if somewhat overgrown, gardens.

As his hired boat neared the landing, Aldo watched the Cavalli gondola bobbing gently at its striped mooring pole. Pasquale, the Cavalli boatman, was sitting on his bench against the palace wall, waiting for the moment when his services would be called for. When the boatman saw a hired gondola heading for the landing, he started toward them with a frown on his face.

"Here you, be gone!" Pasquale called, pointing menacingly to the gondolier. "This is private property. You can't moor here!"

"But, Pasquale, if I can't get off here, where will I sleep tonight?" Aldo called back.

Squinting and putting his hand over his eyes, Pasquale peered out over the canal at the approaching gondola. Then he smiled broadly in recognition. As soon as it was close enough, he reached out to bring the gondola to a landing, helping Aldo ashore.

"One never knows how you are going to arrive, Messer Aldo," Pasquale said. "Hired gondola, family gondola—what will be next?"

"A war galley, with its sails filled, streamers flying, cannons firing, and all rowers manning the sweeps!" Aldo said grandly.

"One wouldn't be surprised," Pasquale said, chuckling, as Aldo paid the gondolier.

Turning from the canal, the youth hurried into the house. He had just started toward the wide marble staircase that dominated the downstairs hall when he heard his mother's voice in the kitchen, talking to the servants. It wasn't at all unusual that his mother should be in the kitchen, though when he had grown old enough to make friends his own age, he had learned that the mistresses of other houses seldom, if ever, visited the kitchen or associated in any way with their servants.

Catalina Cavalli was very different in this way. She not only gave all the servants their instructions, she actually talked with them as if they were her friends, and she genuinely cared about their welfare.

Catalina Cavalli was Portuguese, and her accent was still strong, even though she had lived in Venice for over fifteen years. Though she was now Signóra Cavalli of the very powerful and very wealthy Cavalli family, she had certainly not been born to such a high station. She had once been a serving wench in a Portuguese tavern, which was where she had met her husband, Alessandro Cavalli, and though in the early days some whispered about her, no one whispered now.

There were many reasons why the whispers had stopped. For one thing, whispers were not needed. Neither Catalina nor Sandro had ever tried to hide her background, which made it unnecessary for anyone to whisper behind their backs what the Cavallis were willing to say openly. And, of course, the other reason the whispers stopped was the wealth and influence of the House of Cavalli. No one wanted to make an enemy of such a powerful man as Alessandro Cavalli.

First impression would have it seem most unusual that a man like Sandro, born to immense wealth and power, would marry a tavern wench. But Sandro was himself not without personal knowledge of such a life. When he was just eighteen, an act of the most heinous villainy by his older brother had forced him from his rightful position. The treachery had condemned him for years to a life of slavery, first in the fetid hold of a Genoese ship as a galley slave, then as a stableman, and finally as the trusted assistant of an Arab geographer before he managed to escape back to Portugal, where he met Catalina. Like her, he knew what it was like to be poor, and so they treated their paid servants—neither believed in slavery—with humanity and decency. Their servants loved them for it, and, by extension, they also loved their son, Aldo.

"Oh, Aldo, you are home," Catalina said, coming out of the kitchen just as her son was starting up the stairs. "You must get ready."

"Get ready?" Aldo asked, puzzled. "I don't understand. For what must I get ready?"

"Why, for the celebration at the House of Viviani, of course," Catalina replied. "When the invitation was delivered, it contained your name."

Aldo grinned. "*My* name? *My* name was on an official invitation?" Only adults' names were on such invitations. The fact that Aldo's name was included meant that regardless of how his father might delay in recognizing his adulthood, some were already doing so.

"The invitation specifically stated 'and Aldo Cavalli.' That *is* you, is it not?"

"Yes, it is!" Aldo exclaimed. Then, because he thought showing too much excitement might be construed as being immature, he affected a disdainful look and said offhandedly, "Yes, I suppose I *had* better ready myself."

Francesca Viviani was only thirteen and thus too young, according to her parents, to attend the banquet. Of course, she did not agree that she was too young. Already she was blossoming into young womanhood, although, she readily admitted, the changes were just beginning.

Francesca sat in an upper loggia, peering through the balustrade down at the dancers performing many a fine turn on the lawn in the garden below. The women wore gowns as colorful and bright as Venetian glass, with jewels that sparkled and flashed at the neck or on their fingers, the gold-threaded veils of their cone-shaped hennins catching the torchlight as they danced.

The men were no less brilliantly festooned in bright-colored hose, doublets and cloaks of burgundy velvet with silver brocade or green velvet with gold brocade, gem-encrusted belts, and crimson or black velvet caps on their heads.

One of the most elegantly dressed and, Francesca thought, one of the handsomest of all those at the ball was young Aldo Cavalli. She had left her lessons specifically to search him out, and she saw him, standing near the gate on the far side of the garden, talking to two other young men only slightly older than he.

Francesca could tell just by looking at Aldo how thrilled he was to be there. She could tell because although he was making every effort to keep his expression composed, he could do nothing about the flash of excitement in his eyes. What Aldo did not know, and what Francesca would never tell him, was that *she* was responsible for his invitation. She had offered to assist the *maggiordomo* of the Viviani household in preparing the invitations, and because she was particularly good at her lettering, her offer was accepted. She had seen to it that she made out the invitation to the family of Cavalli, and it was she who had added, on her own initiative, Aldo's name.

"Francesca? Francesca, please, dear, you have not completed your lessons."

Francesca looked around to see one of her tutors standing behind her. Unlike many of her contemporaries, Francesca had not been, and would not be, educated in a convent. Her lessons were being conducted at home with the best tutors Viviani money could buy. In addition to being able to read and write, Francesca was also quite accomplished in all the arts appropriate to a young lady of her class. She could play the lute, was fluent in Latin, could write poetry, and, thanks to the eminence of some of her tutors, even enjoyed some awareness of the events going on in the larger world around her.

"Oh, *signóra,* please, not now!" Francesca begged. She pointed down. "The celebration is in full progress."

"Yes," Signóra Polesine answered, "and that is all the more reason why you should be in your chambers studying. Banquets are for adults, as you well know. Now, you have a chapter of Latin to translate for me, I believe?"

"I have already done so."

"Oh," the tutor replied, slightly nonplussed. "Well, then, you should see to your lace."

"I have done that, too."

"Ah, but have you finished your poem?"

"No. I only started it today."

The tutor smiled broadly, satisfied that at last she had found a task for her young charge. She held up a finger. "Then don't you think you should get started?"

Francesca sighed. "I suppose so," she acquiesced. Dejectedly, she stood up and started toward her room. Then suddenly she brightened. "Oh, but *signóra,* I ate no dinner tonight, and I am *so* hungry! There is so much food; couldn't I just go down to the kitchen and get something to eat?"

"One of the servants could bring you something."

"But how could they do that? They are all so busy. You know how important this banquet is to Papa. Everything must go just right. Suppose one of the servants was needed but wasn't available because I was having her bring food to me? Do you want something like that on your conscience?"

"No, of course not," the tutor agreed.

"Then what is the harm if I go down to the kitchen by the back stairs and prepare myself a small snack?"

"I suppose nothing is wrong with that," Signóra Polesine conceded. "Very well, you may do so. But please, be careful. Please don't do anything that will cause your father to be upset with me."

"I'll be very careful," Francesca promised, and with a barely repressed laugh of joy she scampered along the upstairs hallway to the back stairs.

Too late her tutor noticed that Francesca was wearing her best dress.

Francesca did not go to the kitchen. Instead, she sneaked out the back door to the garden. The door through which she entered was only a few feet away from the gate where she had last seen Aldo, and now that she was down on the level with the others, she looked around for him.

He found her.

Francesca looked shyly down, then curtsied. "Aldo, what are you doing here?" she asked.

Aldo chuckled and stroked his chin—something he had seen older men do. "What am *I* doing here? Why, I might ask you the same thing. Though, to answer your question, I am here because my name was on the invitation to come."

"Oh, how *wonderful!*" Francesca said innocently.

"Yes," Aldo went on, "but, of course, I *have* reached the age where I suppose I will be getting a constant barrage of invitations. I may as well get used to it. You, on the other hand, still have quite a few years to go before you will have to put up with such things."

"Perhaps not as many as you think," Francesca suggested.

Aldo laughed. "Francesca, you are still a child. Don't be in such a hurry to grow up."

"*You* are telling *me* not to be in such a hurry to grow up?" Francesa said angrily. "Oh, Aldo Cavalli, if you knew—" Her words sputtered to a stop.

"If I knew what?"

Tempting though it was to tell him that it was she who was responsible for his being there, Francesca couldn't do it. He was so obviously proud of the fact that he had been invited and so sure that it was because he had reached adulthood that she found she couldn't say anything that would hurt him. Maybe he *was* being a bit condescending to her, but he wasn't doing it maliciously. Besides, she believed that she was in love with him, and one did not hurt the person one loved, did one?

"I just meant, if you knew how I hate to hear those

words, 'Don't be in such a hurry to grow up,'" she explained easily.

Aldo chuckled. "I know what you mean. I have to confess that it hasn't been that long since I heard the words myself. I apologize for using them with you." He smiled sheepishly. "In fact, I have never said them before."

Francesca smiled with pleasure. "Your apology is accepted."

Suddenly a trumpet blared out a fanfare, and all activity stopped as everyone turned to see what was going on.

"Strozzi," someone said, and soon the name was being murmured by everyone in the garden.

"*Strozzi!*"

"*Strozzi!*"

"It's Captain Strozzi!" Aldo said excitedly, moving toward the center of the room. "He was in the battle at Constantinople!"

Francesca knew that Filippo Strozzi was her father's guest of honor tonight; indeed, the purpose of the banquet was to pay honor to his bravery at Constantinople. But at that moment she wished he had been unable to attend. For a brief while she had captured Aldo's attention. But how could she compete for his interest against someone like Captain Strozzi?

As he had at the piazza, Captain Strozzi was the center of attention. He retold the story of the defense of Constantinople, again using his sword to illustrate with thrusts and slashes the excitement of the final moments of the battle. As always, his tale encompassed examples of the craven behavior of the Genoese contingent. At the conclusion of his tale Strozzi was cheered by the envious men and applauded by the admiring women.

One of the women noticed the gold chain he was wearing around his neck and remarked, "How beautiful the chain is. Is there a story behind it as well?"

Strozzi grasped the chain between his thumb and forefinger and held it out to better display it. He turned to face the woman who questioned him and, as she was standing directly in front of Aldo, that meant he was facing Aldo as well.

Aldo's eyes widened in shock.

For an instant, and only for an instant, Strozzi's eyes shone as red as blood due to a reflection from one of the torches—and perhaps the phenomenon was heightened by the fact that the officer had just finished a tale of slaughter and mayhem. Regardless of the reason, Aldo had been drawn to the man by the excitement of his tales and the adventure of his life, but during that instant he could almost believe that he was looking at an apparition straight from hell. Involuntarily he shivered.

"Yes, the chain," Captain Strozzi said. "I took it from the bloody hands of an infidel in the very act of pillaging the city. He was standing in a courtyard, his scimitar in one hand and, grasped by the hair in the other, the severed head of a young Christian girl."

"Oh!" gasped the woman who had asked the question. There were other cries of horror as well, and several of the women, growing faint, began fanning themselves.

"See here, Captain, must you be so graphic with your description?" one of the men asked.

"Graphic? Graphic?" Strozzi replied, raising his eyebrow as if affronted by the remark. "Kind sir, you fear that I might offend the good ladies and more delicate souls by the exactness of my description of what went on in Constantinople. And yet I hasten to remind you that that Christian city was populated by thousands of good ladies and gentle souls who had those terrible atrocities visited upon them. Are we so meek and so mild that we cannot even *speak* of the horrors?"

"No, of course not," Carlo Viviani put in, coming to the defense of his guest. He addressed the others. "We, all of us, owe a debt of gratitude not only to brave men like Captain Strozzi who defended our faith against the heathens, but to those brothers and sisters in Christ about whom he speaks. Pray, Captain Strozzi, please continue with your tale."

"Thank you," Strozzi said, assured now that he had

the undivided attention of the guests. "As I was saying, a Turk rushed toward me, screaming like a demon from hell. His face, teeth, and beard were red with blood, splashed on him no doubt when he took the life of the poor innocent girl whose head he was carrying. Enraged by what I saw, and though beset by other warriors as well, I positioned myself in front of the heathen so that I might force him into mortal battle with me."

During the telling of the story, Strozzi leapt to one side and pointed his sword forward, demonstrating. "He raised his scimitar over his head," he said, "intending to bring it down on me, perhaps severing my own head." Strozzi put a hand to his neck and rubbed gently.

"No!" someone shouted.

"Were you frightened?" asked a woman.

"What did you do?"

Strozzi smiled, and his eyes and teeth reflected the red light so that he appeared like the very heathen he was describing. "I thrust my blade forward," he said, displaying the move. "The heathen," he went on in a quieter voice, "was thus impaled upon my sword. I allowed him to slip free from his own weight, and he fell at my feet, there to die in the agony he so richly deserved. It was then that I saw in his possession this golden chain, taken, I've no doubt, from the neck of the poor girl he had so recently slain."

Strozzi slipped the chain from his own neck and held it out for all to admire.

"It was in sympathy for the young girl that I took this from the heathen's hand, for it is far better that it be kept by a Christian than a Muslim."

As it had been previously in the day, the story was applauded. Strozzi slipped the chain back around his neck.

"Tell me, Captain Strozzi," Sandro Cavalli said, "what will become of our trading routes now?"

"It is easy to see that a great many changes are about to be made," Strozzi replied. "For example, there is no doubt but that all the Venetian trading posts on the Greek islands will fall easy prey to the Turks. And, of course, the Black Sea is closed."

Sandro groaned. "One half of the known world is now denied to our commerce."

"Perhaps not," the officer remarked, raising a finger.

"Oh? That's an interesting comment," Sandro said. "Would you care to explain why you think not?"

Strozzi shrugged. "Because Mohammed II, for all that he is a heathen and a murderer, is also a practical man who understands the need for commerce. He is a man with whom we can do business. I am certain of that. We just need to allow some time to pass, that's all."

"But what are we to do in the meantime?" one of the other guests asked. "Our economy is based upon trade. With so much of the world closed to us, what will we do?"

"We can reach out to discover new areas. For example, I myself have been engaged to serve as master-at-arms aboard a ship being outfitted by a Venetian merchant-adventurer named Alvise da Ca' da Mosto."

"Alvise of the House of Mosto?" Viviani said. "But hasn't he an interest in your merchant fleet, the Galley of Flanders?"

"He does," Sandro said, answering for Strozzi. "He has sailed by way of Portugal before and has made friends there. By the way, the Portuguese call him Cadamosto, running it all together as if it were one name. He has taken to doing so himself."

Captain Strozzi nodded. "I believe Cadamosto is going to call upon the good relationship he has developed with Portugal in order to get their permission to explore and trade in Africa."

"To trade in Africa? But surely there is no profit in such a venture," someone said.

"Oh, but there is," Sandro replied. "My contacts in Portugal tell me the profits in the Guinea trade could quite easily be six- or sevenfold. I can understand why Cadamosto might be so intrigued by the idea."

"I understand that you have spent some time in Portugal," Strozzi said to Sandro. "Indeed, that your own wife is Portuguese."

A few intakes of breath were audible in the awkward silence that followed. Many of the highborn were still uneasy with the fact that Sandro's wife was not only Portuguese, but from a very low station.

"Yes, she is," Sandro answered simply, and because his response was not challenging, the other guests breathed easier.

"I understand, too, that you have a son—a son who is, of course, half Portuguese. Such a young man might be useful to me. Perhaps with a small payment offered to Cadamosto, you could secure a place for Aldo aboard his galley. If such a thing interests you, I would be happy to transmit the bribe for you."

"Father! What a wonderful idea!" Aldo exclaimed. "Could I go? Would you make the arrangements for me? You will pay the bribe, won't you?"

Sandro smiled easily, then put his hand affectionately on his son's shoulder. "I think it would be a wonderful idea for you to go. But a bribe will not be necessary. If Cadamosto is serious about seeking permission to engage in the African trade, then I believe I can offer him something even more valuable. I spent some time at Prince Henry's school in Sagres, working with the navigators and mapmakers, so I am not without influence in Prince Henry's court. I will write a letter to a few of my old friends at Vila do Infante, putting in a good word or two for Cadamosto. That should convince Cadamosto to take you with him."

"But don't you think a bribe would still be in order?" Strozzi suggested. "As I said, I would be most happy to convey it for you."

"No, no, it isn't necessary," Sandro insisted. "I have enough influence to effect the outcome without the need of money changing hands. I do appreciate your generous offer, however."

The officer stroked the scar on his cheek, and for a moment Aldo could almost believe that Strozzi was disappointed that no bribe was being offered. It concerned him because he feared that it might affect his being able to go.

Strozzi's expression of disappointment, which was more visible in his eyes than on his face, passed quickly. It was probable that only Aldo saw it, and Aldo only saw it because he wanted so desperately to go on the adventure that he was sensitive to every nuance.

"Perhaps you are right," the officer said to Sandro. "With your influence no bribe shall be needed." He looked at Aldo. "How long will it take you to get your affairs in order so that you can accompany me to Sagres?"

"How long? No time!" Aldo said. "I can be ready anytime! We can go right now!"

"Surely, Aldo, you will do me the courtesy of finishing the banquet before you rush off to glory," Carlo Viviani said dryly.

Ordinarily the explosive burst of laughter from the other guests at Aldo's expense would have embarrassed him until he had turned brick-red. The only flush on his face now, however, was the flush of excitement. He was bound for adventure!

CHAPTER 3

BRISTOL, ENGLAND

The horse and rider crested the hill and plunged down the far side. Leaving a trail of dust hanging in the air, the animal, its mane and tail streaming and its lathered hide shining with the effort, galloped up the long tree-lined avenue leading to the great stone edifice of Walversham Manor.

Astride his mount, bending low over the neck, the rider shouted into the wind so that those at work on the demesne stopped what they were doing and stared.

"News! I have news! News from Constantinople!" the messenger shouted as his horse rattled over the draw-bridge that had long ago rusted in place, vines entwined on its chains, over a dry moat overgrown with grass.

Tom Giles, Lord Walversham, came out of the manor house to greet the messenger. Holding up a hand in warn-ing to stop the rider from shouting his news to the world, he motioned the man inside.

The workers returned to their duties, disinterested in what the news might be. The rider had clearly said it was from Constantinople, and anything that happened beyond the manse where they lived and worked was rarely of interest to them. Certainly anything that might have happened in Constantinople could not be.

The lord of the manor had an interest in such events because that was his way. It was known that in his youth he had been a wanderer, once traveling as far away as Cathay. And sometimes, when the master had a bit too much to drink, he would grow restless and visit the fields and stables to regale his tenant farmers, freemen, and servants with exotic tales. He spoke of gold- and silk-festooned men, of women of fragile beauty with luminous complexions like fine porcelain, of fleets of one hundred or more ships with each ship as large as ten English cogs, and of black kings of Africa who sat upon thrones made of human skulls. No one believed such tales, of course, but everyone enjoyed them, nevertheless.

This man who shared his old adventures with anyone who would listen now closed the great doors of the chamber where he led the messenger before he turned to face him.

"Now, what is the news?" he demanded eagerly. His straw-colored hair and lanky, nimble body gave him an air of youthfulness that belied his forty-eight years.

"A fierce battle has been waged in Constantinople, m'lord," the man replied, breathing as hard as his horse had been. "Between the Christians and the infidels."

Tom thought wryly how he accepted forms of address such as "my lord" with such easy aplomb now. Not bad for a weaver's get who had been sold into apprenticeship in his youth by his impoverished family, then had run away to escape prison.

"Constantinople has fallen, then?"

The messenger looked up in surprise. "You have heard the news?"

"No," Tom replied. "But I know the size of the army the Muslims can raise, and I know the ferocity of their warriors. Tell me, are there details?"

"A few, Your Grace," the messenger replied. "It is said that when the city fell, the heathens pillaged and slaughtered without mercy. It is a tragedy of the most terrible consequences."

Tom walked over to the sideboard and picked up a small bell. A moment after he rang it, a servant appeared.

"A mug of ale for the messenger," Tom said in a distracted manner. "And a gold coin." Already his mind was focused on the information the messenger had brought.

"Yes, sir," the servant replied.

"Thank you, Your Grace," the messenger said, bowing as he backed out of the room.

When the messenger and servant were gone, Tom opened a drawer on the sideboard and took out a large map of the world. It was a map like none other in existence, for he had drawn it himself using not only information already known to mapmakers, but also what he could add as a result of his own travels.

Unlike all the known maps, which depicted a northern land mass for Africa but ended in the south and east with terra incognita, Tom's map showed that Africa was a continent, with southern and eastern coastlines from which one could sail to China. Tom knew that firsthand, having traveled that very route twenty-three years before as a member of a Chinese expedition, sailing in ships that dwarfed anything used by westerners. The expedition had rounded the bottom of the continent, then started north along the western coast, its destination being England. That it did not complete the journey was only because a change in the political situation in China called the great fleet, known as the Treasure Fleet, back home.

However, before the expedition started back, Tom jumped ship to return to England, trekking up through Africa, relying solely on his wits—which helped him to narrowly escape death at the hands of a cannibalistic chief. Because Tom had not sailed the entire perimeter of Africa, his map did not depict the western coastline. He had been very particular to detail only what he actually knew and surmise nothing else.

For the moment, however, Tom was not looking at Africa. Instead, he was studying the Mediterranean and the Black Sea. With Constantinople in the hands of the Turks, the Italians' trading monopoly could now definitely be challenged. And they could be as easily challenged by

English ships as by ships from Spain or Portugal. Tom, who sustained his fortune as one of the most successful of the Bristol merchant-adventurers, was determined to make that challenge.

"What was that fool messenger spouting off about?" Tom's wife, Margery, asked as she strode into the room, brushing an errant strand of hair back from her oval face. Margery was a plain-looking, clumsy woman, with large hands and feet like a peasant, for all that she was actually the daughter of a nobleman. Tom had married her many years earlier, not from love or even from lust, but because it was politically expedient. Although the girl's father, Sir —later Lord—Eustace, had possessed land and a title, poor management had left him bereft of money. After marrying his daughter, Tom had settled a large enough pension on Lord Eustace to keep him comfortable until he died. In return, Tom had taken possession of Walversham Manor and of the title that came with ownership.

"The Christians have lost Constantinople," Tom said.

"The Christians? Hmph. The Latins, you mean."

Tom rolled up the map, then stuck it back in its leather tube. He walked to the door and shouted down the hall, "Hugh?"

"Yes, m'lord?" his faithful steward answered. Though old enough to retire, Hugh had refused to do so, insisting that Master Tom could not do without his services. There was a degree of truth to Hugh's words, for the social graces Tom had acquired over the years had been painfully taught him by the ever-patient Hugh Peabody.

"Have the groomsman saddle my horse," Tom said. "I have pressing business."

"Very good, m'lord."

"Are you going somewhere?" Margery asked.

"Yes."

"Where?"

"I have business."

"When will you return?"

"When my business is completed."

*   *   *

The jailer rattled the bars of the dungeon cell. Richard Denbigh, who was kneeling in prayer, crossed himself and stood slowly. He was an impressive figure despite the drabness of his prison clothing: a large man of regal carriage and great poise, with a great white beard and a mane of shoulder-length white hair.

Lord Richard, Duke of Clarendon, had been born into power and wealth; however, his bearing was the result of personal integrity and courage. That courage was being sorely tested now, for Richard Denbigh, fourth Duke of Clarendon, was confined to the King's dungeon under sentence of death for treason.

Turning to the bars, he said to the jailer, "Yes?"

"You have a visitor, Your Grace."

"Who would visit me here?"

"It is Lord Tom of Walversham, Your Grace," the jailer answered.

Denbigh smiled. "Pray, let him enter. He has always been an entertaining fellow. And any escape from the weeping stone walls of this dungeon, even by one of Lord Tom's fantastic yarns, would be a welcome respite."

Tom was shown into the cell. In contrast to Richard Denbigh's drab garb, he was dressed in an embroidered red wool tunic festooned with gold chains, a gleaming white surplice, and parti-colored hose. Thrown over the whole was a burgundy cloak with gold embellishments. Tom had always leaned toward the garish in his tastes, but most attributed that to his humble beginnings and his adventurous spirit. Some belittled him for it, but Richard had always rather enjoyed it, for he appreciated seeing someone "tweak the beard" of convention. And because Tom's wealth had been made and was being perpetuated by his own energies, he could tweak the beard as often as he wished, for he did not depend upon the good graces of his peers.

"Tom, it is good of you to come," Richard greeted, coming forward and gripping his friend's hands.

"Your Grace, please forgive me for not coming sooner, but until earlier this very day I had no idea you were here," Tom said, shaking his head in disbelief at finding his friend in such circumstances. "I have been told everything, and the charge of treason is preposterous. You could never be treasonous. How came they by such a charge?"

Richard smiled wanly and threw up his hands. "My crime was attempting to raise an army to go to the support of the Christian defenders of Constantinople," he said. "To that charge I have no choice but to plead guilty."

"But surely that could not be considered treasonous! Would not all Christians pray for a Christian victory against the Turks?"

Richard held up a finger and wagged it back and forth. "It was said that our country has been too weakened by the disastrous French wars to spare any soldiers for foreign adventures. I sought to remedy that by raising the army—and the money it would need—from my own resources. My effort was looked upon as treason."

"But that is preposterous!" Tom exclaimed hotly.

Richard smiled sadly. "My friend, you have traveled so much that you see things from a broader perspective. You do not fully comprehend the myopic point of view of church politics. You see, in some circles a loss by the Latin Christians was welcomed as a weakening of Rome's influence over the Church Catholic. And any weakening of Rome's position could only serve to strengthen those who would have an Anglo-Catholic church, entirely free of papal authority."

"I still do not understand," Tom said. "King Henry himself recognizes papal authority."

"Yes, but it cannot have escaped your attention that our gracious sovereign, King Henry the Sixth, is half imbecile and has lost his power of reason. He is, therefore, subject to the influences of those around him."

"But surely there is something that can be done."

"I have appealed to the archbishop. In matters of religious treason he has the authority to grant a pardon. The archbishop is himself one of those who favor a more English church and thus would be listened to, should he reverse the decision. And in view of the many services I have performed for him, I feel certain that he will show leniency. I am expecting to hear from him at any time now."

The expression on Tom's face grew more solemn, and he looked down at the floor, avoiding Richard's eyes. "I'm sorry, my friend," he said softly.

Richard felt his chest constrict. "What is wrong? Have you heard from the archbishop? Has he made his ruling?"

"Yes. There will be no pardon."

The disappointment that briefly shadowed Richard's face was quickly replaced by a stoical smile of acceptance. "I see. Well, do not be sad, my friend. I must now appeal to a higher authority. My case is in the hands of God. Now, sit you down on what serves as my bed. Find comfort where such can be found and tell me, what has brought you here to me?" He smiled broadly. "You are planning some new adventure, no doubt?"

"It is of no consequence," Tom said.

"But it must have been, or you wouldn't have come to see me. Please, tell me, for such conversations are the only escape I have."

Tom nodded. "Very well. I have come up with a plan to challenge the Italians' trading monopoly in the Mediterranean, and I thought the chances of success would be greater if you and I would combine our fleets."

"And a fine plan it would be, too, I am sure," the Duke said. He sighed. "But alas, I no longer have a fleet. It was seized by the court. My one consolation is that my son has been absent from England for some time and was spared the humiliation. I trust that when he returns, he will be able to rebuild the fleet and restore the Duchy of Clarendon to its position of importance."

Tom cleared his throat. "Your Grace, I'm afraid I have some more news that is . . . distressing." His tone was somber, and his face looked even longer now than it had when he first came into the dungeon.

Studying Tom's discomfort, Richard laughed. "What news could possibly distress me now? The archbishop has upheld the penalty of death, has he not? What more unpleasant news can you possibly give me?"

"Your son has been tried in absentia and found guilty, too," Tom replied.

"*What?*" Richard stared at him. "But—how can that be? My son has been in Spain these past five years, over-seeing trading agreements. He is not even aware of my"—he paused—"*treasonous* efforts. Surely they cannot connect him with the charges against me!"

"But they have. The archbishop feels that your trea-sonous activity would be carried on by your son. Robert has been condemned as well."

Richard bowed his head, unable to speak for a long moment. "I should not wonder at such a thing," he said at last, "for I am innocent of any wrongdoing or thought toward the King or the church, yet here I am awaiting the headsman's ax. But I do feel remorse that this evil scheme to involve me in some treasonous plot has also involved my son. And what of the duchy? What is to become of the loyal people of Clarendon?"

Reluctantly Tom answered him. "The Duchy of Clar-endon is no more."

Richard was stunned. "What do you mean?" he asked weakly.

"King Henry has been persuaded to dissolve the Duchy of Clarendon. Your son is under sentence of death, in absentia, and there are no legitimate heirs."

"And the house and lands?"

"Confiscated and sold."

"There was no mention of this in the trial."

"The lord high sheriff told me that the decision to dissolve the duchy was only recently made, to serve as a warning to others who may consider acts of treason."

Richard's resolve strengthened. "Then it needs be so. Even though I do not consider my act one of treason, if my death and the dissolution of my duchy would discourage anyone who truly did have a treasonous idea, then I will go to my death gladly. In that, I would be content in the knowledge that I had served God, my sovereign, and my country. It may be that it was for just such a thing that God permitted me to be born."

Tom put his hand on the duke's shoulder. "You are a good and courageous man, Richard Denbigh."

"When is the execution to be?" Richard asked.

Tom paled. "You mean you haven't been told that, either?"

"No. No one has said a word to me."

"I cannot understand why you haven't been told," Tom said, sidestepping an answer. "You should at least have time to compose yourself and make peace with your Maker. Perhaps I'd best leave you alone now with your thoughts and prayers, for the time is soon. Very soon."

Again Richard felt a tightness in his chest. "How soon?" he asked. "A week? Less than a week? Days?"

Tom squeezed Richard's shoulder, then pulled the man to him for a long embrace. Stepping back, he looked at him sadly and said, "It is today. You are to be taken to the courtyard at noon, and there, in view of the entire city, you are to be executed."

Richard involuntarily put his hand to his neck. Finally he managed a weak smile. "Then let it be done."

"Guard!" Tom called abruptly. "Guard, let me out! I must go now!"

The guard came to the cell and opened the door without a word. The clanking of the keys and the rattle of the door seemed louder than ever. Oddly, Richard saw things in the guard's face he had never noticed before: a mole, a scar over one eye, several pockmarks, a nose that may have been broken at one time. It was as if all his senses had suddenly sharpened.

"Good-bye, my friend," Tom said from outside the grill in the door. "May God be with you."

"I hope so," Richard answered. "For I shall soon be with Him."

The guard left with Tom, and Richard was alone again. He lay down on his bed and stared at the dank stone walls of his prison. When the authorities had come to Clarendon to arrest him and charge him with raising an army for the defense of Constantinople, Richard had made no effort to deny it. Never could he have imagined that such an action would be seen as treasonous.

The trial was over so quickly that before he had been able to fully understand the gravity of his position, he had been found guilty and sentenced to death. But compared to the bitter news that his son had also been stripped of his title and holdings and sentenced to death, the news that his execution was to be today meant nothing. There was nothing left for Richard in this life, and the sooner he was out of it the better.

The only light in Richard's cell came through the high, tiny barred window. He wondered how many others had lain on that selfsame bunk, staring at the walls as they awaited execution. What had they thought about? Were any of their souls in heaven now? Would he be communing with them soon?

Oddly, Richard felt no wrenching fear. Instead, a strange peace had come over him. Gone was the anxiety of waiting for a possible pardon. He was going to die; it was as simple as that. He lay there awaiting his fate as calmly as if he were waiting for a friend to visit. *After all,* he told himself, *is not Death a friend? He comes to everyone eventually. What difference does it make how long one is able to hold him off? In the end Death must be faced by everyone. And those who are dead but a moment are no different from those who have been dead for a millennium.*

Richard dozed off, sleeping comfortably without dreaming. He was awakened by the sound of his cell door opening.

"Have you your purse, Your Grace?" the jailer asked, upholding the custom that those about to be beheaded pay the executioner for the deed.

Richard reached under his mattress and withdrew a small drawstring bag that contained a handful of gold coins. "Yes, I am ready."

He followed the jailer through the dark stone passageway to a series of worn steps that led up to the courtyard. He could hear the crowd before he could see it, loud and boisterous, the noise reaching back into the passage. As he emerged into the courtyard the crowd roared in anticipation, but still Richard could not see them. His eyes, long unaccustomed to light, were blinded by the bright noonday sun, and he blinked painfully several times. Tears—not of fear or sorrow, but of pain—ran down his cheeks and into his white beard.

His eyes finally cleared as he reached the place of execution: a platform of wood with several steps leading up to it. A guard stood on either side of him, and they grasped his elbows to help him negotiate the steps to the top. There he saw the executioner's block and standing beside it a large, well-muscled man holding a broad-bladed ax. The executioner's face was covered by a black hood that revealed only his eyes.

"This is for you," Richard said, holding out the bag of coins.

"Thank you, Your Grace," the executioner mumbled. He took the bag and shoved it under his waistband.

"Have you any last words, Your Grace?" one of the guards asked.

Richard looked out over the crowd. He had no idea how many were there, but people were crammed into the courtyard all the way back to the gates. Men, women, even small children, were waiting expectantly, all with their heads turned toward him. Because of his newly attained rapprochement with death he was able to observe them casually, objectively, as if someone else were about to die. Many had looks of sympathy or sorrow on their faces. Some faces showed horror; others, curiosity. What surprised him was the great number exhibiting eager anticipation, enjoyment of the gruesome spectacle they were about to witness.

Richard wanted to laugh, to tell them that they were not going to see anything, that only his body would feel the executioner's ax but that his soul would not be participating. But he kept his expression solemn, as if he were playing a role upon the stage.

"No," he replied. "No last words."

"Will you take your place, Your Grace?" the executioner asked courteously.

Richard calmly got down on his knees and laid his head on the block. He closed his eyes and spoke silently to God.

The last sound he heard was the swish of the ax as the executioner brought it down on his neck.

* * *

The table in the great hall of Crestwood Manor could seat over one hundred guests in formal dining, and it was set for its full complement this evening. The serving board was laden with hams and fowl and three spitted steers, and arrayed among the aromatic meats were numerous breads and vegetables. Standing by the table and dressed in impeccable livery, awaiting the diners, was a small army of servants, ready to fill goblets with wine as soon as they were emptied.

A burst of appreciative laughter met the antics of the jesters providing some of the premeal entertainment. Additionally, strolling minstrels played on their lutes and poets recited stirring words in beautifully modulated voices. The music, the laughter, the recitations, and the conversation between guests combined to create a cacophony of conviviality.

To the senses of taste, smell, and hearing was added that of sight as the celebrants, men and women both, flitted about in their luxurious garb, the rich brocades and jewels catching the torch- and candlelight.

The purpose of the evening's festivities was to introduce potential suitors to the daughter of Lord Andrew Barkley, Earl of Crestwood. Diane had been betrothed to Robert Denbigh, but with Denbigh now under sentence of death and his whereabouts unknown, Lord Andrew had gone to the bishop to secure a release for his daughter from the betrothal agreement. Now she was free to enter into another engagement, but because all the other young women of Lady Diane's age had made their matches, there was a sense of desperation to these proceedings. The suitors who had responded to Lord Barkley's invitation to come and declare their intentions toward his daughter were those who had been previously rejected by other young ladies—a fact not unknown by the other guests.

"Why, they're nothing but culls, runts, and wastrels," Tom Giles declared to his wife as their carriage, pulled along smartly by four matched grays, turned onto the long drive leading up to the estate.

"But what other choice has the poor girl?" Margery replied to her husband as their carriage drew to a stop. "With Robert Denbigh no longer available, she must make the best marriage with whoever *is* still available."

Though the carriage was met by attendants, their own liveried footman jumped down from the running board at the rear and hurried around to open the door for them.

After exiting the carriage, Margery slipped one hand through Tom's arm, held up her skirt with the other, and climbed the marble steps leading to the great carved doors. Though she had been born to title and privilege, since her father had squandered away his fortune and practically ruined his own social standing by the time Margery attained adulthood, she had actually enjoyed few benefits of the rank into which she had been born. That she could enjoy them now was the result of her husband's vast wealth, obtained not only through the fortune he had brought back from his world travels, but also through the boldness and daring with which he persued his trading ventures.

Margery realized that there were those among the landed gentry who tolerated them simply because they could not afford to do otherwise. She knew, too, that their entrée into society was a matter of practicality and nothing else. Yet she was so desperate to reclaim her birthright that she accepted it. And rather than being resentful of her husband for his new wealth, she was grateful to him for marrying her and providing her with the opportunity to regain her place.

As they stepped through the door into the great hall the trumpeters played the fanfare of Walversham. Though it had been the fanfare of Margery's family for many generations, it was Tom's now, bought and paid for.

Lady Diane Barkley heard the fanfare being played, but because it lacked flourishes, she knew that no potential suitor had arrived with the party. She looked over toward Tom and Margery, perusing them with little excitement.

It was not fair, she thought petulantly. She had been

engaged to Robert Denbigh when she was ten and he was twelve. It was an arrangement entered into by her father, supposedly ensuring that when she was of marriageable age, she would have a match that was suitable. Those plans so carefully made had gone horribly awry; worse, the field of eligible suitors was narrow indeed.

Diane had cried when she had learned the engagement was off. It was not that she was in love with Robert; in fact, she had not even seen him since she was twelve. But even as a girl she had been quite taken with him, and over the years she had often fantasized about her marriage, imagining herself as the bride of Robert Denbigh so many times that now it felt as if something had been taken from her.

Still, Diane was drawn toward one of the potential suitors tonight, and although there was something familiar about him, she could not place him. She gazed at him speculatively from behind the golden goblet she held to her lips. He was extremely tall, almost six feet, with dark hair, flashing black eyes, and a thick black beard. He was exceptionally handsome, though a bit rugged looking. In fact, if he had not been clothed like a gentleman, Diane might well have taken him for a rogue.

His clothes were the height of fashion. He was wearing a loose tunic of green satin brocade over a tightly fitted doublet. His hose were brilliant orange, fitting his legs as tightly as the sleeves fit his arms, accenting his bulging muscles. Over the green and orange garments he wore an ermine mantle, and around his waist a jewel-studded belt for his sword. Though the sword, with its silver-worked handle, was certainly ceremonial, Diane had the impression that it was also functional, whereas the swords worn by most of the other guests were not.

As Diane studied her guests she was aware that they were studying her with equal interest. She had dressed in her finest gown for the occasion, to make the most favorable impression. The long-sleeved gown was made of cloth-of-gold and edged with ermine, both at the hem and at the neck. The neckline dropped to a V at the belted waist, and though the expanse was partially filled in with a band of gold cloth, sufficient décolletage remained to more than hint at firm young breasts. Her wheat-colored hair, bound up in coiled braids, was draped with a pearl-dotted wimple.

Diane had not realized she was staring at the dark-haired man until she saw that he was returning her gaze with an intensity that matched her own. Their eyes caught, and he smiled and made a leg to her.

Diane felt a foreboding chill pass through her, and she was frightened. Yet beneath the chill, a tiny flame was ignited. A flame of interest? Desire? Or merely one of curiosity? She couldn't be sure.

A trumpet fanfare interrupted the revelry and Diane's confused reflections. It was her father's own fanfare, generally played to announce the arrival of the Earl of Crestwood but played now to call everyone's attention to the fact that Lord Andrew was about to speak.

The noise in the great hall abated somewhat, but the trumpeters were obliged to play the fanfare one more time before everyone quieted enough for the Earl to be heard.

"Hear me!" he began. "On this day I shall select the man of station to whom I will give my daughter's hand in marriage. I ask now that all prospective suitors declare their intentions!"

Lord Andrew took his seat and was immediately handed another goblet of wine. The petitioning began.

Each suitor in his turn approached the trumpeters and had them play his family's fanfare with flourishes. That did two things: It alerted the guests that a prospective suitor was about to make his petition, and at the same time it told them who the petitioner was.

Some of the fanfares Diane recognized immediately. They belonged to neighbors and friends, and she had heard them many times before. But others were new and sometimes strangely discordant—even frightening—as unknown suitors came up to make their petitions.

One such, the twelfth applicant, did so now:

"Here me, Lord Andrew, as I, George Montbatten, petition for the hand of the fair Lady Diane."

The eldest son of the Duke of Weston, George

Montbatten was a powerful and exceedingly wealthy man; he was also quite handsome by any standard. Though Diane had glanced his way many times that day, not once had she caught him looking at her, and it made her wonder peevishly why he wanted to marry her when he did not even care to look at her. What kind of man was he?

"What makes you worthy, Lord George?" the Earl asked, playing out his role.

Montbatten looked around the assembly—or, more accurately, down at them. "I am clearly the most worthy candidate here. My family has more land, greater wealth, and enjoys more favor with the Crown."

"That is true," Lord Andrew said. "But can you make my daughter happy?"

"My lord, if you will forgive me . . . ?" George said. He turned and, for the first time, looked at Diane, giving her a slow, insolent smile. "I should think that at this late date the opportunity for your daughter to acquire a husband of my qualifications would be cause enough for your daughter's happiness. It is I who should ask: Can the lady make *me* happy? Since it would please me to make a marriage of such merit, the answer to that question must be yes."

"Well put, Lord George, well put," Lord Andrew said as Montbatten joined the previous applicants.

Diane, though she had bowed her head demurely, was outraged at his audacity.

"Is there another who would make a bid?" Lord Andrew asked.

An eager buzzing coursed through the room as the guests looked around to see if anyone else would step up to present his case. It seemed that others wanted to, but they felt inferior to those who had already presented their petitions.

"No others, then?"

Diane felt someone's gaze burning into her, and when she turned, she saw the dark-haired man she had been eyeing earlier. When she looked at him, he smiled; then he turned to Lord Andrew.

"Lord Andrew, I would have your ear," he said.

"You are here to petition for my daughter?"

"Not to petition, but to claim that which is rightfully mine."

Lord Andrew looked confused. "I don't understand," he said. "What are you talking about?"

"Trumpeters!" he called jauntily, holding out a sheet of music. "Play my duchy's fanfare, please."

One of the trumpeters retrieved the music, showed it to the others, and then they began to play.

The dramatic music burst forth, high and golden; suddenly everyone, including the trumpeters themselves, recognized the fanfare. One musician stopped, then another, then the third, breaking the fanfare off with a few ragged notes.

"Clarendon," someone whispered.

"*Clarendon!*" another said louder.

"*CLARENDON!*" a third shouted.

"You are—"

The man smiled at Lord Andrew. "Sir Robert Denbigh, Duke of Clarendon." He made a sweeping bow.

There were several gasps, followed by shouts of angry surprise.

"My lord, there's a king's price on this man's head!" a voice shouted above the rest. "He is a traitor! Arrest him!"

Two of the guests approached Robert to take him into custody, but he saw them coming and drew his sword. Pointing it toward them and making tiny circles in the air with the tip of the blade, he said, "Gentlemen, I beg you, stop there. I've no wish to spill blood on such a joyous occasion."

The two men froze.

"They aren't armed, Robert Denbigh, but my guards are," George Montbatten said. He clapped his hands, and four burly men stepped out of the milling crowd. They approached Robert, holding their swords out before them, smiling in anticipation of the quick work they would make of this dandy.

Robert darted toward them. The quick, unexpected maneuver caught them unawares. Certainly most men in Robert's situation would have run away from, not toward, them. Recovering from their surprise, they lunged at him, but Robert parried their thrusts easily and, breaking through their line of advance, leapt up on the table behind them.

There were yells of outrage and screams of fear. Guests seated at the table scattered in all directions. A large vessel of wine tipped over, spreading a broad purple stain.

"My father was wrongly imprisoned and wrongly executed!" Robert shouted. "He sought only to defend the faith. And I am wrongly charged."

"Then stand to trial," Lord Andrew said. The Earl had not moved from his place. "Clear your name."

"Ha!" Robert spat derisively. "My father tried to clear his name and died under the ax. Would my trial be any fairer?"

"Justice will be swift, and death will be slow!" George Montbatten shouted. "I will see to that. I will pay your executioner myself."

"I thought as much," Robert said. He looked at the Earl of Crestwood. "My lord, your daughter is betrothed to me. I have not released her from that betrothal."

"The release is not yours to grant, sir!" the Earl replied angrily. Looking around, he saw at least a dozen armed men rushing into the hall. He smiled. "And now, Robert Denbigh, it appears we have you."

As the men charged the table, Robert turned and ran toward the other end, kicking over goblets and sending plates and food scattering with each step.

"Don't let him reach the door!" someone shouted, and suddenly another group of armed men appeared, cutting off Robert's escape route.

He stopped. At each end of the long table men were closing fast. Escape seemed impossible.

But high up on the stone wall behind him was a large wooden beam. Attached to it was the rope that lowered the candle wheel lighting the table. Across the room, halfway up the opposite stone wall, was a large window, open to the night air.

As his pursuers closed in on him and everyone else

watched, Robert leapt from the table to the rope, pulling himself up to the beam. Gripping the rope, he swung across the room like a giant pendulum, propelling his body through the open window, his laughter rising above shouts of rage and frustration as he vanished into the darkness. A loud splash told everyone in the great hall that he had dropped into the reflecting pool—once a moat—that fronted the manor.

"After him!" Montbatten shouted. "He can't get far!"

But by the time they raced outside, Robert had vanished, the sound of his mocking laughter still ringing in his pursuers' ears.

The excitement and scandal of Robert Denbigh's unexpected entrance was the main topic of conversation for the rest of the evening. It was almost anticlimactic when, achieving the purpose of the evening, Lord Andrew chose George Montbatten from among the suitors. There were some who agreed and some who disagreed, and a brief discussion erupted about the merits of the various applicants. But even that wasn't enough to still the buzz of excitement over the fifth Duke of Clarendon's dramatic appearance and escape.

Tom Giles thought about Robert Denbigh all the way back to Walversham Manor. The young man had shown himself to be bold, resourceful, and as athletic as the most gifted acrobat. Such a man would be an ideal ally for the venture Tom had in mind.

The drive home took just over an hour, and when the carriage stopped in the circular drive in front of the manor Margery yawned and stretched.

"Such entertainments are nice to attend," she said. "But the drive is so long and tiring that I sometimes wonder if they are worth the trouble."

"We can refuse all invitations from now on," Tom suggested dryly, knowing full well just how important such things were to her.

"No, no, we can't do that," Margery said quickly, oblivious to the teasing note in Tom's voice. "We are of the nobility, and as such we are required to fulfill certain obligations."

"We'll attend such occasions if you wish or stay home if you desire," Tom said easily. The social responsibilities that went with wealth meant nothing to him, though they meant everything to Margery—which guaranteed that his reply would exasperate her.

"Are you coming in?" she asked coolly after a moment.

"In awhile. I want to just sit here for a bit."

"Sit where? Here?"

"Yes, here. In the carriage."

"Don't be silly. Why ever would you want to sit in the carriage?"

"Why not? It's made of the finest leathers. Don't you think the carriage is comfortable?"

"Comfortable enough, I suppose," Margery said. "But after a long ride I would think you'd be as anxious as I to get out and stretch."

"In awhile," Tom said.

"Very well, have it your own way," Margery replied, and she stepped out of the carriage and hurried up the front steps of the house, where stood her tirewoman, a pinch-faced spinster named Edilda who had been with her for years, waiting to do her bidding.

Tom dismissed the footman and instructed the driver to disconnect the team and see to the horses but leave the carriage just where it was.

"Shall I come for it later?" the driver asked, looking confused by the puzzling request.

"Tomorrow," Tom said. "Let it sit here tonight."

"Very good, m'lord." Clucking at the horses, the driver walked them toward the stable.

Tom sat in the carriage for some time, just listening to the sounds of the night: the soft sigh of wind, the incessant chirp of insects, and the deep-throated croak of frogs. He glanced up at the moon through the lacy pattern of a towering elm. A limb of the tree caught a breeze, and the leaves passed across the moon, catching its reflection and scattering a burst of silver into the darkness.

Finally Tom sighed. "It's all right," he said aloud. "You are quite safe now. There's no one here but me."

Silence.

"How long do you plan to stay in there?" Tom asked.

There was a muffled chuckling sound; then the back of the seat moved, and Robert Denbigh crawled out.

"It's just as well you discovered me," Robert said. "I couldn't have lasted much longer in the boot. It was very cramped."

"I thought you might be uncomfortable," Tom said wryly.

"How did you know I was in there?"

"That," Tom said, pointing to one of the straps for pulling down the back of the seat to allow access to the boot from within the carriage.

"I was very careful to keep that strap inside," Robert said.

"Yes, but I wasn't," he said. "I noticed that it was hanging out during the drive over, and I hadn't bothered to adjust it."

Robert laughed. "Caught by a man's slovenly habits. So, what do you plan to do with me? I hope you don't think I will just stand idly by and allow you to turn me over to the authorities."

"Why would I waste a good man like that?" Tom asked. "I can use you, if you're interested."

"Use me in what way?"

"A way that can be most profitable for both of us. And it will have the added benefit of getting you out of the country for a while."

Robert grinned. "All right, I'm interested. What do you have in mind?"

"You've been away for a long time, so you probably don't know that your father and I were good friends. Just before he was executed, I went to him with a proposal for a joint venture—which, of course, because of his circumstances, he wasn't able to partake in."

"What kind of venture?" Robert asked.

"I wish to do trading in the Mediterranean. Now that

Constantinople has fallen, I feel that there's an excellent opportunity."

"Do you know what you are letting yourself in for?" Robert asked. "The Genoese ships are heavily armed. They'd not only fight for what they consider their exclusive right to trade there, they'd probably attack your ships and steal your cargo for themselves, considering it theirs."

Tom chuckled. "Yes, I know. That's why I plan to turn the tables on them."

"Turn the tables?"

"I'm going to arm my ships, Robert. I plan to do some profitable trading of my own, and I could use a good man like you. Be warned, however; a man could lose his head in such a venture."

"Better to lose it fighting than to lay it meekly on the chopper's block," Robert replied. He stuck out his hand. "I'm at your service, Lord Walversham."

"Please. I'm far more comfortable being known as Tom of Bristol."

Robert grinned. "Very well. I'm at your service, Tom of Bristol."

CHAPTER 4

FUNCHAL, ISLE OF MADEIRA

Running hard along the narrow street, Diogo da Costa skidded to a stop at the corner and looked down the long boulevard leading to the courtyard of the Church of Our Lady of the Flints. He spied his goal: a small purse of gold hanging from an arm at the top of a thirty-foot pole. He had only to reach that pole, climb it, and grab the purse to claim his prize. However, seven other contestants had the same objective in mind.

Diogo was participating in the yearly Contest for Gold, part of the annual week-long festival giving thanks for the bounty of the island. The festival had religious and social significance, but it was the athletic events that appealed to the *mocos* of the city. The young man who won would claim the prize for the event and win the respect and admiration of everyone, as the athletic champion not only of Funchal, but of all Madeira.

The contestants had started from assigned points on the outskirts of the city and had to successfully negotiate numerous obstacles before getting as far as Diogo had. The preliminary obstacles consisted of temporary constructions such as moats to be crossed, tunnels to be crawled through, walls to be scaled, and ropes to be climbed. With the completion of the first part of the circuit the difficulty was about to increase dramatically; from that point on the contestants would not only face the course obstacles, they would have to compete against each other as well. And anything that prevented ones opponent from reaching his goal, short of inflicting serious bodily injury, was considered fair.

From the onset people had gathered to shout encouragement to the young men. Along this street, the last leg of the circuit shared by all the contestants, there were hundreds, perhaps thousands of cheering spectators, urging their favorites on. They stood lined along the avenue, climbed trees for better vantage points, hung out of windows, and sat on rooftops, enjoying vicariously this game of the young.

"Diogo! Diogo! Diogo!" several shouted in excitement as Diogo, who was now in the lead, prepared to cover the final hundred yards.

Diogo smiled broadly and waved to acknowledge the cheers of the crowd.

"Tome! Tome! Tome!" the crowd began to shout.

Diogo looked over his shoulder and saw that his older brother, Tome, had just completed the first part of the contest, and he, too, was on the final leg. Though Diogo would have preferred to be far in front of everyone, he could not help but feel a sense of pride that the one closest to him was his brother. It did not surprise him, though. Diogo and Tome had always been competitors. Their rivalry was good-natured, however, and each would go to the aid of the other in a moment, should that ever be required.

By now three other contestants were in view, so five of the eight who had started were still in the hunt.

Suddenly a wall of fire flared up in front of Diogo, igniting so quickly and with such ferocity that he could feel the blast of heat. It was a planned obstacle, ignited by one of the game officials, but Diogo had been paying such close attention to those running up behind him that he was not looking ahead, and he nearly ran headlong into the flames.

Gasps and squeals of surprise and excitement erupted from the spectators, and they drew closer to see how the contestants were going to overcome this, the most spectacular of all the hurdles.

The fire served the purpose of stopping Diogo long enough for the others to catch up. For a few seconds the five young men stood there, contemplating the latest in the long series of challenges they had encountered.

"Ho!" one of the young men shouted to his rivals. "Would you have a tiny candle flame stop you now? Stay if you wish. *I'll* claim the prize!"

The young man backed up a few feet, then ran toward the fire. He leapt through it, but even before he disappeared, Diogo saw his clothes catch on fire. He could hear the young man screaming from the other side of the flames, where someone quickly threw him to the ground, rolling him over to extinguish the flames. The *moco*'s direct approach had clearly failed. That was when Diogo got an idea.

"Tome!" Diogo shouted at his brother. "Come here!"

Answering his brother's summons, Tome ran over to him. "What is it, Diogo?"

"We can help each other, if you will trust me," Diogo suggested.

"And why should I trust you?"

"Why, big brother, have I ever given you cause to doubt me?" Diogo replied.

Tome laughed. "Only every time we've ever competed against each other."

That was true. The younger Diogo was a charmer of whom it was said, "He could talk a cat down from a tree." And like many charmers there was a little of the rogue in him, though such was Diogo's personality that he could play the rascal and still be found charming by the very victims of his chicanery. Tome, for all that he knew his brother's faults, was no more immune to them than anyone else.

"Perhaps that is so, but you must trust me now,

Tome," Diogo said sincerely. "For either we work together, or we will surely see the prize go to someone else."

"All right, what would you have me do?" Tome asked.

"That tree," Diogo answered, pointing to one very near the wall of fire. "Neither of us could reach the bottom limb without help. But you could give me a lift up, and once I am there, I could reach a hand down to you. We can climb above the fire, then leap over it. When we are on the other side, it will again be every man for himself."

Tome hesitated. He was probably setting himself up for another of his brother's tricks, but there seemed to be no other choice.

"All right," he agreed with a sigh. "Let's do it."

Quickly, the two brothers ran to the nearby tree, and Tome gave Diogo the boost to reach the lowest limb. Once in the tree, however, Diogo started to climb immediately, with no intention of helping Tome.

"Diogo, you would do that to me?"

Diogo laughed. "I will share the gold with you," he called back over his shoulder.

"Diogo, look!" Tome shouted. He pointed across the street where the two remaining contestants had come to the same agreement at another tree. And, like Diogo, the man who had been helped into the tree betrayed the one who had helped him and was climbing quickly.

"That's Carlo!" Diogo said, recognizing the climbing contestant as the young man who was perhaps his fiercest rival. Diogo would rather have lost to anyone else than to Carlo. "Tome, you don't want Carlo to get ahead of me, do you?"

"Would you forsake me, my brother, as Carlo did his friend? Are you like Carlo?"

"I am *not* like Carlo!" Diogo insisted with a shout of frustrated rage. Trapped by circumstances, he started back down the tree to help his brother.

Tome smiled. His brother was a rogue, true enough, but he did have a degree of self-respect, and Tome had just played upon that, shaming Diogo into seeing that if he abandoned him, he was no better than the hated Carlo.

"Hurry!" Diogo yelled, holding his hand down. "He is getting ahead of us!"

Tome, with Diogo's help, reached the bottom limb of the tree. As soon as he had a good grip, Diogo let go and scampered up as quickly and as agilely as a monkey. Finally climbing above the top of the flames, he then jumped over to the other side, rolling as he hit the ground to break his fall, at about the same time as Carlo. Tome, though he was several seconds behind the other two, got over the top of the flames as well.

The wall of fire had been the last physical barrier to conquer, and now there was nothing but a dash of about seventy-five yards to the churchyard and the pole from which hung the prize purse.

Carlo had a slight lead on Diogo and was almost to the pole when Diogo suddenly launched his body at Carlo's legs, bringing him down in a heap. The unsuspecting Carlo slammed into the ground while Diogo, who had been prepared for the impact, regained his feet as easily as if he were a cat. Now Diogo had the lead over Carlo, and he reached the pole first. Tome was still a good thirty yards behind—though Diogo was sure he could hear his brother groan in frustration.

Diogo started up the pole. He was halfway to the top when Carlo, having recovered quickly, shinnied up the pole, reached up, and grabbed Diogo by the hem of his doublet, then yanked. With a shout of anger and surprise, Diogo was pulled from the pole, falling nearly fifteen feet to the ground.

"I have won!" Carlo shouted in exultation. He looked over his shoulder at Diogo, who, momentarily stunned by the fall, was struggling to his feet and shaking his head to clear it. "Stay there, Diogo!" Carlo called down to him. "Watch me claim my prize!"

Carlo laughed, then climbed the remaining fifteen feet. When he reached the top and stretched his hand out to snatch the purse, however, he discovered that a final obstacle had been put in the way of the contestants. Every time he reached for the purse, it began to bounce around, jerking just out of his grasp. That was because a cord was attached to it, and standing below at the other end of the cord was a man whose job it was to make this, the final task, as difficult as all the rest.

"Hold it still, damn you!" Carlo cursed as he reached for the purse and, again, managed to snatch nothing but thin air. He kept lunging for it, and once he made such a desperate grab that had he not urgently wrapped both arms around the pole, he would have plunged to the ground. The crowd gasped with anticipation, then sighed with relief that the young man had regained his hold, for a fall that far would surely inflict serious injury.

By now Diogo had regained his wits enough to begin climbing the pole as well, and all around the church square hundreds of people who had already counted him out cheered his efforts.

"Ah ha!" Carlo shouted. Though he had not yet grabbed the purse itself, he had managed to get hold of the line being used to jiggle the purse out of his reach. Holding the line fast with one hand and squeezing his legs together to keep himself secure on the pole, he reached out for the bag with his other hand. "Now I've got it!" he declared triumphantly.

Suddenly, like the wings of a swiftly diving hawk, a whirring sound sliced through the air. There was a solid *thunk* as the quarrel from a crossbow buried its point in the bottom of the pole's suspending arm. It quivered mockingly just above the empty space where the purse had been but a heartbeat before. The dangling piece of cord told the story: the crossbow bolt had cut it in two.

Carlo's scream of frustrated rage was joined by Diogo's shout of surprise; then both calls were drowned out by the thunderous roar of approval from the crowd as it realized what had just happened.

Tome, outdistanced in the race to the pole, had drawn up about thirty-five yards short. All had seemed lost until he noticed that one of the spectators was carrying a crossbow, and he borrowed it for one last desperate chance. His shot was true; the purse fell to the ground.

Tome tossed the crossbow back to its owner, then dashed toward the purse. However, just as he was about to reach it, his brother, who had leapt down from the pole, was nearly there as well. Tome dived for the purse, sliding the last few feet on his stomach.

Diogo, too, threw himself to the ground, reaching out for the prize. The hands of both brothers wrapped around the purse simultaneously, and neither would let go.

The roars died in the throats of the spectators. They wanted to cheer for *o vencedor;* the question was, just *who* was the victor? Both young men had apparently reached the prize at the same time. The rules, though very lax as to what impediments the contestants could put in each other's way during the quest, were quite specific about the conclusion: Once the sack was clearly in the grasp of a contestant, the game was over, and the contestant who had possession of the purse was the winner. But *who* had possession of the purse?

Diogo and Tome were both lying on their stomachs, breathing hard from exertion. Though neither would let go, they did not fight each other for possession. Instead, they just lay there to await the decision of those judging the contest.

Tome saw that Diogo was bleeding from wounds on his forehead and lip. He saw, also, the tattered and torn condition of his brother's clothes, and he knew that Diogo, in typical fashion, had thrown himself into the game with such abandon that he had disregarded his own safety.

"Are you hurt, little brother?" Tome asked.

"No," Diogo answered. He smiled. "In fact, I feel wonderful."

Tome laughed. "How can you say you feel wonderful?"

"Because I have won. I always feel wonderful when I win."

Though Tome did not try to take the purse from Diogo, he shook it once to emphasize that his claim of victory was every bit as strong as his brother's. "Don't be so quick to declare triumph."

Diogo looked back toward the pole where the purse had been hanging, and he saw Carlo leaning against it, his head hanging in a posture of defeat.

"Yes, well, at least Carlo didn't win," he said. "There is that to be said for the outcome, whatever it might be."

A trumpet sounded, and when Tome and Diogo looked up from their prone positions, one of the judges signaled that they should stand. By now some of the other contestants were beginning to drag into the churchyard, some limping with injuries, others holding their arms or heads painfully. The colorful costumes they had worn for the quest showed the wear and tear of the ordeal, and their faces reflected their dejection over losing. It was not until Tome stood up that he realized he looked no better than the others. His clothes, too, were badly torn, and blood stained his sleeve, though he was not sure where it came from.

"We have made a decision!" one of the judges declared.

The crowd grew quiet in anticipation.

"There is not one victor; there are *two* victors. Tome and Diogo da Costa will share the prize!"

The crowd roared again, universal in its approval not only of how the game turned out, but of the judges' decision. Tome and Diogo looked at each other for a moment, then smiled and shook hands.

"You look awful," Diogo said. "You had best go home and get cleaned up. You wouldn't want Soledade to see you like that. If she did, she might decide she is in love with the wrong Da Costa."

"Ha," Tome replied, laughing. "You don't think Soledade would ever look at *you*, do you?"

Diogo sighed melodramatically. "I hope not. I would hate to have to break her heart."

Tome laughed and jostled his brother good-naturedly. It was great to be alive and young and a Da Costa on the isle of Madeira.

On the crown of a hill overlooking both the city of Funchal and its sparkling vessel-filled bay sat the Da Costa plantation. The lush, verdant grounds of the estate were dotted with colorful trumpet vines, flowering trees, and orchids, and growing down all four sides of the mountain from the house were the grapes that had already made Madeira famous for its wine.

Though at first glance the plantation house resembled the fine old villas one might find in Lisbon, Seville, Genoa, or Venice, this house was, in fact, quite new. Indeed, not only the plantation, but the entire island had been discovered and developed within the lifetime of its current owner, Pedro da Costa.

Pedro shared the house and wine plantation with his wife, Inês, and their sons, Diogo and Tome. The early days of Pedro and Inês's marriage had included two daughters whom Inês had brought into the union from a previous marriage. When both girls succumbed to a fever that had scourged the island, Pedro's grief was no less than that of his wife, for he had loved and treated the girls as if they were his own. With the birth of first Tome and then Diogo, the pain of the Da Costas' loss had become less acute, and they were able to go on and have happy, contented lives together.

Pedro da Costa was now—quite literally—enjoying the fruits of his early days of adventure, for he was one of the island's discoverers. At the time of its discovery, the island was still wild and covered with virgin timber. In fact, it was named Madeira—wood—because it was so heavily forested. Initially, the greatest hope of wealth Madeira seemed to offer was its trees. The *Infante*, Prince Henry the Navigator, had set his accountants to reckoning the amount of board feet and the profits the trees would bring. He had also directed that certain areas of the island be cleared and colonization begun.

During the clearing operation a foolish accident had started a massive forest fire—a fire that burned for seven years. Enormous sections of timber were destroyed, and the island appeared a blackened wasteland.

That proved not to be the case, however. The burned trees not only made more cleared land available for the original settlers—most of whom were convicts who had been freed from jail on the proviso that they work the land, turning the island into a jewel in Henry's crown—but also greatly enriched the soil. Now Madeira was a veritable garden spot, providing wine, wheat, sugar, dragon's blood resin, and the original prize of lumber from the tracts of woodland that remained.

Pedro was recalling those early days as he stood on the loggia of his house, thanking God for providing him with such wealth and happiness. When he had first set eyes on the island so many years ago, he had never dreamed it could be like this.

In truth, it was not Pedro's dreams that had brought about such a transformation; it was his wife, Inês, who could claim the credit for much of the island's economic success. She was one of those who had helped turn a wild island into the garden it had become, and it was she who was most responsible for Madeira's biggest money crop. Through careful nurturing and grafting, Inês and her first husband had created a new variety of grape. That grape produced the wine now valued all over Europe, earning tremendous profits for the wine growers of the island, of whom Pedro da Costa was one. He was now an extremely wealthy man.

Inês had been one of the island's original settlers, arriving with the first shipload of convict-colonists. Prostitutes, thieves, and murderers were numbered among the founding islanders. Inês, however, was guilty of none of those offenses—nor, indeed, of anything else. Highborn, although her family had fallen on hard times with the death of her explorer father, the young woman had been falsely accused of stealing by a spiteful, jealous cousin and sent to jail without benefit of trial. Her only escape from the terrible prison into which she had been thrown had been by agreeing to join the galleyload of convicts who would settle the newly found island.

Just nineteen at the time, Inês had met and fallen in love with one of the young sailors on the ship that had transported them. That young sailor was Pedro da Costa, and though he had returned her love, he had an even greater passion: love of the sea, coupled with a thirst for adventure.

Pedro had left the young girl on the island while he

continued to sail on an adventurous journey of discovery, undertaken for Prince Henry. He had fully planned to return to Inês after the voyage was completed, and he had thought that she would wait for him.

Inês would have waited had she been allowed to do so, but the island's rules were that the prisoners were there to colonize, and there were to be no unmarried women. Inês had been forced to take a husband.

She had chosen a good and kindly older man, and she had been a good wife to him. Together they had started the farm and orchard that Pedro now regarded as his own. But though Inês was faithful to her first husband during the whole of their marriage, she had locked Pedro away in a secret compartment of her heart. And he would have stayed there, a sweet memory, had not circumstances made her a widow. Then Pedro had come back into Inês's life.

Despite a second opportunity, the course of true love still had not run true. Pedro, whose origins were much lower than Inês's, had felt he was not good enough for her. And he had been ashamed of having deserted her when she had needed him so desperately. If it had not been for Pedro's English friend, Tom Giles of Bristol, he and Inês might never have been reunited.

Tom had practically forced Pedro to go to Inês, and as a result they were at long last married. Pedro would be forever thankful for Tom's insistence, for he and Inês had enjoyed a wonderful life together. Indeed, it was to honor their English friend that they named their firstborn son Tome.

Just as Inês had locked her love for Pedro away in her heart so many years before when she had married another, so Pedro had locked his other love—sailing the sea to adventure—away when he had married Inês. But now, his wealth, position, and family secure, that secret love was again beginning to assert itself.

This time, however, Pedro had no intention of going off on voyages himself. He intended to send his sons out to sea to allow them to see the things he had seen and, perhaps, to even experience something new. He would then realize a vicarious enjoyment from their escapades.

From the time Tome and Diogo were old enough to reason, Pedro had taught them everything he knew about navigation and seamanship. They could use the astrolabe and compass as well as any pilot, could read a map as well as any scholar, and could perform every task on board a ship from setting the topsail to balancing the ballast. They also knew gunnery, archery, and swordsmanship.

Because he wanted his sons to have the benefit of the latest information available before going off to sea, he planned to send them to Prince Henry's school of navigation on the mainland at Sagres. Pedro had spoken to them about it the night before, just after the dinner to celebrate their joint victory in the Contest for the Gold. They had reacted to his news exactly as he knew they would: They were more than willing to be his surrogates in whatever adventure lay before them.

In truth, Pedro realized that Diogo was a bit more eager than Tome. Eager, certainly, to further his studies in navigation and seek out new worlds, Tome was nevertheless reluctant to leave behind his sweetheart, Soledade Bartolomão. No official vows had been made yet, but it was well understood, by both the Bartolomãos and the Da Costas, that the two would marry.

Diogo had no particular girlfriend, so he did not give a second thought to leaving. On the contrary, he was anxious to try his charms on the more sophisticated young ladies he would find in Portugal.

Now all that remained was for Pedro to convince Inês to allow their sons to go. He had arisen early just for that purpose: to ask her in the quiet of dawn.

"It is very beautiful here," Inês said, and her words startled Pedro, for he had not heard her come outside.

"Yes, it is," he said, holding out his arm to invite her to stand with him. Together they watched the sun rise higher, limning the mountain range with a band of brilliant gold.

"Sometimes I think back upon the strange twist of

fate that brought my life to this point," Inês said. "And I thank God for allowing us to share it."

"You were a lady of the court," Pedro said. "I was a lowly ship's apprentice. It is I who thank God every day."

They were silent again, just enjoying the pleasure of the moment, watching as the gold changed to silver and the last morning shadows were driven from the crevices and notches of the surrounding mountains. Finally Inês spoke.

"You wish to ask me about letting Tome and Diogo go to Sagres?"

"It is time," Pedro said.

"Do they wish to go?"

"Yes."

"Tome as well?"

"Tome as well," Pedro confirmed. "Though he will leave a part of his heart here with Soledade."

Inês leaned her head on her husband's shoulder. "You know what it is like, to have your heart in two places. Perhaps you can tell him something to ease the pain."

"Nothing will ease the pain," Pedro said, remembering how he felt when he went to sea and left Inês behind. "But you can learn to live with it."

"Perhaps Soledade will be more faithful to Tome than I was to you."

Pedro gave Inês a squeeze. "You were forced to marry another; you were never unfaithful in your heart."

Inês looked up at him. "That is true. I was never unfaithful in my heart."

The laughter ringing through the tavern had a degree of polish to it, like a piece of blown glass, but it had a harsh, brittle edge, too, as if the work had some imperfection that flawed the end result.

The laughter had come from Carlo Cominho, and his mirth was born of the discomfort of one of the serving girls. The unfortunate girl had suddenly discovered that the hem of her dress was on fire, and to avoid serious burns she had had to rip the dress off. Now she was standing before the crowd in her thin chemise, trying unsuccessfully to shield her ample body.

"Oh, Carlo, that is a wonderful trick," one of Carlo's table companions said, himself a jaded young man of the city. "One never knows what new uses one can make of a candle, does one?"

"It's all a matter of superior intellect, my good fellow," Carlo said, beaming under the praise of his friend. He tapped his head, and the feather in his red cap waved. "I have a brilliant mind and the keenest intellect."

An older man was sitting at a table near Carlo and his friends. He was obviously a sailor from one of the ships in the harbor, and he had been staring into his glass all evening, speaking to no one. He had looked up with only the slightest interest when the girl, screaming, had removed her dress. Now he was once again staring into his wine cup.

"You, sir," Carlo's supportive friend called over to the older man, "do you not believe my friend here is the smartest man on all of Madeira?"

The man mumbled something and continued to stare into his cup.

"What was that? I did not hear you," Carlo said.

The man did not answer.

"Does this ruffian not know who I am?" Carlo asked his companions, who laughed and watched to see what he would do next. He stood up, walked over to the man's table, then with a grand, sweeping motion, brushed the man's cup onto the floor. "Answer me, you buffoon!" he shouted.

The man stood up quickly and grabbed Carlo by the scruff of the neck. "You spilled my drink, friend. Pick up the cup and refill it," he said with simple menace.

"Owww!" Carlo shrieked. "You are hurting me!"

"Do as I say, or I will break your puny neck," the man ordered quietly, speaking in the controlled tone of one who has great confidence in his abilities.

Carlo bent down to pick up the cup.

"And tell me you are sorry," the man added.

"Surely, sir, you do not intend to make the fool of me in front of my friends?" Carlo whined.

"You are already the fool, and I've had nothing to do with it," the man replied.

Those who had been laughing *with* Carlo now laughed *at* him. He felt his face flaming as he replaced the cup on the table, then, with shaking hands, refilled it.

"And now tell me you are sorry," the man demanded.

"I am sorry," Carlo said.

"Thank you. Now, I shall return to my drink, and you, sir, shall return to your friends."

Carlo started back to his table and saw the mirth on the faces of those who moments before had been his accomplices. That their glee should be at his expense was more than he could bear. He stopped halfway to the table, then turned back to face the man who had just humiliated him.

"Sir, you have left my clothes in disarray," Carlo said. "I shall have to arrange them."

The sailor looked up with scant interest, then returned to his drink.

Carlo began to arrange his doublet. Under the cover of making a few adjustments he pulled out his knife. Suddenly he cocked his arm, then threw the knife at the older sailor. Just as suddenly, and seemingly from out of nowhere, Diogo la Costa stepped between Carlo and the sailor, holding up a chair in the path of the knife, interrupting its flight. The knife stuck harmlessly in the bottom of the chair, which Diogo lowered and held out in front of him.

"You!" Carlo shouted angrily at Diogo. "What are you doing here?"

"I came to tell a few of my friends good-bye," Diogo said, and behind him the three young wenches who had been sharing his table giggled. "And it's good that I did. You would have killed this man."

"Would have? I'm going to," Carlo said angrily.

"Not if I kill you first, you little bastard," the sailor growled.

"Sit down," Diogo ordered.

The sailor was half again as large as Diogo and nearly twice his age. He merely laughed at Diogo's order, then, with a roar of defiance, lunged for him. Calmly, Diogo brought the chair he was holding down sharply on the sailor's head. It had the desired effect; the sailor fell facedown to the floor.

"Someone take him back to his ship," Diogo suggested, tossing a couple of coins at the unconscious sailor. Two other sailors, scooping up the coins, hurried to do Diogo's bidding. Turning to Carlo, he said, "You have caused enough trouble for one night. Go home."

"Who do you think you are, ordering me around so?" Carlo asked, his words slurred by drink. "By God, sir, you and your brother robbed me of my prize yesterday. I'll not let you rob me of my pride tonight." He took no more than two steps forward before his eyes rolled back in his head and, with a groan, he passed out drunk on the floor.

Diogo put his chair down, then returned to the table with the three women.

"Tomorrow he will be your bitter enemy," one of the young women suggested.

"Perhaps," Diogo replied. He smiled. "Or perhaps he is so drunk tonight that tomorrow he will remember nothing. At any rate, it doesn't matter. I'll be gone with the morning tide. Will you ladies miss me?"

"Miss you? We'll be devastated," one of them said.

"Show me how much."

She kissed Diogo fully on the mouth. "I'll miss you this much," she said, drawing back.

"As will I," another added, kissing him in her turn.

"And you?" Diogo teased the third. "Will you miss me as well?"

"Even more than they," the beautiful young woman said, climbing onto Diogo's lap to give him her kiss.

"How long will you be gone?" Soledade Bartolomão asked. She was leaning against one of the columns on the veranda of her father's house.

Tome, who had just broken the news that he and his

brother would be going to Sagres to serve Prince Henry and join the school of navigation's ongoing program of exploration, was standing in the shadows behind her, watching the effect of moonlight on her hair.

"I—I don't know," he admitted.

Soledade turned toward him, and he could see the glistening tears on her cheeks.

"I don't want you to go," she said.

"I don't want to go."

"And yet you are going."

"Yes."

"Why?"

"I must."

"Why must you?"

"My father wills it."

"And you are afraid to defy your father?"

"Yes. No. It isn't that," Tome said. He sighed. "I don't *want* to defy him—and in all honesty I must tell you that it's not only by his will that I go."

"Then you *do* want to leave me?"

"No, I don't," Tome said. He groaned in frustration. "If only I could explain it to you. Soledade, from the time I was a very small child my father has told me of his adventures at sea." He stepped beside her and, with a sweep of his arm, he took in the island. "He found this very place, and there are other places yet undiscovered. I feel it is my duty—no, my sacred obligation—to find them."

"What is so important about new discoveries?" Soledade asked, pouting. "Are they more important to you than I am?"

Tome took a deep breath, inhaling the powerful scent of the flowers that grew in lush profusion. "No, of course not. But think, Soledad. Can you imagine how different things would be if this place had *not* been discovered?"

"But it was here," Soledade said. "It was always here. And if Zarco and your father had not discovered it, someone else would have."

"And if someone else had, we would not be here," Tome said. "Please, my love, try to understand."

Soledade gasped. "You—you called me your love."

"Yes, I called you that, and I meant it," Tome said softly. He pulled her to him. He could smell the sweet freshness of her hair. "I love you, Soledade."

"If you truly loved me, you would not leave me merely to find some adventure."

"I told you, it is more than a search for adventure. It is honor as well, for to defy my father, to allow my brother to face the dangers alone, would be dishonorable on my part. Could you love a man without honor?"

"I cannot love a man who would abandon me," Soledade said. "If you go, I will not wait for you."

Tome stiffened.

As if fearing that she had gone too far, Soledade let out a tiny cry of alarm. "No! No, my darling, that is not true! I did not mean that! I will wait for you, I swear to you, I will wait for you for as long as it takes, for I could never love another!"

"When I return," Tome said, "when my obligation to my father is paid, I will speak to him and have him make all the necessary arrangements with your family. I will have you for my wife. This is my solemn pledge to you."

She put her arms around him and lifted up her mouth to his. "And this is my solemn pledge to you: that I will wait."

CHAPTER 5

CAPE ST. VINCENT, PORTUGAL

When drawn on a map, Portugal looks like a profile that is facing west. Sagres was at the very tip of the chin of that profile, sticking out so that it was washed on three sides by the sea. That same promontory had been called Sacred Point by the Romans and was referred to by the English as Cape St. Vincent.

Every ship passing through the Strait of Gibraltar had to pass this place. Sometimes becalmed and sometimes driven in by storms, scores of ships from every nation would sit at anchor while waiting for favorable conditions that would allow them to proceed up the coast of Europe.

Prince Henry, having been made governor for life of the Algarve, the southern province of Portugal, had built at Sagres a church, a school of navigation, an observatory, a palace, and a town for his scholars, students, ship workers, helpers, and attendants.

Aldo Cavalli had heard much about the place from his father. Now, as the galley that had brought him from Venice, along with the other ships of the Galley of Flanders fleet, was working its way toward a place of anchorage, he stood looking at the high cliffs rising from the sea. The top of the cliffs was as flat as a table, and on that table, clearly visible, were the church, palace, school, observatory, and even much of the town itself.

Though much of the journey from Venice had been under sail, the final maneuvering of the galley was requiring a prodigious effort on the part of the oarsmen. Behind him Aldo could hear the beating drum, the clack and rattle of oarlocks, and the sounds of the men as they heaved and strained and sweated at their stations.

"Anchor signal flag hoisted on the lead ship, sir!" the lookout called. Aldo saw the piece of red cloth fluttering in the stiff northwest wind, clearly visible against the great black billowing clouds that were building on the distant horizon.

"Drop anchor!"

The anchor chain clanked as it unwound from the windlass, followed by a loud splash as the anchor hit the water.

"Ship oars!"

A mighty shout of relief went up from the men as the oars were raised, dripping and shining, then pulled back into the sides of the long, sleek galley. Exhausted and hurting, the oarsmen fell forward at their benches, gasping from exertion. On shore there was a flash of light and a puff of smoke, followed a moment later by the report of a cannon. An answering salute was fired from a cannon on the bow of the lead ship of the Galley of Flanders.

"There it is," Alvise Cadamosto said. "Portugal." Cadamosto had come to stand beside Aldo and, like the young bowman of the quarterdeck, was leaning against the railing as he studied the distant shore.

"It's beautiful," Aldo replied.

"Have you been here before?"

"I have not. But, of course, my father has, and my mother is from here. That's why I speak the language."

"It's good for a sailor to have the skills of other languages," Cadamosto said. "I feel you will be very valuable to me."

"Thank you," Aldo said. "It is my wish to serve you."

"You have found the voyage pleasant so far?"

"Oh, yes," Aldo said. "I love sailing."

Cadamosto looked toward the cloud buildup on the distant horizon, noting wryly, "It's fortunate that we could put in before that storm hit us. We would have seen just how much any of us loved sailing, had we been caught at sea under such conditions."

"How long will we be at anchor?" Aldo asked.

Cadamosto looked back toward the brightly colored awning that covered the sterncastle. There his brother, Antonio, the galley's captain, was engaged in conversation with the first mate and the cargo master.

"I hope we are able to remain for a few days, anyway," Cadamosto replied. "I think there's much to be learned from the scholars at the navigation school here. But if my brother has his way, we will weigh anchor as soon as the storm has passed."

"Here come the trading boats!" someone shouted, and the sailors on board the galley began to move about excitedly, for everyone, even the lowest oarsman, was allowed a small trading chest with which he could do business.

Dozens of boats rowed out to meet the fleet, many owned by small merchants and traders seeking to do business with the sailors. One of the boats, however, was protected by an ornate canopy, and two passengers sat comfortably and importantly on cushioned chairs as their rowers propelled the boat across the waves.

"Who are the two distinguished gentlemen?" Antonio asked his brother.

Alvise opened a brass telescope and studied the men for a moment; then he snapped it shut. "One is our own Venetian consul, Patricio de' Conti," he said. "The other gentleman I do not recognize."

"Come, let us prepare to welcome them aboard," Antonio suggested, and the three walked amidships, where a break in the long row of oars would allow the visitors to embark.

Willing hands caught ropes from the approaching boats to make them fast as the occupants climbed the ladders that had been lowered for their convenience. When the two finely dressed gentlemen set foot on the deck, Antonio greeted them.

"Welcome to our ship, Your Excellency," he said with a sweeping bow. "I am Antonio da Ca' da Mosto, and this is my brother, Alvise."

"Which of you is the captain?" De' Conti asked.

"We share the responsibility, Your Excellency," Antonio replied. "We are equal partners in the venture."

"Then, Captains, may I present His Excellency, the secretary to Prince Henry, Antonio Gonsalves."

"Captains," Gonsalves said in greeting. He looked around the ship. "You have come for trading."

"Yes," Antonio replied. "We are bound for England and particularly well stocked for our trading venture, as you can see. We have our famous Venetian glass, brassware, and leather goods of the highest quality."

"An attractive cargo, to be sure," Gonsalves agreed. "While you are here, I hope you will take advantage of the fine bargains to be had: wine, sugar, and, of course, dragon's blood, the special resin dye we process from the trees on Madeira. I have brought samples for you to examine."

"Thank you, Your Excellency. I am sure we will be able to do some business that will prove profitable for both sides," Antonio said graciously.

"And now, tell me, Captain, have you a young man on board by the name of Aldo Cavalli?"

Aldo stood up straight at the unexpected sound of his name on the lips of the Prince's secretary.

"I am Aldo Cavalli, Your Excellency," he said.

"A bowman of the quarterdeck," Alvise added. "And one of the finest young men I've ever had the privilege of serving with. Why do you ask about him?"

"Only so that I may extend the best wishes of the court," Gonsalves said. "Young Cavalli's father spent time with us some years ago and provided the Prince's scholars with most valuable information. The Prince has not forgotten Senhor Cavalli's contribution and wished to be remembered to Senhor Cavalli through his son."

Aldo felt the eyes of everyone who was within earshot

upon him, and he knew that being brought personal greetings from the Prince himself made quite an impression on his shipmates.

After a few more congenialities, Gonsalves and De' Conti were shown the ship, and more importantly the ship's cargo, by Antonio Cadamosto.

"So, my young colleague," Alvise said, rubbing the top of Aldo's head after his brother and the two dignitaries had left, "you are the friend of the Prince. I am honored to serve on the same ship with you."

"Captain, I—I don't even know the Prince," Aldo said, embarrassed as much as he was pleased by the attention.

"Perhaps *you* don't know him, but your father does," Alvise said. "And since the Prince knows and respects your father, he has transferred that respect to you. You would be foolish not to take advantage of this opportunity."

"I would take advantage of it if I knew a way to do so," Aldo said ruefully.

Alvise laughed. "Never you mind, my young friend. I'll find a way for us *both* to take advantage of the situation. By the way, when the secretary and the consul return, I intend to go with them. I plan to take a room ashore and have a look around for the time our ships are anchored here. Would you like to accompany me?"

"Yes!" Aldo said, grinning broadly. "I would love to have a look around."

During the next several days Aldo learned much about the man who had sent his royal greetings. He learned that Prince Henry was a strange and brooding man, and he learned why from an acquaintance he made at the Eye of the Cat Inn.

According to what Aldo was told, Prince Henry, a saintly man who did penance by wearing a hair shirt, passed his life in purest chastity, and neither lewdness nor avarice ever found a home in his breast. Henry's already ascetic life was further constrained by his having formed what turned out to be an ill-advised crusade against Tangier. The campaign had led to the Prince's younger brother, Fernando, being captured and for many years held prisoner in a Moorish dungeon, where he eventually died. Prince Henry blamed himself for his younger brother's captivity, and after Fernando's death, Henry reclaimed his brother's heart, which he now kept preserved in a jar of salt.

Prince Henry's older brother, Duarte, had died of grief over Fernando, and a family fight for the regency had nearly led to civil war. With patience and tact, Henry smoothed over the rift for a while, and the regency went to Prince Pedro, who had always been considered the bright star of the family.

Despite Henry's best efforts, however, civil war had erupted anyway when the boy king, Afonso, grew old enough to want to rule on his own. Pedro's attempt to maintain control had turned into treason.

It had been four years since Pedro's death in an idiotic skirmish that no one had wanted. Henry and his nephew, Afonso, were reconciled now, drawn together by the shock of the fall of Constantinople. When Afonso had asked if any other schemes to take over the throne were in the offing, Prince Henry had assured him that he personally had no interest in changing the situation and made a solemn vow to withdraw from politics for good to devote the rest of his life to his work with the scholars, navigators, and mapmakers at Sagres. That was a vow Prince Henry had not found difficult to keep, for his heart had always been with his cartographers and astronomers.

Aldo had learned all that the first two days they were in Sagres. Within two more days he had explored the entire town, and now he was ready to get on with the voyage to England. He had no idea why the fleet was still there, for the storm and contrary winds that had caused the ships to drop anchor had long since passed. Even the merchants and traders going out to the ships each day were going with less and less frequency, for all the bargains had already been negotiated.

Aldo was not the only one ready to sail. Even the captains were growing anxious, and nearly every day urgent messages were sent back and forth between the galleys, inquiring as to the reason for delay and when the fleet would weigh anchor.

The fleet remained where it was, however, thanks to the influence Alvise Cadamosto had over his brother, Antonio, and the influence Antonio had over the other captains. Alvise had asked Antonio to remain because he wanted more time to look around.

What the other captains did not know was that by sniffing around, Alvise Cadamosto had managed to find out several interesting things. He learned, for example, that the Guinea trade had been opened up by such explorers as Gil Eanes and Antão Goncalves. He was told that the Portuguese had built forts all up and down the African coast, to protect their traders from natives, pirates, and would-be traders from Europe who would not hesitate to take by force what they had not been able to gain by exploration and discovery.

The trade the Portuguese were engaged in was known as the "silent trade," for the Europeans and the natives rarely came in direct contact with each other. Instead, the Europeans would leave their trading goods in a pile on the beach, then return to their ships or forts. The natives would slip out of the jungle, and if they wanted the goods, they would leave a pile of gold beside them as their offer. The Europeans would then return, and if the gold offered was enough, they would take it and leave the goods. The gold was nearly always more than sufficient, because the Portuguese left nothing but the cheapest trade goods: brightly colored cloth, baubles, and beads. Cadamosto was told that this silent trade was netting the Portuguese shipmasters profits of six- and sevenfold.

One afternoon, when they had already been in Portugal for two weeks, Aldo stood at the edge of the cliff, peering down at the many ships anchored below, including the Galley of Flanders fleet, their bare masts like a forest of leafless trees. Compared to the blocky-looking northern European ships, the Venetian galleys were very graceful, lying long and sleek in the water and giving the illusion of great speed even when still.

Gazing at his own galley, Aldo sighed in frustration. Though like his shipmates he was anxious to get on with the voyage, he would never say so aloud. The delay was Cadamosto's choice, and Aldo felt a great sense of loyalty to, as well as admiration for, his young captain. Still, he had grown very bored with the long, enforced idleness. Taking one more wistful look at the fleet, he turned away from the sea, deciding to walk down to the Eye of the Cat Inn for a lunch of bread, cheese, and wine.

When he arrived, he found Captain Filippo Strozzi there, regaling all who would listen with tales of his bravery at Constantinople. Aldo had heard the stories so many times that, even with Strozzi's frequent embellishments, he no longer paid attention to them. Several others in the inn had also heard the stories often enough to have lost interest in them, and they sat at their own tables, paying little attention to Strozzi as they ate, drank, and talked among themselves.

Strozzi did not lack for attention, however, because more than a dozen other customers stood around clutching their drinks, listening spellbound to his stories. For his part, the officer relished their attention and admiration. He also profited by the drinks his listeners were eager to buy for him.

"I stood there," Strozzi was saying, "with my head bowed, praying for the souls of my brave soldiers who had died all around me. I was wounded and tired, for we had fought the heathens, twenty thousand of them, for three days and nights without sleep. That was when I came by this trophy, which I wear in remembrance of all the brave Christians—men, women, and children—who died there."

Discussing his "trophy" was always the high point of Strozzi's stories, and he pulled out the thick gold chain he wore around his neck to display, turning it this way and that to catch the afternoon light.

"He was a big man," Strozzi said. "Fully a head taller and half again as wide as any man I had ever seen. He had a beard as black as the wings of a raven and eyes that glowed as red as burning coals. In one hand he carried a huge scimitar—"

"A what?" someone asked.

"It's a sword," Strozzi explained. "Wider than a man's hand, heavy as a hammer, and curved like the horns of Satan himself. With one swing it can cut through a man's neck as easily as an executioner's broadax. The infidel was moving among the bodies of my fallen men, looking for heads to chop off. I could see that he had already put his scimitar to use because it was running red with blood. Around his neck he was wearing this very chain." Strozzi showed it again. "And in his left hand," he continued, holding his own left hand out before him, "in his left hand, he clutched the dark hair of the severed head of as fair a young Christian girl as you would ever want to see."

"He was carrying a young girl's head?" someone asked in horror.

Strozzi nodded. "I knew then where the gold chain came from. It had been around the neck of that beautiful young girl."

"What happened next?"

"I shouted at him. 'Heathen!' I called. 'Come and see if you find my neck as easy to cut through as the neck of a young girl.' He roared like an angry bull, then held that great devil's sword of his aloft in one hand while with his other hand he swung the young girl's head around over his own head."

Strozzi pulled his sword then and held it out in front of him, standing poised.

"He charged toward me, screaming like all the fiends of hell, but I stood my ground. Then, at the last moment, when the heathen thought he would add one more Christian head to his grisly trophies, I thrust outward and upward!"

Strozzi stepped forward on his right foot, then thrust his foil ahead before drawing it up.

"I opened his belly like gutting a fish, and the food he had eaten for dinner spilled out onto his feet. He dropped the girl's head and his scimitar and grabbed his own belly with both hands, looking foolish as his heathen blood began to spill through his fingers. 'You'll not be needing that,'

I said, reaching for the gold chain. I pulled it from his neck, and he fell dead at my feet."

Strozzi gave a little salute with his sword, then bowed deeply as he returned the sword to its sheath. His rapt audience applauded and cheered lustily.

"So, has our master-at-arms saved Constantinople yet?" a low voice said from behind Aldo, and he turned to see Alvise Cadamosto standing there, a cynical look on his face.

"Good day to you, Captain," Aldo said. He smiled at Alvise's question. "He has killed the heathen who wore the chain, but Constantinople is still in the hands of Mohammed, I'm afraid."

"Perhaps if he tells the story enough times he will be able to change history, and the Christians will have won at Constantinople," Alvise quipped. He held a finger up to signal for wine, and a moment later, as he drank it, he studied Aldo across the rim of his goblet.

"Aldo, my young friend, the Galley of Flanders fleet will be leaving with the afternoon tide. I must return to my vessel. Would you like to go with me?"

"Yes," Aldo said enthusiastically, starting to rise. "I am more than ready to leave this place."

Alvise lowered his goblet. "You don't understand," he said. "The fleet is leaving, but I am not."

"You—you are not going?" Aldo said, sinking back into his chair.

"No."

"But why not? You have goods to trade. Why would you stay here?"

The captain chuckled. "You are anxious to get on with your adventure, aren't you?"

Aldo blushed. "Yes," he admitted.

"Don't be ashamed. I too, seek adventure. But I would not turn away the opportunity for wealth," Alvise added with a sly smile. "And it is my feeling that we will find much more of both commodities if we remain behind after the fleet has left."

"Sagres is an interesting place, I will admit," Aldo

said. "But what wealth is to be found here? And what adventure will we have?"

"Oh, my young friend, our destiny is not to be found here. It is Africa for us. Our fortune will be made in the gold and ivory we will bring back. And our adventure will be in sailing to the end of the sea."

Aldo's eyes widened. "To the end of the sea?"

Alvise laughed. "To the end of the *known* sea," he explained. "Unlike so many superstitious sailors, I do not think the sea drops off at the end like the edge of a table. Rather, I am convinced, as are most learned men, that the world is round. And I intend to sail farther around this globe than anyone has ever gone. What do you say, Aldo? Have you the spirit for such an endeavor?"

"Yes! Yes, I will gladly go with you!"

"Excellent. A voyage such as the one I am contemplating demands that I be surrounded by good and loyal men. I can think of no one I would rather have sail with me than you. Now, let us go out to the ship and tell my brother of my decision. I fear that he will not greet it with the same degree of enthusiasm you have shown."

As the boat carrying Aldo Cavalli and Alvise Cadamosto approached the galleys, Aldo could see that the fleet was indeed making ready to get under way. Fresh kegs of water were being loaded, and the food larders were being restocked. On board the Cadamosto galley, carpenters were busy with last-minute repairs, while the sailmaker was making a final inspection of his repairs to sheets damaged by the high winds that had plagued the fleet during the first part of the voyage. Sailors hurried to and fro in a flurry of activity, and Alvise and Aldo had to pick their way through the industrious men to the awning-covered cabin on the sterncastle. Known as the "carosse," it served as the captain's cabin, or, in this case, the captains' cabin, since it was shared equally by Antonio and Alvise Cadamosto. There Antonio was also engaged in presailing activity, for spread out on the table before him were all the charts of the seas and coastline between Portugal and England. Antonio smiled at his brother's approach.

"Ah, Alvise, good, good," he said. "I was beginning to think you wouldn't return to the ship before we got under way. And you brought young Cavalli with you, I see." Antonio poured a goblet of wine and handed it to his brother. "The wine from Madeira is very good," he said. "I'm sure we'll turn a fine profit on it in England." He laughed. "Provided, of course, that it isn't all drunk before we reach there."

"It is good," Alvise agreed, taking a swallow. He wiped his mouth with the back of his hand, then turned to look at the preparations. "The crew looks busy."

"Yes. In fact, we're nearly ready to weigh anchor," Antonio said, taking in the scurrying sailors with a sweep of his hand. "By this time tomorrow, if these favorable winds hold, we'll be a hundred miles or more up the coast."

"*You* will be, my brother," Cadamosto replied. "Not I."

Antonio looked at his brother with a shocked expression on his face. "Alvise, what are you saying?"

"I intend to stay here."

"*What?* For God's sake, man, why would you stay here?" Antonio exploded in frustration and confusion.

"Because it is my intention to sail on seas never before sailed and discover strange races and marvels never before discovered."

"A noble ambition, I will admit. But why not wait until you have enriched yourself from a few trading voyages first?" Antonio suggested, calming down some. "We have a fine cargo here, one that should bring us a handsome price from the English. After you've made your profit, there will be plenty of time to think about adventure and honor."

Alvise shook his head. "It isn't just adventure and honor I seek. In fact, I believe that what I intend to do will prove to be even more profitable than the most successful English voyage."

"Dangerous and unproven is what it is," Antonio said,

trying to talk him out of it. "Why not stay with something you know is worthwhile? Why not complete the voyage to England?"

"I know you mean only to warn me of the risks of my undertaking," Alvise replied, "but you can't talk me out of it. I am going to Africa."

Antonio sighed and rubbed his chin for a moment. "What about all this?" he asked, gesturing at the ship's hold. "Half the cargo on this ship is yours. What will you do about that?"

"I will sell it to you."

"I can't pay the profit now, not before we get the goods to England. I am too heavily invested in the expenses of the voyage."

"I want no profit," Alvise said. "Pay me just what I paid for it."

"But—you would be cheating yourself out of a great deal of money!"

"No, I wouldn't. I haven't made the voyage to England and thus haven't earned the profits. I will be happy to recoup just the money I have already invested, if you will buy me out."

"Captain, signal flags have been hoisted by the flagship," a crewman shouted.

Aldo turned his attention away from the two brothers to see the small red cloth that fluttered from the top of the mainmast of a distant ship.

"There is the signal flag ordering all ships to weigh anchor," Antonio said. "For God's sake, Alvise, give up this foolishness and come with me now."

"I'm sorry, my brother, but my mind is made up," Alvise said resolutely. "I am going to stay."

"And the boy?" Antonio asked, nodding toward Aldo. "What will he do?"

"Aldo Cavalli is his own man, free to do as he wishes," Alvise said.

"And what is your wish?" Antonio asked Aldo.

"I wish to stay with Alvise," Aldo replied.

"But we promised your father we would take you to England," Antonio said.

"No," Alvise put in. "We promised his father that we would find some meaningful service for him to do. What could be more meaningful than the discovery of new lands —with the turning of a profit thrown into the bargain?"

The sound of a cannon report rolled across the water, and when the three looked toward the lead ship, they saw the "weigh anchor" flag coming down and the sails going up.

"Captain, the fleet is getting under way!" the lookout called.

"Antonio, you must not tarry," Alvise warned. "You must leave now to keep up with the fleet."

"And you will not come with me?"

"I can't," Alvise said. He put his hands on his brother's shoulders. "Antonio, please understand. I must do this. I feel that God is leading me to do this. It would mean much to me, my brother, if you would give me your blessing."

"Very well." Antonio opened his arms to Alvise, and the two brothers embraced. "Go on your adventure, if you must. And go with God."

"Thank you, Antonio. I will not shame the family name."

Aldo Cavalli and Alvise Cadamosto scrambled down the rope ladder to the chartered skiff that had brought them out to the fleet, then settled back as the boatman began rowing them back to shore. As soon as their small boat was clear of the oars of the great galley, the coxswain started his cadence. The oars dipped into the water, came out with a splash, shining and wet, then, in perfect synchronization, dipped in again. The galley shot forward, leaving a wake as it cut through the waves after the rest of the Galley of Flanders fleet, now fully under way.

The fleet had been gone for three days before Alvise Cadamosto managed to get an audience with Prince Henry. He asked Aldo if he would like to come with him, and, of course, Aldo was honored to be invited. The youth did not yet fully comprehend how instrumental he'd been in Cadamosto's having gotten the audience in the first place.

The Venetians were instructed to present themselves at the map building of the school at Sagres. On the appointed day they dressed in their court finest, for it was extremely important to make a favorable impression on the man who held the key to their future.

"Will we be taken from here to Prince Henry's palace?" Aldo asked as they paced nervously, waiting as instructed for someone to come for them.

"Yes, I suppose we will," Cadamosto replied. He looked around the building at all the long tables, most of which were cluttered with strange instruments and dusty charts. They had passed through some cobwebs upon entering the building, and Alvise brushed them from the rich wine velvet of his mantle. "I must confess, however, to some confusion as to why we were asked to wait here and not summoned to the great room of the palace."

"I've never met a king before," Aldo said. "Maybe this is the way they do things."

"He isn't a king, he's a prince," Cadamosto reminded him.

Aldo chuckled. "It doesn't matter. I've never met a prince before, either."

A man wearing a brown sackcloth robe and rope sandals approached Aldo and Cadamosto.

"Senhor Cadamosto and Senhor Cavalli?" the man asked.

"Yes," Cadamosto replied, somewhat relieved. He had begun to fear that they might have gone to the wrong place.

"Come with me, please." The man turned and began to walk away. For a moment Cadamosto and Aldo remained where they were. When the man realized they were not following him, he turned to look back at them. "Please," he said again.

"We're supposed to meet Prince Henry," Cadamosto insisted. "Are you taking us to him?"

"Come," the man in sackcloth said again.

Cadamosto and Aldo exchanged a glance; then Cadamosto shrugged. "All right. We'll go with you."

They walked through the building, out across a large garden, and into another building fully as large and as cluttered as the one they had just exited. The major difference between the second building and the first was that several people were working there. Some of the workers were cartographers, drawing meticulously detailed landmasses and coastlines. Others were artists, adding their own flourishes to the maps, depicting camel caravans, rivers, mountains, and trees. There were artisans as well, working on strange-looking devices that Aldo could only assume were instruments of navigation.

Four men sat at the far end of a long table. All four were dressed in as nondescript a fashion as the man who had led them there from the other building.

"Wait," the man said.

"Wait? We can't wait here," Cadamosto said. "Don't you understand? We are to be taken to the palace for an audience with the Prince."

Even as Cadamosto was protesting, Aldo noticed that one of the four men at the far end of the table was the same Antonio Gonsalves who had come aboard to welcome them to Portugal when bad weather had forced them to drop anchor off Cape St. Vincent. He pointed him out to Cadamosto.

"Captain," Aldo whispered, "isn't that—?"

"Gonsalves, the Prince's secretary, yes," Cadamosto replied, his face registering his surprise at seeing a man with such a noble position in a place like this.

Gonsalves left the little group and came to greet them. "Captain Cadamosto, it was good of you to come here to our modest school," he said, reaching out to take Cadamosto's hand in his.

"Modest? There is nothing modest about it," Cadamosto replied. "It is the grandest school of its kind anywhere. It is an honor to meet you here. But I also wish to meet with Prince Henry. Will you be taking us to him?"

"No need for that. Prince Henry is here."

"What? He is here?"

"I will introduce you to him," Gonsalves said.

To Cadamosto's astonishment Prince Henry was one of the men in sackcloth working at the table. Smoothing his mantle to make certain he presented the neatest possible appearance—although under the circumstances he could not help but feel that personal appearances were unimportant—Cadamosto, with Aldo just behind him, followed Gonsalves across the room.

"Gentlemen, may I present His Excellency, Prince Henry."

Cadamosto noticed that while Prince Henry was dressed in a sackcloth robe as the others were, peeking out from under the robe were bright bits of color, indicating that the Prince was also wearing his court finery. And just visible beneath the court finery was another shirt, one lined with hair to press irritatingly against bare flesh. This was the shirt of penance he wore at all times.

Both Cadamosto and Aldo bowed.

"Welcome, gentlemen, to Sagres," Prince Henry said. He looked at Aldo. "You are Aldo, son of Sandro Cavalli, are you not?"

"I am, Your Highness."

"Yes, I can see the resemblance"—he grinned—"though the infusion of Portuguese blood makes you perhaps a bit more handsome than your father."

Aldo blushed.

"And now, gentlemen, what can I do for you? Why did you request an audience with me?"

"Your Highness, your work here among your scholars and navigators is known and admired throughout the world," Cadamosto said.

"Thank you."

"What is also known is the boundless generosity you have shown to men of courage willing to expand the known limits of the sea. And I wish to ask, would this generosity be extended to courageous men of other nations?"

"Anyone who wishes to sail for me may do so under either of two conditions: He may fit out a caravel and load it with his own merchandise, in which case he would pay me one fourth of the proceeds, or he could go in on one of my own caravels and pay me one half the proceeds. These arrangements are true for men of other nations as well as for men of my own."

"Then I wish to sail for you, Your Highness," Cadamosto said.

"And I," Aldo quickly added.

"Very well," Prince Henry agreed. "And which of the two conditions will you accept?"

Cadamosto cleared his throat. "Your Highness, if you will permit a slight alteration to your generous offer . . . ?"

"And what would that alteration be?"

"I have sold my trading goods to my own brother so that I could undertake this venture. I sold them at a loss and therefore have little money of my own to invest in merchandise. I will, however, invest my adventurous spirit, my courage and dedication, and my loyalty in this venture. And to that I will add my pledge to sail farther than any man has ever gone, to expand the known limits of the world, and to explore lands never before seen."

"A worthy ambition," Prince Henry said. "And admirable traits upon which to base your pledge. What do you expect from me for such a pledge?"

"A ship, Your Highness," Cadamosto said. "One of the new caravels your shipbuilders have developed. And I want you to supply all the provisions and stores as well as the money to pay a crew to sail her. I want you also to fill the ship's hold with goods for trading so that I may engage in commerce with any new peoples I may encounter. If the venture is successful, Your Highness, one half of all the profits shall be yours. If the venture fails, all of the cost shall be borne by you. That is my proposal."

There was a moment of stunned silence, and then Gonsalves spoke.

"Senhor Cadamosto, that is the most arrogant, selfish, ill-mannered, and ill-conceived proposal I have ever heard! How dare you suggest such a covenant with the Prince!"

Prince Henry raised his hand to still his secretary's

outburst. "He dares to do so because he is a man of courage and vision," he said.

"But, Your Highness—"

The prince cut off Gonsalves's protest with a wave of his hand and proceeded to say, "You shall have your ship, Senhor Cadamosto. The keel is being laid for a new one even now. I will send word that it is to be yours. That way you will be free to visit the shipyard during the vessel's construction so that you may be satisfied as to its seaworthiness. If you are to expand the horizons of our world, I want you to have all the confidence you need in your ship."

Cadamosto was beaming. "Thank you, Your Highness."

Aldo Cavalli went with Alvise Cadamosto to the shipyard in Lagos directly after their meeting with Prince Henry. Although the shipyard was a place of much industry, it was not nearly as large or as impressive as the Arsenal in Aldo's home city where, behind a walled-in complex, the Venetians had been building galleys for four centuries.

However, it was not the shipyard complex that now dampened Aldo's spirits. Three ships were under construction: one with the keel just laid, which was the one Prince Henry had promised to Cadamosto; a second, which was half completed; and a third so nearly completed that it looked almost exactly as it would when it began sailing.

The design of the caravel was radically different from that of a Venetian galley. A galley was long, low, and sleek, with a rakishly slanted lateen sail. A well-crewed galley with a brisk following wind could make twelve knots. Even without a wind, a crew rowing at twenty-six strokes per minute could make a dash of seven knots. And it looked fast even at anchor.

The caravel, by contrast, looked anything but fast. The ungainly, slab-sided, bulky, square-rigged block of a ship could not possibly keep up with a well-crewed Venetian galley. Aldo wanted to groan.

"What do you think?" Cadamosto asked. "Beautiful, isn't it?"

"Beautiful?" Aldo replied, surprised that Cadamosto would think so.

"Of course she is beautiful. Her hull is made of two-and-a-half-inch oak planking fastened with wooden pegs and iron bolts, making her sturdy enough to withstand winds and seas that would beach a galley, and her hold will carry two and a half times what a galley could. We'll put square sails on the mainmast and foremast and a lateen sail on the mizzenmast so she'll answer any breeze. But, most of all, she is beautiful because this is the ship, Aldo, that will take us to fortune and fame."

Aldo laughed. "Yes, when you think of it that way, she *is* a beautiful ship, isn't she?"

That evening Aldo wrote a long letter to his father and mother. He extended Prince Henry's greetings and described the quarters he had been provided in Prince Henry's court. It was a heady experience for a young man away from home for the first time, he knew, but he promised not to commit any indescretion that might reflect disfavorably upon the family.

The news that excited him most, however—beyond the upcoming adventure itself—was that Alvise Cadamosto had provided him with a small trading chest of his own. He would be making the voyage not just as a crossbowman of the quarterdeck, but as a merchant in his own right.

"I vow to you, Father, to make you proud of me, and to bring honor and riches to the house of Cavalli."

CHAPTER 6

IN THE WATERS OFF MALTA, MAY 1454

Giovanni Ruggi stood near the bow of the Genoese merchantman, leaning on the *moschette*. The breech-loading, swivel-mounted gun could be brought to bear to repel boarders, though he considered it very unlikely that the ship would be boarded. In fact, he believed *he* was much more likely to board one of the English cogs that they were expecting.

Almost a full year had passed since the walls of Constantinople had been breached and the infidel army of Mohammed II had rushed in to plunder, rape, and murder. Christians everywhere marked the defeat as a serious setback to the faith, though Giovanni's keen sense of loss was of a far more personal nature, stemming as it did from the death of his beloved, Iole Zarous.

Sometimes in the quiet moments just before sunset, such as now, Giovanni would look at the horizon. There, where the sky and the sea came together, he could almost see Iole's face. And then, no matter how hard he tried to block it out, that vision would be replaced by another: the demonic eyes and evil grin of the one who had killed her—not one of Mohammed's warriors, but a Venetian. A Christian soldier sworn to defend the faith had instead defiled it by murdering and robbing one of the innocents who had put their trust in him.

Giovanni would never forget that repulsive countenance. He had seen it in his mind's eye every day now for nearly a year. Sometimes he pressed his fists hard against his temples, trying to rid his mind of the agonizing image by replacing it with physical pain. At other times, however, he lost himself in it, studying every facet of the devil's face, committing to absolute memory every line and plane. He would not chance overlooking him if he ever encountered him again.

Giovanni's reverie was broken when Antoniotto Usedimare, the merchant-owner of the ship, came over to stand beside him. This was Giovanni's first voyage with Usedimare; as an experienced warrior he was more accustomed to sailing on battle galleys than on merchant ships. However, by now all of Genoa knew of Captain-General Giovanni Giustiniani's deathbed declaration. The dying words of the commander of the Genoese forces of Constantinople's defenders, repeated many times by those who had been close enough to hear, were, "I am glad you escaped, Giovanni Ruggi. You were the bravest and best of all my men."

Giovanni's military experience was what prompted Usedimare to enlist him for this voyage, for though Usedimare was first a merchant, he was now expected to be a military man, too, having been pressed into service by the Genoese government. His duty was to take his position in a line thrown up against the English "pirates," and he felt that some military experience among the members of his crew would be beneficial.

"Have you seen anything, Giovanni?" Usedimare asked, leaning on the ship's railing.

"No sign of the pirates," Giovanni replied.

"*Pirates*," Usedimare growled with disgust. He spat over the rail into the sea. "The English are no more pirates than we."

"Then why do we stand duty against them?" Giovanni asked.

"Because they have defied our government's edict and are trading in the Mediterranean; the English have breached that which was closed to them."

"But I have heard that we, and the Venetians as well, trade in England."

"That is true," Usedimare said, stroking his chin. "But trade is not necessarily reciprocal. At least, not according to the Doge of Genoa." The merchant looked back over the length of his ship at the trading chests full of cargo. "And so here I am, with my own holds bulging with trading goods and my debts piling up, running low on water and supplies, while I wait for the English merchant ships to show."

"Are we certain that they will be here?" Giovanni asked.

"According to the Doge's agents in Bristol, three English vessels loaded with wool and tin are supposed to be sailing into our waters."

"Perhaps the English ships had already achieved their destination by the time the message reached us," Giovanni suggested.

"I wouldn't think so. The message was sent by a swift galley that would have reached us several days before the English ships could get here . . . although we *have* been here for four days with no sight of the English convoy."

"How much longer will we anchor here, waiting for them?"

"I wish I could answer that," Usedimare replied. He looked at the five other Genoese galleys on sentinel duty with him. Four of them, like his own, were but armed merchantmen. The fifth was a war galley, well armed and larger than the merchantmen. The war galley was the flagship of the small blockade fleet, and according to Usedimare's instructions, the merchant galleys were supposed to remain on station until the warship flew a red and gold pennant, signifying that the line was being disbanded.

No such pennant was flying, and Usedimare swore angrily.

"I am going broke protecting the Mediterranean from the English so that Portuguese, Venetian, and Genoese merchants can get rich. I say we should let the English have their trade. Our goods are as valuable as the English goods, and our merchants are as astute at business as the English merchants. If we must fight the English, then let us fight them in the field of commerce. I am a merchant, not a warrior."

He put both hands on the railing and looked at the western horizon. By now the setting sun was a great orange disk, balanced on the horizon. Stretching from the horizon all the way to the ship was a wide band of red, laid out like a carpet on the sea. The few clouds dotting the western sky had purpled, and the lateen sails of the other ships were rimmed in gold.

Usedimare abruptly turned away from the colorful vista with a wide smile on his face.

"We'll wait no longer," he said.

"I beg your pardon?"

"Giovanni, be a good fellow and gather the officers for me, will you? Tell them to hurry, before the sun is below the horizon. Do you understand? *They must be here before the sun is below the horizon.*"

Moving through the ship, Giovanni had the other officers assembled quickly. The men, all of whom had their own trading chests on board, were as anxious to get under way as Usedimare. They looked expectantly at the captain to learn why he had summoned them.

"Gentlemen," Usedimare said, smiling slyly, "our signal to get under way is a red and gold pennant atop the warship's mainmast, correct?"

"Yes," the others agreed in unison.

"I ask you to look now at the mainmast of that vessel. Does not the setting of the sun paint it red and gold? Could that not be mistaken for a pennant of the same color?"

One of the officers grinned. "Captain, I would *swear* that I see a red and gold pennant."

"As do I," another said.

Usedimare nodded. "I only called you together so that I might have verification of my sighting. Now, having seen the pennant, I propose that we weigh anchor and get on with our voyage."

"But that will do no good," one of the others suggested. "As soon as we begin to leave, we will be signaled back into position."

"Ah, but as we have been at anchor for such a long time, I am certain there are many things we must do to get under way. So many things, in fact, that it will more than likely be quite dark by the time we actually leave. And if they don't see us leave, they won't be able to signal us to return."

"Captain, may I offer a suggestion?" Giovanni ventured. Though technically not one of the ship's officers or a merchant, he had been given a small trading chest as compensation for his military contribution. As a result, he felt he had a vested interest in the success of the voyage.

"Yes, of course, Giovanni."

"Having stood watch during the night many times, I can tell you that the sail, when deployed, will catch the light of the moon, thus making us visible to the other ships. I suggest you allow the sail to remain furled and have our rowers pull us away."

"An excellent suggestion, Giovanni. That is just what we will do," Usedimare said. "Gentlemen, it is my belief that the departure pennant has been shown. Make ready in all respects to get under way. We'll weigh anchor after darkness."

The coxswain's drum had pounded a steady twenty beats per minute for two hours. No matter where Giovanni was on the galley, he could not escape the constant *thump-thump-thump* of the drum. The pounding moved into his soul and resonated with his pulse and heartbeat. He became a part of it and it a part of him. He could hear also the rattle of the sweeps in the oarlocks and the grunts and groans of the rowers at their work. He could virtually feel their aching muscles and tired limbs, and he couldn't help but feel sorry for the men who had to sit at their station hour after hour, stoically sweeping the oars through the water in a steady twenty strokes per minute.

Though the rowers of this particular galley were not slaves, they were men of the very lowest station, and their lot was the most difficult of all. To many of the merchants and officers who served on board or took passage on the galleys, the rowers were scarcely human. They were thought of as fixtures of the ship, no different from a windlass, anchor, or sail. Giovanni did not think of them that way, however, and he was pleased that Usedimare did not either, for after the men had sweated and strained for two hours, Usedimare ordered the drum silenced, and he passed the word that the rowers could rest for the remainder of the night.

"We have come far enough away from the others that we are quite safe now," the captain-merchant said. "At sunrise we'll get under way again, only this time our voyage will be one of trade, not of war."

"Captain, what about the night watch?" Giovanni asked. "Should I double it?"

"No, why should we double the watch?" Usedimare shrugged. "On the contrary, I believe we can reduce the watch to one person. After all, we are no longer on sentinel duty."

"Perhaps not. But if the English convoy is in these waters, wouldn't it be better to be on the alert?"

"Suppose they *are* in these waters?" Usedimare asked. "They wouldn't want to be seen, so if they see us, they would turn and run. And since I have no more wish to confront them than they do me, I am perfectly content to let them run. No, my military friend, I can understand that your training and experience would make you believe that increased vigilance is necessary, but remember, you now have a trading chest as well, so it's time you began to think not as a warrior, but as a merchant."

Giovanni smiled and nodded. "You are no doubt right. But old habits are hard to break."

Usedimare stretched, then looked at the position of the stars. "We have at least six more hours of darkness.

Plenty of time to get some sleep. Rest well, Giovanni. I know I will."

Usedimare walked back toward the sterncastle, where he and the other merchants of high station slept. The common seamen were beginning to drift belowdecks to the large hold where the cargo was kept and where the sailors had hung hammocks or spread blankets out for themselves. Giovanni slept there, too, when the weather was foul. On nights like tonight, however, he preferred to sleep on the deck.

The oarsmen had no such leeway. Good weather or foul, they worked, ate, and slept at their benches, and when Giovanni looked down the length of the starboard bulwark, he saw that most of them had already collapsed across their oars and were sleeping the sleep of exhaustion. The few still awake sat quietly, the occasional movement of their heads being the only indication that they were not asleep.

It was nearly midnight, and Giovanni had been on duty since before midnight the previous night. Seeing so many yawning, stretching, and sleeping men made Giovanni now realize how tired and sleepy *he* was; he, too, stretched and yawned, then found himself a place to lie down near the bowsprit bitts. Within moments he was sound asleep.

Giovanni didn't know what caused him to awaken. It might have been a sound, though now he heard nothing. He sat up to look back down along the starboard gunwale of the ship, but a thick early-morning fog made it impossible to see even a quarter of the way down the deck.

Getting to his feet, he walked over to the gunwale on the larboard side and peered into the fog. The scene had such a dreamlike quality that it was hard to distinguish fantasy from reality. He thought he perceived movement on the ship, no more than shadows gliding through the fog, vapors drifting soundlessly about.

At first he wasn't sure if he had really seen them, and then he wasn't sure if they were real or if he was dreaming them. Initially there were only two or three, then five, then several; then, his hair standing on end, Giovanni saw one of the figures materialize right in front of him.

"You are armed with a rapier, sir. Use it," the figure challenged. These were not apparitions after all but real people, and his very life was in danger.

"Boarders!" he shouted. "All hands! We're under attack!"

The fight put up by the galley's crew, if indeed it could be called a fight, was short and ineffective. The rowers at their benches were at a distinct disadvantage since the boarders already controlled the coursier, the planked walkway that ran the length of the rowers' benches. Anytime one of the rowers attempted to come up from his station, he was clubbed back down. The sailors who had been sleeping belowdecks were of no more use than the rowers; boarders had positioned themselves by all the hatches, keeping the sailors trapped below. That left only the officers and merchants free to wage the fight, and they were badly outnumbered by well-armed men.

"Quarter! Quarter!" Usedimare shouted, and, raising his hands meekly, he, the other merchants, and the officers of the Genoese galley surrendered.

The short battle was over, yet throughout the ship the ring of blade on blade continued as two opponents engaged in a struggle at the bow of the ship.

Giovanni Ruggi was surprised by the tenacity of his adversary. He had thought himself the match of any Englishman, yet this Englishman was more than holding his own. His foe was nearly six feet tall, considerably bigger than Giovanni and stronger as well. He had dark hair, flashing black eyes, a thick black beard, and a smile that could only be described as insolent.

"You're putting up a good fight for a Genoese dog," the Englishman said. "But you are losing. Ask for quarter."

"No," Giovanni replied. "*You* ask for quarter!"

Giovanni thought he saw an opening, and he moved quickly to take advantage of it. But his thrust was parried easily, and then, in a whipping motion, the sword of his opponent clashed with his and jerked it free from his hand.

It flew across the rail, and Giovanni heard a faint splash as it hit the water.

"Now, my belligerent friend," the English swordsman said, holding the tip of his blade against Giovanni's neck, "beg for mercy and I'll let you live."

"Go ahead and kill me, you English bastard!" Giovanni spat. "I'll not beg you for my life."

The Englishman's eyes flashed in anger for just a second; then they sparkled with humor, and he laughed loudly.

"Kill you? No, by God, I'll not kill one as brave as you." He stepped away from Giovanni and slipped his sword into its scabbard. "Step over there with your captain and the others," he said. Facing Usedimare and the merchants and officers standing helplessly under guard, he announced, "Let it be noted that I, Robert Denbigh, granted this man his life out of respect for his bravery and not as an answer to his plea."

"Where did you come from, Captain Denbigh?" Usedimare asked. "We have been watching the west for many days."

"Have you, now?" Denbigh replied, laughing in appreciation of the Genoese's plight. "Well, that's just what my friend Tom of Bristol thought you would be doing. So we decided to come the long way around, between the toe of Italy and Sicily."

"Impossible," Usedimare said. "Such a route would carry you through the narrow Strait of Messina. How could you avoid the fleet of Naples?"

"How could we indeed?" Denbigh replied. Again he laughed. "Perhaps the merchants of Naples are not as frightened of English commerce as are the timid little peddlers of Genoa and Venice."

"What are you going to do now?" Usedimare asked. "Are you going to kill us?"

The Englishman laughed again. "No, my good fellow, I'm not going to kill you—even though I know that Genoese ships would give no quarter if the situation were reversed. I am, however, going to extract some ransom from you. You will not mind, I'm sure, if I help myself to the choicest of your merchandise. I will leave the bulkier items."

"How did you find us in the fog?" Giovanni asked, unable to hold back the question any longer.

"Oh, we saw you long before the fog set in," Denbigh replied easily. "At first we were going to sail away as quickly as we could; then we realized that you were not only alone, you were also without a posted watch. That was when we decided to take advantage of the situation. After that it was a very simple matter to just lie to and wait for the morning fog, then take advantage of it to cover our boarding party. It worked out well, don't you think?"

"The devil take you, pirate. I will not offer you my congratulations," Usedimare grumbled.

"Oh, you don't appreciate my ingenuity?" Denbigh asked, smirking. "What a shame. One does want to be appreciated, you know. What do you say, my good men?" he hollered to his men. "Let's lighten the ship for our Genoese friends."

With a shout of victory, Denbigh's men began rifling through the cargo chests and hold. By the time they had the choicest freight loaded onto their skiffs, the fog had lifted, and Giovanni could see the three English ships lying less than fifty yards off the larboard bow. Though not as sleek looking, and certainly not as fast, as a galley under way with all sweeps manned, the English ships were, Giovanni had to admit, impressive-looking vessels.

Along the rails of the English ships were rows of shields. They were placed in groups of four and decorated alternately with the cross of Saint George on a silver background, a golden fleur-de-lis on a blue background, the Tudor rose on a green-and-white background, and the golden portcullis on a red background. Long, forked pennants flew gaily from the mastheads, yardarms, and other parts of the vessel, and they, like the sails, were marked with the cross of Saint George. Though loaded with cargo, the ships also bristled with cannon, a fact of which the faster, though more lightly armed galleys on blockade duty were unaware. Giovanni decided that the blockade fleet was lucky it had not encountered the surprisingly heavily armed English convoy.

Robert Denbigh supervised the loading of the last of the pirated cargo, then started over the railing, the last man to leave the galley's deck. He paused with one leg over the rail and looked back at Usedimare.

"Would you like some advice, my good fellow?"

"I ask for no advice from an English pirate," Usedimare fumed.

"Then I give it to you without need of your asking," Denbigh said lightly. "Try your hand at trading with the Portuguese. They have no qualms about dealing with Genoese, Venetians, or us English. And while it is not yet generally known, some real bargains are to be had in wine, Madeira sugar, and dragon's blood resin." Denbigh grinned. "Who knows, this little encounter might prove equally profitable for *both* of us."

Laughing, he scrambled down the galley's side into the last skiff. The boats, loaded with sailors and looted cargo, then started across the open water toward the three English ships.

"The arrogant bastard," Giovanni said. "We'll see who has the last laugh." He ran toward the *moschette*. The swivel gun was still loaded, having been unfired during the boarding.

"Giovanni, no!" Usedimare said sharply, sticking his hand out to restrain him. "Look," he said, nodding toward the nearest English ship.

Though two of the three ships in the convoy were merchant ships, the nearest one, named the *Golden Hawk*, was primarily a war vessel. Looking closely, Giovanni could see that several of the warship's cannons were trained on them. Behind the cannons stood English sailors, a slowly burning wick in each of their hands. It would take but a touch of the wick to fire the cannons, and one broadside would in all likelihood sink the galley.

"The bastards!" Giovanni swore in frustration.

*   *   *

When Robert Denbigh returned to the *Golden Hawk,* he was met by his first mate.

"Any trouble, sir?"

"No trouble at all," Robert replied, smiling broadly. "Send signals to the other ships, Mr. Cooper, and make ready to get under way."

"Aye, aye, sir," Nigel Cooper replied, his smile as broad as Robert's own.

Tom Giles had made good on his promise to equip a fleet of ships to trade in the Mediterranean and had even gone one step better by making one of them not just an armed merchantman but a genuine man-of-war, captained by Robert Denbigh, erstwhile Duke of Clarendon and now, as he liked to call himself, a "gentlemen of the sea." While perhaps not as sleek or as fast as a galley, the *Golden Hawk* did have graceful lines and was a beautiful sailer. Her forecastle ended at her stem, and a long, slim prow projected far forward. The stern was pitched up, square and narrow. The sides of the ship were reinforced with skids, giving the vessel the strength needed to withstand heavy seas without greatly increasing her weight. Her fore- and mainmasts were equipped with round tops and carried courses and topsails, while the mizzenmast was lateen-rigged.

Robert thought the *Golden Hawk* a sight to quicken the pulse of any seafaring soul who set eyes on her. She was especially beautiful when running before the wind, with billowing courses, flowing topsail sheets, fore-and-aft mizzens swollen, and boiling foam and iridescent spray surging beneath her prow.

The *Golden Hawk,* like the other two ships of the convoy, was manned not by impressed sailors, as was so often the case on English vessels, but by volunteers. Robert had had no trouble recruiting them for his venture, going from grogshop to tavern to waterfront inn, promising a voyage of "adventure, excitement, danger, and perhaps a little gold." His recruiting efforts netted more sailors than the three ships could accommodate. That favorable circumstance enabled him to pick and choose among the volunteers; as a result, all three ships in the convoy were manned by experienced, fearless seamen in perfect physical condition. That many of them also had a price on their head had been of no consequence to Robert in making his selection. When the men discovered that the captain they had agreed to serve under was himself condemned by the Crown, they took a pledge of "loyalty until death" to him.

By extension, their loyalty to Robert Denbigh included Tom Giles, Lord Walversham, for Robert was careful to point out that their venture was being made possible by the generous support of their benefactor. There was no question as to Robert's personal loyalty. Tom of Bristol had not only provided Robert a means to escape King Henry's "justice," he had also given him a means to recover his wealth and self-respect. Even without the sentence of death over his head Robert would have been in difficult straits, for the confiscation of his land, title, and wealth would have left him a pauper. Now, Robert actually allowed himself a dream: to return to England by stealth and claim the Lady Diane, then hie to some country where his newly found wealth would allow him and his bride to live as well their stations decreed that they should—and allowing him also to keep his head on his shoulders.

"What is our course, Captain?" Cooper asked as Robert watched the pirated booty being stored.

Robert looked back at the Genoese galley, which had called upon its rowers and was now beginning to widen the gap between them, getting out of range of the *Golden Hawk*'s cannons. *Let them run*, he thought. He had what he wanted from them. There was no need to sink them.

"Captain?" the first mate asked again.

"East by southeast, Mr. Cooper," Robert replied. "Fortunately for the merchants who were waiting for these trading goods, they will still be delivered, despite the fact that the Genoese lost them." Robert chuckled. "They'll just have to pay a bit more for them, that's all."

"Three cheers for our captain, men!" the first mate shouted, and the crew responded resoundingly.

*   *   *

Even across the widening gap of water Giovanni could hear the English sailors' cheers, and he gripped the rail in anger as he watched the English ships' sails fill with the freshening wind.

"You were right, my young military friend," Usedimare said, stepping up to the rail alongside Giovanni and putting a hand on his shoulder. "We should have doubled the watch last night."

"I should have been more alert," Giovanni said. "That was my responsibility."

"No," Usedimare said. "I am the one who ordered that the vigil be relaxed. You have nothing to blame yourself for."

"What will you do now?"

Usedimare shrugged and stared out toward the three English ships growing noticeably smaller as they pulled away. "I don't know," he said. "I went very deeply into debt for this voyage. I have nothing left to work with."

"You have your skills at sea and your experience in dealing with foreign traders," Giovanni suggested.

Usedimare laughed mockingly. "What good is my skill and experience without the money to stock and equip a ship?" He stroked his chin for a moment, then added, "Unless . . ." The word hung, inviting a response from Giovanni.

"Unless?"

"The Englishman," Usedimare answered. "He *did* say that the Portuguese were trading Madeira sugar, wine, and dragon's blood at bargain rates, didn't he?"

"You believe the Englishman?" Giovanni asked.

"Yes. Why not?"

"Because all Englishmen lie."

Usedimare laughed. "There is no more truth to that than there would be to a statement that all Genoese tell the truth."

"Then *this* Englishman lied," Giovanni insisted.

"Why should he lie?"

"Why? He attacked us, that's why. He attacked us, and he stole our cargo. He could have sunk us."

"But he didn't," Usedimare said, holding up a finger

and smiling. "And that's my point. He could have sunk us, but he let us stay afloat. I believe that the same code that kept him from sinking us also compelled him to provide us with useful information. He is right, you know. With Alexandrian sugar cut off by the Turks, and with Mohammed advancing on Greece, the sugar on Cyprus will be threatened. If we could buy Madeiran sugar at a good price in Portugal, we could recoup our losses here many times over."

"That may be true," Giovanni said. "Though it makes one wonder why an Englishman would show compassion."

"Compassion?" Usedimare replied with a snort. "No, not compassion, my young friend. What he showed was arrogance."

Giovanni looked at Usedimare for a long moment; then a slow smile spread across his face. He turned to look back at the three English ships, now beyond cannon range.

"Arrogance," he repeated. "Yes, that I could see. Perhaps the Englishman thought it would be a good jest to provide you with some valuable information, all the while believing that you couldn't, or wouldn't, use it."

"Yes, well, he may very well be right in his belief that I *can't* use it," Usedimare said, concern edging into his voice. "Because to take advantage of those opportunities, I'll have to return to Genoa for more supplies and provisions. And that means I'll have to tell my creditors that I can't repay them because an English pirate raided the ship. Then, after I tell them I have lost their investment, I'll ask them to lend me even *more* money, and when they ask why, I'll tell them that the Englishman told me of bargains to be had by trading with the Portuguese." He grinned wryly. "That shouldn't be too hard."

"You are a man of great respect, Captain," Giovanni said. "I think they will listen to you."

"Do you?" Usedimare asked thoughtfully. "Good. I will first try it on you. Would you sail with me again, Giovanni Ruggi?"

Giovanni looked at Usedimare for a long moment before he answered. When Usedimare lost everything, Giovanni lost everything as well, for one of the trading chests the English took with them was the one he had been allowed for his own. Now he not only had no trading chest, he wouldn't be paid for it since Usedimare didn't have the money. And all this because Usedimare had not listened when Giovanni counseled doubling the night watch. It was frustrating to know that he had been signed on to the voyage to provide protection against just such a thing, yet when he attempted to do what was necessary to fulfill his obligation, he was overruled. By all reason he should say no to Usedimare; still, he found him a man difficult to say no to. He smiled. Perhaps Usedimare's backers in Genoa would find it equally difficult to say no.

"You are smiling," Usedimare said, his voice hopeful. "Does that mean you'll go with me?"

Giovanni nodded. "I will sail to Portugal with you, Captain."

CHAPTER 7

SAGRES, PORTUGAL

To make good on the promise to Alvise Cadamosto that the next caravel to be launched would be his, Prince Henry had his shipwrights, carpenters, and artisans concentrate all their efforts on the vessel's completion. However, Aldo Cavalli, provoked by the impatience of youth, still felt that despite the amplified activity, construction was going painfully slowly. He went down to the shipyard nearly every day, ostensibly to help, but in reality to measure the progress being made. For the first few weeks it seemed that progress could barely be measured. Now, however, with the ship's strakes in place, the vessel was finally beginning to take shape.

Though Cadamosto had been an early convert to the qualities of the caravel, Aldo continued to compare it to the galleys with which he was more familiar, finding it hard to believe that this bulky-looking box would be the means by which they went to sea. Gradually, however, his appreciation of the new ship design grew as he heard tales of its sturdiness. Sailors told of riding out storms that Aldo knew would have swamped a galley. And if, as Cadamosto had said, they really were going to sail to "the end of the sea," it would be comforting to do so in a craft as sturdy as the caravel.

While waiting for their ship, Aldo and Cadamosto were given positions in Prince Henry's court. Though little more than titular in nature, the positions did nonetheless require them to be present for official court functions, such as the banquet being given that night honoring Pedro and Inês da Costa, who were returning to Madeira after seeing to the installation of their sons at Sagres.

Aldo had lingered a bit too long at the shipyard and nearly didn't make it back in time to get ready. His tardiness forced him to dress so quickly that he was still making last-minute adjustments to his clothes even as he hurried through the stone corridor that led from his apartment to the great hall.

It was at an earlier such event that Aldo had met the Da Costas and their two sons, Tome and Diogo. Aldo was younger than the Da Costa boys, but they were much closer to his age than anyone else at the court. That a friendship developed between them was, in Inês da Costa's view, not unexpected, particularly since Pedro and Inês had once been close friends of Aldo's mother and father. In fact, over the past several days Pedro had regaled Aldo with stories of some of the experiences he and Inês had shared with Aldo's parents years before.

Aldo felt comfortable with the Da Costas; their marriage reflected that of his own parents, with one partner—in this case, Inês—being highborn and the other from a much lower class. To Pedro's credit he had risen far above his modest birth station to become a highly influential person on Madeira. That prestige, coupled with his past services to the *Infante*, had earned for his sons a position at Prince Henry's court.

Tome and Diogo were students at the navigational school, a fact that impressed Aldo because he was particularly intrigued by the technical advances that had been made by the learned scholars at the school. For their part the Da Costa brothers were impressed by, and perhaps even a bit jealous of, the fact that Aldo would soon be sailing off on a great adventure with the charismatic Alvise

Cadamosto. They had even hinted that they would like to be invited to come along, but Cadamosto, though friendly toward them, was not disposed toward inviting too many, as he put it, hands to cut the pie.

The long, twisting corridor was lighted only by torches placed at long intervals, sufficient light to show Aldo the way, but rendering the corridor for the most part in shadow. As Aldo neared the great hall, however, the corridor grew brighter, for the hall was brilliantly illuminated by seemingly hundreds of torches and candles.

The great golden bubble of light that waited at the end of the hall was filled with laughter and conversation that all but drowned out the lutes and lyres of the court musicians. Aldo saw Tome waiting for him just inside the room.

"You are nearly late. Were you at the shipyard again?" Tome asked.

"Yes," Aldo replied, smiling self-consciously. "Has anyone noticed my absence?" He looked around anxiously.

"I noticed it—but only because I was impatient to see you. I didn't speak of it to anyone," Tome added.

"Thank you."

"How is the work progressing on the ship?"

"Slowly," Aldo answered. "Sometimes I think I could build it faster myself."

Tome laughed. "Oh, you think so, do you? And tell me, my Venetian friend, would you really want to go to sea in a ship of your own construction?"

Aldo laughed with him. "I wouldn't even want to cross the Grand Canal behind my father's house in a ship of my own construction." He looked around for Diogo.

"You are looking for my brother?" Tome asked.

"Yes. Where is he?"

"Look no farther than Luisa," Tome suggested.

"Luisa again? Is this the same Diogo who boasted that there are too many beautiful young girls to waste time with but one?"

Tome sighed. "He did say that, didn't he? I wish he still felt that way. I've never seen Diogo so entranced before. Luisa has some strange power over him. Diogo, the fierce, independent one, has now become a tethered puppy. He is so distracted by the beautiful Luisa Canto that he pays no attention to his studies or me or anything else."

"But surely you can understand such a reaction," Aldo said. "Are you not equally in love?"

"Yes, I am," Tome admitted easily. "But it isn't the same thing. Soledade Bartolomão is a modest, generous girl who wants only to become a wife and raise a family on Madeira. Luisa is vain and selfish, and I can't help but feel that no good will come of Diogo's infatuation with her. And I know that my mother and father feel the same way."

"Why don't you speak to him about your concern?" Aldo asked.

Tome smiled and shook his head. "You don't know my brother. If I told him I disapproved of what he was doing, he would do it all the more. No, my friend, all I can do is hope that he will tire of her—or, what is more likely, that she will tire of him, and the liaison will be ended."

"There he is, standing near the door that leads out to the portico," Aldo said. He waved, then lowered his hand. "He doesn't see me."

"Of course not," Tome replied. "Can't you see that Luisa is with him? He sees no one but her."

Luisa Canto saw Aldo and Tome—but she didn't want Diogo to see them. Diogo's eyes were fastened on her, so she shifted position slightly, knowing the move would direct his line of sight away from where Aldo and Tome were standing.

"I am very angry with you, Diogo da Costa," she scolded.

Diogo's eyes widened in surprise. "Angry? Why? What have I done?"

Luisa pouted. "If you don't know, I'm not going to tell you." She turned and walked through the open door onto the great stone veranda.

"Luisa, wait!" Diogo called. "Please, don't leave!"

Luisa smiled triumphantly to herself. She didn't even

have to look around. She knew he would be hurrying after her, following her outside, which was just what she wanted. Inside the great hall there were too many distractions, like his friend Aldo. Out here she would have him to herself. She walked over to the waist-high stone wall and looked out at the sea.

Below the promontory upon which the castle sat, the sea was a great, black void, given texture by a carpet of moonlight that stretched from the distant horizon under a great silver orb to immediately below, where the waves burst with a luminous froth on the shore.

"Luisa, please, be fair and tell me what I have done to offend you," Diogo said, coming up behind her.

Luisa sighed. "And to think I wore them just for you." Her hand touched the jeweled fasteners in her hair in a seemingly artless manner.

"Those?" Diogo asked. "But yes, I think they're beautiful."

"Do you? Then why did you say nothing about them before now?"

"I—I was so dazzled by your own beauty that your adornments are insignificant by comparison," Diogo said.

Luisa turned toward him, smiling prettily. "Why, Diogo, how sweet you are."

Diogo beamed proudly, then reached for her. "Come," he said. "Let us return to the celebration. I want to display you to my friends."

"By your friends, do you mean your brother, and those—those awful Venetians?"

"Awful Venetians? Do you mean Aldo and Cadamosto? They're hardly awful. In fact, they're very fine fellows, and soon they'll be sailing off on a tremendous voyage."

"Yes, and I suppose you would like to go with them," Luisa complained.

"But of course. Who wouldn't want to go with them? They are going to have a wonderful adventure, discovering new lands and seas. I'd give anything to go with them."

"How do you think that makes me feel?" Luisa asked, sulking.

"I would hope it would make you feel proud of me," Diogo replied.

"Proud of you? Should I feel proud at having you sail off and leave me here, all alone, to fend for myself? Diogo, you have no idea what it is like for a girl alone at court. And if that girl happens to be well placed and pretty," she added immodestly, "it is all the more difficult."

"But you aren't alone," Diogo protested. "You have your father to look out for you."

"My father has his own ideas of who I should marry," Luisa said. "He wants me to marry Duarte d'Afonso."

"Duarte d'Afonso? Do you mean that ridiculous popinjay? *That* Duarte d'Afonso?" Diogo laughed. "If he's my competition, then I have no worry."

"Why do you laugh?" Luisa asked, peeved at the unexpected reaction. "Don't you realize that it would be a good marriage? He is the great-great-nephew of King Afonso the Fifth. If you were gone, I might not be able to resist my father's determination—and the idea of having a title."

Diogo stopped laughing. "But, Luisa, no!" he gasped. "You can't be serious?"

Having regained control of the situation, Luisa smiled benevolently and put her hand to Diogo's cheek. "But why are we worrying about such things?" she asked coyly. "You are here, studying. You aren't off God knows where on some voyage where your ship is likely to sail right over the edge of the world."

Diogo laughed again.

"Now what is so funny?"

"You can't sail over the edge of the world."

"Why not?"

"Because there *is* no edge. The world isn't flat, like a table. It's round, like a ball."

"Yes, I've heard that ridiculous theory, but I don't believe it. Not a word of it. And anyway, what if the world *were* round? What difference would that make? You could still fall off if you sailed too far around it."

"No."

"Why not?"

"I don't know," Diogo admitted. "And neither do any of the scholars at the school. But they all seem to believe that there is something—some type of force—that keeps everything bound to the earth so that even if one were to sail to the very bottom of the globe, he wouldn't fall off."

"But how do they know that? Has anyone ever sailed to the bottom of this thing you call a globe?"

"Well, no."

"No, nor are they likely to, because we don't live on a globe with a bottom."

Movement behind Diogo caught Luisa's eye, and she glanced back toward the entrance to the great hall. Tome was heading toward the doorway, no doubt in search of his brother.

"Diogo, we've talked enough about the sea," she said, thrusting out her lower lip in what she felt was an irresistible pout. "Couldn't you be a little more romantic? As far as I'm concerned, the sea is good only for reflecting the silver light of the moon. Come, let us enjoy a walk."

Diogo hesitated. "I don't know. I really should be getting back inside. You know, my parents are returning to Madeira tomorrow, and I should spend some time with them."

"But you've spent your entire life with your parents," Luisa protested. "Can't you spend this little time with me?" She wrapped a coil of his long hair around her finger, then played lightly with his ear. He shivered. "Wouldn't you like to take a walk along the shore?" she whispered seductively.

"Yes," Diogo replied thickly. "Very much."

Luisa put her arm through his and started toward the long row of stone steps that led from the veranda down the side of the steep hill to the shore below. Her graceful, expert maneuvering had him out of sight by the time Tome reached the terrace to have a look around for his brother.

"Did you see him?" Aldo asked when Tome returned.

"No," Tome answered. "I don't know what happened to him. I was certain I saw him go outside."

"Perhaps he'll turn up later."

"Perhaps," Tome said. "Well, whatever Father has to tell us, he can just tell me. Come, we'll see him together."

"But he sent for you and Diogo," Aldo pointed out, "not for me."

"No matter. You know that he likes you very much. He won't mind saying whatever he has to say in front of you. Besides, aren't you curious?"

"Yes, very curious," Aldo admitted.

Tome smiled. "Then let's see what his summons is all about."

Pedro and Inês da Costa were receiving well-wishers who had come to tell them good-bye. For all his fine garments, Pedro still had the look of a rugged sailor about him, and Aldo knew that there were some who found Pedro's appearance distasteful and whispered things behind his back—knowing better than to say anything to his face, for he was as tough as his countenance indicated.

There were no such whisperings about Inês, a woman as beautiful in aspect as she was graceful in deportment. Watching her as she stood conversing with her fellow guests, Aldo thought her poise and bearing regal.

As the youth approached Pedro, he noticed someone standing beside the Portuguese, a man shorter, younger, and every bit as rugged looking. There was something familiar about him, but Aldo couldn't place it. He knew for a fact that he had never met the man, but he couldn't rid himself of the feeling that he had seen him before.

"Ah, Tome, here you are," Pedro said as Aldo and Tome approached. "And, Aldo, how are you this evening?"

"Very well, thank you, Senhor da Costa," Aldo replied. He made a leg to Inês, who smiled sweetly.

"Where is your brother?" Pedro asked.

"I can't find him, Father."

Pedro's gaze swept around the great hall. "But surely he's here," he said. "I thought I just saw him."

"I'm sure he's here somewhere." Tome chuckled. "But you know how Diogo is. He's everyone's friend, and he must speak to them all."

"I wouldn't be surprised if he wasn't with that Canto

girl," Pedro muttered. "I wish he would find some other distraction."

"Luisa Canto *is* very pretty," Tome said, defending his brother.

"I suppose she is. But I don't trust her." Pedro sighed. "But never mind all that now. I have someone I want you to meet." Pedro turned to the man standing beside him. "Captain Diogo Gomes, this is Tome, the older of my two sons."

"Captain Gomes," Tome said, shaking the sailor's hand.

"Your father tells me that you and your brother are skilled in the arts of sailing and navigation."

"Any skill we have is thanks to my father," Tome replied modestly. "He has trained us in seamanship nearly from the time of our birth."

"Has he now?" Gomes said. "Well, then, you must be fine seamen, indeed, for I've great respect for the man who piloted the ship that discovered Madeira. And I've no doubt that his sons will make contributions that are just as valuable. That's why I agreed to take you with me."

Tome shook his head, confused. "I beg your pardon?"

"I'm going to take you and your brother with me on the Guinea trade," Gomes said. "That is, if you have a wish to go."

An ecstatic grin spread across Tome's face. "Do I have a wish to go? But of course I do! By the saints, this is wonderful!" he said. He grabbed the captain's hand and shook it vigorously. "Thank you, Captain Gomes! Thank you very much!"

"Before you sign on, be warned: I'm a master who must have his way," Gomes said gruffly. "I am called Vinagre Gomes, and the name is not without some justification. Do I make my point?"

"Yes, Captain," Tome said, stifling a grin. He couldn't have thought of a better nickname himself for this acerbic seadog than Vinegar. "And don't worry! My brother and I will do all that we can to please you."

"Just be true to your father and be the good seamen that he assures me you are," Gomes said. "That's all you need do to please me." He looked at Aldo. "And what of you, young man? Are you looking for a berth as well?"

"No, *signóre*," Aldo replied.

"He *has* a berth," Tome put in quickly. "He is Aldo Cavalli, and he will be sailing with Alvise Cadamosto."

"Ah, yes, the Venetian," Gomes said. "I have seen you at the shipyard, checking on the progress of the caravel."

"Yes," Aldo said, realizing now where he had seen Gomes. "I have been there a few times."

"A few times? Aldo, I think you practically live there," Tome suggested, and the others laughed because Aldo's impatience was well-known throughout Sagres.

"Now that *you* have a ship, you will discover what it's like to have to wait," Aldo countered.

"I will make you a bet, Aldo," Tome said. "I will wager that Captain Gomes will sail farther for Prince Henry than your Captain Cadamosto. And my brother and I will make more discoveries than you."

"I accept your wager," Aldo replied enthusiastically.

After a few minutes of small talk, Aldo excused himself to the others. "I must return to my room to finish the letter I am writing to my parents. A ship is leaving for Venice in the morning, and I have arranged for it to carry the letter back."

"You will extend our kindest regards to your mother and father, won't you?" Pedro asked.

"Indeed I will, Signóre da Costa. It will be an honor to do so," Aldo replied.

"I will excuse myself, as well," Tome said. "I will try again to find Diogo. He will be thrilled to hear the news I have for him."

Diogo and Luisa were sitting on a shelf tucked into a depression in the rocks about two thirds down the towering escarpment upon which Prince Henry's castle had been built. Still above the sea, the shelf afforded a view of the foaming, rolling breakers and the dim yellow glow of lamps on the several dozen ships riding at anchor. The couple listened to the relentless sound of surf as it rolled in from a dark sea, boomed against the shore, then retreated, leaving a shimmering smear of iridescent bubbles.

Just below them was a phenomenon created by a quirk of geology: A cavern and a fissure had been formed in the rocks, and this forced the incoming sea to spew a fountain of spray up through the fissure, making it resemble a whale coming to the surface to blow. Occasionally, when the incoming breaker was particularly large, water burst through the fissure with such pressure that it spewed up as high as the shelf where Diogo and Luisa sat, spraying a fine mist.

"Perhaps we should start back now," Diogo said. "I am sure we have been missed—and already our clothes are more than a little damp."

"I told you, I don't mind. I don't want to go back," Luisa said. "I would much rather stay here. Don't you like the view?"

"Of course. But we're getting wet."

"Are you afraid of a little water?"

"No, of course not," Diogo replied, stung by her chiding. "I just think we should go back, that's all."

"Well, if you like the view and you aren't afraid of getting wet, I can only surmise that you don't like my company," she said, pouting.

"Luisa, you know that isn't true."

"How do I know?" she asked. "You have done nothing—" Her words were drowned out at that moment by the explosive thunder of an incoming wave bursting through the fissure and spewing high into the air. Another cool spray of the water blew over the couple.

"I'm sorry," Diogo said. "I didn't hear you."

"I said, how am I supposed to know that you enjoy my company? You have done nothing to show me."

Diogo was confused. "What would you have me do?" he asked.

Luisa began unbuckling the belt that cinched the waist of her dress. She smiled coquettishly. "If you don't know what a man and woman can do together, then perhaps you should ask Duarte d'Afonso."

Diogo had sown a few wild oats back on Madeira, so

he certainly needed no instruction from the likes of Duarte d'Afonso. However, his oats had been sown with serving wenches. He had no idea that young ladies of rank would be interested in such things. And yet Luisa certainly seemed to be indicating that that was exactly what she was interested in.

"Luisa . . . ?" Diogo asked.

"You *would* like to lie with me, wouldn't you, Diogo?" she asked in a sultry voice.

The water again erupted through the hole, sending another fountain roaring high into the sky.

"Yes," Diogo answered thickly. He reached for Luisa and pulled her to him for a kiss. She responded eagerly, letting him know in no uncertain terms what she wanted.

Diogo lay her back on the ground, then slipped his hand under the bodice of her wet dress, exposing and cupping the firm breast. The feel of her smooth, dampened skin under his hand was extremely erotic.

Somewhere between the pounding of the blood in his ears and the surf below him Diogo could hear Luisa's whispers of love. They removed their clothes so that they were lying together, side by side, their nude bodies shining in the fine mist of the spray that continued to gush like a fountain.

Diogo moved over her, pressing his muscular legs against her smooth calves and his hard thighs against her resilient flesh. She rose to meet him, and they began to make love. Below them the surf crashed and the blowhole boomed, Nature's timpani the rhythm for their intimate ballet.

Lying beneath her lover, Louisa smiled victoriously. She had achieved just what she had sought.

VENICE

The gondola carrying Carlo Viviani, his wife, Alva, and their daughter, Francesca, crossed the placid waters, heading for the Borgo *palazzo*. The Vivianis were as yet several hundred yards away, but two of the Borgos' servants were standing there, awaiting their arrival.

"Oh, Francesca, how lovely you look," Alva Viviani said, beaming proudly at her dark-haired young daughter. "Don't you think our child has grown into a beautiful young woman, my husband?"

"Of course," Viviani replied. "And so does Vitale Borgo. His father has told me many times that Vitale has an eye for our Francesca."

"Well, no wonder they were so anxious to have Francesca attend the banquet this evening," Francesca's mother replied, smiling broadly. "Did you hear that, child? You have caught the young Borgo's attention."

"Yes, Mamma, I heard it," Francesca replied. "But I'm too young to think about anyone just yet."

"Too young?" Viviani asked. "Nonsense. You're fourteen now—certainly old enough to become betrothed. And an excellent alliance would be forged between the House of Viviani and the House of Borgo. A marriage between the families would be a financially sound move."

"What of an alliance between the House of Viviani and the House of Cavalli?" Francesca asked. "The Cavallis are wealthier than the Borgos."

"But who in the House of Cavalli would be a potential groom?"

"Why, Papà, you know perfectly well who," Francesca said, surprised to hear her father say such a thing.

Viviani shook his head. "Are you thinking of Aldo Cavalli?"

"Yes, of course."

"He *is* a nice young man," Alva said. She looked at her husband. "And Francesca is certainly correct about the Cavalli wealth," she added. "Their house is stronger even than the Borgos."

"That may be true," Viviani replied. "But Aldo Cavalli is not a marriage prospect for our daughter. He isn't in Venice. Vitale Borgo is."

"Yes, but you said last week that the Galley of Flanders has set sail from Portugal. Aldo will be back soon," Francesca said.

"The fleet set sail, yes, but Alvise Cadamosto left the fleet and remained in Portugal. He plans to sail for Prince Henry. Imagine that, will you? A Venetian, willingly offering his services to a Portuguese sovereign—why, such a thing is almost treasonous. And Aldo Cavalli is with him. It is my understanding that they plan extensive explorations."

"But he will be back," Francesca insisted.

"Perhaps so, but when? You are of the age for us to start seeking a husband for you. If we wait too long, it will be impossible to make a match that would be beneficial to our enterprise."

"Papà, is a good business match the only reason for one to get married?" Francesca asked. "Does love play no role?"

"Love? Ah, don't worry about love. The young are always worrying about love. What you don't understand is, if the match is good, love will come."

"But suppose love comes *before* the match?"

"Ha," Viviani said, laughing, "that isn't very likely to—" He suddenly stopped and frowned at his daughter. "Daughter, are you trying to tell me that you and Aldo . . . that is, has anything happened between the two of you that I should know about? Has he said anything or done anything improper?"

"No, Papà!" Francesca colored at his suggestion. "Actually, he hardly knows that I exist."

"Then I don't understand. What is all this talk about Aldo Cavalli?"

"Nothing in particular, Papà. I was just using him as an example of what might also be considered a good match. We don't have to rush into anything, do we?"

Alva Viviani put her arm around her daughter and gave her husband a scolding look. "Of course we don't, my child," she said to Francesca. "And you, my husband, don't be so impatient to marry our daughter off. She is still a comfort and a joy to her mother."

Viviani sighed. "As she is a comfort and a joy to her father, as well," he said. "Don't worry, my little one. I'm not sending you to the altar yet. At least not until you're

sixteen. But we must start planning these things now. To
delay could be disastrous. Marriage is what counts for you,
after all. We cannot casually make a decision of such important consequence without lengthy scrutiny. Negotia-
tions must be conducted between all parties, after all.
There are so many considerations to take into account: the
dowry, your prospective groom's status and occupation, his
family's political influence—" He broke off. "Ah, here
comes Vitale to greet us. I want you to be nice to him.
That's all I ask. Just be nice."

"All right, Papà, I'll be nice," Francesca promised.
She looked at the callow, pimply-faced young man who
strode importantly down the grounds behind the *palazzo*,
then stood, smiling, by the bank of the canal.

The gondola touched the bank, and the two Borgo
servants scurried into action. One took a line from the
gondolier and held it fast to keep the craft from drifting,
while the other offered his hand to help the occupants
disembark.

Carlo Viviani accepted the man's assistance, then
turned to help his wife, Alva, and his daughter, Francesca.
Just at that moment the servant who had been lashing the
Viviani gondola fast to its mooring pole flicked the rope in
such a way that its dripping water sprinkled Vitale Borgo.
A wet spot appeared on the young man's blue velvet tunic.
His smile disappeared, and his face twisted with rage.

"You stupid idiot!" he screamed. "Look what you've
done!"

"I'm sorry, Messer Vitale," the servant said, falling to
his knees in supplication. "Please forgive me."

"Forgive you, you clumsy oaf? Why, I'll thrash you
within an inch of your life!"

Vitale picked up the rope's knotted end and began
lashing the hapless servant. The first blow caught the man
across the face, leaving a huge welt on his cheek and opening up a cut on his lip. He fell forward, protecting his face
by pressing it to the ground. Vitale, his rage growing, continued to scourge him with the rope, hitting him across the
shoulders and back.

"Oh, Papà, do something!" Francesca cried. Her father was very gentle with their servants, and she had never seen a man so cruelly abused.

Viviani stepped between young Borgo and the whimpering servant just as Vitale drew back his hand for another lash. Vitale immediately dropped his hand to his side.

"Won't you show us into the house, Vitale?" Viviani asked lightly.

Vitale's face was red with anger, and a blood vessel pounded in his temple. His eyes were wide, the pupils small, and a line of spittle ran from his grim mouth down the side of his chin.

"Show you into the house?" he asked, still trembling with anger.

"Yes. Don't you normally welcome your guests?"

The look that Vitale gave the prostrate servant said that he would have preferred to continue administering punishment. But Viviani had put him on the spot. He had no choice but to play the role of gracious host. Reluctantly, and with one last angry sigh of frustration, he tossed the rope aside, then turned toward Francesca and her mother. A smile crossed his face, though his eyes remained cold.

"Yes," he said. "Yes, forgive me. Welcome to our home. Let me show you in."

He reached for Francesca, but she took her mother's hand instead, doing it in such a way as to make it seem a natural move on her part and not a rejection of Vitale's overture. She saw a flash of anger appear in his eyes and smiled sweetly at him; the anger disappeared.

Francesca's smile, in fact, was at the thought of Aldo Cavalli and how wonderful it would be when he came back to her. Whether he really would come back or not, and particularly to her, she had no way of knowing. But the agreeable thought would help her get through the difficult evening—and perhaps even more difficult months—to come.

CHAPTER 8

SAGRES, PORTUGAL

This was the most exciting day in Aldo's life. He had thought previously ascribed that the day he had left Venice aboard one of the galleys of the Fleet of Flanders was the high point of his life, but even that event couldn't compare with this one, and the excitement he had felt then paled beside the euphoria he was feeling this morning. He was bound for adventure in places not only new to him, but to mankind. Just before setting sail, Alvise Cadamosto had renewed his vow to Prince Henry that he would take his ship and crew into uncharted waters and unknown lands. And he welcomed the presence of Filippo Strozzi and his *balestrièri* on any explorations undertaken on terra firma.

The actual sailing of the ship was to be handled by Vincente Dias, a Portuguese who had been appointed by Prince Henry as shipmaster. That position gave Dias authority over the entire crew, subordinate only to Cadamosto, the ship's captain. The *Infante* had made this arrangement because Cadamosto's previous sailing experience had been limited to Venetian galleys, and the Prince decided Cadamosto should have someone expert in the operation of the caravel.

The differences between caravel and galley were immediately made apparent by the absence of rowers' benches. Without rowers to move the ship out into the current, maneuvering it away from the docks required skilled, experienced seamanship. Dias was already proving his value to the voyage by the smoothness with which he got them under way.

"Aldo! Aldo! Good luck to you, Aldo!" a voice called from shore, and Aldo, looking back toward the dock, saw his friends Tome and Diogo waving at him. The Da Costas' own ship would be departing within a few days, though Aldo knew they envied him for leaving first.

"Tome! Diogo! Good-bye!" Aldo called back to them, waving expansively.

"Say hello to our parents!" Diogo shouted, cupping his hands around his mouth.

"And to Soledade!" Tome added.

"I will!" Aldo promised, for Madeira would be the ship's first port of call.

Madeira was not a new land in an uncharted sea, of course, but Aldo found the prospect of visiting the island exciting nevertheless. He was looking forward to seeing Pedro and Inês da Costa again and eager to meet Tome's betrothed, Soledade.

"Here, *moco*, you can watch, but stand to the rail, if you please," Dias ordered. He was neither gruff nor insulting with his instruction, but Aldo felt his face flush, embarrassed at having gotten in the way like some novice traveler.

"Loose the topsails," Dias called.

Sailors climbed aloft on the main- and main-mizzenmasts, then crawled out onto the arms. Aldo had studied the ship during its construction to be thoroughly familiar with the rigging and could call each component by its proper name.

The four masts were: the foremast, the main, the main-mizzen, and the bonaventure. The main and the main-mizzen were the two middle masts and the larger of the group. The foremast and the aftermast, known as the bonaventure, were considerably smaller. The foremast was steeped slightly forward, while the bonaventure mast was raked aft. The main and the main-mizzen were square-rigged with a mainsail and topcourse. The foremast and bonaventure were lateen rigged.

The topsails filled and the ship began to move.

"Loose the mainsails," Dias ordered.

The mainsails were unfurled; then the filling canvas thundered, and the ship felt as if it were leaping forward under the press of sail.

"We've a good following wind, Captain," Dias reported. "We're under way, sir."

"Excellent, Signóre Dias," Cadamosto replied, a grin lighting his face. It was then that Aldo realized that Cadamosto, though older and charged with the awesome responsibility of being the captain of this voyage, was just as excited over the adventure ahead as he was.

"Senhor Dias," a sailor suddenly called. "The main-mizzen topsail halyard is fouled."

"Can you shake it loose?" Dias asked.

"We cannot, sir."

"Very well, send a man aloft."

"It's on the outer tip of the yardarm itself, sir," the sailor reported. "It would take a slight man to crawl out without breaking off the arm, and none of our crew is so slender."

Dias sighed with frustration. "Very well, prepare to put about," he ordered. "We'll have to go back to rig some way of getting up to it."

"Go back?" Cadamosto said. "Surely you can't be serious."

"We've a crippled ship, Capitão Cadamosto, and no way to repair her at sea," Dias explained. "It won't take long, once we're docked."

"But we'll lose the tide."

"Yes, that's true," Dias agreed.

"And if we lose the tide we won't be able to sail until tomorrow."

"That is also true."

"So what you are saying is, it doesn't matter how long

it takes to effect the repair, once we put about, we're going to be in port overnight."

"Yes, I'm afraid so. I'm sorry, Capitão, but there's nothing else to be done."

"Senhor Dias!" one of the sailors shouted, and both Dias and Cadamosto turned to look toward the main-mizzenmast. Aldo was nimbly climbing it.

"It's the Venetian *moco!*" someone said, and all the sailors halted their tasks to watch the young man. He reached the very top, then started working his way out on the arm toward the fouled rope.

"You aloft!" Dias shouted, cupping his hands around his mouth to make himself heard. "Get back down here! You've no business up there! You'll get your fool self killed, and I'll have to answer to the *Infante* for your death! Get down, I say!"

Aldo ignored the order. He had always been agile, and he had always been a climber. The moment he had heard that it would take a man of his size to free the line, he decided to give it a try. The youngest person on the crew, he was also the lightest, and he felt that he would have a good chance of getting the job done.

"Get back down here at once! Do you hear me?" Dias shouted again.

"Capitano, I think I can get it for you," Aldo yelled back down.

He had started on the task with absolute confidence in his ability to reach the end of the arm and free the fouled rope. Suddenly, however, he was having second thoughts about the wisdom of the attempt. Though for the past several months he had climbed all over the masts and rigging of ships, the ships he had thus explored had been at anchor, and their masts had been as steady as trees growing in a forest. That was certainly not the case now. This ship was under way, and as it climbed up, shuddered, then slid back down each rolling wave, its masts dipped and swayed so that Aldo was nearly tossed off. Still, he didn't want to spend one more day ashore—and besides, he couldn't turn back now without facing the ridicule of the other crewmen. He had no choice. He had to go on.

Wrapping himself tightly around the yardarm, he inched his way out to the end. He glanced down; he saw the pitching deck of a ship that seemed very small to him now and the upturned faces of all the sailors watching him. Foreshortened by his angle, they looked even smaller and farther away than they really were.

Looking down was a big mistake. Aldo began to get nauseous. He closed his eyes to blot out the image, and when he opened them again, he forced himself to concentrate only on the fouled rope dangling just a tantalizingly few feet in front of him. Taking a deep breath, he continued on his task, moving slowly but steadily forward until he reached the errant rope.

Fortunately the knot was very easy to loosen, and within a moment Aldo had the fouled halyard freed. A cheer floated up from the sailors, and Aldo glanced down again just long enough to acknowledge their cheers. He gave a quick wave, then started back.

At that moment the ship hit a particularly large wave. The vessel was tossed up, holding its position for a long, quivering moment before crashing back down sharply. The movement was so turbulent that before he realized what was happening to him, Aldo was thrown off the mast.

"Look out!" someone shouted from the deck below.

Aldo fell through space, his hands flailing out in front of him. He closed his eyes, not wanting to see the deck that seemed to be racing up to meet him, the deck that would smash every bone in his body. . . . As luck would have it, he managed to grab one of the stays. He desperately clutched it, stopping his fall with an arm-snapping wrench. He hung there for a moment, his gasps for breath barely audible above his pounding heart. He wouldn't be smashed against the deck after all.

Finally, his breathing now more or less normal, it was just a matter of sliding the rest of the way down to step lightly onto the deck.

"Good man!" Cadamosto said, beaming proudly and hurrying over to shake his young friend's hand. The rest of the crew was cheering lustily. It seemed that they believed he had purposefully leapt rather than fallen, and they were impressed with his steady nerves and catlike agility. Grinning self-consciously, Aldo decided to keep the truth to himself.

FUNCHAL, MADEIRA

Although Madeira had become a regular port of call for both English and Portuguese ships, the residents of the island still felt isolated enough that the arrival of a ship was a great event. Ships brought mail and visitors. They also brought many luxury items, purchased with the wine and sugar and dragon's blood for which Madeira was famous.

Since many residents of the island had come as *degredados* in the days of colonization, a common touch remained to even the wealthiest of the citizens. This served them well when they were dealing with the seafaring men of many nations who called there. The islanders might have grown wealthy, but they had not grown fat and complacent with their success.

Though a Portuguese possession, should the need have ever arisen for Madeira to field an army, the citizens were perfectly capable of doing so without help from the mainland. They were justifiably proud of their *cavaleiros* and could put eight hundred armed men in the field if necessary, one hundred twenty of whom would be mounted. Many of these armored *cavaleiros* were on hand to greet Cadamosto's ship, adding to the welcoming festivities.

When the ship was safely in the harbor, Vincente Dias furled the sails and allowed the tenders sent out by Funchal's harbormaster to pull the caravel up to the pier. Aldo stood at the rail and watched the rowers in the small boats sweat and strain to pull the big ship across the bay, reminding him of the galleys in which he had originally gone to sea, depending as they did as much on the muscles of men for their motive power as they did on the wind. By contrast, this passage from Portugal had been made in its entirety by harnessing the force of wind in the sails. It was so much more efficient a way of doing things that the straining efforts of the men in the small boats suddenly seemed archaic, and Aldo wondered if he could ever go back to ships that depended upon the pain and strain of human labor for their locomotion.

"Stand by the bowline!" Dias shouted as he steered the big ship to a gentle landing at one of the empty docks.

"Bowline ready!"

"Stand by the stern line!"

"Stern line ready!"

"Make fast all lines!"

The recipients of Dias's shouted orders were two sailors holding hawsers at either end of the vessel. At Dias's command they tossed their lines to men waiting on the dock, who then slipped the looped rope's ends over pilings, making the ship fast.

Almost immediately after the ship was docked gangplanks were lowered to begin taking on some of the produce of Madeira that Cadamosto had contracted for even while awaiting the completion of his ship in Sagres. Sweating dock workers rolled each barrel aboard, then stowed them securely at various places on the deck and in the cargo hold.

After all the casks of sugar and kegs of wine were loaded, they began lading on cattle. A few pigs and a handful of chickens were brought aboard to provide for the crew's dietary needs, but what caught Aldo's attention were the horses—six mares and six stallions led up the gangplank in pairs by handlers keeping the horses in check with short halter ropes.

"Here, careful with those horses, now!" Cadamosto shouted. The warning was elicited when the first pair of horses shied at the gangplank and began to stamp around, resisting the efforts to get them aboard. "Those animals are worth their weight in gold in the Guinea trade," Cadamosto added.

Aldo did not know if the horses were really worth that much, but he had heard from the Portuguese who had been carrying on a brisk commerce with the Africans that of all trading goods offered by the Europeans, horses were the most prized.

They were also the most difficult cargo, requiring constant tending for the duration of the voyage. Aside from having to be fed and watered, they didn't take well to sea travel and thus would have to be watched closely to keep them from injuring themselves or each other during times of fright or discomfort.

Aldo helped with the loading of the horses. When the animals were secure in their stalls, he went ashore, intending to honor the promise he had made to Pedro and Inês da Costa that he would pay them a call when his ship reached Madeira.

As it so happened, a messenger had met the ship upon its arrival. He carried with him an invitation from the Da Costas to Aldo Cavalli, Captain Alvise Cadamosto, and shipmaster Vincente Dias to dine at their villa. Pressing ship's business prevented Cadamosto and Dias from accepting the invitation, leaving Aldo with the sole responsibility of carrying out the ship's social obligation.

Noticeable by its omission was an invitation to Filippo Strozzi. Strozzi made light of the matter, saying that it made no difference to him, but Aldo was sure that he was actually quite miffed by the slight.

"I am certain it was a mere oversight on their part, Capitano," Aldo told the strutting *balestrièri* commander. "I would be amenable to speaking to the Da Costas about it."

"No," Strozzi said, holding up his hand. "I have no wish to attend such a boring event. Besides, I don't have the time. I plan to make the maximum use of our stay in port to institute drills for the *balestrièri*. I have no doubt but that we will be engaged at some time during the voyage, whether by Moorish corsairs or strange creatures from unknown lands I don't know. But when that occasion arises, I intend that I and my men will be prepared for it."

"I hope it comes soon!" Aldo said in youthful excitement. He held up his crossbow. "I would like the opportunity to demonstrate my skill."

Cadamosto, overhearing Aldo's enthusiasm, laughed. "I'll certainly be glad to have such a stalwart warrior with me," he said.

Embarrassed for having sounded like a braggadocio, Aldo flushed and quickly excused himself from the ship to accompany the messenger to the Da Costa home.

From the vantage point of the Da Costa estate on the crown of a hill overlooking both the city of Funchal and its sparkling, vessel-filled bay, the fifty-five-ton caravel that had brought Aldo and Cadamosto to this island was clearly visible from the Da Costa's veranda. Having completed its loading at the dock, the caravel had been towed out some one hundred yards offshore, where it now rode at anchor. Standing on the veranda, Aldo looked down at the ship, which, like the others in the harbor, had its masts free of sail. Also like many of the others, the red and gold flag of Portugal flew from atop its main-mizzenmast. But it did have one distinction: Cadamosto's green and white personal ensign fluttered from the bonaventure, making the ship easily identifiable from all the others.

Just beyond the profuse flowering vines and shrubs that surrounded the Da Costa house were the vineyards. The wine grapes growing down all four sides of the mountain had transformed the Da Costa family from a lowly status to one of high regard.

Aldo found to his surprise that he was the guest of honor at a gala banquet. In attendance with her parents was Soledade Bartolomão. Aldo now had the opportunity to meet the young woman who had captured Tome da Costa's heart.

He met Carlo Cominho as well. Aldo knew from Tome and Diogo that Carlo was the one they had defeated during the Contest for the Gold, and though neither Da Costa youth had spoken ill of Carlo, Aldo had gotten the distinct impression that they were not overly fond of him.

"So," Carlo said, approaching Aldo as he stood talking to Soledade, "tell me about my good friends Diogo and Tome. Have they both lost their hearts to the ladies of Prince Henry's court?"

Aldo glanced at Soledade and saw a twinge of hurt flicker across her face. Carlo was certainly callous, if nothing else.

"No, of course not," Aldo said quickly. "They have

both been very busy with their studies. And by now they've most certainly already set sail on the voyage with Captain Gomes."

Carlo laughed. The sound was brittle and without mirth. "You can't convince me that two young, healthy men with prodigious appetites for women can be set loose in Sagres without sampling as many of the delights as such a place would have to offer," he scoffed. "If so, then you don't know Tome and Diogo as well as I thought."

"Well, Diogo is quite the bon vivant, of course," Aldo said. "But not Tome."

"You don't really expect us to believe that Tome is staying true to—" Carlo stopped in midsentence and looked over at Soledade, who was now staring at the floor in flushed embarrassment. He cleared his throat. "Oh, please forgive me, *senhorita*," he said to Soledade. "I am sorry if I spoke out of turn. Tome pledged himself to you, and I am sure that he is honoring that pledge. What man would not?"

Though Carlo's tone was ingratiating, it was quite obvious that he wasn't in the least sincere, and Aldo felt that he had raised the subject simply for the purpose of casting doubt upon Tome's fidelity. Aldo's impression was further buttressed after dinner when, while taking a walk through the gardens, he overheard a conversation between Carlo and Soledade.

"I only tell you these things for your own good, Soledade," Carlo was saying. "You are foolish to keep your vow to Tome when it is obvious that he isn't keeping his vow to you."

"But that isn't obvious at all," Soledade said. "You heard Senhor Cavalli say that Tome is being true to me."

"I am afraid Cavalli is speaking out of his loyalty to Tome, not from any regard he may feel for you," Carlo said.

"Yes, I am loyal to Tome," Aldo said, stepping out from behind a large bush to confront Carlo. "But I am also loyal to the truth. Tome has been absolutely faithful to Signorina Bartolomão, and I will not stand by and listen to you cast doubts."

"You will not stand by?" Carlo challenged. "Am I to take that as a threat?"

Aldo squared his stance and looked at Carlo, prepared for anything he might try. "If you wish to take it as a threat, so be it," Aldo said quietly.

Carlo looked at him for a long moment, then shrugged. "I am not going to fight you, Venetian," he said casually. "I meant only to spare the fair *senhorita* the pain of heartbreak. I'll be taking my leave now."

Soledade watched Carlo's retreating back, then turned to Aldo and smiled. "Thank you for reassuring me."

"No thanks are needed for speaking the truth," Aldo replied.

"Would you walk me back to the house, please?" she asked.

"It would be my pleasure."

THREE DAYS LATER

"We're running full and by at your command, Captain Cadamosto," Vincente Dias reported.

"Thank you," Alvise Cadamosto replied. "How many days until we raise the Canaries?"

"Three."

Cadamosto nodded, pleased, then walked to the stern of the ship, where Aldo stood watching Madeira sink into the sea behind them.

"Did you hear Dias's report?" Cadamosto asked. "Three days and we'll be in the Canaries. They are the gateway to the unknown, my young friend. Beyond that place we shall be charting new territory."

"Yes," Aldo said, a wistful tone in his voice.

Cadamosto looked at him in surprise. "I must say, that's a rather subdued response. I thought you'd be excited by the prospect."

"I *am* excited. Truly, I am. I was just thinking—"

"Of the lovely young lady you left behind?" Cadamosto offered.

"The lovely young lady? Of whom are you speaking?"

"Soledade Bartolomão, of course."

Aldo shook his head. "You are mistaken, Capitano. I did not leave her behind. She is betrothed to my friend Tome."

"Yes, I know, and you are far too much the gentleman to ever do anything but admire his taste," Cadamosto said. He tousled the youth's hair. "But that doesn't keep you from thinking about her, does it?"

"No," Aldo admitted. "She was most gracious to me during the time we were on the island, and I couldn't help but admire her."

"And she you?"

"I—I don't know," Aldo said. "I hope not."

"And yet, the possibility does exist, does it not?"

Aldo nodded. "Our parting was bittersweet. And fortuitous," he added. "For indeed, if we had lingered a bit longer, I fear I would have been unable to leave her behind. Now . . ." He let the word hang.

"Now," Cadamosto said, speaking for him, "you can clear your mind of her and dedicate yourself anew to the quest that lies before us."

As the shipmaster had predicted, they raised the Canary Islands in three days. Here, at the gateway to the unknown, Cadamosto had the ship's complement refill all the water kegs, both for the crew and for the horses. Dias suggested also that they lay at anchor for a few days while the ship's carpenters and sailmakers went over the caravel prior to the next leg of the voyage.

"But why should we do that, Signóre Dias? The ship has suffered no damage as a result of our transit to this place," Cadamosto complained. "I can see no purpose in delaying for any longer the onset of our exploration."

"Permit me, Capitão," Dias said, "but I am charged with the safety of the men and of Prince Henry's ship. I have sailed into these waters before, and I know that there are whirlpools, contrary winds, and boiling seas that can tear apart all but the sturdiest of ships."

"Are you trying to convince me to go no farther?" Cadamosto asked.

"No, Capitão," Dias replied. "But you are a young man with an adventurous spirit, and sometimes men like you act in haste. The *Infante* assigned me to you to be a modifying influence against such hasty acts." Dias smiled and put his hand on Cadamosto's shoulder. "Please believe me, *senhor*, I am as anxious as you to explore new territory for Prince Henry. But my many years at sea have taught me the value of prudent behavior. What would be the harm in spending a few days here to make certain that all is in readiness?"

Cadamosto sighed. "Very well. Do what you must." He looked over the railing at the rocky crags of the island. "Perhaps I will look around for a bit. It is *my* first time here, even if I am not the first."

"Be very careful of the natives, Capitão," Dias warned. "Only a few have been Christianized. Many still live in the mountains and are wild and dangerous."

Filippo Strozzi, who was listening in on the conversation, laughed.

"Oh, come now, Dias, how dangerous can a handful of savages be?" he asked. He took in his *balestrièri* with a wave of his hand. "My fellows should certainly be able to handle them with little difficulty. Don't worry, Capitano Cadamosto, if you want to explore any of this island, I'll provide you with the protection of a mounted guard."

"No, not mounted," Cadamosto said, holding up his hand. "We'll take no chances with the horses."

"God's beard, Cadamosto, you think more of those horses than you do of the men," Strozzi complained.

"That is as it should be," Cadamosto answered coolly. "I can trade the horses, not the men. Now, if you would, please, get a small shore party ready. I would like to have a look around, and I will follow our good friend Dias's advice to be prudent, so I will have you and your *balestrièri* accompany me."

*   *   *

It had been nearly two hours since Cadamosto, Aldo, Strozzi, and the shore party left the ship. They were climbing a narrow, twisting path that hugged the edge of a cliff on one side, while on the other side was a sharp, steep drop of over a hundred feet. The expedition was being led by one of Strozzi's soldiers, a strong man with broad shoulders and rippling muscles. Even he was panting hard from the exertion of the climb.

It was very hot, and sweat streamed down the explorers' faces. Aldo felt sorry for the soldiers, who were baking inside their metal breastplates, helmets, and leg protectors. They were also carrying heavy shields as well as from their crossbows, making walking, and especially climbing, quite an effort.

"Where are these Canarian savages?" one of the soldiers grunted disgustedly. "I haven't seen anything."

"Maybe there aren't any," one of the others suggested.

"They're here, all right," another put in. "I've seen them."

"You've seen Canarians since we arrived here?" Cadamosto asked.

"No, not since we arrived," the man answered. "But I have seen them as slaves. Many slaves come from these islands. They bring a good price, I'm told."

"Cadamosto," Strozzi said, "suppose we capture a dozen or so? Would that not allow us to turn a profit on this voyage?"

"It might," Cadamosto replied. "But it isn't slaves we're after. It's gold and exploration."

"I've heard slaves called gold," Strozzi said. "Black gold," he added with a sinister laugh.

Suddenly a hailstorm of rocks and stones hurtled down from the cliffs above. Several fist-size rocks hit the big man who was leading the party, the first one knocking off his helmet and the others slamming into his head. He tumbled over the edge of the steep path, crashing into the boulders far below. That he made no sound on the way down suggested he had been knocked unconscious, perhaps even killed, by the rocks that had struck him.

"Look out!" someone shouted, though his warning wasn't needed, for by now everyone was aware that they were under attack.

Aldo ducked just as a rock whizzed by his head, missing him by inches. Many others of the hurled missiles were more accurate, as attested to by the rattle of stones against metal breastplates and helmets.

"Strozzi! Strozzi! Rally your men!" Cadamosto shouted to the captain, who had been one of the first to take shelter.

Aldo looked up to the top of the cliff and saw a naked man painted in green and yellow stripes standing on the edge of the cliff, angrily shaking his fist at the group of soldiers and yelling. The man was well formed and tall—taller than most Portuguese—with light skin and fair hair. At first Aldo thought the native was talking in his own tongue; after a moment, however, he realized that the Canarian was shouting to them in Portuguese.

"Não escravo!" the Canarian shouted over and over. "Não escravo!" His last shout was followed by another fusillade of rocks thrown by the more than two dozen men who were with him, all of them naked but brightly painted.

Cadamosto cocked his head. "What is he saying?"

"He is saying 'no slave,' " Aldo said. "Maybe he thinks we're slave traffickers."

Cadamosto cupped his hands around his mouth and yelled back up toward the native Canarians as loudly as he could, "No slaves! We have not come for slaves!"

The natives looked back down toward the group of explorers for a moment longer; then they backed away from the edge of the cliff so that they could no longer be seen from below. Aldo started to stand, but Cadamosto held out his hand, motioning for him to stay put.

"Wait a minute," he said. "Strozzi," he called. "This is your area. Take a few men and go up there to have a look around."

Strozzi hesitated, looking up at the top of the cliff wall. Then slowly, cautiously, he stood and waved at a couple of his men, and they silently started climbing to the top.

Aldo joined them.

"What are you doing here?" Strozzi asked.

"You might have need of a crossbow," Aldo said, holding his weapon up.

Strozzi gazed at him for a long moment, then grunted and nodded. "Come along," he said.

Holding his crossbow at the ready, Aldo started up the side of the cliff with the others. It took them almost ten minutes to reach the top, but when they did, they were rewarded with a memorable vista. From here they could see the entire island and the sea surrounding it as well. Their ship far below was but a tiny carving, bobbing on a great background of blue.

"Where are they?" someone asked. "Where did they go?"

"I've no idea," Strozzi answered gruffly. "They just appeared, and then they disappeared."

"But weren't they magnificent creatures?" Aldo said.

"Magnificent? They're nothing but savages," Strozzi snorted. "They would be magnificent only if Cadamosto would change his mind and let us capture a few for slaves."

"How would we capture them? We couldn't even catch up with them," Aldo pointed out.

"If we shot a few of them in their naked asses, we'd slow them down sure enough," Strozzi growled. "Come on, men," he said to the others. "We'd best be getting back to join our captain. We wouldn't want to leave him unprotected, now, would we?"

Aldo glanced over at Strozzi. The tone of Strozzi's words made Aldo believe that that was exactly what he would like to do: leave Cadamosto unprotected. But why? Aldo wondered. Unless Strozzi coveted Cadamosto's position for himself. If something happened to Cadamosto during this voyage, Strozzi was already letting it be known, he would take over.

Aldo shivered. He had been around Strozzi long enough now to know that under no circumstances would he want to be part of an expedition under the soldier's command. And the best way to avoid that, he decided, was to make absolutely certain that nothing happened to Cadamosto.

Aldo had signed on as a bowman of the quarterdeck during a routine trading voyage with the Galley of Flanders. Now he was taking upon himself the responsibility of personal bodyguard to Captain Alvise di Ca' da Mosto on a voyage to the end of the sea. Six months ago, perhaps, such a prospect would have daunted him. But no longer. Now he was perfectly prepared to perform whatever service was required of him—and absolutely confident that he could do it.

As the ship proceeded south from the Canary Islands, the sun grew warmer and warmer until it beat down upon the ship and its crew with an oppressive ferocity. Cadamosto and Dias allowed the crew to strip down to their breeches to find some relief, but Strozzi insisted that his soldiers continue to be fully dressed, including their armored breastplates. When Cadamosto suggested that Strozzi might allow his men some relief from the heat, the soldier replied that the *balestrièri* were under *his* command.

"A soldier who surrenders to the elements is a soldier without discipline," Strozzi insisted. "And a soldier without discipline is a soldier without worth."

For two more days Strozzi's men sweltered under the blast of the sun; then they began to pass out, and one of them died.

Cadamosto took personal charge.

"Captain Strozzi, you may be the commander of the military contingent on board this ship, but I remind you that the military contingent and its commander are here to serve the needs of the voyage. They will not be able to serve the needs of the voyage if they are unconscious from the heat. Or dead. You will permit them to remove the armor and excess clothing."

Strozzi glared at Cadamosto, showing his displeasure at Cadamosto's interference with his command. Finally he said in a hostile voice, "Very well, Captain. I will allow the men to remove their armor. But if they fail us in a time of need, the fault will be upon your shoulders."

"I will accept culpability."

Strozzi called his men together on the middeck of the ship. He had them stand at rigid attention while he strutted back and forth, preaching the need for military discipline. Two more men passed out during this exercise before he finally relented and allowed the rest of the company to remove the heavy breastplates, which were now so hot from the sun that they blistered the fingers of anyone who touched them barehanded.

The soldiers' morale improved decidedly after that, though Strozzi, always sullen and moody, became even more so. For the rest of the day he kept to himself as much as was possible on the small ship.

That night Aldo stood at the starboard rail at middeck, looking out over the sea. He could hear the sea slapping against the ship's hull. Wood groaned and ropes creaked, and now and again a sound like a thunderclap filled the air as one of the billowing sails spilled wind.

The night was clear, and the moon hung like a huge lantern. The sea stretched out to the horizon, a gently rolling deep purple topped by whitecaps flickering like a hundred thousand candle flames.

"A beautiful sight, is it not?" a voice asked.

Aldo turned. Cadamosto had come down from the sterncastle to stand at the rail beside him.

"Yes, it is," Aldo replied. "And all the more beautiful because no one has seen it before."

Cadamosto sighed. "That isn't true, I'm afraid. The Portuguese have been here before."

Aldo looked at him in surprise. "But I thought the Canary Islands were the gateway to unknown waters."

"To the west, perhaps; not to the south, of course," Cadamosto said. He nodded toward the quarterdeck where Dias stood, hands on his hips, staring up at the main and main-mizzen topsails. "Portuguese explorers, our own Shipmaster Dias included, have sailed south for quite some distance. All the way to Prince Henry's trading post at Arguim. Surely while at Sagres you learned of the European-style houses at Arguim and of the fort, established to guard the commerce forever. No one can trade with the

Arabs there except those who hold a license from Prince Henry."

Aldo winced with embarrassment. "I suppose I do vaguely recall hearing such things, but for some reason I got it in my head that I would be the first person to see what lay in the sea beyond the Canaries." He laughed sheepishly. "Well, at least I will be the first Venetian—other than you, of course."

Cadamosto laughed with him. "That much *is* true."

"This Arguim, what sort of trade can be conducted at such a place?" Aldo asked.

"A very profitable one," Cadamosto said with a chuckle. "About three hundred fifty miles inland, I am told, is the great trading city of Wadan, where caravans from Timbuktu and other Arab trading centers terminate. There caravans divide up the gold for transport to Tunis, Oran, and the other North African ports, which are now closed to Christian traders. But much of the gold from Wadan is now sent to Prince Henry's factory at Arguim."

"And we are going to trade for that gold?" Aldo asked.

"Yes. Although how successful we shall be there I do not know. It would seem that too many people already know of this trade. And of the equally lucrative trade in slaves," he added.

"Are there many slaves from there?"

Cadamosto nodded. "About a thousand per year, I understand. The Arabs and the Berbers carry on quite a traffic in that particular commerce." He nodded toward Strozzi, who was standing morosely on the larboard side of the ship. "Of course, Strozzi is trying to talk me into taking a raiding party ashore to capture slaves for ourselves."

"Are you going to do it?"

"No, I don't think so. Actually, Prince Henry has specifically forbade the practice of raiding parties. He hopes that, by kindness, those being sold might be converted to Christianity."

"Whether the people are captured or bought by us, it would hardly seem a kindness to be taken as slaves," Aldo observed.

"True enough, I suppose," Cadamosto said. "But as

long as there is a profit in slavery, the business will be maintained." He put both hands on the rail and stared far out to sea. "However, there are more things to be considered than the making of a profit," he finally said. He pointed west. "We are going south now, but someday, Aldo, a stout ship and a brave crew will chase the setting sun as far as they can go, until they reach the end of the sea."

"The end of the sea?" Aldo said with a smile. "Captain, you sound like one of those people who think the world is riding upon the back of a turtle, with an edge over which one could sail."

Cadamosto laughed. "No, my young friend, not an edge," he said. "But an end, yes, for the sea must end somewhere. The question is, does it end on the shores of some new land? Or, by sailing far enough in that direction, will we circumnavigate the globe to reach India?"

"What a unique idea," Aldo said.

Cadamosto shrugged. "Yes, well, it's not a question for us to decide. That will be a voyage for another explorer. What we are going to do is sail south—farther south than anyone has ever gone before. So I have promised Prince Henry, and so shall we do."

"And so shall we do," Aldo repeated.

CHAPTER 9

IN THE WATERS OFF AFRICA

Aldo was asleep, curled up near one of the canvas lockers. His body had learned to make unconscious adjustments to the pitch and roll of the ship as it plowed through the sea so that, under normal conditions, he would sleep right through it. However, one particularly violent pitch and roll penetrated through the fog of his sleep, and when he awoke, he discovered he was unconsciously hanging on to a stanchion to keep from being thrown across the deck.

"Capitão Cadamosto, we're getting into very heavy seas," Dias shouted through a loud, whining wind. "With your permission, I'll be reefing the sails."

"Do whatever you think best, Signóre Dias," Cadamosto shouted back.

The sea had been as calm as a millpond when earlier Aldo had lain down to take his nap. Amazed at the sudden change, he leapt to his feet to have a look around. As he did so, the bowsprit dipped and poked through a large swell. The wave broke over the bow, throwing spray the entire length of the deck.

"Reef the main topsail!" Dias shouted into the wind,

and a handful of sailors scrambled up the mainmast. "Bosun, see that there is a proper furl!"

"*Sim, senhor!*" the bosun called back, his voice sounding thin in the tempest that buffeted them.

The wind was blowing with nearly gale force now, and the ship was crashing violently through the waves. Aldo steadied himself at the rail and watched the men work. They furled the topsail with authority, but the wind continued to build until suddenly the great mainsail on the mainmast ripped open from top to bottom.

"Bosun! Put some men on that sheet before it blows to tatters!" Dias yelled.

"*Sim, senhor!*"

The sailors who had been working on the main topsail now clambered back down the mast to work on the torn mainsail, but no sooner had they finished with it than the main-mizzen topsail tore loose and began flapping in the breeze, threatening to pull away and take with it the top part of the main-mizzen mast, now vibrating like a wand.

"Damn!" Dias swore. "I'd better get up there."

"I'll go," Cadamosto volunteered, heading for the main-mizzen mast. Within moments he was climbing the rigging and nearly to the errant sail.

The howling wind grew even louder, nearing hurricane velocity, and the mountainous waves were battering against the hull of the ship with the impact of cannonballs. The caravel would be lifted by one swell, hang quiveringly over the trough between swells, then slam back down into the sea, only to be caught up by another, even larger wave. The vessel was knocked to the side, slapped about as if it were prey caught in the claws of some great beast.

Cadamosto was stepping from the braces to the weather spreader just as a violent move of the ship jerked the spreader away. He had already transferred his weight from one foot to the other, so he lost his balance. Fortunately he grabbed the gaff, preventing a fall. Aldo stood on the deck, looking up with his heart in his throat. Finally, after what felt like hours, Cadamosto managed to improve his position until his feet were braced again. Gripping the mast, he cut the topsail loose, and it flew back in the wind, landing in the frothy sea several hundred feet behind the ship. Carefully, and holding on for dear life, Cadamosto climbed back down to the deck.

Finally Dias had the ship's sails reefed so that the masts were bare, like winter trees prodding the dark gray sky. Shortly after the sails were reefed the rain began, large, heavy drops that blew in sheets across the deck and mixed with the salty sea spray.

"Signóre Dias!" Filippo Strozzi shouted into the wind, "you must head for shore! You must put in to land or we will all be killed!"

"I can't head for the shore," Dias replied. "There are shoals and rocks that would wreck the ship. We must stand out to sea!"

"You're a madman!" Strozzi screamed. "We'll all be killed!"

"Strozzi, if you can be of no help here, then I must order you to go below. Go below, *senhor*!"

"No!" Strozzi shouted back. "I'll not be below deck aboard a sinking ship!"

"By God, we have not sunk yet, *senhor*," Dias snapped. "And if you will allow my men to do their jobs, we will not sink. Now, get you below!"

Strozzi glared at Dias for a long, angry moment; then, when the ship made another particularly violent roll, he relented and started below.

"That goes for all hands! If you aren't helping, go belowdecks to ride out the storm!" Dias ordered.

"Aldo! Come with me!" Cadamosto shouted. "We must check the horses!"

Aldo started below with Cadamosto, but progress was not made easily. He scrambled wildly across the deck toward the hatch, holding on to whatever he could find. At one point the ship rolled hard to larboard, nearly heeling over. Had Aldo loosened his grip on the stanchion he clung to, he would have slid from the deck almost straight down into the boiling ocean.

The vessel righted itself again. Aldo dashed to the hatchway just as the ship made another great roll. It took nearly superhuman effort, but he finally managed to make it down the ladder to the second deck. It was quite dark there, with the only light washing in through the gray openings of the small portholes. Even in the dim light, however, Aldo could see that three of the horses were already down. The eyes of the other horses reflected their terror.

"Help me, Aldo!" Cadamosto shouted against the screaming wind of the violently tossing ship. "We'll lose them all if we don't do something!"

It was almost impossible to work. Although there was no danger of being thrown overboard, the furious lurching continued unabated as the caravel dipped and climbed on monstrous swells, rolling back and forth as it pitched through the sea. The condition of the horses themselves made helping them almost impossible. They stood stiff-legged, fighting the rolling action of the ship to avoid being dashed against the sides of their stalls and thus fighting against the efforts of Aldo and Cadamosto as well.

"We must get them tied!" Cadamosto shouted, hurrying to the first stall.

His strategy was to get each horse as close to one wall of the stall as possible, then to shorten the rope so that the animal couldn't be thrown to the other side. Despite the conditions, the two Venetians persisted, until finally the nine remaining horses were securely tied.

"There!" Cadamosto shouted as they got the last animal taken care of. "I don't know how much help this is going to be, but it's the only thing we can do."

"What about the three horses that are already dead?" Aldo called. "The other horses smell death, and it's terrifying them."

"I know. But there's nothing we can do about it now. When the storm breaks, we'll toss the carcasses overboard. For now we need to get somewhere where we can ride out the storm without being tossed overboard ourselves!"

"How about the galley?" Aldo yelled back.

Cadamosto nodded. "Excellent idea! The tables are nailed down there!"

The idea of riding out the storm in the galley was such a good one that several other crewmen had come to the same conclusion. They were there sitting quietly, staring out through eyes eerily similar to the horses' terrified eyes.

The galley itself was a shambles. The benches were securely mounted around the tables, so they and the tables, also secured to the deck, were still in place. But nothing else was fast. All the cabinet doors had swung open, emptying their contents onto the floor in a jumble of broken crockery and piles of sugar, flour, and beans. With each roll of the ship the crockery slid from side to side, tinkling, cracking, and breaking into smaller and then still smaller pieces.

Strozzi, who was one of the men in the galley, was sitting at a table with his legs wrapped securely around the leg of the bench and his hands gripping the table edge. His face was gray, his mouth was set, and, like the others, his eyes were full of horror.

The ship rolled hard to starboard, far beyond a forty-five-degree angle. It hung in place for a perilously long time, and Aldo felt his heart come up to his throat as he truly believed that they were about to founder. He glanced at everyone else to see if they shared his fear, and he saw that Strozzi was so ashen-faced that he had no color at all. Finally, just when he thought the ship would complete its roll and go hull up, it shuddered and creaked, then righted itself. Aldo heard a dozen quickly mumbled prayers—his own included.

"Cadamosto! You have brought us too far," Strozzi suddenly shouted. "We have come to the place of boiling waters! We are going to sink!"

"The waters aren't boiling," Cadamosto scoffed. "This is only a storm."

"A storm? A storm, you say? Have you ever seen a storm like this? No, it is no storm!"

Another sudden lurch of the ship brought water crashing through the hatch above, wetting down everything in the galley. Strozzi got up from the table and ran over to the corner, where he lay facedown, his arms covering his head.

"We're all going to die!" he shrieked. "Oh, God in

heaven, have mercy on us! I don't want to die! I don't want to die!"

Aldo looked contemptuously at the soldier. He contrasted the groveling coward he was looking at now with the bragging popinjay who would strut so gloriously at parties while entertaining all who would listen with tales of his bravery in battle. Strozzi did not fare well in the comparison.

"Do you think he will be all right, Captain?" Aldo asked, nodding toward the whimpering Strozzi.

Cadamosto looked at Strozzi with ill-concealed contempt. "He'll fare no worse than the rest of us. Let us just hope our brave military commander shows more courage in the face of real dangers than he has shown in the midst of a little rain and wind," he snorted.

The storm continued through the remainder of the long gray afternoon and into the night. Occasionally Aldo would doze fitfully, though he could not be sure when he was asleep and when he was awake. Sometimes Cadamosto would say something to him, and he would respond, but for the most part the night was spent in silence.

"This is quite a ship," Cadamosto said.

"I beg your pardon?" Aldo replied, startled by the statement, coming as it did at the end of a long period of silence.

Cadamosto was standing by the ladder that led up to the deck. Strangely, Aldo had not seen him stand, and he did not know how he had gotten over there.

"I said, this is quite a ship," Cadamosto repeated. "Such a storm would have sunk a lesser vessel."

Aldo became aware then that the rolling of the ship had nearly stopped. And through the hatch at the top of the ladder he could see the gray light of dawn. He had been asleep and did not even realize it.

"Is the storm over?" he asked.

"Yes," Cadamosto replied. He sighed. "We lost two

more horses during the night. That's five. We've only seven left now."

"I suppose we're lucky we didn't lose them all," Aldo said.

"It wasn't all luck," Cadamosto said. "It was thinking quickly enough to get them tied down." He smiled. "And having someone help me do the job."

"Have you been on deck?" Aldo asked. He stood up somewhat shakily on legs cramped and sore from holding tightly to the bench leg.

"I went atop after I checked the horses."

"I think I'll go up and have a look around—if Senhor Dias doesn't mind."

Cadamosto chuckled. "I don't think he'll mind a bit this morning," he said.

Aldo climbed the ladder and stepped out onto the deck, looking around. It was a shambles. Sailors who had stayed awake all night fighting the storm were lying exhausted on every space available, paying little attention to the wet boards. There were broken fixtures and dangling stays but, to Aldo's amazement, the sails had already been reset, and the ship was under way once more, still sailing south.

The sea was a dirty green, jagged and frothy but not boiling as wildly as it had during the night. Overhead the sky was gray, with low-lying scudding clouds that appeared to be held off by the very masts themselves. To the east, their larboard side as they proceeded south, was the verdant coastline of Africa.

"On the deck!" the lookout suddenly called from the crow's nest atop the mainmast. "*Capitão Cadamosto!* A river! I see a river coming from the inland!"

"Perhaps it is the river of gold!" Cadamosto said excitedly. "Strozzi! Prepare your men! We'll be putting in to land today! I shall explore that river!"

"We had better anchor here," Dias said when they later drew even with the mouth of the river.

"Anchor here? But can't you get any closer? We are a thousand yards away!" Cadamosto protested.

"Yes, I know," Dias replied. "But the rocks and shoals between here and the beach are treacherous. One mishap and we could tear out the belly of the ship. You wouldn't want that, would you, *senhor*?"

"No," Cadamosto agreed. "No, of course not. Very well, you may remain here while we go ashore."

"How long should we remain?" Dias asked.

"How long? Until the shore party returns to the ship, of course."

Dias cleared his throat discreetly. "*Capitão*, I do not wish to be an alarmist," he said, "but there was a practical reason for my asking the question. If you and the landing party were to be set upon by savages and . . . killed, we would have no way of knowing what had happened. How long should we wait before we assume that—uh—some evil has befallen you?"

"Oh," Cadamosto said. "Oh, yes, I see now what you're saying. In that case, I should think one month would be long enough for you to wait." Cadamosto turned to his young friend. "And to that end, Aldo, perhaps it would be best if you didn't go with me."

"Not go with you? Sir, how could you even ask such a thing of me? That is my whole purpose for being here! I couldn't stay on board while you're ashore, facing danger. How could you deny me that right after all this?"

"I am concerned for your safety."

"And I am concerned for yours," Aldo replied. "And may I remind you, Captain, as bowman of the quarterdeck, my concern for your safety has more merit than your concern for mine."

Cadamosto laughed. "Does it, now? Well, perhaps what you say is correct. Very well, *Messer Balestrièri della Poppa*, you may accompany me ashore."

A wide, excited smile spread across Aldo's face. "Thank you, Captain," he said. "Thank you!"

The caravel carried two skiffs. One was left with the ship, which would enable the crewmen remaining behind to make brief forays ashore to replenish their supplies of

food and water. Into the second skiff piled the ten men—
Aldo, Cadamosto, Strozzi, and seven soldiers—who would
be undertaking an inland trek of discovery.

It took the rowers several minutes to pull the great
distance from the ship to the beach, and for the last two
hundred yards they had to fight their way through a
pounding surf. As they reached land, a soldier jumped out
of the boat and hauled on the rope, pulling it out of the
water and well up onto the wet, black sand.

Aldo stepped out of the rear of the skiff and walked on
up the beach, noting that after so long at sea, the solid
ground felt almost unnatural. While the boats were being
made secure behind him, he studied the tree line, which
was about sixty yards back from the water's edge.

He saw a movement, a shadow within a shadow. At
first he wasn't certain that he had even seen anything, so
well did the onlooker's dark skin blend in with the deep
shadows of the tree line. Then he saw the movement again,
and he felt his own skin begin to tingle.

"Cadamosto! Cadamosto!" he hissed, forgetting in his
excitement to address his captain by his title.

"What is it?"

"There, in the trees," Aldo said without pointing. "A
man is watching us. Do you see him?"

Trying not to appear too anxious, Cadamosto also began studying the tree line.

"Shall I point him out to you?" Aldo asked.

"No," Cadamosto replied. "If he sees you pointing at
him, he'll know he has been discovered. Just tell me where
he is."

"He's standing near the clump of trees that juts out
into the sand," Aldo said.

"If you don't see him, Cadamosto, I do," Strozzi put
in quickly. He laughed derisively. "Just look at him, standing there in the shadows, watching us. He thinks he's im-
pervious to us, but don't you worry about that. A quarrel in
his heart will set things right. Bowmen, prepare to shoot!"

"No!" Aldo hissed. "Don't shoot him!"

Strozzi sniffed. "Have you gone soft? Set your bolts,"

he ordered, and three of the soldiers began to arm their crossbows.

"Look behind him!" Aldo said.

The small shore party suddenly realized that the man in the trees was not alone. There were dozens, perhaps scores, of men with the mysterious watcher, all armed with bows and spears.

"Don't shoot, Strozzi," Cadamosto ordered. "You might get him, but the others would surely get us."

Strozzi held his hand out toward the crossbowmen, motioning for them to lower their weapons. When they did so, the man who had been watching them walked out of the shadows and into the bright light. He was as black as the sand upon which he walked, and as he approached the ten men, he displayed no fear at all.

"Look at him!" Cadamosto whispered. "Have you ever seen anyone so tall, so muscular, so handsome? What a magnificent specimen he is!"

"I am King Budomel. You are Christians from Portugal," the tall black man said. It was not a question, it was a statement, and it was made in Portuguese.

"Yes," Cadamosto answered. He was astonished, and disappointed, that the man could not only identify them, he was speaking to them in Portuguese. Cadamosto had harbored some hope that he was in new territory. That was obviously not the case. Prince Henry's sailors had been this far before.

"You have horses?" King Budomel asked.

"Yes, I have horses," Cadamosto replied. He pointed back to the ship. "They are still on board."

"Good, good," King Budomel said, smiling broadly. "You bring them to me. I will give you good trade for your horses."

"What sort of trade?"

"I will give you many things that are prized by your people. I will give you many slaves."

"I do not want slaves."

King Budomel looked surprised. "You do not want slaves?"

"No."

"But all Christians want slaves," Budomel said. "Why do you not want them?"

"I will be going farther south," Cadamosto explained. "My ship is not equipped to provide shelter, food, and water for many slaves for a long time."

"I see. You do not want slaves. Do you want gold and ivory?"

"Yes!" Cadamosto said excitedly. "Yes, gold and ivory. I will trade the horses for gold and ivory!"

"Come to my village. Visit with me for a while. I will show you how to get your gold and ivory. But now I have a present for you."

King Budomel turned toward the trees and shouted something. The people waiting back in the shadows talked among themselves. There was some commotion, till finally one of their number was pushed forward and began walking across the beach to join King Budomel.

"Since you do not want many slaves, I will give you one slave," the potentate said.

"But you do not understand, King Budomel," Cadamosto said. "I don't want any slaves at all."

"This is not slave for work. This is slave to warm your bed." He held his hand out toward the young girl who approached them.

The girl, who was totally naked, moved across the ground in an effortless glide. Her skin was ebony and her eyes a deep, deep brown. Her hair was blue black, and her lips shone almost as if they were coated with some type of paint. Her small, well-formed breasts and the gentle curves of her body suggested that she was somewhere between a pubescent girl and a young woman.

"Tell your master your name, girl," King Budomel said.

"My name is Harau," the girl said.

Her voice fell on Cadamosto's ears like the tinkling of wind bells stirred by the breeze. He was thunderstruck. Never in his life had he seen anything quite like this. Never had he heard a voice quite so appealing. And she had spoken to him in a language he understood.

"She—she speaks Portuguese!" he said, startled by that fact.

"Yes," King Budomel replied, grinning. "I had her instructed in the language and in the ways of your people so I could make a present of her. Are you pleased?"

"Yes," Cadamosto replied with some effort. He had intended to send the young girl back, to tell the King that he was not interested in either the trading or the practice of slavery. But he found himself so stricken with the girl that he could not make himself give her up. Instead, he held his hand out toward her, beckoning her to come to him. "I am very pleased."

The girl rewarded him with a broad smile and a lilting laugh; then she ran the rest of the way across the beach to him and, leaning into him, put her arms around him. Cadamosto could smell the sun on her skin and feel the warmth of her naked body against his. He found himself wishing no one else was there except for himself and this delightful young creature from another world.

"Come," King Budomel invited. "I will take you to my village now." He looked at the soldiers. "Men with weapons must stay here," he added.

"Careful, Captain, it may be a trap," Aldo warned.

Harau was now holding Cadamosto's hand, closely examining the skin color and holding her own hand up for the contrast.

"No," he said. "I don't believe it is a trap. But, just to be safe, perhaps I should go alone."

"No," Aldo said quickly. "I'm going as well."

"And I," Strozzi said.

"You, Captain Strozzi? You are that worried about my safety?" Cadamosto asked skeptically.

"Yes," Strozzi said. "And about the gold and the ivory he has there."

"You are confused, Captain Strozzi. He did not say he had gold and ivory. He said he would tell us how to find it."

Strozzi smiled. "When he tells you where it is, Cadamosto, I want to be there to hear. It's better that both of us know, don't you think? That way, if one of us forgets, the other will remember."

Cadamosto smirked. "Ah, yes, and of course you are only concerned for the good of us all. Very well, you can go. You both can go." He turned to one of Strozzi's men. "You and the others take the boat and return to the ship. Inform Shipmaster Dias of our plans, and tell him to rig up a way to offload the horses. It will take some doing, of course, but I see no need to keep them on board until we return, since eventually they will be traded to King Budomel anyway and they will be far less distressed once back on land."

"Yes, sir, I will tell him."

"I should think that by using an arrangement of harnesses, he can lower them into the sea one at a time beside an awaiting skiff," Cadamosto continued. "The men stationed in the boat can guide the animals through the breakers to the shore. Construct a rudimentary enclosure for the horses, and guard them carefully until word is received from me via one of Budomel's men that the exchange can be made. At that point the men on shore duty should return to the ship."

"Yes, sir," the man he had been addressing replied again.

"Well, I guess that covers matters. Aldo, Strozzi, let us be off. But you'd best leave your weapons here."

Strozzi put his hand on the hilt of his sword. "That, sir, I will not do," he said.

"Then you, sir, will not go," Cadamosto said easily but with finality.

Strozzi glared at Cadamosto for several long moments; then, grumbling, he removed his sword and handed it to one of his soldiers. Aldo did the same thing with his crossbow. When they both held their hands out to show the potentate they were unarmed, Budomel grunted, turned, and began walking inland. Cadamosto, Strozzi, and Aldo followed.

*   *   *

They trekked through the jungle for hours. Sometimes the passage climbed up slopes so steep that scaling them was nearly impossible. Other times Budomel led them through brush so thick that had his entourage not hacked a rough pathway, they wouldn't have made any progress at all. Toward the end of their journey the Europeans heard a roaring, rushing noise coming from ahead. As they got closer the roar began to sound familiar.

"It is a huge waterfall," Aldo said. "I am sure of it."

"Yes, yes," King Budomel said, smiling and making a motion with his hands, demonstrating a waterfall. "It is much water going down."

A large lake had formed beneath the waterfall, and a village had grown up on its bank. The village consisted of a hundred or more thatched huts, built to enclose a huge square. In the center of the square the villagers were gathered around what seemed to be a marketplace. The settlement was bordered by the lake on one side and by a high bamboo fence on two other sides. The fourth side, the side by which King Budomel and his entourage approached, was open.

The arrival of three white men created a great deal of excitement. The villagers abandoned their marketing and rushed out to see the visitors, calling to each other, pointing and laughing. The younger children, having never seen a white man before, were especially curious about the visitors' skin color, and the more courageous youngsters would dart up to them, reach out with a finger to touch them, then race back to the safety of their own and check their fingertips to see if the Europeans' odd coloration had come off.

During it all, Harau walked proudly beside Cadamosto. When she saw how much interest the children evinced in the skin color of the three visitors, she made a big show of spitting on Cadamosto's hand, then using the moisture to try to rub off the pale shade.

"It does not come off!" one boy gasped.

"They are devils!"

"No," another said. "They are gods!"

"Are you not afraid, Harau?"

"I am not afraid," she replied. Having already known white men, from whom she had learned their language, she was not frightened of them. In fact, she was fascinated by them, especially by Cadamosto, whom she correctly assumed to be their leader.

Although the three visitors were treated with the utmost respect for the rest of the day, there were still those younger villagers whose curiosity got the best of them. They continued to dart up, touch the skin of one of the men, then turn and dash back into the crowd. Cadamosto and Aldo took it all good-naturedly, but Strozzi became annoyed, and he started swatting at them, cursing them loudly when one dared approach him.

"Captain Strozzi, I would think you could show more courtesy to these people," Cadamosto suggested. "After all, the information they share with us may make us rich men."

"I don't like them to touch me like that," Strozzi growled.

"It does no harm," Cadamosto replied.

Strozzi scowled, but he refrained from other overt displays of his aversion.

The visiting continued through the afternoon and through the golden blaze of sunset into the soft dark blanket of evening. That night there was a huge communal feast. Aldo did not know if communal meals were the norm or if this feast was in celebration of their arrival. He suspected the latter, especially in light of the sheer volume of foods displayed. Surely the villagers did not eat this sumptuously every day.

There were numerous fruits and vegetables that he had never seen before, some of which he found particularly palatable. There were several different kinds of meat as well, with which he had a bit more difficulty since some of the meat had a very strong flavor, while other cuts were tough and hard to chew. Nevertheless he, Cadamosto, and Strozzi got through the meal with little trouble.

After the meal there was entertainment. Again Aldo couldn't be sure if that was normal or something special to celebrate the visit of the white men. The entertainment consisted of dances and songs, the singing made up of nasal hums and deep guttural barks. There were instruments, too, from drums to stringed instruments to a type of wind instrument that was played by holding it up to a nostril.

Beautiful young girls, their naked skin shining gold in the fires, began to dance. Harau hurried out to join them, showing off her skill in a wild, powerful display of energetic yet graceful movements. Cheers and laughter greeted her flying feet and fluidity, and she kept up her performance until all the other dancers fell out in exhaustion and even the musicians begged her to stop.

Finally, full of food and slightly intoxicated by the strong liquor they had been drinking, the likes of which they had never tasted before, the three Europeans were led off to their own private huts. When Strozzi showed some apprehension, King Budomel put him at ease by promising to keep a guard posted outside their huts all night long to keep at bay any beasts of the jungle.

Aldo was nearly asleep when he was roused by a gentle voice speaking in Portuguese.

"King Budomel has sent me to you. I hope I am worthy."

Aldo opened his eyes in surprise and looked at the girl standing by his bed. He recognized her as one of the dancing girls he had watched earlier; now, as she had been then, the girl was totally nude.

"Worthy? Worthy for what?" Aldo asked.

The girl knelt beside his pallet. "Worthy for you. I am here to please you," she answered, boldly reaching between his legs.

"What are you doing?" Aldo asked, jumping up and shoving her hand away.

"You do not like?" the girl asked, surprised by his unexpected reaction.

"It's not that . . ." Aldo said, still stunned.

Tears sprang to the girl's eyes, and she covered her face with her hands. It was not until then that Aldo realized how young the girl really was.

"Please," he said, reaching for her. "Don't cry."

"I have been schooled to please my master," the young girl said. "If I do not please my master, I will be killed."

"Killed? No, surely you're wrong about that."

The young girl reached for him again. There was such a desperate look on her face and an anxiousness to her actions that he could not bring himself to push her away again. Nor, within a moment after she started her ministrations, could he have pushed her away if he had wanted to. The beautiful young nude girl, her skills, the pulsating thump of jungle drums, and the excitement of the moment all combined to take his freedom of choice away from him. It was the most erotic experience of Aldo's young life; it was also his first time.

Some four weeks later, just before they left to return to the ship, Cadamosto wrote in his journal:

> It seems to me a marvelous thing that just beyond the river the people should be extremely black, tall, and have large, well-formed bodies, and the country is green, fertile, and heavily timbered, while to the north the people are mulatto-colored, lean, dried up, and short, and the country is desert and poor.
>
> I believe the river we have discovered, which the natives call the Senegal, is but another branch of the Nile. From what I have been able to discern, it flows through all of Ethiopia and, passing through Cairo, it irrigates on this coast of Africa.
>
> The King of these people is a man named Budomel, a very friendly man and one in whom we can place our faith and trust. He offered me 100 slaves for 7 horses. As I shall not be returning right away, I refused the offer of slaves—except for four natives who are familiar with the Portuguese language as well as the language of people who live farther south. I am taking the four trans-

lators with me because King Budomel assured me that south of here are villages rich in gold who will trade that commodity for beads, knives, and other such goods as we are carrying. The four slaves, by virtue of their knowledge of the language, will enable us to bargain.

Budomel also presented me with a gift I have come to prize very highly: a girl, quite young and very beautiful for being so black. I wish I could take her home with me, for she has learned to please me in many ways. I cannot, however, for the men and women of Venice would hardly hold her in as high esteem as do I.

The treatment of Budomel by his subjects is worthy of note here. He is installed with great ceremony, surrounded by his wives, slaves, and subjects in a village of grass huts. The King displays great haughtiness toward his people, who are allowed to approach him only nude and prostrate, all the while throwing dirt over their heads and backs. For the slightest offense against their ruler, they and their families might be seized as slaves.

Aware of my sacred duty to expand the word of Christ as well as enlarge the realm of commercial trade, I spoke at length with the King about the true faith. Budomel is a Muslim, though he has expressed an opinion that he believes both religions are good. It is interesting to note that he once consulted with me because "being a Christian I know so many things and am so wise, as Christians are" as to the best way to satisfy his many wives.

Decorum and modesty preclude my recording my answer in this journal. Suffice it to say that King Budomel's opinion of the wisdom of Christians did not suffer for my answer.

I have recorded in the pages of this journal detailed drawings of the plant and animal life to be found here. I am bringing back some of the

*more exotic animal skins, as well as several very
colorful birds I have heard called parrots. Amazingly, the birds will mimic human speech, though,
of course, there being no intelligence behind the
words, they are random and often make no sense
at all.*

*Despite all that I have found of interest, I am
greatly disappointed to note that except for those
who wish to do a brisk business in the slave trade,
there is very little of value here. We found no
gold, no precious gems, and no ivory. We did
trade for several measures of tin, which the natives prize very highly. Though not as valuable as
gold, the tin might be put to some use by the
mechanics and craftsmen of the Christian world.*

"Captain Cadamosto? Captain, are you ready?" Aldo
Cavalli called through the open door of Cadamosto's hut.
Alvise Cadamosto closed the cover of his journal, then
turned to look at his young friend.

"Is everyone ready?" he asked.

"Yes, sir," Aldo replied. "King Budomel will accompany us back to the coast, and he has a number of bearers
to carry our supplies."

"It's a pity they won't be carrying gold," Cadamosto
said with a sigh. He stood up and put his journal into a
leather pouch, then reached for the walking stick he had
learned to use since coming into the jungle. "However,
we'll take back a wealth of experiences, won't we?"

"Yes, sir!" Aldo agreed enthusiastically.

"And perhaps the knowledge of where the gold might
be found. What about Strozzi? Is he out there?"

"Yes, sir, he's there, ready to depart."

"Then what do you say we get under way?"
Cadamosto said, stepping out of the hut and into the dazzling morning sun.

*   *   *

"They've left us!" Strozzi exploded in fear and anger. "Blast their hides, they've gone running!"

It was many hours after they had left the village, and Cadamosto, Aldo, and Strozzi were standing on the beach, looking out at the sea for their ship. The caravel was nowhere to be seen.

"They wouldn't have left yet," Cadamosto said. "I told them to wait for one month. It has only been twenty-eight days."

"A lunar month," Strozzi pointed out. "That's all Dias needed, that Portuguese coward. Now we are stranded here for God knows how long!"

"There!" Aldo said, shielding his eyes against the glare that rose from the bright surface of the water. "I can see the ship! They haven't left!"

With Aldo pointing it out to them, Cadamosto and Strozzi were also able to see the ship. They hadn't noticed it initially because it was anchored so far out to sea. The fact that its masts were free of sail made it even less conspicuous, for from that distance they made only the lightest mark against the sky.

"Why are they so far out?" Strozzi asked.

"Well, just look around," Cadamosto said, gesturing at the beach, which was scattered with limbs, leaves, and other debris from the jungle. "You will recall that we had a storm last night. Look how the wind littered the beach. Dias probably deemed it best to anchor far from any rocks and shoals that could have damaged the ship, had the vessel been blown into them."

"Dias!" Strozzi yelled, waving his arms over his head. "Dias! Over here!"

Aldo began to shout and wave as well, but Cadamosto merely laughed.

"What are you laughing at?" Strozzi asked angrily.

"You two," Cadamosto answered. "Do you really think he can hear you? Or even see you, for that matter?"

"He could see us if he looked," Strozzi said.

"Don't be foolish. Look at the ship. Can *you* see anyone on board?"

"No," Strozzi admitted. "No, I can't."

"Of course not. They're too far away. And if we can't see them, then they can't see us."

"Unless they have a lookout posted, keeping watch for us with a telescope," Strozzi said.

Cadamosto shrugged. "After so many weeks, it seems unlikely that Dias would keep a man on constant watch for us. And even if he did, the distance is too great for anyone to be able to tell that we are who we are, not simply three of the natives."

"Then how are we to get their attention?" Strozzi asked.

"We could build a fire," Aldo suggested. "They might see the smoke."

"They might," Cadamosto agreed. "But even if they did, again they would probably think the smoke is just a cooking fire prepared by the natives."

"Then what are we going to do?" Aldo asked, anxiety creeping into his voice.

"I don't know," Cadamosto admitted, stroking his chin as he stared out toward the ship, made minuscule by the distance.

"You want to reach men on ship?" King Budomel asked.

"Yes. Do you know a way?"

Budomel laughed. "Is simple. I will send someone," he offered.

"Send someone to the ship? What are you talking about?" Strozzi asked. He pointed to the caravel. "You can't just take a stroll out there, you know."

"Swim."

"Swim? Are you crazy? That ship must be three miles offshore. If you sent someone swimming out there, he would never make it. He would drown before he got there," Strozzi said.

King Budomel held up two fingers. "I send two men," he said. "Maybe one will not make it. Maybe one will." He turned and shouted something to the bearers, and all of them put down their loads, then ran over to answer his bidding.

"Are all these men volunteering to swim out to the ship?" Cadamosto asked.

"Yes," Budomel said. He grinned. "I have told them you will pay two measures of tin to the two men who will go."

"Yes," Cadamosto agreed quickly. "Yes, I will. But who will go?"

"It is your choice."

Cadamosto looked at the six eager young men for a long time, then pointed to two of them. The two who were selected smiled proudly, while the other four, with downcast faces, returned dejectedly to their burdens.

"Wait," Cadamosto instructed. "I will write a letter to the captain, instructing him to meet us at the mouth of the Senegal River."

A moment later the two swimmers, each with a copy of Cadamosto's letter carried in a small corked bottle dangling from a thong around their necks, waded naked into the surf. Aldo, Cadamosto, Strozzi, and the soldiers watched for a long time until they could no longer see the natives' heads in the sea.

"Do you think they'll make it?" Aldo asked Cadamosto.

"I don't know, but I will tell you this: If they *do* make it, they are the finest swimmers in the world."

"They *have* to make it," Aldo said.

"Of course they have to make it," Strozzi put in. "We'll be stranded here if they don't."

"I meant that they'll be dead if they don't," Aldo said.

"Better them than us," Strozzi muttered.

"Come along, gentlemen," Cadamosto said. "If we are going to meet the ship at the mouth of the river, we should get started now."

At an order from King Budomel, the bearers picked up their cargo, adding the loads of the two swimmers, and they started hiking down the beach toward the mouth of the river.

They had been walking for nearly two hours, periodically checking back over their shoulders at the ship. One of the bearers suddenly let out a shout. Aldo turned to look out to sea.

"Look, they're putting on sail!" he cried. "The swimmers made it!"

"Perhaps," Strozzi said. "Or perhaps Dias has decided to leave us."

Aldo had not considered that possibility, and he watched the ship closely as it moved down the coastline. Finally, with a sigh of relief, he realized that the vessel was proceeding just as Cadamosto had directed, for if it was leaving, it would have turned about and begun beating up the coast. Any doubt at all was totally dispelled when the ship turned toward them, heading directly for the mouth of the river.

The ship made better speed than the walkers so that by the time Cadamosto and the shore party reached the river's mouth, the ship was lying at anchor just a few hundred yards offshore. One of the ship's boats was beached, and Vincente Dias himself was pacing back and forth nervously on the beach. One of the two native swimmers was sitting on the beach, breathing heavily.

"Signóre Dias!" Cadamosto shouted, waving expansively as they approached. "You got my instructions, I see."

"Yes, I did," Dias said.

Cadamosto pointed to the native. "That man's a hero. As is the other one."

"The other one?"

"Two swimmers left the beach for the ship."

"Two, you say?" Dias shook his head glumly. "Only one made it."

Cadamosto looked at King Budomel. "I'm sorry, my friend," he said.

Budomel smiled. "No worry. Now you have to pay only one measure of tin."

Cadamosto shook his head. "No. I will pay a measure of tin for the man who died as well. Has he a wife?"

"Yes, yes, he has a wife," Budomel said. "You may give the measure of tin to me. I will pay his wife."

Harau, who had made the journey with them, whispered in Cadamosto's ear. "He had no wife, master."

Cadamosto smiled at her. "Thank you for your loyalty," he said. "But it does not matter. I feel that I should pay the measure anyway. Besides, I can more than afford it. So far this voyage has made quite a tidy profit." He turned to Dias. "Signal the other boat ashore," he instructed. "We've a prodigious amount of booty to take on board."

Dias, his eyes shining in excitement at the treasure trove, nodded. "Yes, I can see that your visit has been quite worthwhile."

The loading of goods and exchanges of good-byes went smoothly until Harau realized that she was not to be taken, and she began crying. King Budomel, believing that his "gift" was found unsatisfactory as a result of some offense by Harau, glared coldly at the young woman.

"Captain," Aldo whispered urgently, remembering the fear expressed by the young girl who had come to share his bed that first night, "if you leave her here, she may be killed."

Cadamosto studied Aldo for a long moment, contemplating the possibility; then he nodded. "You may be right," he said.

"Hold on, Captain! You aren't planning on taking her with us, are you?" Dias asked.

"No, I can't do that either," Cadamosto said. Finally he smiled and snapped his fingers. "But I do have an idea."

"What?" Aldo asked.

"You'll see." Cadamosto cleared his throat, then called out to King Budomel, "Your Excellency, I would like a word with you."

King Budomel had been keeping a respectful distance. Now he came over to see what had transpired.

"King Budomel, I would like to marry Harau," Cadamosto said.

"Marry her? Have you gone crazy?" Strozzi asked, speaking not in the Portuguese that King Budomel could understand, but in Italian.

"I won't be marrying her by the laws of the church," Cadamosto replied in Italian. "And so in the eyes of God we won't be married. But in King Budomel's eyes we will be, and that should grant the girl protection, for he will know with absolute certainty that his gift gave me great pleasure. I'm certain I can leave her behind without fear of her being harmed."

Cadamosto's plan seemed to have worked, and as the ship weighed anchor to continue its journey, he waved at his young "wife," who stood on the shore, covered with wedding trinkets, waving back.

"Does she understand that you won't be coming back?" Aldo asked, coming to stand beside his captain and friend.

"Oh, she understands," Cadamosto said.

"And she isn't upset?"

Cadamosto chuckled. "Contrary to what you might think, my young friend, this was not the love of the ages— for her or for me. By marrying her I have freed her from the bonds of slavery—and she'll have the right to choose any man she pleases to keep her bed warm until her husband returns." He laughed. "No, I don't think she is upset at all."

"Cadamosto," Strozzi said, coming up to them. "Dias tells me we are proceeding farther south."

"Yes, we are."

"But why?" Strozzi asked. "We've had a successful trade, we've done what we set out to do. Let us return while we still can."

"We have not done all that we set out to do," Cadamosto retorted. "I told Prince Henry that we would sail farther than any man has yet gone, and that is exactly what I intend to do."

Aldo had just awoken the next morning when he heard the news: A ship's sails had been spotted on the northern horizon. Cadamosto, Dias, and Strozzi were discussing it.

"Who is it, do you suppose?" Dias asked. "Christian or Moor?"

"I have no idea," Cadamosto replied. "But there seems to be only one vessel, so perhaps even if it's a Moorish one, we can avoid an armed confrontation."

Strozzi said, "We can wait for them, showing nothing to arouse their suspicion, then fall upon them with my bombards and crossbowmen. After that it'll be a simple matter of sending a boarding party over to finish any remaining resistance. We'll loot them for whatever valuables they have managed to acquire, and then we'll burn and sink the ship."

"We'll do nothing of the kind," Cadamosto said fiercely. "We will wait until they have drawn close enough to us to determine their intent. Then perhaps I shall put a boat over and go to meet them. Would you like to accompany me, Aldo?"

"Yes, I would," Aldo said. Although he said nothing, he couldn't help but harbor the hope that it was, in fact, a Christian ship—that of Diogo Gomes, on which the Da Costa brothers sailed.

"Don't plan on asking *me* to go with you," Strozzi said, his tone churlish.

"Don't distress yourself, Strozzi," Cadamosto answered. "I didn't intend to ask you."

CHAPTER 10

IN THE WATERS OFF AFRICA

Giovanni Ruggi was in the crow's nest, looking through the spyglass at the skiff crossing the hundred yards between his caravel and the one they had overtaken. He had been surprised to see another ship so far south, though they had heard before leaving Portugal that a Venetian merchant-adventurer named Alvise Cadamosto had preceded them. He held Venetians in such low esteem, however, that he would not have believed one courageous enough to venture this far. Apparently he was wrong.

"Aloft!" Antoniotto Usedimare shouted, cupping his hands around his mouth. "Was our count from here on deck the correct one? How many men are coming aboard?"

"Four, as we thought, Captain. Two rowers and two gentlemen," Giovanni called back.

"Very well," Usedimare replied. "Return to the deck. Prepare to receive visitors."

Giovanni clambered back down the mast, then armed two men and had them stand by at the ready. When Usedimare saw the armed men taking their positions, he held up his hand.

"Here, Giovanni, we've no need for that," he said. "We'll welcome them as friends."

"Friends, sir? If, as we suspect, one of the gentlemen is Alvise Cadamosto, he is Venetian. Since when did Venetians become friends of Genoese?"

"Giovanni, may I remind you that we are both sailing under the flag of Prince Henry? Besides, when we find ourselves this far from Christian waters, we are neither Genoese nor Venetian. We are all brothers in Christ, and, accordingly, we will welcome the Venetians as if they were our own kinsmen."

"I beg your pardon, Captain, but when we are this far from civilization, I feel we should be even *more* careful."

"I respect your feelings, Giovanni, and given that I overlooked your caution once before and allowed the Englishman to attack us, I can understand why you would feel it necessary to warn me this time as well. But I have a feeling that we are in no danger from these people, and I will not insult them by having them set foot on my deck only to be threatened by the presence of armed men. Now, have your men put down their weapons and make no show of hostility to our guests."

"Very well, Captain," Giovanni said. "You two," he said, signaling the men he had just put into position, "stand down."

However, Giovanni did not tell the men in concealed positions to relax *their* vigil. On the contrary, he indicated to them with a pointed glance that they were to stay exactly where they were without giving themselves away—either to the visitors or to Captain Usedimare.

The small boat pulled alongside Usedimare's caravel, scraping lightly against the side of the ship. A line was thrown down by one of the sailors on deck, and one of the rowers caught it, then secured the boat to the ship. The line was followed by a rope ladder for the visitors to climb up onto the deck. Cadamosto was the first to board.

"*Buon giorno, signóre,*" Usedimare greeted in Italian. "You must be Alvise Cadamosto."

Cadamosto was doubly surprised—to be addressed in

his native language by the captain of a Portuguese vessel *and* addressed by name.

"I *am* Cadamosto," he replied. "But you seem to have the advantage of me, Captain. Who would you be?"

"I am Captain Antoniotto Usedimare, at your service, sir," Usedimare answered, giving a slight bow of his head.

"And how is it that you know who I am, Captain Usedimare?"

"When I arrived in Portugal to seek a commission to sail for Prince Henry, you were the talk of the court. Oh, yes, Captain, I heard all about you. I am sure that Prince Henry will be pleased to learn that you, too, have journeyed so far south."

"Apparently I have not come as far south as I thought," Cadamosto replied wryly. "We are evidently still in waters being plied by the Portuguese trade."

Usedimare grinned. "That is perhaps so. However, I, too, intend to expand the boundaries. And now that we have encountered each other, may I propose that we continue our exploration together?"

Cadamosto smiled, then looked around the ship. "I see," he said. "You wish to join us for protection, do you?"

"I would rather think that it is for our *mutual* protection. After all, our vessel carries a military complement, commanded by a true hero of the battle at Constantinople." He pointed toward Giovanni Ruggi, who was standing near the mainmast with one arm resting in the rigging. Giovanni stared, unblinking, at the visitors.

"You were a hero at Constantinople?" Cadamosto called, his tone pleasant.

"We lost the battle," Giovanni said flatly. "There are no heroes when the battle is lost."

"Oh, I disagree with you," Cadamosto replied. "Whether the cause is won or lost has nothing to do with individual heroism."

"Giovanni is being very modest," Usedimare said. "But I have it from one who was there that the dying words of Captain-General Giustiniani were in praise of Giovanni Ruggi's bravery."

"A *modest* hero at that," Cadamosto said to

Usedimare. "All the more commendable." He smiled. "We, too, have a hero of that battle sailing with us. His name is Strozzi. Captain Filippo Strozzi. Perhaps you have met him or heard of his exploits?"

"I may have met him at one time or another," Usedimare replied. "But if so, I know nothing of his exploits."

Aldo chuckled. "If you had met him, Captain, you would have heard all about his exploits."

"I beg your pardon?"

"What my young friend means is that in contrast to the commendable modesty of your own military man, our Captain Strozzi is a man of considerable verbosity."

"Do you know Captain Strozzi, Giovanni?" Usedimare asked, turning toward his young military commander.

"No, sir, I do not," Giovanni replied. "But then, I met very few Venetians during the battle—and those I did meet, I had little regard for."

Usedimare scowled. "Giovanni, I'll not have anyone on my ship displaying impudence to guests."

"I beg your pardon if I have offended you," Giovanni said to Cadamosto and Aldo, though it seemed fairly obvious that he wasn't sorry at all. "If you'll excuse me, I have work to tend to."

Usedimare, Cadamosto, and Aldo watched Giovanni saunter toward the back of the ship.

"I beg of you to forgive his rudeness," Usedimare said. "You see, his own story of the events that happened in Constantinople is quite tragic. He was in love with a young Greek girl who was killed."

"How unfortunate. I know that the casualties were high, for our own Captain Strozzi has told how Mohammed's warriors committed wholesale slaughter of the citizens of Constantinople—men, women, and children alike."

"That is true," Usedimare said, "and by itself would be quite terrible enough. But there is an even greater tragedy to Giovanni's story, for his beloved was killed not by an infidel, but by a roguish band of Venetians who were

roaming through the defeated city, killing and looting with
as much alacrity as the heathens themselves."

"A *Venetian*, you say?" Cadamosto gasped.

"Yes."

Cadamosto sighed. "I am very sorry. And greatly
shamed that any of my fellow citizens would do such a
thing."

"Yes, well, we can't all be responsible for everyone
who just happens to share the place of our birth, can we?"
Usedimare replied. "As I told Giovanni, one bad Venetian
does not make all Venetians bad."

"Of course not," Cadamosto replied. "But I can see
that he will always be distrustful of us." He shook his head
as if clearing it of unpleasantness. "Despite all that, you
still want to sail with us?"

"Yes, I would very much like to, if you will accept the
company."

Cadamosto smiled and extended his hand. "As you
wish, Captain. Our single-vessel voyage has just become a
two-ship fleet. Let us proceed south."

"A minute, if you would, sir," Usedimare said. He
gestured toward Cadamosto's ship. "Judging from their
color and their costume, I would guess that you have some
native people sailing with you."

Cadamosto glanced over at the caravel, then turned
back. "Yes, we have four native interpreters aboard."

"Truly! I wonder, sir, if I might petition you to share
with me."

Cadamosto was silent for a moment, contemplating
the notion. Then he nodded. "I'll have two of them sent
over to you."

"Thank you," Usedimare said. "That is most generous
of you. And now, sir, south to riches—and south to glory!"

Cadamosto, Aldo, and the two rowers climbed down
into the skiff for the trip back over to their own ship. As
Aldo took his seat in the boat, he looked up at Usedimare's
ship and spotted Giovanni Ruggi. The muscular sailor was
leaning in the rigging, watching the Venetians leave. His
expression was one of ill-concealed hate.

*   *   *

It took nearly thirty minutes for the Venetians to return to their own ship, send the two black men across the water to the other ship, then recover the boat. When all that had been accomplished, Vincente Dias raised a signal flag to his counterpart on Usedimare's ship, and both ships hoisted anchor, then put on all sail to get under way. The ships proceeded south, though always in sight of land that lay off their larboard side.

Giovanni Ruggi was glad to get under way again. He did not like to be idle. When he was idle, he had too much time to think and too many painful memories. . . .

The two black men were not very good sailors, as evidenced by the fact that they spent most of the day at the rail, throwing up. Many of the sailors laughed at their misery, but Giovanni, taking pity on them, gave them each an orange, explaining that it would help settle their stomachs. When one of the natives tried to eat it without removing the skin, Giovanni showed him how the orange should be peeled.

Giovanni's friendly overtures resulted in the natives' responding in kind to him. The taller of the two told Giovanni that his name was Targumo. The shorter man was Utembe.

"You are good man," Targumo said as he worked on the orange. "Not like Strozzi."

"You don't like Strozzi?"

Targumo and Utembe both shook their heads. "He is most evil," Targumo said.

"He is Venetian," Giovanni replied. "All Venetians are evil."

Targumo shook his head, then spit out orange seeds before he spoke. "Not true," he said. "Cadamosto is good man. Cavalli is good man. Only Strozzi is evil."

Giovanni would have preferred for Targumo and Utembe to agree with him that all Venetians were evil, but he did not press the issue. Instead he left the two of them to fight their seasickness, while he returned to his own duties, drilling and preparing his men for whatever dangers they might encounter.

As the sun started setting far off to their starboard side, the sailors grew visibly nervous. At first Giovanni did not know what was troubling them; then he overheard some of them grumbling.

"It's a foolish thing to attempt, if you ask me," one sailor complained.

"That's because Usedimare and Cadamosto care about nothing but riches and glory," one of the others replied. "They don't care a *ducat* for the safety of their ships or their men."

"You're being unfair," one of the sailors defended. "Usedimare is risking his own neck as well."

"Yes, well, he can risk his neck if he so chooses, but that gives him no right to risk *mine.*"

"What is it?" Giovanni asked, coming over to stand among them. "What is troubling everyone?"

"What is troubling everyone? Do you have to ask, Giovanni? Can you not see the sun is setting?"

Giovanni was puzzled. "Of course it's setting. It sets every day," he said. "What's so unusual about that?"

The sailor spit over the rail, then wiped his mouth with the back of his hand. "I'll tell you what's unusual about it," he said. "When the sun sets, it gets dark. And when it gets dark, a body can't see."

"So?" Giovanni replied, still confused.

"What he's trying to tell you, Senhor Ruggi, is that if we proceed under sail through the night in uncharted waters, we could very well run into danger without seeing it."

"Shoals, whirlpools . . ." a second sailor said.

"Sailing off the end of the world," another put in.

Giovanni laughed. "You don't really think we could sail off the end of the world, do you?"

"Who is to know, sir?" the sailor replied. "Already we have seen many strange things in the sky. The North Star is so low on the horizon that it has nearly disappeared. And what of the star formation we've been seeing? The one shaped like a cross? Is that not a portent of danger?"

"I don't know," Giovanni replied. "Perhaps just the opposite is true. Perhaps it is a sign of God's blessing."

"No, I don't believe that. I believe it is a warning to go no farther."

"You must talk to the captain, Giovanni," one of the sailors said. "You must tell him to turn back now."

"I'll do no such thing," Giovanni said.

"What is it that you will not do?" Usedimare asked, suddenly coming upon the knot of men.

"Nothing, Captain," Giovanni said.

"Begging your pardon, sir," one of the sailors said. "We were trying to get Senhor Ruggi to plead our case before you."

"Oh? And just what is your case?"

"It's the darkness, Captain. We are afraid."

"Of the *dark*?" Usedimare scoffed.

"Of what danger may lie before us in the dark this far south," the sailor replied, unperturbed by Usedimare's mockery. "Who can say what lies before us? Perhaps some men are right when they say the world is like a table and the waters fall off at the edge. And if that is so, it would be foolish to sail on in the night when we can't see."

"And you, Giovanni? Do you believe we are in danger of sailing over the edge?" Usedimare asked.

"No, Captain," Giovanni replied.

Usedimare smiled. "More of you should be like Giovanni," he suggested.

"But," Giovanni added, "as we *are* in uncharted waters, the men are correct. It is entirely possible to run upon rocks in the dark and wreck the ship."

Usedimare nodded. "Yes, we might at that. Very well, I shall signal Cadamosto and recommend that we make anchor during the hours of darkness."

When Usedimare left to look for the signalman, the sailors looked at Giovanni in gratitude.

"Thank you," the most vocal of them said. "All the men will appreciate the extra caution."

"Just see to it that all the men remain loyal to the captain," Giovanni replied.

*　　*　　*

The next day they were becalmed. The sails drooped and the water was flat and glassy, without so much as a ripple. The lack of wind and the heat and glare of the sun wrought a terrible effect upon the men, and when the simmering tar began to run in the caulking, some began to fear that they had come too far south.

"We should put about and return to our own latitudes," one of the sailors warned. "Otherwise we shall remain becalmed here, never to escape."

Giovanni laughed, trying to make light of the situation, though he was as uncomfortable as everyone else. "I hardly think we will remain here forever," he said.

"You scoff at such a notion? Well, I myself have seen ghost ships, rotting at the seams with the skeletons of their crews still at their stations, doomed to remain becalmed for all of eternity. My ship stayed only long enough to behold that horrendous scene; then we put about and left immediately."

No one thought to ask the sailor how his ship could maneuver easily while the ghost ship was becalmed. Some of the younger sailors shivered in fear, and though Giovanni did not believe the doomsayer, even he did not like to hear such talk—particularly when the wind had completely failed.

The doldrums lasted for three days, and though Usedimare and Cadamosto fired cannons—hoping to stir up the air to create wind—and wet the sails, not a breath of air appeared. Giovanni watched the crew walk the deck, keeping their voices low as if somehow even loud talk might keep the wind away. One after another the sailors would look up at the flat sheets. But all the looking and wishing and cursing and praying and cannon firing and wetting of sails—even the backbreaking labor of putting the ships in tow behind the rowboats—did nothing to raise a breeze. They entered the fourth day still becalmed.

"Oh, how I wish for a galley," Usedimare said, wiping the sweat from his face. "Why did I ever let myself be talked into undertaking such a voyage in a ship like this?"

He looked up at the limp sails and sighed. "If we were in a galley, we could stroke our way out of this soon enough."

"But would the galley have held up to the terrible storm we came through last week?" Giovanni asked.

Usedimare wiped his face again. "I don't know," he admitted. "But anything, even a storm, is better than this. It's as if the very atmosphere had died. Perhaps there is no wind in these latitudes."

"Captain, you don't really believe that," Giovanni said.

Usedimare smiled sheepishly. "No. No, I don't believe it."

Giovanni looked out over the flat, glazed sea. Flying fish propelled themselves across the calm water alongside the stilled ship, and Giovanni watched them frolic. Behind him, men were loading a bronze cannon, preparing to fire another charge into the still air. Giovanni didn't understand how such a thing was supposed to get the air moving, but twice a day the cannon was fired, a routine as regular as any other duty the men had.

The fourth morning dragged on with the men moving, if they moved at all, as listlessly as the empty sails. Then at about noon someone shouted.

"Wind! Captain Usedimare, there is wind!"

The listlessness fell away, replaced by a great rush of energy, everyone turning from their places on the deck to see for themselves if the calm had indeed broken. Anxious faces peered up at the sail sheets, lips moved in silent prayer, and hands made the sign of the cross as, with a report like a cannon shot, the great sheets suddenly filled. Ropes creaked, masts swayed, and the ship heeled over in answer to the wind. The sailors cheered, and their cheer was echoed by the men on Cadamosto's ship.

Once again they were headed southward, toward the unknown.

It was midday the next day when the lookout spotted the mouth of another river, one as large as the Senegal had been. The land here appeared more lush than the land they had been passing for the last several miles, due, no doubt, to the presence of the river. At a signal from Cadamosto's ship, both caravels reefed sail and dropped anchor. A few minutes after the anchor was dropped, a skiff crossed the distance between the two ships, bringing Cadamosto to Usedimare's ship.

"Do you see any sign that this river has been visited by Christians before?" Cadamosto asked his fellow captain as he climbed onto the deck.

"No," Usedimare replied. "There is no cross marking passage. Nor did I hear of any visit this far south while I was still in Portugal."

"Nor I," Cadamosto said. He rubbed his hands together excitedly, then walked over to the rail to look at the distant shore. "What say you? Shall we send a party ashore to have a look around?"

"Yes," Usedimare agreed. "And, Captain, perhaps we should send an interpreter with the shore party. Should we encounter any natives, our interpreter could inquire about gold."

"Excellent idea. But in case there is danger, we shouldn't risk too many men."

"All right. Suppose we draw lots?" Usedimare suggested. "Whoever wins the draw will send the landing party ashore."

Cadamosto agreed to the suggestion, and after lots were cast, it fell upon Usedimare to provide the shore party. Giovanni was selected to command the landing party, and he chose Targumo as his interpreter.

The ships were anchored no more than a few hundred yards offshore, so the rowboat taking the landing party to the beach managed to close the distance quickly.

Eight men were in the boat—six sailors, Giovanni, and Targumo. They hopped out of the boat while still on the seaward side of the breakers, then began pushing it ashore. Just as they landed, a group of natives emerged from underneath the canopy of trees. They were armed with short curved swords, similar to the scimitars with which the Muslims had been armed at Constantinople. For a moment Giovanni had a feeling of déjà vu, and the pounding of the surf and the screech of a jungle creature caused his blood to run cold. He could see again the fires of hell and hear the devilish shouts of the Muslim warriors and the terrible, wrenching screams of the beleaguered citizens of Constantinople.

"Are you all right, Giovanni?"

"What? Oh, yes, of course. Why do you ask?"

"I spoke to you, and you didn't answer."

"I'm sorry, I didn't hear you. It must have been the noise of the surf. What did you say?"

"I asked, what should we do now?"

"Targumo, do you think you can talk with those people?" Giovanni asked.

"Sim, senhor," the African replied.

Giovanni waved his hand toward them. "All right, go tell them who we are and ask them if they have any gold to trade."

Targumo grunted, then started across the beach toward the small group of natives who had come to watch the landing. The natives, like Targumo, were large, well-muscled men. And, like him, they were naked except for the beads around their necks and the tattoos that decorated their bodies.

"What should we do?" one of the sailors asked.

"Nothing," Giovanni replied. "We'll stay here and watch."

Targumo began talking to the natives. As he was fifty yards or more distant from the boat, Giovanni could not hear what was being said. He wouldn't have been able to understand the words even if he had been able to overhear them, but he would have at least been able to judge Targumo's progress by the tone and intensity of the conversation. Had he been able to do that, he would not have been surprised by what happened next.

"Mother of God!" one of the sailors gasped, his mouth hanging open.

One of the natives abruptly raised his scimitar. The thick-bladed sword sliced through Targumo's neck, and his head fell like a large black ball to the ground. His body remained upright for a full second longer, gushing blood from the stump of the neck. Then, even as the body was falling, the natives began hacking it to pieces.

"Back to the ship!" Giovanni yelled, and he and the sailors pushed the boat quickly back into the surf, climbing aboard only after they were on the other side of the line of breakers.

None of the natives were armed with bows and arrows, so they could only stand on the beach and shout and wave their swords at the sailors paddling desperately into the surf.

"What in God's name happened?" Usedimare asked when the shore party returned. He already knew that the interpreter had been killed because he had watched it through his telescope. But he did not know why.

"I don't know," Giovanni replied. "Targumo was just talking to them one moment, and then the next moment they began chopping him to pieces. It didn't seem prudent to stay and try to find out what angered them."

"Of course," Usedimare said. "Better that we lose one slave than seven men."

"Should I take a larger landing party ashore?" Giovanni asked.

"No. The natives far outnumber us, and undoubtedly, having shown themselves so barbarous to one of their own, they would be no less to strangers."

Usedimare and Cadamosto held a brief council to decide on their best course of action. When Cadamosto returned to the ship, Aldo Cavalli helped him from the boarding ladder, anxious to find out what decision the two captains had made.

"Are we going to send more men to land?" Aldo asked. He was holding his crossbow, ready to go ashore if need be and do battle with the natives.

"No," Cadamosto replied. "We have decided to proceed farther south, in hopes of finding friendlier people."

"But perhaps we can beat them," Aldo said.

"To what purpose?" Cadamosto replied. "We are here to trade with the natives, not war with them."

Aldo sighed, then laid his bow down. "Yes, I suppose that is best." Though he did not speak his thoughts aloud, in truth he was hoping Cadamosto and Usedimare had decided to send a war party ashore. He would have welcomed the opportunity to prove himself in battle.

The ships hoisted anchor and continued to sail south. Some twenty-four hours later they came upon the mouth of another large river. It formed a very large basin as it emptied into the sea, as if inviting the ships to leave the ocean and sail upstream. Usedimare and Cadamosto accepted the invitation.

Although they were sailing against the current, the vessels had a following wind and thus were able to make fair headway. Aldo felt it a strange sensation to be hemmed in so closely on both sides by towering trees, twisting vines, and elephant grass that grew right to the river's edge. This was especially so after having spent so much time on the open sea.

The youth studied the high, magnificent trees and the beautiful flowers growing in such colorful profusion around and in them. There was a great abundance of visible animal life as well, for numerous creatures came to drink from the river. Once they sailed past what seemed to be a great, green island. As they neared it, it suddenly came alive, beating the water into a frothy frenzy. Aldo realized with a start that the "island" was a huge colony of crocodiles.

Monkeys swung through the limbs and vines of the trees, occasionally stopping to stare with unabashed curiosity at the two ships slipping by so quietly. Flocks of brilliantly hued birds fluttered in colorful, living clouds, sometimes filling the trees like flowers. Then, startled, they would all take flight at once.

Accompanying the strange and wondrous sights were strange and wondrous sounds. The jungle was filled with high-pitched screeches and chortles and deep, frightening roars.

"Captain! Negroes off our starboard bow!" someone suddenly shouted.

Aldo, hearing the shout, hurried across the deck to look in the direction indicated by the lookout. Three dugout canoes were swiftly cleaving through the water toward the ship, propelled by a dozen or more muscular young men who rowed with rhythmic strokes.

"Do nothing to frighten them!" Cadamosto shouted. "Remember, we are here to trade!"

Obeying their captain, no one raised a weapon or threatened the approaching natives in any way. Despite the explorers' peaceful intent, however, the natives suddenly launched an attack of their own, sending a cloud of arrows across the water to land on the ship. One of the shafts stuck in the deck just beside Aldo, and he looked at it in surprise as it quivered in the boards.

Aldo reached for the arrow, but Utembe let out a shout. "No, *senhor*! Do not touch the arrow! Do you see here?" Utembe pointed to a wet, sticky substance on the arrow's tip. "Poison! If you touch, you die!"

"Don't touch the arrows!" Aldo shouted to the others, and the warning was passed from man to man in time to prevent any harm from being done.

"Strozzi!" Cadamosto shouted. "Strozzi, get your crossbowmen on them!"

"Crossbowmen! Engage the heathens!" Strozzi shouted in a high-pitched voice.

At Strozzi's command, Aldo grabbed his crossbow, fitted a quarrel into the slot, then took careful aim at one of the Negroes, himself in the act of drawing back his own bow. Aldo flicked the trigger release, and his bolt sped through the air, then buried itself in the native bowman's chest. The native dropped his bow and, a surprised expression on his face, reached for the short shaft protruding from his chest. He tried to pull it out but couldn't, then fell from the canoe and floated facedown in the river.

Suddenly there was a frenzied commotion, and the water frothed around the floating Negro warrior. A moment later the turbulence ceased, and the water turned red. Aldo saw a crocodile swim away with the prize of a severed arm in its jaws. The sight gave him chills, the more so knowing that it was his missile that had felled the warrior.

Seeing one of their number in the water, the natives turned their canoes about and paddled away quickly. Cadamosto would not allow his men to shoot at the fleeing natives, but they did belittle them with hoots and catcalls to celebrate their victory.

The ships continued to sail upriver, stopping for the night by anchoring in the middle of the river. Both Cadamosto's ship and Usedimare's kept a double guard on duty all through the hours of darkness. Aldo drew the watch from midnight to four, and he stood attentively at the rail, staring out into the dark jungle and listening to the sounds. The jungle wasn't at all quiet during the day, but at night the sounds were almost deafening. And terrifying. As a result, even when it was time for Aldo to go to sleep, he found that he could not.

About midway through the next morning, the lookout's shout again gave notice that Negroes had been sighted.

"Where away?" Cadamosto asked.

"Off the larboard after rail," the lookout said. "God's blood, Captain! There are *hundreds* of them!"

It was clear the natives had no interest in negotiating trading deals, for a cloud of poisoned arrows came flying toward the ship.

"Engage! Engage!" Strozzi shouted, and the crossbowmen went about their duty.

Aldo saw his quarrel zip by the lead canoe without finding its mark, splashing harmlessly into the water. As he watched his own bolt miss its target, a missile shot by one of the other crossbowmen buried itself in the neck of the warrior who had been in his sights.

An exchange of arrows resulted in a number of warriors being struck by the more accurate missiles of the crossbows. Then, after the first exchange of arrows, Cadamosto loosed a salvo of artillery.

The cannons flashed like lightning, then boomed like thunder. A huge cloud of acrid smoke rolled across the flat water. When it cleared, Aldo saw that the natives were so dumbstruck by the fire and noise and the heavy stones that raised geysers of water as they struck near the canoes that many of them threw their bows and arrows aside.

For a moment there was a lull, and Utembe, taking advantage of it, shouted to them.

"Why did you attack us, my brothers? These strangers from a distant land have come in peace to trade with you!" He interpreted his own shout for Cadamosto and the others.

One of the natives called back, and again Utembe interpreted the words.

"We have heard of white men and of black men who go with them," the native said. "You cannot fool us! We know that all white men eat human flesh! They come to buy black men to eat them."

After the exchange of shouts, the natives launched one more attack. Cadamosto had the cannons reloaded and run out to fire a second salvo. This time one of the stones struck a canoe full of natives, smashing it into several pieces and scattering the hapless men in the water. That was enough to frighten the remaining canoes away, and the men on board the two caravels let out another shout of victory.

The battle had cost the natives dearly, with at least a dozen of their number floating in the river. Yet despite the ferocity of the fight, not one Christian was even slightly wounded.

The two caravels drifted close together, and Usedimare and Cadamosto consulted with each other, shouting across the distance between them.

"What do you think we should do?" Usedimare called, cupping his hands around his mouth.

"I think we should follow the river for as far as it can be navigated," Cadamosto replied. "We may find friendlier, perhaps wealthy, people."

"I agree," Usedimare said.

"Signóre Dias," Cadamosto said to his sailing master, "proceed upriver as far as possible."

"*Capitão*, I would have a word with you," Dias replied. "It is about the crew."

"What about them? None of them were injured during the battle, were they?"

"No, *Capitão*."

"Then what is there to discuss?"

Dias sighed. "It shames me to speak of this," he said. "But they have refused to sail any farther."

"They'll go where I tell them to go," Cadamosto said sternly.

"I am sorry, *senhor*," Dias said. "But the crew has agreed, to a man. They will work no more."

"What? You mean they have made a mutiny?" Cadamosto sputtered.

"No, *senhor*," Dias explained. "They just refuse to sail any farther, that's all."

"But that's mutiny!" Cadamosto shouted. "On a Venetian galley I could have them broken for this!"

"Yes, *senhor*, but we are not on a Venetian galley. We are on a Portuguese caravel, governed by the Portuguese rules of the sea. And the Portuguese rules of the sea allow the sailors the right to decide their own fate."

"And just what is the decision of these pigheaded and obstinate men?"

"They wish to return to Portugal."

"And leave Usedimare to go on alone?"

Dias shook his head. "Usedimare's crew is in agreement with our own."

Cadamosto was startled. "How can that be? When have they had the opportunity to confer? Only Usedimare and I have spoken to shape decisions."

Dias smiled wanly. "Who can know the ways and means that the lowest sailor has of communicating with his kind?" he said. "But you need not take my word alone. Inquire of Usedimare. See if his sailors have not come to a mutual agreement."

"Very well, Dias, I shall do so," Cadamosto replied. "And if I find that they are willing to continue on, I will leave this ship and travel with Usedimare. I will not be turned back from wealth and glory by the cowardice of rigid, shortsighted men!"

Cadamosto signaled again for a conference with Usedimare, but he could tell from the moment the two ships drew abreast that Dias was right. The expression on Usedimare's face mirrored his own, for the captain of the other ship was as displeased with the unexpected turn of events as he was. Finally, with a sigh of disgust, Cadamosto turned away from the rail and spoke to Dias.

"Put about, Signóre Dias," he said. "We are going home."

CHAPTER 11

MADEIRA, SIX MONTHS LATER

Three maids were attending Soledade Bartolomão,
and as they worked around her, the young woman fidgeted
nervously.

"Would you please hold still, Soledade?" Inês da
Costa said. "I'll never get this finished with you twitching
about so." Inês was on her knees on the floor beside
Soledade, who was wearing a gown exquisitely fashioned
with lace and intricate beadwork, all done by Inês.

"But what are you doing, attending to me like one of
the maids?" Soledade asked. "I am very embarrassed that
a great lady like you would sew for me."

Inês chuckled. "I am not a great lady," she said. "I am
only a simple vintner's wife."

"Surely you are teasing me. The Da Costa vineyard is
the finest on all Madeira, and Madeira has the finest vineyards in the world," Soledade said.

"No matter," Inês said, dismissing Soledade's logic. "I
love to sew and make beautiful things. You wouldn't deny
me the opportunity to do so, now, would you? Especially
when it means working on the gown for one soon to be my

own daughter-in-law. Besides, when I was a young girl, I was quite proud of my needlework."

"You do me a great honor. And you have every right to be proud of your needlework because it is certainly the loveliest I have ever seen."

Inês finished the stitch, then tied off the thread. She stood up, brushing her hands together as she did so, and smiled with pleasure at the picture Soledade presented.

"Oh, my dear!" she gushed. "You truly will be the most beautiful bride Madeira has ever seen. What an honor for our household to have someone like you."

Soledade blushed. "The honor is all mine, *senhora*," she said. "The more so after the successful voyage of Tome and Diogo. The entire island is talking about the exploits of Captain Gomes and his crew. Their ship brought back over one hundred and eighty pounds of gold dust."

"Yes," Inês agreed. "Their father and I are quite proud of them."

"Ah, Inês, there you are," Pedro da Costa said, coming into the sewing room. "Hello, Soledade. May I say you are looking particularly lovely?"

"Thank you, Senhor da Costa," Soledade replied demurely. "But who would not look beautiful in the lovely gown Senhora da Costa has fashioned?"

"It is pretty, all right," Pedro said. He turned to his wife. "Inês, guess whose ship has landed?"

"I have never been very good at guessing, Pedro. You know that."

"It is a vessel belonging to our old friend, Tom Giles."

Inês's face lit up. "Tom is here on Madeira?"

"No, not Tom himself. But it *is* his ship, making it the next best thing. The captain of the ship, a man named Robert Denbigh, has come calling, bearing Tom's greetings. You must come and meet him."

"Of course," Inês said. She signaled to one of the maids who had been helping with the fitting of Soledade's dress. "You can finish with it now, can't you, Maria?"

"*Sim, Senhora*," the young woman said, reaching for the hem of the beautiful gown almost reverently.

"Now," Inês said, smiling and offering her arm to her

husband, "you may take me to meet our guest. We must offer him some liquid refreshment."

The man standing in the front room of the Da Costa villa was tall, tanned, well dressed, and very handsome. He smiled broadly, then made a leg and gave a sweeping bow to Inês as she entered the room.

"Gracious madam," he said, "I bring you greetings from a mutual friend, Lord Walversham"—he grinned—"or as he prefers to be known, Tom of Bristol."

"And how is our friend Tom?" Inês asked.

"Prosperous," Robert said, laughing. "And pursuing a sea trade that is making him even more prosperous."

Pedro joined in the laughter. "Yes, Tom has always been successful at making money." He gestured to a large oak table and bade Robert to sit. Then he uncorked a decanter of Madeira wine and poured a substantial amount into a goblet for his guest.

Robert sampled it, smiled with pleasure, then drank some more before picking up the thread of the conversation. "On the subject of being successful at making money, your two sons are as well, I have heard," he said. "The voyage they recently completed is the talk of Prince Henry's court."

"Yes, I'm sure the *Infante* is pleased with them," Pedro said, pouring two more goblets of wine for himself and Inês. "Though it's my understanding that the voyages of Cadamosto and Usedimare have caused more of a stir at Sagres."

"Perhaps so. Certainly they sailed farther south than anyone has ever gone before and have brought back knowledge and extended the boundaries of the known world. But in their expressed purpose of making a fortune they were sadly deficient."

"That was particularly unfortunate for Usedimare," Pedro said. "He is having such a difficult time with his creditors that he wrote a long letter to them, requesting that they have patience with him for six more months. I understand he has even taken out insurance."

"Indeed?"

"Yes," Pedro replied. "And even now he is back in Genoa, trying to raise funds for another voyage."

"I wish him luck," Robert said.

"I am sure Usedimare would find your best wishes most heartening . . . particularly since all his troubles seem to have begun when he was attacked by an English pirate in the Mediterranean."

Robert stroked his chin as he studied Pedro's face. Did Pedro know that it was he who had relieved Usedimare of his cargo?

"And yet wasn't it that same English pirate who suggested to Usedimare that he could do business with Prince Henry?" Robert asked.

"That is the story I heard. By the way, Captain Denbigh, have you had the pleasure of meeting Usedimare?"

"Uh, no," Robert said. "He had already returned to Genoa when I arrived at Sagres."

"I have not met him either," Pedro replied. "But I shall soon remedy that. My eldest son is about to be married, and Usedimare, Cadamosto, and Diogo Gomes are all coming to Madeira to attend the wedding."

"Ah, yes, when I was in Sagres, I heard that Tome was about to be married," Robert said. "I haven't had the pleasure of meeting the young lady who is to be his bride, but she is certainly getting herself a fine young man."

"It strikes me, Captain, that this would be an excellent opportunity for you to meet Usedimare," Pedro said. "You will be staying for the wedding, won't you? As my guest, of course."

Robert thought quickly. "Thank you for your generous invitation, but I fear I must decline. As soon as the water kegs and larders of my three ships are restocked, I must be on to England. My holds are bulging with cargo, and, if you remember Tom, he will want a timely delivery so that he can take advantage of every business opportunity."

"That's too bad. I'm sure Usedimare would have liked to meet you," Pedro said, his tone guileless. "You might even have been able to shed some light on who the English pirate is and where he might be found."

"I would think a man like that more to be avoided than found," Robert suggested, trying to read Pedro's expression.

"Quite so," Pedro agreed with a chuckle. "Quite so. Tell me, Robert, have you a lady waiting in England? If so, I could understand that your own need to reach home port would be every bit as urgent as Tom's need to have you there. I was once a sailor like yourself, you see, with someone waiting at home for me." He glanced at Inês. "Only I was nearly fool enough to let her get away. I hope you won't ever make the same mistake."

"I hope not as well," Robert replied.

He thought of his betrothed, Lady Diane Barkley, daughter of Lord Andrew Barkley, Earl of Crestwood. He wondered what had happened after the debacle at the Earl's estate, when he had to so ignominiously flee on the heels of his foolish act of cockiness. At the time it had seemed such a splendid idea: Defy the King's counsel and appear at Crestwood to claim what was rightfully his—the hand of Lady Diane. All it actually accomplished was a greater firing of Lord Andrew's determination to wed his daughter to anyone suitable, just as long as it wasn't Robert.

He had learned that Lord Andrew had issued orders to all in his employ that in the event that Robert Denbigh were to be so foolish as to again try to force the issue of his marriage to Diane, he was to be arrested and delivered to the King for execution. If Robert resisted arrest, Lord Andrew's orders read, he was to be killed.

Robert had heard through a mutual friend that Diane shared neither her father's attitude nor his desire to find her a new marriage partner. In fact, she was doing all she could do to delay the process, for after his bold act that night she found herself thoroughly in love with Robert and knew that he was in love with her. It was her fervent belief that if she could put off marrying another long enough, then someday she and Robert would be reunited.

Robert hoped that she was right.

He bade farewell to the Da Costas and headed down the mountain to the harbor, where his small fleet of three ships was moored, the crews taking on provisions and making ready to return to England. He stood on the quay and looked proudly at the *Golden Hawk*, the armed warship that was his own flagship, and the two unarmed merchant ships. Their holds were nearly spilling over, filled with enough silks, spices, gold, and other treasures to make Robert a wealthy man, even after Tom's healthy fifty-percent cut. Not only Tom and Robert stood to gain from the trade and piratical voyage through the Mediterranean. Each man of the crew would get a share of the bounty, as specified by the "Gentlemen of the Sea" charter under which they were sailing. Every man aboard—from the fiercest soldier brandishing a sword on the decks of the *Golden Hawk* to the meekest sailor manning the bilge pumps on one of the merchant ships—would be wealthier than he had ever imagined being in his life.

"Did you see your friends, Captain?" first mate Nigel Cooper asked as Robert stepped back aboard.

"Aye," Robert answered. "And I was invited to stay around for the wedding."

"And will you be doing so?"

Robert chuckled. "I think not. One of the guests is the captain of the Genoese galley we did business with some months back."

"Usedimare?"

"Usedimare." Robert looked up at the masts, now free of sail. "I wouldn't be at all surprised if Tom's friend Pedro didn't suspect more than he let on. And friend of Tom's that he is, he just might have been telling me something. Mr. Cooper, I think it would be best if we sailed with the evening tide."

"Aye, aye, Captain," the first mate replied.

SAGRES, PORTUGAL

Diogo da Costa and Luisa Canto were sitting on what Diogo considered hallowed ground: the rock escarpment below Prince Henry's castle where, just prior to Diogo's voyage with Captain Gomes, Luisa had given herself to him. That rapturous experience had been one of the thoughts that sustained Diogo during the long expedition with Gomes. However, if he had entertained the idea that they would recapture that rapture upon his return, he was mistaken. Luisa, so approachable before, was now very distant.

As it had for thousands of years, including the last time Diogo and Luisa had been there, the incoming sea just below them spewed up through a hole in the rock, misting them with spray. Diogo looked over at the beautiful young woman sitting beside him and remembered the sight of her naked skin covered with droplets. That memory was so erotic that, with an aching groan, Diogo reached for her.

"No!" Luisa said sharply, twisting her body enough to move out of his grasp.

"But, Luisa, I don't understand. You weren't like this the last time."

"That was different."

"What was different about it?"

"You were about to embark upon an adventure," Luisa said. "I—I wasn't sure you would ever return, and my heart went out to you. I wanted to comfort you."

"There will be other adventures equally as dangerous," Diogo said shamelessly. He reached for her again. "I may not return from them, either, and my need for comfort is just as great now as it was before."

"But I am not the same girl now that I was then," Luisa replied, pushing his hands away.

"You're not the same girl? What are you talking about?"

"I have a responsibility to my rank now," Luisa said. "My father has found favor with the Prince, and his standing has gone up. I am a lady of the court. I am fond of you, Diogo—very fond of you, as I am sure you are aware. But you are a person with no official position, and my parents do not approve of you."

"But surely I can win them over," Diogo said. "I don't want to sound arrogant, Luisa, but since our voyage with

Captain Gomes, my brother and I have also won favor with the court."

"Nevertheless, you are still a commoner."

"Nonsense. My father is a wealthy man," Diogo defended. "He owns the finest vineyard on Madeira."

"Perhaps so," Luisa replied. She looked at Diogo, then put her hand on his arm. Somehow his desire for her made her fingers feel cool and hot at the same time, and he didn't know how that could be. "But don't you see, Diogo? No matter how wealthy your family may be now, your mother was a *degredado*—as, indeed, everyone on Madeira was—and your father was a lowly seaman." Luisa sighed. "Please understand, I don't share my parents' opinion. I find you"—she smiled sweetly at him—"to be a fine young man, most worthy of my attention. And I want to continue seeing you, I really do. But it must be on my terms."

Diogo lifted Luisa's hand to his lips and kissed her cool-hot fingers.

"Whatever terms you set," he said. "For I am madly in love with you, Luisa, and I must see you, whatever the cost."

"Very well," Luisa said. "I will allow you to continue to call on me, but only when it is convenient for me. We must keep our real relationship secret from my father, and that means—" She paused. "I'm afraid this will be most difficult for you."

"Go on," Diogo urged.

"Very well. In order to make it appear to my father that I have no particular interest in you, I will have to continue to see those men of whom my father does approve. That means that you will often see me at court festivities with another. Will you be terribly jealous?"

"Yes."

"Oh, dear, I knew it wouldn't work."

Diogo smiled and raised her fingers to his lips again. "I will be jealous," he said. "And I won't like it. But I do understand. And if that's the only way our relationship can continue, then, God help me, so be it."

"There will be many, many men," Luisa warned, "for,

now that my father is a man of such importance, I have become a most desirable prize."

"If your father were a swineherd, you would still be the most desirable prize in all of Portugal," Diogo said gallantly.

"Diogo, really," Luisa said in a disgusted tone of voice.

"What is it? What did I say wrong?" Diogo asked.

"You will never be anything more than a commoner," Luisa said coolly. "Perhaps we are making a big mistake by even continuing to see each other."

"Luisa, no, please! I'm sorry if my words offended you. I meant only to make it clear to you how much I truly love you. *You*, not your position."

"Very well, I shall overlook it this time," Luisa said. "But please try to be less offensive in the future."

"I will, I promise. I will do anything you say," Diogo pleaded.

"Then take me back to the banquet. There are several eligible young men there, and I must make myself available to them."

"Available to do what?" Diogo challenged.

"Diogo," Luisa scolded, "remember our agreement. I will talk with them, walk with them, perhaps dance with them, and you are not to interfere in any way."

"I remember," Diogo said sullenly.

"And you understand that it is for my parents?"

"Yes," Diogo said.

"Good." The expression on her face grew sweet and concerned, and she reached out to touch his cheek. "I will smile and be pleasant to all my suitors, but remember, I care only for you." She moved her face close to his and he kissed her, feeling her lips move under his, and suddenly all his sullenness and resistance melted. At that moment he was her abject slave, anxious to do her bidding no matter what it might be. His eyes were so full of stars that, when they separated, he did not even notice that her expression of sweetness had turned into one of triumph.

*   *   *

Aldo Cavalli and Tome da Costa stood on one side of the brightly crowded great hall, watching the other revelers while holding a conversation of their own. The friendly rivalry between the two youths had continued, though each had been most generous in his appraisal of the other's achievements. Aldo envied Tome's success in bringing back large quantities of gold, while Tome envied Aldo his adventures, particularly the battles he and his shipmates had waged with natives.

"We, too, encountered canoes full of armed natives," Tome explained. "But they fled as soon as they saw us." He sighed. "I had hoped to be able to prove myself in battle, but I didn't get the opportunity."

Aldo put his hand on his friend's arm. "May I share something with you?" he asked.

"Of course."

"The excitement of battle is not all one expects."

"Were you frightened?"

"Yes," Aldo admitted. "At first. But it's more than that."

"What else?"

"I don't know if I can explain it," Aldo replied. "But the sight of a man mortally injured by your hand is most disconcerting." His mind conjured up the grisly sight of the first man he killed floating facedown in the river, then being dismembered by the snapping teeth of crocodiles. He shivered. "It isn't a scene one can easily erase from one's mind," he added.

"But it isn't as if you had killed a Christian," Tome said. "It was only a Negro."

Aldo recalled the ebony-skinned young girl who had been sent by King Budomel to warm his bed. She was his first sexual experience, and though he could not say he had fallen in love with her, during the time they spent together he had grown very fond of her, and even now he wondered how she was doing.

"Yes," Aldo said quietly. "It was only a Negro."

"I'm sorry," Tome replied quickly. "Of course he was a human being, and it cannot be an easy thing for any decent man to kill another human being."

"Let us speak of something else," Aldo suggested. He grinned. "Let us speak of your marriage. You are a very lucky man, Tome, to be marrying someone as beautiful and wonderful as Soledade."

"Yes, I am," Tome agreed. He looked intently at his friend. "I know that when you met her on Madeira, you fell in love with her."

"Tome!" Aldo gasped.

Tome laughed easily and put his hand on his friend's arm. "Don't worry," he said. "I also know that you were the perfect gentleman, for Soledade told me so. And how can I blame you for falling in love with her, for didn't I do the same thing? She is so wonderful that it's a mystery why *everyone* doesn't fall in love with her."

Just then Luisa Canto stepped through the great door leading from the loggia into the great hall. She made a quick adjustment to her clothes, another to her hair, then fixed a smile upon her face and started across the floor toward one of the well-dressed wastrels who made no greater contribution to court life than to lend his presence to the many celebrations.

Diogo came into the room a moment or two behind Luisa. He looked over at her as she glided toward the young popinjay; then, with a morose yet determined look on his face, he glanced away.

"I wish only that my brother could find someone as wonderful," Tome said with a sigh. "Luisa Canto is no good for him."

"I agree," Aldo said. "But I fear that is something he'll have to discover for himself. We would only incur his ire if we made such a suggestion to him."

Although from where Diogo stood on the far side of the room he couldn't possibly have overheard Tome and Aldo talking, he suddenly looked right at them. For just a moment the hurt expression on his face lingered, but then he smiled broadly and came across the room to greet his brother and his friend.

"So," he said when he reached them, "have you managed to dissuade my brother from the folly of getting married?"

"If I could do so, it would only be so I could have her for myself," Aldo replied.

"I agree," Diogo said. "I was only jesting. Soledade is a wonderful girl, and my brother is a lucky man. I will be most honored to be witness at his wedding next week."

"I would like to say," Aldo put in, "that I hope Diogo and I are as fortunate when we take our own brides."

"Indeed," Diogo said. His eyes searched the room for Luisa, then found her . . . kissing Duarte d'Afonso.

CHAPTER 12

ENGLAND

At cock's crow, the sun, its disk blood red, seemed to be resting momentarily on the tree-crowned hill. At the foot of the hill, in the middle of some one hundred acres that ran down to the sea, lay a manicured estate of sculptured hedgerows, elegant statuary, sparkling fountains, and walkways lined with sweet-smelling flowering rosebushes. In the center of the garden was a large reflecting pool, and mirrored in it, the image perfect on this still morning, was Crestwood Manor.

The three-story manor house was one of the finest examples of current architecture in England. Constructed of pink brick with rows of huge, mullioned windows, it had over one hundred rooms. In a setting of exquisite beauty, the house was the crowning jewel. Approached from the sea, silhouetted against the sky, it was an awesome sight, and this was what greeted Robert Denbigh as he had himself rowed ashore. Behind him the *Golden Hawk* lay at anchor. The other two ships of the small fleet had already sailed through the Bristol Channel and up the Mouth of the Severn, headed for Bristol.

"You're sure now, Cap'n, that you won't be wantin'

Gil and me to come with you, just in case there's a mite of trouble?" one of the rowers said.

"Thank you for your offer," Robert said. "But I know the grounds very well. If there *is* trouble, I'd have a better chance of getting away on my own. You fellows get on back to the ship and have Mr. Cooper put in at port. We've got some cargo we need to turn into money, eh, lads?"

"Aye, sir. A coin or two would be nice," the sailor agreed. "Still, I can't help but be worryin' about you."

"Don't," Robert assured the man. "I'll be there with you by the time you hoist your second mug of ale."

"And then the ale will be on me, Cap'n," the sailor said with a grin. "For 'tis that proud I am to have sailed with you."

"And we'll sail together again, I promise," Robert said. He pointed to a slip that led off the cove. "Head there," he said. "A gully leads from there to the back of the house. That'll let me get there without being seen."

"Aye, sir. All I can say is, I hope the lady is worth the risk you're takin'."

"Oh, she is, Gil, she truly is," Robert replied.

Moments later the boat bumped gently ashore, and Robert stepped out without getting so much as the soles of his boots wet. Grabbing a vine, he pulled himself up the bank, then turned and waved to his two men as they pushed the boat back into the water.

"Hurry back to the ship now, lads," he said. "I wouldn't want her seen lying offshore in one place for too long."

"Aye, aye, sir. We'll tell Mr. Cooper to get under way the moment we're aboard. Good luck to you, sir."

Robert turned and started up the gully, moving quickly, wanting to reach the manor and climb up to the third-floor window while it was still early. With any luck he would be in Diane's room before anyone else in the house was even awake.

The climb up the side of the house was made easy by a well-placed trellis, and the window opened easily as well. Robert slipped through it into the shadowy corridor. As he moved quietly down the long, wide hall, he could hear the snores and measured breathing of the sleepers behind the closed doors. He did not have to look for Diane's bed-chamber; he knew which one it was, having once when he was fifteen, in a bit of youthful bravado, embarked upon this same adventure. She had welcomed him eagerly enough then, infatuated as only a girl of twelve could be. He could only hope she would do so now.

When Robert reached Diane's door he tried it, discovered to his relief that it was not locked, then crept in.

The curtains around Diane's bed weren't fully drawn, and he looked down at the sleeping young woman, lying with her hair fanned out on the pillow around her, the soft morning light falling upon her face. To Robert it was as if she were lighting the room itself with the radiance of her beauty.

A vase of freshly cut roses sat on a table, and Robert plucked one. He laid it on the pillow beside Diane, then smiled when her nose twitched at the rose's fragrance.

Her eyes opened. At first she stared with bewilderment at the rose lying on the pillow, but then she smiled as she reached for it and brought it closer to smell it.

"Good morning," Robert said softly.

Diane's eyes grew wide with fright, and she drew in a quick breath, preparing to scream. Robert clamped his hand across her mouth.

"Diane!" he said. "Diane, it is I! Robert!"

The fear in her eyes was replaced by surprise, then by joy. Robert pulled his hand away.

"Where did you come from?" she asked in a rush. "How did you get here?"

"I am a ghost from the sea," Robert joked. "And, as you know, a ghost can go anywhere he wants, anytime he wants."

"Lady Diane?" a woman's voice called from the hallway just outside Diane's door. "Lady Diane, did you call me? Are you all right?"

Diane put her finger across her lips to silence Robert, then motioned for him to get down. He scurried around to the far side of the bed and was hidden by the curtain just as the door opened.

"Do you need anything, m'lady?" the maid asked, sticking her head into the room.

"No," Diane answered. "I must have called out in a dream. Go away, please, and close the door. I would like to sleep a little longer."

"Yes, m'lady," the maid replied contritely. "I'll see that you aren't disturbed." She curtsied, then backed out of the room, closing the door behind her.

Robert pulled open the curtain and sat on the bed beside Diane.

"You did this once before, as I recall," she said, taking his hand in hers.

"Yes, I did," Robert replied. "And do you remember what ransom I demanded?"

"You demanded a kiss," Diane said.

Robert raised Diane's hand to his lips and kissed it, then smiled roguishly. "Yes," he said. "But I was very young then, and a kiss was all the ransom I required. I am much older now, and much wiser. I'm afraid a kiss isn't enough."

Diane drew in a breath, and her skin flushed with passion.

"It isn't?" she asked in a low voice.

Robert shook his head. "Not nearly enough."

"Then, pray, what will the ransom be?"

Slowly, gently, Robert began undoing the fasteners that held the bodice of Diane's chemise closed. She offered no resistance, but just lay there, her pupils dilated, saying nothing. A moment later the bodice lay open, framing her naked breasts. The nipples tightened in the morning air.

"I haven't yet decided what my ransom will be," Robert said. He bent down to her breasts, taking one of the nipples between his lips. His hand touched her between her breasts, then slid beneath the gown down her smooth skin to her stomach, then lower, then lower still. She gasped from the pleasure of his touch. He lifted his head to look at her. "I thought perhaps you might have an idea," he said.

Diane put her hands on his head and pulled him up to

kiss him deeply, hungrily. Consumed by an overpowering heat, she tore at her chemise to get it off. She then lay back, naked, watching through smoky eyes as her ghost lover from the sea removed his own clothing. He came to her, falling upon her, and they began making love—finally realizing the fantasies they had each entertained ever since Robert had made his daring appearance—and getaway— now nearly a year ago.

When the door to Diane's bedroom burst open, Robert sat up quickly, but he could do nothing. Six armed men rushed in to surround the bed.

Startled awake, Diane screamed, though the scream died in her throat.

"What is the meaning of this?" Robert shouted, hoping by bluster to bluff his way out. He had not intended to fall asleep; he thought only to lie beside his beloved for a moment or two longer to feel her soft skin, to smell her sweet scent, to listen to her rhythmic breathing. That had been a mistake—one that might well cost him his life.

"You rapscallion!" Lord Andrew Barkley shouted angrily, storming into his daughter's room. "You dare to defy me? You dare to defile my daughter?"

"Father, please! What are you going to do?" Diane asked.

"Do? Why, I won't do a thing, my dear. The King's counsel will do it all for me. This man is a traitor, and like his treasonous father before him, he will go to the executioner's block."

Diane was sitting up, holding the covers to her chin to shield her nakedness from the guards. But they kept surreptitiously glancing at her, which gave her an idea.

"Robert," she said, so quietly that no one but he heard her, "get ready."

Robert felt her tense as she prepared to act. He primed himself mentally and physically to react to whatever she might do.

"Well, might I at least get dressed?" Diane asked. Not waiting for a response, she boldly threw the coverlet aside and stepped out of the bed, displaying her luscious nakedness.

As one, all the guards stared hungrily at her.

"How *dare* you gaze upon my daughter!" Lord Andrew bellowed. "Close your eyes, you swine!"

Obediently, the men turned away, covering their eyes. That was Robert's needed chance. He leapt from the bed and dashed past the guards, out the door. Several servants were standing in the corridor just outside Diane's room, listening to the drama being played out inside. So startled were they by the spectacle of a nude man suddenly bursting upon them that they jumped away rather than toward him, giving Robert even more of an advantage.

He ran to the winding staircase, encountering two maids coming up the stairs. One of them, an old woman, averted her eyes in embarrassment, but the much younger one smiled broadly and enjoyed a long look at the muscular young man as he raced down to the ground floor.

"*Stop him!*" Lord Andrew screamed, coming to the top of the stairs. "*Someone stop him!*"

Fortunately for Robert there was no one left to stop him; Lord Andrew had already summoned every manservant in the house to help secure the arrest in the first place—and they were just now recovering from the trick Diane had played on them. Robert ran unmolested through the front door of the mansion, so far ahead of everyone that there was no chance that anyone would catch him.

"I would love to have seen Andrew Barkley's face," Tom Giles said, laughing uproariously as Robert recounted his tale. "And the face of the maids as you ran by," he added. "So, tell me, my bold young friend: How long did you entertain the countryside with your bold display?"

Robert was laughing with him. "It seemed like I was naked for the livelong day," Robert said. "Though in truth I found some clothes airing on a line behind the gameskeeper's house and purloined them. I was not the epitome of sartorial splendor, to be sure, but no more young maidens were shocked by my appearance."

"Nor beguiled either, I wager," Tom added, and once again both men were convulsed with laughter.

A servant came into the room, standing quietly just inside the doorway until Tom acknowledged him.

"Ah, Charles, good fellow, have you news?" Tom asked, noticing him.

"Yes, m'lord," Charles answered. "The Lady Diane is being confined at Our Lady of Sorrows convent. It's on the coast near Cardiff, sir. There she is to make amends for her wanton behavior by placing herself in lasting servitude to our Lord."

"Yes, I have seen the place," Tom replied.

"Barkley accused her of being a trollop and had her incarcerated?" Robert said angrily. "What sort of man would do such a thing to his own daughter?"

"The same sort of man who would behead you, if he could find you," Tom reminded him.

"Tom, you must help me. I must get her out of there."

"And if you do, my friend, what then?" Tom asked. "Where will you take her? Lord Andrew will offer a reward so large that she will be safe nowhere."

"I will take her to sea with me," Robert said simply.

"You would subject her to the perils you face?"

"Only if she would do so willingly," Robert replied. "And between the perils of the sea and the slow, silent death of confinement in a convent, I have no doubt as to the choice she would make."

Tom thought about it for but a second before breaking into a wide smile. "Nor do I, my friend, nor do I," he said. "Very well, I'll help you. Now, let's see what kind of plan a couple of smart gentlemen like you and I can come up with."

Late afternoon shadows darkened the room, but bars of sunlight fell on Lady Diane Barkley. Even without the sun she would have been the bright spot in the otherwise drab cell that was now her world.

She was no longer referred to by her secular name. Now she was Sister Magdalene, a name pointedly chosen to suggest the need for contrition and humility.

Diane looked around the bleak cubicle and could not help but make the comparison between this place and her bedchamber at Crestwood. The centerpiece of her bedroom at home had been a great four-poster bed with ornately carved head- and footboards, brocaded curtains, and beautiful silk and wool coverings. There was a huge chifforobe, a large gilded cheval glass, a dressing screen, a padded bench, a small table by the window where she often had breakfast served to her, a golden harp, a workstand for her needlework, several paintings and pieces of statuary, a delicate porcelain washbasin and vase, rich draperies, and exquisitely woven carpets to take the chill off the floor.

It took much less time to inventory the contents of this room: a quilt that she rolled out as a sleeping pad by night and a small three-legged stool that served as a chair by day.

There was nothing else in the room.

Diane was expected to attend prayers six times a day —and except for her spoken prayers, not one word could pass from her lips. Along with the virtual confinement to her minuscule room, the gregarious Diane had been given the additional penance of silence.

"You will not speak, nor will you be spoken to, for a period of eighteen years," the bishop had declared. "After such period you will be allowed to speak, but only in praise of Christ."

Though there were members of the convent who had voluntarily taken vows of silence, Our Lady of Sorrows was not a silent order. Therefore, Diane often heard the low murmur of voices as others talked among themselves, and whenever possible, she would strain to hear the words, for never had she known how sweet could be the sound of the human voice. And yet it was a bittersweetness, for to hear words not meant for her and to know that she could not speak herself pained her almost to the point of death.

The last vestige of evening light had faded now, and she heard a call for prayer.

> "Eternal Father, I offer Thee the
> Sacred Heart of Jesus, with all Its
> Love, all Its sufferings and all Its merits:
> To Expiate all the sins I have committed
> this day, and during all my life."

The words of the prayer leapt to her tongue, not so much for the religious comfort such words would bring as for the pure joy of speech itself.

The *Golden Hawk* lay at anchor in Bristol Bay, a dark shadow against the sea. Halfway between the ship and shore a small luminous wake marked the passage of the ship's longboat being propelled by muffled oars. Sitting in the bow were Robert Denbigh and Tom Giles, distinguishable from the others by the hooded cassocks they wore, for both were disguised as traveling priests.

"All right, lads," Robert whispered as the boat bumped ashore. "Wait here for us."

"Aye, aye, Cap'n," one of the oarsmen replied. "Good luck to you, sir."

"Thanks," Robert replied. "We'll be needing plenty of that, I'm afraid."

It was no more than a quarter of a mile from the boat to the front gate of the walled convent. By pulling on a dangling rope, a section of log suspended in a rope cradle could be manipulated to strike against the heavy timbers of the double gate. Tom pulled the rope, and the log struck solidly, sending a resonating boom throughout the convent. A few moments later a small window opened in the gate, and someone peered out.

"What do you want here?" a woman's voice asked.

"The Lord be with thee, Sister," Tom said.

"And with thy spirit," the woman replied.

"I am Father Tucker, undertaking a journey on behalf of His Eminence the Bishop of Bristol to carry a message to the Bishop of Cardiff. This is my traveling companion and aide, Friar Gillis. We ask only for a bit of bread and a place to sleep for the night."

"This is a convent, Father. We have no men here. Except, of course, when Father Mullins comes to say mass and hear our confessions."

"Yes, yes, indeed," Tom replied. "But we are all servants of God, are we not? And my companion and I have no place else to go. Would you turn us out?"

"Wait here. I will see Mother Superior."

The window closed, and Tom and Robert stood impatiently for several minutes before they heard timbers being slipped through brackets to allow entry. A moment later the gate opened, and an old woman stood just inside the grounds.

"Welcome, Father. Welcome, Brother," she said. "I am Mother Mary Margaret, abbess of this convent. You may take supper with us."

"The Lord's blessings be upon you," Tom said.

"Follow me," the abbess said. "I would caution you about speaking to any of the sisters. Many of them have taken the vow of silence, most voluntarily, some as an act of penance."

"We will abide by your wishes, Mother Superior."

The expansive refectory was as cold and dreary as the rest of the place. It had walls of unadorned stone blocks, lighted by a dozen candles burning in wall sconces whose dim glow barely managed to push back the deep shadows. Twenty or more women sat on long wooden benches on either side of the thick planked table. The evening meal consisted of black bread and porridge, and the women stared at their bowls when Robert and Tom came in, as if looking at them would be a sin.

Robert had no such compunction. Taking his seat, he stared at each woman in turn. To his frustration he found that all the staring in the world did him no good. The wimples of the women's habits obscured their faces so completely that he could see nothing of their features.

Then he heard a slight gasp, so delicate as to be barely discernible. Turning, he found that the very nun who had been selected to serve him was none other than his own sweet Diane.

Diane recovered quickly from her own shock and began to spoon the porridge into Robert's bowl.

"Thank you, Sister," Robert said.

"Father, please remind your acolyte that he is to speak to no one," the abbess said sternly to Tom. "Sister Magdalene's penance is that she can neither speak nor be spoken to for a period of eighteen years."

"*Eighteen years?*" Robert was unable to restrain his outburst at hearing the severity of the sentence. "That is inhuman!"

"It is not our place to question the penance prescribed by the Bishop," the abbess said coldly. "Especially as the bishop in question is your very own superior."

"Forgive him, Mother Superior," Tom said quickly. "He is new to our order and still needs a bit of acclimation."

The abbess sighed. "Yes, such things can be very trying. But now, please, no more talking."

The meal was consumed in a silence that offered no distraction from food so bland and tasteless that it was all Robert could do to eat it. He fumed at the severity of Diane's punishment, vowing to take her out of that awful place no matter what. If the stealth he and Tom had planned did not work out, then he would remove her by force—an easy enough task since the place had but women and was too far from the city for them to summon help.

The first problem was to locate exactly which cell was Diane's. That turned out to be no problem at all; after the meal each nun put her bowl in a particular position on the shelf, and Robert deduced that the placement corresponded with the position of their rooms. Diane's bowl was on the top shelf, the third from the right.

She was waiting for him when, an hour later, he slipped along the long, dark corridors, feeling his way through the shrouding shadows, and found her room. They embraced hungrily, though in complete silence.

Parting reluctantly, Robert took her over to the far side of her room. The narrow, mullioned window pushed open easily and noiselessly. He leaned out and felt along the stones. It was as he had hoped: A capped bolt projected from the wall, securing the beam within. Taking a rope from under his cassock, he secured it to the bolt, then dropped it to the ground one story down. A moment later the rope jerked, Tom's signal that he was waiting below, standing by to help.

Robert did not have to prompt Diane. She climbed onto the windowsill and, securing the skirt of her habit between her knees, took hold of the rope, then let herself down. Robert waited until he was sure she was safely on the ground. Then he wedged himself through the narrow window, finding that the most difficult part of the entire escape, and lowered himself to the ground.

"Let's go!" Tom urged in a hoarse whisper the moment Robert's feet touched soil. "With any luck I'll be back in Bristol and you'll both be far at sea by the time anyone realizes she is gone."

"At sea?" Diane asked.

"Yes, my darling, at sea," Robert replied. "Will you go with me?"

"Of course I will go with you," Diane answered. "I can think of nothing that would make me happier. Oh, listen!" she said.

"Listen? Listen to what?"

"To my voice. To yours. To yours," she added to Tom. "Do you know what a beautiful thing the human voice is?"

"I know how beautiful *your* voice is," Robert said.

"No, not just my voice. *Any* voice," Diane insisted.

Robert laughed. "Wait until you hear the growl that is my first mate Mr. Cooper's voice," he said.

"I'm sure it will be as beautiful as harp music," Diane said.

"Which we'll all be hearing if we don't make haste," Tom said. "Angel's harps, I mean. I imagine the penalty for stealing someone from a convent, even if she is willing, would be quite severe."

"Yes," Robert agreed. "Come, my love. The boat is waiting for us."

"Robert?" Diane said.

"Yes?"

"I love you."

Robert chuckled. "Now, *that* is the most beautiful sound in the world."

CHAPTER 13

1456, NORTH OF ARGUIM

"We're running full and by, at your command, Senhor Cavalli. But some of the men are nervous. They've never been on a ship running under full sail after nightfall."

Aldo Cavalli had been leaning on the taffrail, watching the rolling wake. By contrast with the black sea, the wake was so white as to appear phosphorescent; Aldo found that watching it relaxed him.

He turned to face the sailor who had come up behind him. "Have we a man aloft?" he asked.

"*Sim, senhor,*" the Portuguese seaman said, pointing to the crow's nest at the top of the mainmast.

"You told him to keep a sharp lookout for rocks and shoals?"

"*Sim, senhor.*"

"Then put the men at ease. The moon is bright. If we exercise all the proper precautions, we'll have no problem running in the darkness," Aldo said. He leaned back against the railing and surveyed the deck. A lantern was lit on the quarterdeck to allow the helmsman to see the compass, and it splashed yellow light onto the deck and the main-mizzen- and bonaventure masts. The ship was heeled over under a fair breeze, a billowing white sail blossoming from every stick and line.

This was Aldo's second voyage with Alvise Cadamosto, and this time, as evidenced by the sailor's deference, the young Venetian wasn't a mere bowman of the quarterdeck. This time he was shipmaster, Vincente Dias having been given a ship of his own to captain by Prince Henry.

Aldo's responsibilities were, of course, much greater on this voyage—and with his increased responsibilities came a greater share of any profits the voyage might earn.

"And this time, my friend," Cadamosto had promised, "we will not come back without a profit."

Although at just eighteen Aldo was very young to hold the rank of shipmaster, he had already earned the respect of the entire crew. For one thing he had sailed on Cadamosto's previous voyage, which had traveled farther south than any ship had ever gone before, and the sailors regarded anyone who was associated with that voyage a hero. For another, Aldo obviously knew his business: He understood seamanship and navigation, he had proved himself in battle, and he was a good trader and an astute businessman. Sailors, who were allowed small trading chests of their own, generally found that their trading opportunities were enhanced if their ship was commanded by officers who were themselves good businessmen.

In addition to being the sailing master, Aldo was also the *balestrièri* commander. When the previous voyage had returned to Portugal, Captain Filippo Strozzi, the old crossbowmen commander, had formed a partnership with Gonzalo Canto, Luisa Canto's father—an alliance spoken of in some circles as an unholy one because of the somewhat unsavory reputation of both men.

Canto had risen to his position within Prince Henry's court either by toadying or by deceit. He was jealous of the financial success reaped by Captain Diogo "Vinegar" Gomes and the accolades awarded to Alvise Cadamosto and Antoniotto Usedimare as a result of their explorations. Canto craved wealth and glory—without having to go to sea for it. He and Strozzi had formed the perfect symbiotic relationship: Canto's money and position provided Strozzi the ship and the license he needed from Prince Henry to operate in Portuguese waters, and in Strozzi, Canto had a captain who was as ruthless a man as himself. Strozzi, Canto knew, would never turn away from a profit, even if the method of obtaining it were unscrupulous.

Strozzi had invited Aldo to sail with him on his new ship, promising the young man that he would make a far greater profit with him than he could ever make with Cadamosto. However, Aldo, long weary of Strozzi's boasting and aggrieved by his mistreatment of everyone under him, declined the invitation.

When Strozzi began assembling his crew for his new ship, Aldo was relieved that he had judiciously refused to sail with the soldier. Strozzi seemed to reject reputable sailors in favor of the dregs of the sea, filling his ship's complement with wharf rats, louts, drunkards, thieves, and cutthroats. Questioned about it, he had replied that such a crew could be hired for less, ensuring greater profit for himself and for the ship's owner. When his ship had sailed two weeks before Cadamosto's, Strozzi, never a man to be restricted by modesty, boasted that he would return with his cargo holds bulging with gold, precious jewels, silks, and rare spices.

Now, as Aldo stood upon the quarterdeck of Cadamosto's ship, listening to the water lapping against the hull and the gentle creaking of ropes and wood in motion, he found himself wondering if Strozzi would make good on his boast. He wondered, too, if, as Cadamosto had promised, this voyage would prove to be more profitable for them than the previous adventure had been. It wasn't a question he would have to ponder long; tomorrow they would raise Arguim.

ARGUIM, NORTHWESTERN AFRICA

It had been two years since Aldo had last seen Prince Henry's fortified trading factory at Arguim. He had been surprised then to see European-style houses built in this part of the world. Now he was beyond surprise. Arguim was no longer just an armed trading post with a palisaded wall and a few western houses to set it apart; it was a bustling coastal city of crowded markets, taverns, and inns, teeming with people of a dozen nationalities.

In addition to being the shipmaster for Cadamosto, Aldo was also an official representative of the House of Cavalli. While wandering through the marketplace, he sought out those trading goods he felt would be most profitable to his father's business in Venice.

The marketplace at Arguim was about the most wondrous sight Aldo had ever seen, filled with virtually everything that anyone could ever need or covet. The huge, open site was stacked with baskets overflowing with fruits and vegetables of every hue, size, and shape. Juxtaposed among the produce were intricate wood carvings, splendidly wrought utensils of copper and tin and brass, lacquered pottery, and precious and semiprecious gems. Some of the stones were inlaid in gold and silver medallions and rings, though most were lying unset on straw mats, where they caught the sun and gave back the light in flashes of red, blue, green, and yellow.

Ivory tusks were stacked up like so much cordwood. Some pieces had been intricately carved, including several showing men and women copulating in explicit detail.

Exotic scents accompanied the dazzling sights, from the smell of spices to the bouquet of perfumes to the aroma of food cooking over open fires and offered by enterprising peddlers making their living by feeding the hungry marketers.

Even if a visitor to the market were blind or had no sense of smell, a visit would still be a compelling aural experience. Shoppers and peddlers haggled in a half dozen languages, flutes keened melodically or mysteriously, drums pounded, cymbals jangled, men sang, children shouted, women laughed. . . . Aldo decided at that moment that Prince Henry, by building this trading metropolis, had made a contribution to the world that far exceeded any profit motive. For in Arguim all the cultures of the world could come together in a spirit of friendly barter.

"*Hola, amigo! Hé, ami! Saluto, signóre!* Hello, friend!"

"*Saluto,*" Aldo replied in Italian, turning toward the voice. He saw no one.

"*Hola, amigo! Hé, ami! Saluto, signóre!* Hello, friend!"

"Hello," Aldo said again. "Where are you hiding? Come. Show yourself."

An old African man sitting cross-legged on the ground between two piles of straw baskets burst out laughing. "But he *is* here, *senhor.* Do you not see him?"

"He *is?*" Aldo asked in confusion. "Where? I *don't* see him."

The multilanguage greeting was repeated, and it was then that Aldo realized it came from a parrot sitting on a perch just above the black man's head. Aldo was startled at first; then he laughed aloud and pointed to the bird.

"So, a parrot!" he said. "What a wonderful thing! He can say hello in four languages."

"In seven," the black man said, holding up his fingers. "He speaks the language of three African peoples as well."

"It's too bad that I couldn't use him as an interpreter," Aldo quipped.

"Oh, I'm afraid he would not make a very good interpreter, *senhor,* since he does not really know what he is saying. However, he does make a good amusement, yes?"

"Yes," Aldo said. "He is wonderfully amusing." He said hello to the bird, and the bird replied.

"You would like to buy him, perhaps?"

Aldo stroked his chin. If he found the bird entertaining, then so would those who did not have the opportunity to visit exotic lands. Talking parrots could become the amusement of all the moneyed families in Venice. He could see a genuine possibility for profit in such a thing.

"Yes, I would like to buy him. And many more," he said. "Perhaps more than you can supply."

The merchant smiled broadly and nodded vigorously. "Do not worry, my friend," he said. "As many parrots as you want to buy, that is how many I will get for you."

Aldo and the merchant haggled for a while before finally settling on what each of them considered a fair exchange for fifty birds. If Aldo could keep them alive until he got back to Venice, he figured to make a profit of tenfold on each bird.

He next visited one of the merchants who dealt in ivory. The man had many beautiful pieces made from ivory —not just erotic pieces, but objets d'art—and several dozen rough tusks, as well. Aldo was torn between the finished pieces, which were magnificent, and the raw tusks. He finally settled on the tusks, surmising they would less likely be damaged in transit and the raw ivory would be a medium for which Venetian artists would pay well.

Besides the parrots and ivory, Aldo managed to trade several cases of Venetian glassware for gold dust at a rate that made the glassware far more profitable than it would have been anywhere else.

He had just left the market area after a successful three hours of bargaining when a naked young black boy darted out from between two warehouses. The boy's eyes were wide with fear, and he kept looking back over his shoulder as he ran. Not watching where he was going, he tripped over a rope and slid facedown across the hard ground, winding up at Aldo's feet.

"Stop him! Stop that boy!" someone shouted. Emerging from between the same two warehouses were two well-armed white men. One was brandishing a sword, the other carrying a crossbow. Seeing the boy lying at Aldo's feet, the one with the crossbow raised the stock of the weapon to his shoulder and took aim.

"Hold on there!" Aldo shouted, stepping in front of the boy. "What are you doing?"

Whimpering, the boy got to his knees, then wrapped his arms around Aldo's legs, hiding behind them.

"Get out of the way!" one of the two pursuers commanded, waving his arm impatiently at Aldo. "You've no business here!"

"If you are aiming that bow at me, you are making it my business," Aldo said. By now the commotion had drawn an encircling crowd, which contained a number of Aldo's sailors. At the sight of their shipmaster beset by trouble, the crewmen edged toward the two armed men.

"My, such brave talk coming from one lone unarmed fellow," the one carrying the sword scoffed.

"He is not alone," one of Aldo's sailors spoke up.

"That's right," another called from the other side of the crowd. "And we *are* armed."

"There are many of us here," a third said, from still another location.

The two pursuers jerked their heads back and forth, locating the sources of the challenge. Finally the one who was holding the crossbow lowered it.

"Look," he said to Aldo, "I don't wish any trouble with you or your companions." He pointed to the young black boy. "But this is a runaway slave, and I have my duty. I am to recapture him—dead or alive."

"It appears that you have no interest in recapturing him alive," Aldo said.

The man holding the crossbow flashed an insincere smile. "Of course I would rather have him alive, sir," he said. "After all, no one wants to pay for a *dead* slave."

The boy began whimpering as the man with the sword walked over to grab him. He held his hands out to Aldo, pleading with words that were unintelligible and eyes that needed no translation.

"I'm sorry," Aldo said, though he knew the boy would be no more able to understand his words than he could the boy's. "I'm sorry," he said again. "There is nothing I can do." He looked away from the boy, unable to meet his gaze.

The two armed men hauled away the screaming, weeping boy, and Aldo watched until they disappeared behind the warehouses. He had planned to do some more marketing, but the plight of the young boy stayed with him until he found himself being inexorably drawn toward the "factory" where he knew slaves were being bought and sold.

Coming upon the place, Aldo was stunned. There, arrayed in an enormous square, were hundreds if not thousands of natives, their nude bodies coated with palm oil so that they gleamed in the midday sun. The young Venetian was surprised at the diversity of skin color among the cap-tives, ranging from golden copper to nearly ebony. But it wasn't just the skin color or the fact that they were all naked—men, women, and children—that affected him. For a long moment he couldn't figure out what it was. Then he realized that never before had he seen such a huge body of people so unremittingly the picture of grievous despair.

Some of the Negroes, their heads hanging, were crying piteously; others merely looked mournfully at each other. Some stood moaning, looking up at heaven and calling out with shrieks of agony, entreating their gods for deliverance. Some groveled on the ground, beating their foreheads with their hands, while others sung a sorrowful dirge. Every now and then there would be a particularly poignant outbreak of wailing, the result of families being wrenched apart—husbands from wives, mothers from children, sibling from sibling. Aldo was glad that he had nothing to do with it.

When he reboarded the ship later that day, however, he discovered, to his surprise, that he *did* have something to do with it. Sitting on the middeck were numerous black men, women, and children, including, by coincidence, the same boy who had pleaded to him for help.

The slaves were chained together in groups of ten, their bodies still naked and oiled, and looking even more terrified than they had while on land.

"What is this?" Aldo asked, looking around. "Who brought these people on board?"

"They were brought aboard by our crew," Cadamosto said, stepping out onto the deck from his cabin. "As you know, we promised them a share of the trading activity. They decided to pool their money and buy slaves."

"But I thought we weren't going to do that," Aldo protested.

"Well, you and I aren't doing it," Cadamosto replied. "But we can't let our convictions affect the right of our men to make a profit from this voyage, can we? And you know as well as I that slaves are the single most profitable venture."

"But this is inhumane!"

Cadamosto gestured toward the crew. "Can you offer them a more profitable enterprise?"

Aldo sighed. "I suppose not. But I don't approve of it. Not at all."

"Close your mind to it," Cadamosto suggested. "That is what I do."

VENICE, THREE MONTHS LATER

Alessandro Cavalli stood at the windows of his warehouse looking out across St. Mark's Canal, watching luminous clouds scud across the blue sky, casting their shadows against the imposing architectural facades of Venice. Behind Sandro, going over the latest figures in the ledger book, was Leonardo Ippolito, the *contabile* of the House of Cavalli.

"My, my," Ippolito said. "My, oh, my, oh, my. Messer Aldo has been most successful with his enterprises, hasn't he, sir?"

Turning toward the old man, Sandro shook his head and chuckled. "Parrots," he said. "Can you imagine something as foolish as parrots? If I had been with him and he told me he wanted to buy parrots, I would have stopped him straightaway. And if I had . . ." Sandro sighed. "And if I had, I would have made a big mistake," he admitted. "The profit from the parrots alone has doubled the investment of the entire voyage. The ivory, the gold"—Sandro waved toward the warehouse, the action encompassing its contents—"is all extra. And it would have been enough to make the year a profitable one for the Ca' di Cavalli even if we had done no other business at all."

Ippolito smiled broadly. "That is true, sir. And it is easy to see how Aldo comes by his great trading skills, for we *did* do other business—a great deal of business. I am pleased to tell you that this has been the most profitable year in your family's history. But even aside from that accomplishment, of course, the House of Cavalli would still be one of the wealthiest and most successful trading houses in all of Venice."

"Yes, I suppose it is that," Sandro said. "Yet somehow it doesn't seem enough for Aldo."

"Surely, Signóre Cavalli, you are not suggesting that your son is not satisfied with the level of success of the House of Cavalli!"

"Frankly, I don't think satisfied or unsatisfied has anything to do with it," Sandro replied. "In fact, I'm quite certain that if we had a serious reversal of fortune, it wouldn't matter much to Aldo. It's not that he isn't satisfied, Leonardo. He isn't *interested.* All he is interested in is the sea and exploration."

"Yes, sir. But if I may point out, Signóre Cavalli, were you not also quite the wanderer in your youth?"

"I had no youth," Sandro said flatly.

Chastened, Ippolito looked down at the ledger. "To be sure, sir," he said softly.

Seeing that he had inadvertently upset his *contabile,* Sandro sighed. "That was a misguided thing for me to say. Of course I had a youth, and if it was much more difficult than that of any of my peers, then so be it. I sincerely believe that my life is more successful now because of the hardships I endured then."

Sandro's mind briefly rushed back to the time when, at eighteen, the same age his son was now, his treacherous brother, Matteo, wanting total control of the family business and fortune, had had him kidnapped. He was forced into slavery, first laboring for more than two brutal years as an oarsman on a Genoese galley and then, after the galley was taken by Barbary pirates, toiling as an assistant to a relatively humane old Arab geographer in Damascus. When the old man had died while traveling to Mecca and Sandro's life again took a brutal turn, the determined Venetian managed to escape and make his way back to Europe, first to Portugal, where he met his wife, Catalina, and then home to Venice and a final confrontation with Matteo.

It was almost impossible to comprehend, but the man who guided one of the most successful enterprises in Venice, the head of one of its most esteemed families, once occupied a station beneath that of anyone in the entire city. Lesser men would have been broken by his experiences, but Sandro Cavalli had been strengthened by them. He not only had a far deeper appreciation of his own blessings, he felt a keen awareness of the rights of others and was proud of the fact that though some of the other trading houses were becoming heavily involved in the slave trade, he was able to turn his back on it and still show a handsome profit in his operation.

"Will Messer Aldo be returning to his position here soon?" Ippolito asked.

Sandro sighed and shook his head. "I'm afraid not," he said. "In the last letter we received from him, he told us that he would be sailing with Cadamosto again in May."

Ippolito smiled. "It is as they say: Like father, like son."

Summoned from his cabin, Captain Filippo Strozzi stepped out onto the quarterdeck, and Giuseppi Remilio, his first mate, passed him the telescope. Strozzi put it to his eye and focused on the merchant ship on the horizon.

"She is English," he said. "Her cannons are shipped, and she is riding low in the water. That means her hold is full." Strozzi snapped the telescope shut, tapping it against the palm of his hand as he continued to stare at the ship with his naked eyes. "Certainly they have seen our Portuguese flag, and so her captain suspects nothing," he said quietly, almost as if speaking to himself. Then, eyes gleaming with anticipation, he looked at Remilio. "Show signals, Remilio. Ask her captain for a friendly parley."

"A parley? But, Captain, aren't we going to attack?" Remilio asked.

"Of course we are going to attack," Strozzi replied. "But there's no need to let the English captain know of our plans before it's necessary, is there?"

Remilio smiled. "Ah, I see. No, Captain, I suppose not."

"Remilio?" Strozzi called, as his first mate started down from the quarterdeck to transmit the captain's orders to the men.

Remilio paused and looked back. "Yes, my captain?"

"When we open fire, tell the men to take care only to shoot away the sails and the masts. Don't hole her. If she sinks, her cargo sinks with her. Whatever she is carrying will do us little good if it's lying at the bottom of the sea."

Remilio smirked. "Yes, Captain."

The order was passed, and every man on the ship went to battle stations. Some scampered into the rigging to bring in all but combat-necessary sails. A swivel gun was taken to the top and put in position to fire broken chain and grapeshot down onto the merchant ship. Deck cannon were loaded with heavy stones and run out. Hands who weren't part of the gun crews stood by with loaded muskets and crossbows. All this activity was carried on while signal flags, requesting a parley, fluttered atop the mainmast.

In compliance, the English captain flattened some of his sheets, spilling air and losing headway to facilitate Strozzi's approach. Strozzi watched the Englishman through the telescope as his own ship closed quickly on the hapless vessel.

The ships had now drawn close enough for the Portuguese caravel's preparations to be clearly visible. Strozzi's telescope revealed the English captain looking first at the cannons and then at the men standing by, armed and ready. The Englishman's expression of curiosity left his face, replaced by one of surprise, then anger, then fear. He shouted to his men, and the English sailors scuttled about the ship, trying to ready themselves to fight off an attack.

It was too late. At an order from Strozzi, his cannon hurled a broadside across the water into the English ship. Masts were broken, sails were cut loose to come fluttering down, and nearly a dozen English sailors lay dead or dying on the deck, felled by the devastating effect of grapeshot and chain and stone.

"Do you ask for quarter?" Strozzi shouted, cupping his hands around his mouth.

The English captain answered by firing his pistol, more out of rage than any hope of actually inflicting damage.

"Helmsman, bring us alongside!" Strozzi ordered.

"Bowman to the rails! The rest of you into the shrouds, prepare to board!"

Strozzi's men let out a ghastly shriek and climbed into the shrouds, some wielding sabers, others holding ropes with grappling hooks, preparatory to securing their ship to the English merchantman.

The two ships crashed together with a horrific, grinding crunch; then the grappling hooks were tossed across and the ships secured. Strozzi's men gave another ferocious shout and leapt or swung across to the merchantman.

"Quarter! Quarter!" the English captain shouted, realizing that all was lost. "By all that's holy, Captain, call off your attack!"

"Have your men drop their weapons," Strozzi ordered.

The few Englishmen who were still standing did as they were directed.

"Now, over to the railing with you. All of you."

"What—what are you doing?" the English captain asked, paling.

Strozzi laughed, the sound the cackle of a demon from hell. "Why, we are going to kill you, of course."

"But surely you are not! We asked for quarter!" the English captain protested. "We have put down our arms!"

"And I appreciate that," Strozzi replied. "It does make our task easier." He finished his statement by abruptly plunging his sword through the Englishman's heart. The captain died with an expression of disbelief on his face.

As if that were a signal to the others, Strozzi's men finished off the rest of the English crew in a short, furious killing frenzy. Within moments no one was left alive on the English ship.

"Into the hold, men," Strozzi said as he wiped his bloody sword on the English captain's doublet, then sheathed the weapon. "We'll empty her of her cargo, then open the petcocks and send her to the bottom. As far as her owners back in England will know, she'll be just another ship lost to the dangers of the sea."

SAGRES, PORTUGAL

As Filippo Strozzi paraded about the town—which he seemed to do whenever and wherever possible—Aldo Cavalli, newly arrived in port himself, couldn't help but notice that the onetime *balestrièri* commander had made good on his promise. Even after giving one half of his share to Gonzalo Canto, Strozzi had made more profit than the combined total earned by the ships of Alvise Cadamosto and Antoniotto Usedimare.

"I told you you should have come with me," Strozzi bragged to Aldo when the two men met in the Eye of the Cat Inn. Strozzi was dressed like the finest gentleman, and he carried a sword with a gold-and-ivory handle. The gold chain that he had worn since his time in Constantinople was almost lost among all the other chains and medallions with which he now adorned himself.

"We had a very successful trading voyage," Aldo said. "But I must confess that we were not as successful as you. How is it that you are so prosperous?"

"Do you think because you were born into the Ca' di Cavalli that you have some God-given talent for trading?" Strozzi replied coldly.

"No, of course not," Aldo said, taken aback by Strozzi's aggression. "I have to work hard for every profit."

Strozzi took a long swig of his wine, then wiped the back of his hand across his mouth. "Yes," he said, "and if you want to beat me, you will just have to work even harder."

Aldo smiled. "I shall work harder. Tomorrow we leave on another voyage."

Sailing together once again, Cadamosto and Usedimare set out from Sagres. It was early May, and a favorable wind took them quickly by the Canaries, which they passed without stopping. There, picking up the Canaries current, which had been discovered by previous Portuguese navigators and documented in the charts at the school in Sagres, they proceeded south to Cape Branco, going farther out to sea than they had on any previous trip to take the fullest possible advantage of the current.

The two ships were so far out that they had completely lost sight of land. This was an unusual experience for most of the sailors; though many of them had sailed with Cadamosto before and had pushed the southern limits, they had generally done so within sight of land. It was one thing to sail out of sight of land in known seas, such as on the voyage to Madeira; doing so in unknown seas was an ominous prospect.

They could control their fear as long as the sea was calm; however, when the ship abruptly began to lift and fall, when the long ocean swell gave way to a choppy sea, the crew got skittish. Ancient superstitions that Aldo thought had been laid to rest once and for all began to be whispered about. More than once Aldo would come upon a knot of men muttering among themselves. Finally he could take it no more, and he asked them about it.

"What is it?" he asked. "Why are you gathering like this? What sort of mischief are you plotting?"

"No mischief, Senhor Cavalli," one of the sailors replied. "Only mystery."

"Mystery? What do you mean, mystery?"

"Have you not noticed that the sea is beginning to boil here?"

"Don't be silly."

"But it is true," the sailor insisted. "You can't deny that the heat is greater than anything we have ever experienced. Why have we tacked so far from land? Perhaps out here the sea ends, just as some people say."

Aldo laughed. "Do you think we would just tumble off?"

"No," the sailor said. "I don't believe, as some do, that the world is flat or that it sits upon the back of a giant turtle. I have heard the learned men at the observatory and the navigation school at Sagres say that the world is round, and I believe that." He gestured toward the other sailors. "And most of these men believe that as well."

"Well, thank goodness you have learned a little something for all of your sailing with us," Aldo replied dryly.

"But you must admit, *senhor*, that since we are in territory not visited before, we can't know for certain that even if the world does not end here, perhaps the sea does."

"What do you mean?"

"Suppose it gets hotter and hotter until the water does boil away? Suppose we are left sitting on the bottom of the ocean? You have seen ponds in the summer, after the sun has dried the water. You have seen how the mud cracks and cakes on the bottom, leaving everything in the pond high and dry."

"Yes, of course."

"Suppose we reach a point in the sea where the same thing happens. Suppose we find ourselves high and dry on a cracked and caked ocean bottom. Suppose we could not get the ship into the sea again. What would happen to us if we were stranded in such a salty swamp? What sort of creatures might we find inhabiting such a place?"

Aldo laughed, unable to help himself.

"Can you tell me for certain that this isn't so?" the sailor asked defiantly. "You can't dismiss this out of hand as if it were some tavern sailor's superstition, *senhor*. I have heard this very thing discussed by the most learned men at Sagres."

Aldo took a deep breath. The sailor was right; this was not an easily scoffed-at earth-as-flat-as-a-table superstition. This was a well-reasoned theory that, without any proof to the contrary, had as much validity as any other. Which made it much more difficult to deal with.

"All right," he said, "what is it you want? Do you want to go back to Sagres with an empty hold?"

"No," the sailor replied. He took in all the men with a wave of his hand. "We have sailed with you and Cadamosto before, and we're honored to sail with you this time. And to a man we'd be pleased to sail with you again. But we would feel better if, when we are in unknown waters, you would keep us always in sight of shore. That is no different from what you did before."

"I'll talk to Captain Cadamosto about it," Aldo promised. "I'll see what he has to say."

Suddenly the swelling of the waves became even

more pronounced, and the wind began to whip into a frenzy.

"Senhor Cavalli, the wind is getting ahead, sir," the helmsman noted.

"Furl all sails," Aldo commanded.

His order was transmitted to the crew, and men leapt into the shrouds and began furling sail so that nothing was aloft but bare masts and loose lines whistling in the sudden rushing wind.

"That's no good, *senhor*! We're still being blown out to sea!"

Alvise Cadamosto, who had been leaving all the sailing to Aldo, came on deck. He looked over the railing and saw waves running nearly as high as the ship itself.

"What is it?" he shouted. "What's going on?"

"We're being blown farther out to sea!" Aldo shouted back. The wind was now a mad howl, and the gigantic swells were roaring like thunder.

"Drop anchor!" Cadamosto shouted, and Aldo passed the order on. The anchor chain rattled as the heavy anchor fell into the sea, but even that didn't stop the ship from being pushed.

"*Senhor*, the jib!" the helmsman shouted, and Aldo saw then that though the other sails had been furled, the jib was still flying from the bowsprit.

"We'd better get that in," Aldo said. Without a moment's thought to his own safety or rank, he climbed out onto the bowsprit to work alongside the other men.

By now the ship was tossing and slamming around more severely than anything Aldo could remember experiencing. She was lifted up and thrown back down, knocked along her larboard beams, then wallowed over and thrown backwards. She shuddered and slipped through the waves, sometimes giving the illusion of coming completely out of the water and other times going down by the bow, plunging the forward part of the vessel deep into the water.

Aldo and one man were on one side, while two other sailors were on the other. Their feet were in the footropes, and they held on to the spar as they worked their way out. Although he hadn't purposely chosen it, Aldo was on the most dangerous side, for the great sheet was flying with the wind and puffed out so that it was all he could do to keep from being thrown off the boom.

At first the men could do nothing but hold on. Finally they succeeded in furling the jib enough to prevent it from tearing off the bowsprit. They were preparing to come back onto the ship's deck when two towering waves broke over the ship. The first wave brought the men in water up to their chins. The bow then raised up out of the ocean, suspending the men high over the water, dripping wet and clinging desperately to the spar. Then the ship plunged back down again, and this time the men went completely under the water. Aldo was taking a breath just as they went under, and he got a mouthful of salt water, tasting the burn of the brine. He shut his eyes tightly, expecting at any moment to be forcibly ripped away from his perch. To his astonishment, when the ship lifted out of the water again, he was still managing to clutch the spar, coughing desperately to get his breath. Opening his eyes, he saw that the two men on the other side of the jib boom were gone.

In spite of the impulse to just stay where he was and hold on, he knew that he had to get back or he would be swept off like the other crewmen. Summoning up the nerve to move, he worked his way back down the jib, inch by inch, until he was close enough for strong hands to grab him and pull him onto the deck. He lay there for a long moment, gasping for breath. When at last he could sit up, he found that the men were watching him. They were still frightened, though now more of the storm itself than of the unknown waters, he suspected. However, mixed with the fear he saw admiration and respect, for Aldo had put his life on the line with the others, and the sailors recognized and honored that. Aldo knew he would now be able to call on them to stay with him a while longer, and they would do so.

That was good, he thought wryly to himself. Because, in truth, he had no idea where they were going to wind up once this storm blew itself out.

*   *   *

"*Terra!*" the lookout aloft called two days later. "*Terra!*"

"Land? Out here? To the west?" Cadamosto said, surprised at the lookout's shout. "How can that be? Africa lies to our east."

"Captain, perhaps we have discovered a new land!" Aldo said excitedly.

Cadamosto grinned. "A new land! Yes, that's it, isn't it? We've discovered a new land!"

"It's an island!" the sailor in the masthead called down to them. "No, there are two islands!"

As the ship approached the islands, Aldo and Cadamosto studied them through their telescopes.

"Aren't they beautiful?" Aldo asked. "Look how verdant and lush they are."

"*Si, verde,*" Cadamosto replied. He snapped his fingers and gave a triumphant laugh. "*Verde!* That will be their name! The Cape Verde Islands!"

Sometime later, when the ship dropped anchor off the lush shore of the larger of the two islands, Aldo led ten men on an exploration. All were armed with crossbows, and Aldo cautioned them to have the bolts set so that they could react quickly, should the need arise.

With one man walking ahead, chopping through the thick underbrush with a large machete, the party eventually made it to the top of the tallest mountain. Here Aldo walked out onto a rock overhang and was rewarded by a view so encompassing that he could see the entire coastline of the island they were on and quite a bit of the neighboring island, as well.

"What do you see, *senhor*?" one of the sailors asked.

Aldo took a swig of water from the flask he had carried. Because of the latitude and the exertion, he was very hot and thirsty. In fact, he noticed, he had nearly drunk the entire flask. He wasn't concerned about that, however, for earlier in the day they had come across a deep, clear pool of water that seemed to be fed by an underground spring.

"Nothing of note," Aldo said, answering the question

as he recorked the flask. "Trees, trees, and more trees. Not the faintest sign of life."

"Look over there," one of the others said, pointing out across the sea.

Following the man's finger, Aldo saw thin blue lines on the horizon—three more islands. "We'll have to tell Cadamosto," he said. "Perhaps we'll find something over there. There doesn't appear to be anything here."

As it turned out, nothing of significance was to be found on any of the islands, nor any sign that they were inhabited or that they had ever been inhabited. After a few days of what he considered "fruitless" exploration and anxious to establish a profitable trading relationship elsewhere, Cadamosto was ready to move on. He was waiting for Aldo when the younger man returned from a full day of exploring.

"What did you find?" Cadamosto asked.

"Another source of water. And some beautiful rock formations. And trees."

"Any sign of gold? Or silver?"

"No," Aldo said. "Nothing like that."

"Any inhabitants?"

"No one."

Cadamosto sighed. "We've been wasting our time here."

"But, Captain, how can you say that? We are gazing upon land that has been unseen by human eyes since the day of creation!"

Cadamosto chuckled and put his hand on Aldo's shoulder. "Would that I had your enthusiasm," he said. "But I don't. I am fueled by but one desire now: to return to Venice rich. Unfortunately, I see nothing on this island that will help me attain that goal. Therefore, while you were exploring today, Usedimare and I were making ready to get under way. Already we have refilled our water kegs and provisioned our ships with salted fish and turtle meat. We will sail with the morning tide."

"Yes, sir," Aldo replied, disappointed that they would have to leave before all the islands had been fully explored. That disappointment was still evident in the letter he wrote to his father several weeks later, after he returned to Sagres:

> After leaving the Cape Verde Islands, we returned to the coastline of Africa and began coasting until we reached the River Gambia. We sailed up the Gambia, where we traded for gold, handcrafts, and exotic animals. It was there, Father, that I saw an elephant for the first time. It is a creature bigger than anything you can imagine.
>
> Another animal we encountered was something that Cadamosto calls the horse fish, although I have heard it referred to as a hippopotamus. Though not as enormous as the elephant, it is nonetheless quite large, and its habit of standing about in the water makes it strange, indeed.
>
> Cadamosto was very disappointed in the quantity of gold we were able to acquire, and he feels this voyage was a failure. I don't share his feelings. I believe we have found something far more important than a new supply of gold: new land and new knowledge. I am very pleased to have been a part of this voyage.
>
> There is, however, one aspect of the adventure that I am not pleased with. On our last two voyages—the first time without Cadamosto's participation, the second with it—our ship transported Negroes from Africa to Portugal for the purpose of slavery. I know how much you abhor this gruesome practice, and I despise it with you. Therefore, because of my loathing of slavery and because Cadamosto, like so many others, has succumbed to the profits to be made in the foul practice, this will be my last voyage with him. I have determined that when next I put to sea, it shall be in command of my own ship.

CHAPTER 14

NEAR ARGUIM

Aldo stood at the stern, watching the three Moorish corsairs through his telescope. The lookout had sighted them several hours earlier when they were no more than tiny dots on the distant horizon. Now they were close enough that he could see their bows dipping and plunging through the waves under full press of sail.

Aldo snapped his telescope shut. "More speed, Signóre Vivaldi!" he shouted urgently. "More speed!"

"Captain, we are flying every rag we can fly now!" Frederico Vivaldi replied. Vivaldi, also a Venetian, was Aldo's shipmaster on this, Aldo's first voyage as captain of his own caravel.

"It would be a fine thing, wouldn't it, for me to lose my very first ship?" Aldo replied.

"Lose your ship? Captain, I don't wish to be an alarmist, but losing the ship would be the least of our worries. It has long been suspected that Moorish pirates are operating in these waters, but there have been no survivors to tell the tale. If they catch us, they will kill us all."

"Well, we certainly can't let that happen, can we?" Aldo said.

"But what is to stop them, Captain? There are three of them, and their ships are faster."

"If we are not stronger or faster, then we must be smarter," Aldo countered.

"Captain, do you have a plan that will get us out of this?"

"I have a plan. Whether it will get us out of this situation is another question," Aldo admitted. "Muster the crew, Signóre Vivaldi. We are going to have to work quickly."

"*Sì, signóre,*" Vivaldi replied, happy to be doing something—anything—that might have an effect on their fate.

A moment later the entire ship's complement stood at middeck, looking up at their young captain standing on the sterncastle, his hands on his hips and a defiant smile on his face.

"I have an idea," Aldo told his crew. "It will require courage, but there isn't a man among you who hasn't already demonstrated courage to me. It will require strict obedience of orders, but there is not one among you who has ever been the laggard. I can count on you?"

The sailors shouted enthusiastically as one.

"Excellent." Aldo looked over at the cook. "Luigi, I'll need your help."

"*My* help, Captain?" Luigi said. "I am but a cook. How can I help?"

"By doing exactly as I say, despite how strange it might seem," Aldo said. "And that goes for the rest of you. Keep your courage and your wits about you, and we should get out of this all right."

It was another forty-five minutes before the corsairs closed to within artillery range. When they were near enough, the Moor commander ordered his cannoneers to open fire; the thunder of all the guns firing at once rolled across the waters. The gunpowder created a huge cloud of smoke that, running before the wind propelling the ships, lingered for almost two full minutes. Meanwhile, the pirates readied their guns for a second barrage, and the

Moorish captain waved at the smoke impatiently, anxious for it to dissipate so that he could loose another broadside.

Finally it thinned out enough for the pirate to raise his telescope to assess the damage of his first fusillade. What he saw astounded him, and he gasped and jerked away the telescope.

"Wait!" he shouted. "Gunners, do not fire again!"

His orders were conveyed to the gunners on his ship, then signaled to the gunners on the other two ships. Sweating pirates in the act of refilling charges or lifting stones in place stopped in midtask, puzzled by their captain's strange order. Were they not to disable and capture the Christian ship?

"Look," the Moorish captain said, pointing to the caravel. "The infidel dog's ship is down by the stern! By the Prophet's beard, we must've holed her! She's sinking!"

"Look at her crew!" the first mate said. "They have been devastated!"

The Moorish captain raised his spyglass again for a closer look at the deck of the Portuguese ship. Nearly a dozen men were lying about, all of them covered with blood. In fact, on the entire deck of the Christian ship there appeared to be but one man left alive, and he was moving—crawling, actually—toward the stern of the ship. Like the others, he was soaked in blood, and he appeared to be carrying a piece of white cloth.

"Praise be to Allah!" the Moor shouted excitedly. "We have wiped them out with one barrage!"

On the Christian ship the wounded man laboriously began raising the white flag. The Moorish sailors chortled the high-pitched ululation that was their battle cry, and many of them grabbed scimitars and held them aloft, twisting them back and forth so that the blades flashed in the sun.

"Lead us, O mighty one," one of them said to the captain. "Let us board the infidel ship!"

"Signal our comrades," the Moorish captain ordered. "The wind is such that they cannot surround the caravel. Have them come alongside this ship, then send their men across to join us. We'll board her with every man we have."

"Will we not leave anyone at the guns, Captain?" his first mate asked.

The Moorish captain pulled at his beard and smiled at his first mate. "There is no need for that. Allah guided the stones of our cannon well . . . too well," he added. "The infidel ship is sinking, and we must move quickly to empty it while we can."

Responding to the signals, the other two corsairs pulled alongside the third; the men of the other two ships swarmed across to the inside ship, where they climbed into the shrouds, preparatory to boarding the stricken Christian ship. Grappling hooks were then thrown fore and aft, fastening together the corsair and the caravel.

On board the stricken caravel Aldo Cavalli was slumped over the stern tiller. The arm that trailed down to the deck was streaked with blood already drying and turning brown in the hot sun. Through half-open eyes Aldo surveyed his ship, peering into the shadows where a dozen of his men were standing by, crossbows at the ready. Twelve well-placed quarrels, plus twelve more loosed before the pirates could react, would take down a goodly complement of the boarders. That would about even the odds between the attacking pirates and Aldo's men, perhaps even skew them slightly in Aldo's favor, under the circumstances.

He watched the pirates come aboard—ten, twenty, thirty of them. Another six were yet to come across, and Aldo waited patiently, praying that none of his men would act too quickly. Finally, when all the pirates were aboard, stepping around and over the scattered bodies, Aldo stood up.

"Attack, men! Defend the faith!" he shouted at the top of his voice.

His command was followed instantly by the booming thunder of the caravel's six guns, firing at point-blank range into the side of the Moorish ship that was drawn alongside.

The side of the pirate ship was staved in, and it began

to founder immediately. Two stones went all the way through the first pirate ship and holed the second, and it, too, started going down, though not as fast as the first one. The first corsair sank so quickly that the few men left on board wound up in the water.

Concurrent with the broadside of the caravel's guns was a well-aimed unleashing of crossbow bolts. Twelve pirates grabbed at their chests or necks in pain and surprise as the swarm of arrows sank into them.

"It is a trick!" the Moorish captain shouted, his warning patently unnecessary in its obviousness. What was not obvious was what the pirates should do. While the second rank of boarders was trying to make up its mind, the still-hidden crossbowmen released another fusillade of arrows. Twelve more pirates crumpled to the deck, mortally wounded.

"*Now!*" Aldo bellowed, and all of his "dead" crewmen leapt up to face with the remaining pirates. After a brief but furious battle, the Moors, unaccustomedly outnumbered, suddenly threw down their arms. The captain was among them. Of the thirty-four pirates who had boarded Aldo's ship, only eight remained alive.

"Stop!" Aldo commanded, and his men, with difficulty, pulled back at the last moment. To a man, the pirates sank to their knees and begged for mercy.

"Don't kill us!" the pirate captain pleaded. "Your Christian god asks that you show charity to your enemies!"

"We're not going to kill you," Aldo said.

"Thank you, thank you, thank you! A thousand blessings upon your house!"

"Get up," Aldo commanded, disgusted by the Moor's groveling.

The pirates all stood.

"May I ask the name of the one who defeated me?" the pirate captain asked, his tone obsequious.

"His name is Captain Aldo Cavalli," Frederico Vivaldi called proudly. "And he is the bravest and smartest captain on the sea."

"To have won such respect and admiration from your men at such a young age is truly an accomplishment blessed by Allah," the Moor told Aldo. He touched his forehead, chin, and chest in a gesture of respect. "And if you would live to see another year, had we not better abandon this ship before it sinks?"

Aldo smiled. "What makes you think we are sinking?" he asked.

"Feel the deck, Captain! Do you not feel the slant?"

"Captain, shall I reposition the ballast now?" Vivaldi asked, a sly grin on his face.

"Yes."

"The ballast?" the pirate captain asked, eyes widening. Then he laughed. "Oh, but you are the clever one, my young Christian warrior. You shifted the ballast and made it look as if you were going down by the stern! That is why I threw caution to the wind. I thought we had holed you."

"Yes," Aldo said, grinning. "That is exactly what I wanted you to think."

"And the blood? What about all the blood? If you are not truly wounded, where did the blood come from?"

"From our cook."

"Your cook? I do not understand. Was *he* wounded?"

"No. It is from our food stores," Luigi himself replied. He tossed a small flask of blood on the Moorish captain's doublet. "It is pig's blood."

"*Pig's blood?*" the pirate captain screamed. He brushed at the spots of blood on his clothing. "*Get it off! Get it off!*"

Aldo's crew laughed uproariously at the Moor cringing in horror at having the blood of an unclean animal on his person.

"What are we going to do with them, Captain?" Vivaldi asked.

"I don't know," Aldo said.

"We could lay out a plank and make them take a walk," one of the sailors suggested.

"Yes, there's a good idea. They can swim back home," one of the others agreed.

"What about it, pirate?" Aldo asked the Moor. "Would you like to go for a swim?"

"No, please, no!" the pirate captain pleaded. "Let us live, Captain Cavalli!"

"Pirate, were you going to let *us* live?" one of Aldo's sailors shouted.

"I beg of you, Christians, be merciful! Allah smiles upon those who are generous to their defeated enemies."

Aldo looked at the one remaining corsair. "I suppose I could allow you to leave in that ship," he said after a while.

"Thank you, young master, thank you! A thousand blessings be upon you," the pirate said.

"Vivaldi, take some men with you and see to it that all the cannon are slipped overboard."

"Wait!" the Moor called. "Surely you would not leave us defenseless? We aren't the only pirates plying these waters. There are Christian pirates as well."

"Then you had best sail as fast as you can for home waters," Aldo said. "And to lighten your load to speed your journey, we'll relieve you of whatever spoils you may have aboard."

"That ship?" the pirate captain said, his tone derisive. He shrugged. "It carries nothing of value. Our real treasure went down with the other two ships."

"You won't mind if I just have a look for myself, will you?"

"Look if you wish," the pirate captain invited. "But when you find our hold empty, do not take your anger out on this poor miserable servant of Allah."

Accompanied by several of his men, Aldo went across to the corsair, then down belowdecks to have a look around. As the Moor had claimed, the hold was empty except for two trunks, carefully covered by sailcloth, sitting in a corner.

"What is in the trunks?" Aldo asked.

"Nothing, young master, nothing," the pirate captain replied quickly. Too quickly, Aldo thought. "Only some rope and a few tools."

"Why would you cover such things so carefully with tent cloth?" Aldo asked.

"No reason," the pirate captain answered lightly.

"Open them," Aldo said. "I want to see for myself."

"As you wish." The Moor opened them. "As you can see, it is as I said: rope and tools."

"Open the one beneath," Aldo ordered.

"Of course, of course," the Moor replied. "Abdul, lift off this trunk."

One of the captured pirates, a giant of a man, glared at the sailor who was standing guard over him.

"Let him move the box," Aldo said.

With a nod, the Portuguese sailor indicated that Abdul could move the box. The pirate easily picked up the top chest, then set it on the floor. The Moorish captain then opened the bottom trunk to show that its contents were similiar to the other one's.

"Are you satisfied?" he asked. "I told you, what treasure we had sank to the bottom of the sea with my other two ships."

"So it would appear," Aldo said.

Abdul lowered the lids on the two chests and picked one of them up so that he could restack them. As he did so, Aldo noticed his huge biceps bulge.

"Wait a minute!" Aldo ordered. He nodded toward the pirate captain. "I would like for *you* to restack the boxes, sir."

"What?" the pirate captain protested. "Why, that is an insult to have me, a captain, do such labor."

"I suppose it is," Aldo said. "All right, I'll have one of my own men do it." He pointed at one of his sailors. "Pedro, pick up that chest."

"*Sim, Capitão,*" the sturdy Portuguese replied.

"That isn't necessary, young master," the Moorish captain said. "Abdul will do it." He smiled ingratiatingly. "It would not do to have one of the victors do the toil of the vanquished."

Aldo smiled as his suspicion grew. "No. We'll take care of it."

Pedro bent to his task, but he couldn't lift the box. He looked up his captain.

"What is wrong, Pedro?"

"The box, *Capitão,* it is far too heavy."

Aldo was not surprised. "Well, now, how can that

be?" he asked. "Surely a bit of rope and a few tools should not weigh so much."

Opening the chest, Pedro removed the top layer of rope, then gasped at what was exposed. *"Ouro, Capitão! Ouro!"* he shouted excitedly.

Aldo looked into the box. Beneath the concealing layer of rope and tackle, the box was filled with bars of gold bullion.

Pedro quickly threw aside the top contents of the other trunk. It, too, was filled with gold bars.

"Well, Captain," Aldo said to the pirate, "you thought to trick us, did you?"

"The gold is not mine. It is the property of my caliph."

"It *was* the property of your caliph," Aldo replied. "Now it is booty that belongs to me and my crew."

"How did you know, you infidel dog?" the pirate growled, all semblance of obsequiousness gone. "How did you know the gold was there?"

Aldo smiled slyly. "It seemed strange that someone as strong as your giant would display such bulging muscles just from lifting a small chest." He turned to his sailors. "Transport these trunks to our ship. Thanks to our Moorish friends, this has been the most profitable voyage of any we have thus far undertaken."

The treasure chests were transferred, all weapons were removed from the corsair, and the Moors were returned to their ship. That done, the securing ropes were released, and the ships began to drift apart. Aldo stood on deck, watching the pirate ship fall away.

"Captain Cavalli!" the Moor shouted across the widening space of water. "You will encounter Allah's warriors again. By the beard of the Prophet, you will see the soldiers of Islam again!"

"If that is so, Captain," Aldo called back, "I hope they are as generous with Allah's gold as you."

VENICE

"Francesca! Francesca! Come quickly!" Maria Polesine called through the door of Francesca Viviani's bedroom.

Francesca, who was doing needlework on a coverlet, looked up from her work. "You sound so urgent, Signóra Polesine," Francesca said. "What is wrong?"

"It is Signóre Borgo," the maid said. "He is coming to the house."

"The father or the son?"

"The son. Vitale Borgo."

Francesca hurried out of her room and across the landing to look over the railing down into the entry foyer of the Viviani house. Francesca was no longer just a pretty girl. Now she was a beautiful young woman, and as she strained to peer over the balustrade, her breasts pressed against the bodice of her dress.

"You are mistaken, *signóra.* He is not here," Francesca scolded.

"He has not yet arrived, but he is coming," the maid said.

"Fie," Francesca responded. "Let him come. I will just tell Papà that I am not feeling well, and he'll send him away again."

"No, Francesca, that won't work this time," Maria said.

"Of course it will. It has always worked before." As if dismissing the entire incident, Francesca turned to go back to her needlework.

The maid reached out to stop her. "Not this time," she repeated.

Something in the tone of Maria Polesine's voice frightened Francesca. "What is it?" she asked. "What is different about this time?"

"Young Borgo is bringing with him a side of mutton," Maria said.

Francesca gasped. "No! It cannot be! Papà has said nothing to me about this!"

"Your father does not know it. As you know, I have a

cousin who works in the Borgo house. It was my cousin who sent word that the young *signóre* is coming, and it was my cousin who sent word that he will be bringing a side of mutton. Francesca, if your father accepts the meat . . ."

"I know, I know," Francesca acknowledged. "I'll be promised to Vitale." She looked at the woman who had been her handmaid and before that her nursemaid for as long as she could remember. "Oh, Signóra Polesine, what shall I do? I don't want to marry Vitale Borgo! I can't marry him! I am in love with another!"

Maria Polesine reached out and touched her young charge's face. "Child," she said softly, "I can understand if you do not love Vitale Borgo. But do not eat your heart away for Aldo Cavalli. Cavalli is the eternal wanderer, as remote to you as the moon and the stars."

"How—how do you know it is Aldo Cavalli that I love?" Francesca asked, blushing.

The maid laughed. "Dear girl, am I not with you every day? Do I not see the way your face lights up when you hear others talk of his exploits? Of the voyages he has taken to places where no one has ever before gone? Of the gold and treasure he has won for his father's house by his brilliant trading?"

"You are right, I confess. I do love him," Francesca replied. She sighed. "And you are correct when you say that he is as remote to me as the moon and the stars. Oh, *signóra*, I don't know if Aldo even realizes that I am alive. If so, he would come and marry me now and save me from a life of pain and despair as the wife of Vitale Borgo."

Inexplicably, Maria Polesine smiled.

"Why are you smiling?" Francesca asked. "I am about to be betrothed to someone I do not love, while my heart is breaking because the one I *do* love does not return my feelings."

"I can't do anything about the unrequited love. But on this day at least I think I can keep you from becoming betrothed to Vitale Borgo."

Francesca brightened. "Oh! Signóra Polesine, can you?" she said in delight.

"Come to the window," Maria said conspiratorially.

Curious, Francesca accompanied the older woman to the window.

"There," the maid said, pointing to the gamesman. "Do you see Rico?"

"Yes."

"He has not yet fed the hounds."

"But what is he thinking?" Francesca asked, appalled. "Those poor animals must be famished. They should have been fed hours ago."

"They *are* terribly hungry," Maria said. She looked at the young woman and grinned slyly. "They are so hungry that if they caught the smell of something good to eat—for example . . ."

"A side of mutton!" Francesca said quickly, giggling.

"Such a temptation for those poor creatures might be more than they can stand," the maid concluded. "Why, there is no telling *what* they might do."

"Look there, coming up from the front landing," Francesca said then.

Vitale Borgo, dressed in his finest toggery, was at that very moment coming up the stone steps from the canal. Over one shoulder he carried a large wrapped package.

At almost the same moment that Francesca saw Vitale, the four game hounds also saw him—or, more likely, smelled the fresh meat.

The dogs began barking and tugging at their leashes. Rico gave the impression of trying to hold them back, struggling with them mightily, before suddenly letting go of the leather restraints.

Apparently Vitale had paid no attention at all to the animals. They, like the servants themselves, were part of the background to Vitale, so self-centered was he that he seldom noticed anything going on around him. As a result, the dogs were nearly upon him before he realized what was happening.

"*No!*" he suddenly shrieked, his shout loud enough to carry all the way up to Francesca's room. "*Get away from me!*"

The four dogs leapt as one, and their combined weight and the shock of their attack knocked Vitale down.

Before he could recover, the dogs had ripped the wrapping off the package and were tearing at the great piece of meat.

"*No!*" Vitale screamed again. He tried to reach for the meat, but the snapping teeth and jaws of all four dogs kept him at bay.

Carlo Viviani, overhearing the commotion, ran out of the house. Seeing what was happening, he called to the houndsman.

"Rico, call off your dogs!"

The servant shouted a few orders, and the dogs left, though each was carrying a large chunk of meat. All that was left of the side of mutton Vitale had been carrying was a few jagged red chunks and some scattered bones.

"Are you all right, Vitale?" Carlo Viviani asked solicitously, hurrying over to the young man.

"No!" Vitale replied angrily. "No, I am not all right! Look at me! Look at my clothes! Look at the gift I was bringing you!"

"I am terribly sorry," Viviani said, helping Vitale to his feet. "I don't know what got into those animals. They are very well-trained and well-behaved dogs. I just don't understand."

"They are neither well trained nor well behaved!" Vitale spat. He wiped his hands across his chest in a vain effort to cleanse himself. "I want those dogs put to death, Signóre Viviani."

"Put to death? No, I'm sorry, but I would never consent to such a thing," Viviani replied.

"You have no choice, *signóre*," Vitale said coldly. "I will not bring meat back onto these grounds until those animals are properly disposed of."

"That is your prerogative, Signóre Borgo," Viviani said, smiling easily. "But the loss is yours, not mine. I am perfectly capable of feeding this household."

Vitale paled, realizing that his anger had gotten the better of him. His plan had been to force the issue of getting Viviani's permission to marry his daughter by means of the old Venetian custom of bringing to the father a gift of fresh meat. If Viviani had accepted the gift, it would be recognized that he had just given his daughter's hand in betrothal. As it was, Vitale had yet again suffered the consequences of his temper.

Seething, his fingers curling into fists, Vitale turned red and then purple with rage. He finally managed to get control of himself long enough to bid Viviani farewell.

"Good-bye," Viviani replied pleasantly as if nothing untoward had passed between them.

Francesca, who had been watching everything from her window, suddenly gasped. Vitale was looking longingly up at her window, and she knew that he had seen her. She jerked away from the glass, then began fanning herself.

Maria Polesine came over to her. "It is all right now, little one," she said gently. "He is walking back to his gondola."

Francesca took her maid's hand and kissed it.

"Oh, Signóra Polesine, my dear, dear friend," she said. "Where would I be if it weren't for you? You saved me from him."

"This time. Unfortunately, Vitale Borgo is a determined young man, and I fear he will try again—and again and again and again until finally he wears your father down. And why shouldn't he?" she added. "Your father has always sought a strong alliance for his trading house, and an alliance between the Viviani and Borgo houses would be an extremely profitable one."

"As would an alliance between the House of Viviani and the House of Cavalli," Francesca insisted.

"I have told you," Maria said gently. "To think such a thing will only bring you heartbreak."

"And yet," Francesca said, putting her hand to her breast and looking out the window as if seeing someone far, far away, "I can think of nothing else."

CHAPTER 15

SAGRES, PORTUGAL

Aldo Cavalli's defeat of the Moorish pirate and his seizure of the gold booty was much admired in Prince Henry's court. The worth of the gold was so great that after giving Prince Henry his due, Aldo could still be extremely generous to his sailors—increasing his popularity even further with them.

Yet despite his success, he was still far short of Filippo Strozzi's accumulated wealth. Strozzi was so successful that the rumor being spread throughout the court was that he had discovered a village of natives who had their own gold mine.

The soldier's success in accumulating wealth did not translate into social success. To the contrary, he was very much the outsider, for most of those at the court had grown tired of his constant boasting. Strozzi was openly resentful of the popularity of his peers. Even Antoniotto Usedimare was still spoken of highly in the *Infante*'s court, which was particularly galling to Strozzi, for Usedimare had long since returned to Venice to pay off his debts and re-establish himself as a citizen of wealth.

Aldo's ventures remained the talk of the court until

Captain Vinegar Gomes returned from a highly successful voyage. At that point Gomes's exploits became the topic on everyone's lips, and Gomes, as well as everyone who had sailed with him, basked in the glow of popularity. That included the brothers Tome and Diogo da Costa.

While the Gomes voyage had not discovered any new territory, it had established more favorable relations with some rulers who had previously been hostile to Christians. This particular afternoon found several members of the court gathered around Diogo, who, because of his charm and sense of humor, had become the raconteur of choice to detail the expedition's exploits. Filippo Strozzi, standing and watching with increasing irritation, made a disparaging comment.

"The difference, Strozzi," someone told him, "is that when you tell stories, you boast as if you are the center of the entire world. When Diogo da Costa tells stories, he gives others their due. Listen to the tale he tells now. Who is the hero of the story? Diogo? No. Tome? No. The hero is Captain Gomes. And that, my friend," the speaker said, holding up his finger to make the point, "is how a story *should* be told."

Adopting a bored, disinterested expression, Strozzi nevertheless wandered over to stand on the periphery of the assemblage so that he could listen. Luisa Canto was there as well, hanging on Diogo's every word—and practically his person—and looking at him as if he were the only man in the world.

Strozzi grunted. He could tell Diogo a thing or two about Luisa, if he wanted. He knew how she bent with the wind, showing interest in whoever might enjoy the privilege of the court at the moment. Why, she had even flirted with *him* a few times, but he had discouraged her interest. It wasn't that he didn't find her attractive or her attention flattering. It was just that he could have as many women as he wanted, as long as his pockets were lined with gold. And his pockets would be lined with gold only as long as he was able to continue the relationship with Luisa's father. It would, therefore, be foolish of him to jeopardize his situation by dallying with the daughter of his colleague —no matter how tempting the prospect might be.

"We were in a place called Al-cuzet," Diogo was telling the others. "Now, every sailor knows that Al-cuzet is an infidel land, with much hatred for Christians. But it is a place of sweet water and lemons and ivory, and our captain decided that we should not pass up the opportunity to trade there.

"We stayed at the mouth of the River Gambia for three days, during which time Captain Gomes sent presents to the Negro king Nomimansa. Nomimansa, if you do not know, was one who had done great mischief to the Christians."

"Hold on. Did you say Gomes sent *gifts* to this ruler?"

"Yes."

"Why would he do such a thing, knowing of the King's mistreatment of Christians?"

Diogo smiled. "Because Captain Gomes is a smart man and knows that honey makes a better lure than vinegar." He laughed. "Despite his nickname. At any rate, when King Nomimansa received the gifts, he actually came to us, rather than wait to be paid homage, and sat down on the riverbank to meet with the captain."

"What was Nomimansa like?" someone asked.

"Ah, he was a magnificent specimen. Very tall and well-proportioned, a man of quite regal bearing. He was accompanied by a mullah of the Islam faith," Diogo continued, "but he listened most attentively as Captain Gomes told him about Christianity. Then, when the discussion was finished, King Nomimansa was so pleased with what he heard that he sprang to his feet and ordered the mullah to leave his country within three days, and he swore he would kill anyone who should speak the name of Mohammed from that day forward. He even asked Captain Gomes to baptize him and all his people."

"But Gomes could not do that, could he?"

"No, he's a layman, after all, and we had no priest sailing with us. However, he did promise the King that a priest would be sent to perform the rite. To celebrate Nomimansa's conversion, Gomes invited the King, his twelve chief men, and eight of his wives to dine with us the following evening on board the caravel."

"That must have been a sight," someone said in a wry voice.

"Oh, it was, it truly was," Diogo replied, laughing. Immersed in the role of storyteller, he gestured and minced broadly. "The entourage came aboard in a great procession. Nomimansa and his chiefs were painted and tattooed, and they wore great, colorful headdresses."

"What did the women wear?"

Smiling, Diogo answered with eyes sparkling in devilment, "Only their beauty."

"You mean they were naked?"

"As the day they were born," Diogo said.

Luisa gasped and her eyes flashed, but Diogo knew her well enough to know that it wasn't from anger. She was enjoying the ribaldry of the conversation.

"Go on with the story, Diogo," someone urged. "What happened next?"

"Captain Gomes and his officers, including Tome and myself, sat around the table with our visitors, eating fowl and meat and drinking wine—as much wine as they could hold. The Negroes found the wine odd-tasting though enjoyable, quite different from their usual fermented brew. When they finally left some hours later, they were singing our praises, saying that no people were better than the Christians."

"So Gomes made a small conversion," Strozzi said, stepping forward. "But it wasn't truly significant, since a priest can at least baptize his converts, whereas your captain could not." Strozzi examined the ends of his fingers as if bored with the entire tale. "The voyage left little enough to talk about, I would vouchsafe."

"Oh, but I haven't finished the story," Diogo said.

"There is more?"

"Not with Nomimansa. But with Bezeghichi."

"Bezeghichi?" someone said. "Even I have heard of him. On one voyage it is said that he fell upon eight Christians who had gone ashore for water and killed them all. I daresay he was not handled as easily as Nomimansa."

"Ah, but you underestimate the cleverness of Captain Gomes," Diogo rejoined. "It was a few days after we left Gambia that, while coasting near to the shore, we saw two canoes putting out to sea. Captain Gomes ordered that we sail between the canoes and the shore, cutting off any chance they might have of escaping us by returning to land. Then the interpreter told the captain that Bezeghichi, the lord of the land, was himself in one of the trapped canoes."

"What did Gomes do?"

"He ordered the Negroes to come aboard the caravel. To their surprise, for they were expecting to be mistreated at best, they were given food and drink. Then, pretending he did not know the chief, Gomes had his interpreter ask, 'Is this the land of Bezeghichi?' And when the chief answered that it was, Captain Gomes asked, 'Why is he so bitter against Christians? He would do far better to have peace with them so that they might trade in his land and bring him horses and numerous wonderful things as they do for other lords of the Negroes. Go and tell your lord Bezeghichi that I have taken you and could easily kill you, but for love of him I have let you go.'

"At this, the Negro chief was very pleased. When he and his men returned to their canoes, Gomes stood at the rail and instructed his interpreter to call, 'Bezeghichi, I am aware of who you are. I could have done anything to you I wanted, but I let you go. And as I have done for you, so shall you do for all Christians.'"

"And did Bezeghichi agree?"

"He did," Diogo replied. "And now Christians have allies in lands where once we had only enemies."

"That may well be to our advantage," a member of the court said, "since Pope Calixtus the Third has called for all Christians to conduct another holy war against the Turks, and no one but King Afonso and Prince Henry has agreed to fight."

Diogo nodded. "Yes, my brother and I will be departing with the war fleet."

"You are going, Tome? And your wife back on Madeira, what does she think of this?"

Tome smiled self-consciously. "I am sure that the prospect of my doing battle does not please her," he said. "However, she is a loyal subject of the King and a good Christian. She understands that sacrifices must be made."

"What about you, Aldo? Will you be going to war?"

Aldo shook his head. "As a Venetian I can trade on Prince Henry's license, but I cannot go to war. I will be returning home."

"And you, Captain Strozzi?"

"I have served my time in the Holy Wars," Strozzi replied self-righteously. He looked around at the gathering. "While the rest of you were safe and comfortable in your own beds, I was risking my life on the walls at Constantinople. This time I will let *you* go and fight the war for me. I have more important things to do."

"Yes, like bringing more gold out of the secret mine you have discovered," someone suggested.

"How much gold is there, Strozzi?"

"Is there enough for the rest of us?" someone quipped.

Strozzi smiled slyly, pleased to be once again the center of attention—and pleased, as well, that the real source of his wealth, piracy, was unsuspected.

"I have no gold mine," he said. "I am merely a very astute trader."

The others laughed; then someone said, "Someday someone should follow you, Strozzi, just to see where you get your gold."

Strozzi glared at the speaker. "That would be a big mistake," he said menacingly. "Perhaps even a *fatal* mistake."

The laughter died on the lips of the man who had made the suggestion, and his eyes flashed with fear. He looked at the others; they, too, were surprised by Strozzi's dire reaction to a few words said in jest.

"Strozzi," the man said, "I was only making a joke."

The soldier smiled coldly. "Yes, of course, you were joking. And so was I," he said. "And now, gentlemen," he added, holding his cup of wine out toward Diogo, "let us toast Diogo and Tome da Costa and all the other soldiers and sailors who will go to defend the faith for Christians the world over."

Diogo lifted his own cup. "And a toast to our brave Prince Henry, who has vowed to lead us personally into battle."

OCTOBER 1458

The ship stood just off the coast of Alcácer, sails folded and anchor dropped, rocking gently on a smooth sea. To the west the sun was sinking, a great, flaming ball that spread its color across the water and onto the sails of the other 279 ships of Prince Henry's war fleet.

Tome da Costa was leaning into the shrouds, looking ashore at the walls of Alcácer, thinking of the attack that would be launched tomorrow. The fortified city had been chosen as the target for Prince Henry's attack because of its proximity to Ceuta. Prince Henry controlled Ceuta, and the Moors controlled Alcácer. As long as the Moors held Alcácer, Ceuta was under constant threat.

The taking of Alcácer would be of twofold benefit for the *Infante:* He would be following Pope Callixtus's edict to mount a holy war—thereby satisfying a sanctified obligation—and at the same time he would be protecting his own interests in Ceuta. It was too good an opportunity to disregard.

"Are you thinking about tomorrow?"

Tome had not heard anyone come up behind him, and he was startled by the unexpected sound of a voice. When he turned, he saw Giovanni Ruggi standing there.

"Yes, I am," the young Portuguese admitted. "I guess you think it's cowardly of me to be frightened, but I can't help it."

Giovanni replied softly, "I think it would be foolish of you *not* to be frightened."

"Are *you* frightened?" Tome asked.

"Of course."

"But how can that be? You were at Constantinople. You have seen battle before."

"That's precisely why I *am* frightened," Giovanni said. He stepped up beside Tome and looked at the shore. Though the sun was sinking quickly, enough light remained to see dark figures slipping in and out of the shadows, making preparations for the forthcoming siege.

"Why did you come again?" Tome asked.

"To defend the faith," Giovanni answered easily.

"Giovanni, why did you *really* come? When the Pope called for a holy war, only the Spanish and the Portuguese responded. Every other Christian nation declined. Why did you not go back to Genoa like Aldo went back to Venice?"

"I don't know," Giovanni replied. "Perhaps I am no longer Genoese."

"No longer Genoese? What do you mean? Of course you are Genoese."

"Perhaps I am a new man—not Genoese, not Portuguese, but a man of the world."

"Yes, well, for whatever reason you stayed, I'm glad you did. It will be good to have someone near who has been to war before."

A sudden burst of laughter sounded from the front of the ship, and when Tome looked in that direction, he saw his brother, Diogo, surrounded by several soldiers.

"Your brother doesn't seem to be worried about tomorrow," Giovanni noted.

"Oh, he's worried enough, all right," Tome replied. "He's just much better at hiding it than I. And when the time comes, he will fight bravely."

"So will you," Giovanni said. "And so will most. And when the battle starts, you will find that the fear goes away."

"Why?"

"I don't know. Maybe it's because there's no longer time to be frightened—or maybe it's because you are more frightened of what others may think of you than you are of dying."

"Yes," Tome agreed. "Yes, I can believe that. Even as I stand here, watching the Moors prepare their defenses, I know that what I'm really afraid of is showing myself for a coward."

"I don't think that's something you'll have to worry about."

Laughter again erupted from the front of the ship.

Tome looked out across the water at the hundreds of dark shapes and winking lights. "Twenty thousand men are riding these ships. I wonder if they are feeling as we are."

"They are men, aren't they?" Giovanni said simply.

"And the ones ashore, the Moors?" Tome said. "As they prepare their defenses, they can see us out here. What do they think? Are they frightened?"

"They, too, are men."

The two men were silent for some time after that. Finally Tome rubbed his hands together, then stretched. "I suppose I'd better get some sleep tonight," he said, knowing full well that he wouldn't sleep at all. "Do you have any advice for me before we do battle?"

"Yes. You had better relieve yourself before the battle starts," Giovanni said sagely.

"Why?"

"Those who do have no problem," Giovanni replied. "Those who don't soil their pants."

The following day found the ships of Prince Henry's huge war fleet anchored as close to the shore as they could get, but several hundred yards of heavy surf rolled between them and the beach. Beyond the beach was the walled city of Alcácer, and visible along the walls were the cannons and bowmen the Moor defenders had placed. From here and there within the city, columns of thick, black smoke rose.

"I don't understand," Tome said, pointing to the smoke. "Is the city burning? Why is there so much smoke?"

"They are heating oil," Giovanni said matter-of-factly. "To pour down on us as we attack."

"Oh," Tome replied, the word barely audible.

Giovanni chuckled. "Don't worry about it. It doesn't hurt if you don't stand under it."

"Look!" someone shouted. "The flag on the *Infante*'s ship! There is the signal!"

"Let's go!" another shouted. "Into the boats!"

The men who would be going ashore, including Tome, Diogo, and Giovanni, raised a great cheer, then started over the side of the ship into the several skiffs bobbing on the sea alongside. Once the men were settled, rowers started pulling them toward the shore, and Tome stared at the walls of the city, which loomed ever higher with every oarstroke.

The first boats reached the shore, and the men clambered out and waded through the surf, then dashed across the beach to form into companies. Tome's boat landed, and with his brother and his friend Giovanni he splashed through the breakers to join the ranks of the men from his and other Christian ships. By now a mighty Christian army had been massed beneath brightly colored, fluttering flags, led by officers in shining helmets and breastplates.

"There is the Prince!" one man shouted. "And look. He wears the sword given him by his mother on her deathbed, when she commanded him to conquer Ceuta. Just as he took that infidel city, he now will lead us to take Alcácer by the power of that consecrated weapon!"

With the powerful invading army ashore and the men in their positions, the Christians waited for Prince Henry's command to launch the assault.

"Why don't we attack?" Diogo asked impatiently after what seemed like an eternity had elapsed.

"We are waiting for the siege machinery to be put into place," Tome explained. He pointed at the cannons, ferried across from the ships. They were now in position, and the officers were giving their gunners instructions.

Suddenly the siege cannons were all fired with a deafening boom. The heavy stones hurtled black against the sky, toward the wall of the fortified city. A few hit the wall, raising dust and chips. Others flew over the wall to fall inside, where they would demolish anything—or anyone —they might land on.

A narrow black cloud came arcing across from the top of the walls, and Tome watched it with curiosity. Suddenly he realized what it was and shouted, "Arrows!" Immediately afterward came a whooshing sound as a score of arrows fell on the attackers. One hapless soldier took an arrow through his neck, and Tome watched in horror as the mortally wounded man tugged in vain to pull it out before he fell. A couple of other men were hit in the arm or leg; the rest of the arrows fell harmlessly to the ground. One stuck up in the sand a few feet away from Diogo.

"Here come more!" someone warned.

"Move in closer!" one of the officers shouted. "We must move in closer to shorten the angle for their bowmen."

"Yes," Diogo said, "and to give me a chance to get a shot at one of those heathen bastards."

The army of Prince Henry moved closer to the wall. Behind the foot soldiers the artillery continued to fire, answered now by artillery from the top of the walls. With specific targets to shoot at, the Christian artillery became more effective, and two of the Moor cannons were hit and disabled by stones hurled by Christian cannons.

The Moors were still effectively defending their position, however, and Tome saw firsthand the effect of boiling oil as a weapon. A dozen Christian soldiers who had carried a scaling ladder to the bottom of the wall were doused from a large kettle of the scalding, viscous liquid just as they started to climb. Some were severely burned, and their cries of pain were hideous. Others were only negligibly splashed, and although they shouted loudly, the shouts were as much of anger as pain.

One of the Moorish bowmen raised up and loosed an arrow. It flew true, felling a soldier near Tome. A moment later the Moor shot a second time, finding a second victim.

When he raised a third time, however, Diogo was ready for him, having raised his own crossbow to his shoulder and waited patiently. As soon as the Moor raised again, Diogo released his quarrel; it struck the Moor in the heart. Grabbing his chest, he tumbled forward, falling off the wall to the cheers of hundreds of Christian soldiers.

Diogo's well-placed shot seemed to mobilize the rest of the Christians, for hundreds of arrows were suddenly launched toward the top of the wall—so many that the defenders were driven back, including those who stood ready to dump more oil. With the tops of the walls clear, the Christians brought scaling ladders into place, and soon scores of attackers, including Diogo, Tome, and Giovanni, were climbing up. Battering rams assaulted the great doors of the city gate at the same time. The noise of battle was horrendous: the explosion of artillery; the clanging of scimitar against sword; the screams of pain, rage, and fear from men engaged in life-or-death struggle.

Diogo was the first to reach the top of the wall, and the Moors converged on him. He got one with a slashing thrust of his sword, a second was brought down by an arrow from Tome's bow, while Giovanni fell upon a third with his battle-ax, knocking him off the wall with a well-aimed blow.

A loud cheer erupted. When Tome looked down he saw that the great doors had been breached, and hundreds of Christians began pouring through, led by Prince Henry himself, who was thrusting, slashing, and hacking away with his sword.

Within minutes all the Moor defenders they had thus far encountered were subdued. The guns grew silent and the shouts died. The Christians, their knives, swords, and pikes stained with blood, looked in vain for more infidels to quell, but the defenders had abandoned the field. Those Moors who hadn't been killed or captured had joined with the remaining elements of King Fez's army to take refuge and defensive positions inside a fortified mosque. Though a major victory had been won in breaching the walls, the Christians still faced a formidable enemy. Prince Henry called his army together and began laying plans for the final siege.

"Burn it, sire," someone suggested. "Burn the mosque."

"No," replied Prince Henry, a chaste knight of mystical fervor. "I will not burn a place of worship."

"A place of worship? It is a place of infidels!"

"There is but one God," Prince Henry replied. "And He is God over us all."

"But how will we ever get them out of there?"

"We will get them out," the Prince insisted. "The advantage is ours now."

During that night, as the Christians slowly improved their own positions and moved their siege machinery and scaling ladders into place around the fortified mosque, the Moors realized that all was lost. At midnight they sent word that they wanted to surrender, and, to the cheers of his army, Prince Henry accepted.

"My fellow warriors for Christ," the *Infante* said, addressing his men, "the stain of my brother Fernando's martyrdom has been expiated. Constantinople is avenged!"

Prince Henry's terms were quite generous. His object, he declared, was the "service of God," not to take goods or to force a ransom from the defeated Moors. All he required of them was that they depart Alcácer immediately with their wives, children, and possessions. However, he added forcefully, they must leave their Christian slaves behind.

VENICE

As the gondola glided effortlessly down the Grand Canal, Aldo Cavalli looked out over the city of his birth. It was a city of incredible beauty, with its network of canals crossed by marble bridges, bordered by Gothic palaces, and overhung by villas and churches whose reflections stared back from the dark waters.

Rich, busy, and cosmopolitan, Venice saw a constant succession of revelries. Aldo, who had been back home for nearly a month now, was heading to one such celebration, this one at the palazzo of a very wealthy Venetian merchant, Marco Bellini.

Bellini's stately dwelling was one of Venice's showplaces. It sat well back from the canal, the intervening distance taken up by an elaborately designed garden. A broad path flanked by a geometrically shaped hedge wound past an ornamental pool. The garden was embellished with bronze statuary created by leading artisans of the city, and several peacocks strutted regally around the grounds, lending their raucous cries to the occasion.

Arrayed on the enormous loggia were linen-covered tables laden with hams, fowls, muttons, and various vegetables and fruit, food provided for the celebrants' hearty appetites. Several lutenists provided food for their souls, as well, and the lilting music greeted Aldo as he was helped out of the gondola by a servant. He started up the marble steps to join with others gathered in the garden, including his father and his host.

"Ah, Sandro," Marco Bellini said, "here is your illustrious son. He has come after all, despite your worry otherwise."

"It isn't that I was worried he wouldn't come," Sandro Cavalli replied. "I merely said that he has returned to Venice with such an independent mind that I couldn't say whether he would come or not."

"Well, the young man has a right to be of an independent mind," Bellini said. "After all, he has been most successful in the Guinea trade, has he not?"

"Yes," Sandro said proudly. "And he has done so with no help from me."

Aldo smiled as he joined them.

"Welcome, my young friend," Bellini said, offering his hand. "It is not often one gets the opportunity to congratulate a young man of but twenty years who has already made a vast fortune."

"It is most gracious of you to invite me, Signóre Bellini," Aldo said, shaking the merchant's hand.

As Aldo greeted Bellini, he caught sight of a young woman standing across the garden. She had blue-black hair, flashing dark eyes, high cheekbones, and the most beautiful smile Aldo had ever seen. She was talking to three other highborn young women, and though the three others were pretty, the one who had just caught Aldo's eye was like a rose among vegetables. Her beauty fairly robbed him of his breath.

". . . don't you agree?" someone said.

Realizing that he was being asked a question, Aldo pulled his eyes away from the beautiful young woman.

"I beg your pardon?" he said to the speaker.

"I said, it is a particularly lovely day, don't you agree?"

"Oh, uh, yes," Aldo said. "Excuse me, but do you see that young lady standing over there, near the pool? Could you tell me who she is?"

The man looked around. "Which young lady? There are three of them."

"That one—" The young woman Aldo had been eyeing was gone. "Never mind," he said.

He excused himself and walked up to the loggia, where he partook of the food and drink. The wine was Madeiran, and as he drank it, he couldn't help but think of the Da Costas, particularly the brothers, Tome and Diogo, who were off fighting the Moors.

"Aldo, perhaps you could settle an argument for us," a young man said, coming up beside him.

Aldo smiled. "I'll do what I can, but it has been my observation that most people who argue are so convinced in the rightness of their case that the matter can't be settled by soliciting a third opinion."

The other debater laughed and then said, "Normally that is true. But you more than anyone else here are uniquely qualified to address this issue. Therefore, we have decided that we will abide by your opinion, whether it agrees with ours or not."

"All right. What is the argument?"

"It has to do with the relative merits of ships," the first man said. "Now, I say that the Venetian galley, with its dependable source of motive force, is far superior to the caravel, which must depend for its movement upon the vagaries of the wind."

"And I say that the caravel, which does not depend upon the muscle of men, is the superior vessel," the other replied. "You have sailed on both. What say you?"

Aldo considered his answer. Knowing that Venetian merchants were great believers in the technical superiority of Venetian shipbuilders and craftsmen, if he said anything that could be construed as disloyal, they could take offense. On the other hand, he couldn't be dishonest about his feelings, and he was now very much a proponent of the caravel.

"There are admirable qualities about each of them," Aldo replied, being as diplomatic as possible.

"But you have settled nothing," one of the debaters said.

"I am sorry," Aldo said. "But settling which is the better ship is like comparing the relative merits of an apple and an orange." Suddenly he saw the young woman again, and she appeared to be looking at him. When he smiled at her, however, she glanced away. "Excuse me," Aldo said quickly. "There is someone I must see."

The two men bowed politely, and Aldo returned the gesture. He was about to make his way down from the loggia to the garden to where he had seen the beautiful young woman standing; however, she had disappeared again.

Damn! Who was she? And was she deliberately playing a game with him? It was maddening, and yet he knew that he had to seek her out and meet her, for she was, without doubt, the most glorious creature he had ever seen.

He began walking through the garden, his eyes searching everywhere.

"Aldo," a voice called, and he had to respond. It was his father.

"Yes, sir," Aldo said, going to the elder Cavalli's side.

"Aldo, I want you to meet some gentlemen who are crucial to our business," Sandro said.

He introduced them, but Aldo was so preoccupied with thoughts of the beautiful young woman that their names failed to register. He did manage to learn that they were important bankers and frequent customers of the House of Cavalli.

"So, have you finished with your adventuring?" one of the bankers asked.

"Of course he has," Sandro replied. "He has had a

fine adventure and has brought many rewards to our house. But now it is time to settle down."

"Oh, I hope not," Aldo replied. "There is still much to see in the known world—and much to discover in the unknown world."

Sandro frowned over the unexpected answer, but he didn't press the issue, and Aldo knew that he would not under these circumstances.

"I am, however, very much enjoying my time here," Aldo added quickly, partially for his father's sake, though there was much truth to the statement. If—or perhaps when—Aldo returned to Portugal to resume his adventures at sea, there would almost certainly be a confrontation with his father. However, Venice, with all its attractions and excitement, would hold his interest a bit longer, which would stave off the confrontation for a while.

Sandro's frown turned into a smile, and he put his arm affectionately around his son's shoulder. "He will be a great asset to the House of Cavalli."

"There!" Aldo said aloud, pointing. "There she is again! Father, who is that girl?"

Sandro looked in the direction Aldo was pointing, and this time the girl did not escape notice.

"Why, you know her, Aldo. That is Francesca Viviani."

"*That?*" Aldo said, shocked by the revelation. "That is Francesca?" The last time he had seen her, she had been a somewhat irritating child. "But I can't believe it! I thought she was—" He let the sentence hang.

"A little girl?" Sandro finished for him, laughing. "Well, in all your great adventures, have you not learned that little girls grow up?"

"Into beautiful women," Aldo said.

Sandro glanced at Francesca again. "Yes," he agreed. "Francesca is indeed a beautiful young woman. She is also betrothed."

"Betrothed? To whom?"

"Vitale Borgo."

"Vitale Borgo? I remember him. He is a somewhat

dim-witted fellow, as I recall, with a most unpleasant personality. Surely she doesn't love him."

"My dear Aldo, you have not been so long gone from Venice to have forgotten that when a union of two trading houses is made, love doesn't enter into the marriage. The House of Viviani wants to secure its relationship with the House of Borgo, that's all. Francesca is but an instrument of the arrangement."

Aldo sighed. "No, I have not forgotten. Or, rather, I *had* forgotten—until now."

"Yes, well, it's a matter done, so my advice to you is to not get interested in the girl."

"How can one not get interested when one has looked into those eyes?" Aldo groaned. He excused himself from his father and started toward Francesca.

This time she waited for him, a smile on her face.

"I didn't think you would notice me," she said when he came up to her.

"How could I not notice the most beautiful woman here?" Aldo replied gallantly. "Indeed, the most beautiful woman in Venice—in all the *world*."

"Good sir, such talk will sweep me off my feet," Francesca said, blushing.

"That pleases me, for that is just what I intend to do," Aldo said.

"No, young man, that is exactly what you will *not* do," Francesca's father said suddenly.

Coloring, Aldo turned. "Signóre Viviani! How do you do, sir?"

"I would do better, young man, if you would mind your place," Viviani replied.

"Father!" Francesca said. "Aldo was only being pleasant to me. We *were* childhood friends, after all."

"You are children no more," Viviani said coolly. "And it would behoove you not to seek each other's company. Have you forgotten, daughter, that you are to be betrothed to Vitale Borgo?"

"To *be* betrothed?" Aldo asked, his voice rising in hope. "You mean you are not yet?"

"In all but the formal announcement," Viviani said.

"Signóre Viviani, until that announcement I ask permission to call on your daughter," Aldo said.

Viviani shook his head. "It would serve no purpose." He put his hand on Francesca's elbow. "Good day to you, Signóre Cavalli," he said and led his daughter away.

In the week that had passed since encountering Aldo at the Bellini palazzo, Francesca tried putting him out of her mind. But it was impossible. After seeing him again, she was more in love with Aldo than ever—and she had to know if he was in love with her. Therefore, despite the risk, she sent word to him via her trusted maid and confidante, Maria Polesine, to meet her in the small garden house at the back of her father's *palazzo*.

Now, as she stood waiting for him, she wondered if she was making a big mistake. But when she saw him coming toward her, her heart raced in her breast, and she was certain that she had made the right decision.

"I thought perhaps you would not come," Francesca said, looking quickly around the garden to see if anyone was watching.

"Why would you think such a thing?" Aldo asked. "Would I not want to see the most beautiful girl in the world?"

"Could that be true?" Francesca asked. "In all your travels about the world, have you really seen none prettier than I?"

"None, Francesca, and I'll swear to that."

"Have you a sweetheart in Portugal?"

"No," Aldo replied, smiling. "I've no sweetheart in Portugal, Africa, or anywhere else I have been."

"Why, pray?"

"Why? Because I was waiting for you," Aldo said. His tone was playful, but what he did next was not. Without warning, he put his arms around Francesca and pulled her to him, crushing her mouth against his. At first she struggled, out of surprise and fear. She had never been kissed before.

Then the surprise changed to surrender, the fear to curiosity—and excitement. A pleasure, sweet and forbidden, began to overtake her. Her body was warmed with a heat she had never before experienced. The kiss went on, longer than she had ever imagined such a thing could last, and her head grew so light that she abandoned all thought save this pleasure.

"Francesca!" a woman's voice suddenly hissed.

Startled, the lovers broke their embrace.

"Signóra Polesine!" Francesca exclaimed. "What is it? Has someone sent for me?"

"No, but they will. The Borgos, young Vitale and his father, they are here."

"The Borgos?" Aldo asked.

Francesca looked at him with a pained expression on her face. "I fear I know why they have come. They want my father to give his consent for my marriage to Vitale."

"Is that what you want, Francesca?" Aldo asked.

"No!" Francesca said. "Aldo, it's you I—" She put her hand to her mouth to keep from saying more.

"Love?" Aldo asked. "Were you going to say that you love me?"

Francesca answered him with a nod.

"But can you have fallen in love with me in but a week's time?"

Francesca forced the words out. "I have not been in love with you for a mere week's time. I have been in love with you for five years—even before you left to sail with Alvise di Ca' da Mosto."

Aldo's expression was one of shock. "But you said nothing."

"And if I had spoken, would you have listened to the words of a thirteen-year-old child?" Francesca asked.

He smiled. "I suppose not." He sighed. "Besides, my story is no less improbable, for though I first took notice of you—as a woman, not as a girl—only last week, I know that I love you with all the depth of my heart, and I will not let Vitale Borgo have you."

"Very pretty words, Aldo Cavalli. But there is nothing you can do about it," a deep voice said.

Francesca gasped. The Borgos and her father had come upon them, their approach unnoticed by either the rapt lovers or their eager accomplice.

"Francesca," Carlo Viviani said sternly, "you are to go into the house immediately."

"Please, *signóre*," Maria Polesine said meekly, "do not be hard on her."

"I'll deal with you later, *signóra*," Viviani said, even more sternly. "And you, Signóre Cavalli, are not welcome at my house. Not now, not ever."

"Father, please!" Francesca begged.

"Go!" Viviani demanded, his voice nearly a shout.

"Francesca, don't worry," Aldo said. "Everything will be all right."

"Cavalli, shall I have my servants throw you out?" Viviani warned.

"You won't need servants," Vitale said, lifting his sword an inch in its scabbard.

"Vitale, if that sword leaves its scabbard, I'll kill you with it," Aldo said coldly.

It was well known in Venice that Aldo had proved himself in battle against formidable enemies. Vitale Borgo let the sword slip back down.

"He threatened me," Vitale said. He looked at his father and the others. "You all heard it. He threatened me!"

"Guards!" Viviani called.

"No need to call the guards; no one will be hurt," Aldo said. "I'll leave." He looked at Vitale. "But you will not marry Francesca," he added menacingly before turning and striding down the steps to the canal and the gondola waiting for him there.

"How much gold is in the sack?" the sailor asked. He was an unsavory-looking man, with a badly broken nose and several ugly scars on his cheeks. His companion was equally frightful looking.

"Enough for you to do the job," Vitale Borgo said. "And you can have anything you find on him."

"You want him beaten and robbed?"

"I want him *killed* and robbed," Vitale said.

The sailor eyed the young knave, then looked into the sack at the jumble of gold coins.

"I don't know," he said slowly. "Beating and robbing someone is one thing. Killing is another. Why don't you call him out and fight a duel? He *is* a gentleman, isn't he?"

Vitale hesitated. "I have no intention of fighting a duel with him," he finally said.

"And we have no intention of killing him," the sailor said, shoving the sack back. "Not for this amount."

Vitale scowled at the man. "How much will it take?"

"There are two of us," the sailor said, holding up his fingers.

"So?"

The sailor grinned slyly. "That means two measures of gold coin. One for each."

"Very well," Vitale agreed. "But hear me well: Aldo Cavalli is to be killed, and then I will never see either of you again."

The sailor weighed the two measures of gold in his hand, then handed one to his partner. Both men stuck the gold sacks into the waistbands of their breeches.

"You need not worry about that, *signóre*. After we complete our job, you'll never even know we existed."

Leaving the Cavalli warehouse after a full day's work, Aldo wandered to the docks, lost in thought, passing the dark, dank warrens full of whores and taverns that catered to the lowest level of sailors from the many ships that called on Venice. Many among Aldo's class had never, and would never, come this way. Aldo did so frequently because the foreign tongues and exotic aromas reminded him of the sea and an adventurous way of life.

Crowding the docks was a forest of masts on ships from all over the world. Aldo looked upon them as comforting and somehow more home to him than home itself.

"Well, now," came a low, grating voice from just inside a dark alley as Aldo walked by. "What have we here?"

The voice startled Aldo, the more so because of its

challenging tone. He stopped short, his hand moving to cover his sword.

"What do you want?" he asked.

His question was met by an evil chuckle. "Just your burden, *signóre*."

Two men emerged from the shadows, each carrying a sword. Aldo pulled his blade from the scabbard, assuming a stance for a formal duel.

One of the men, whose face bore ugly scars, laughed derisively. "Well, I do believe he wants to fight like a proper gentleman." The cruel smile left his face. "The only trouble is, *signóre*, we aren't gentlemen, so we don't fight like them."

As the first man was raising his sword hand, Aldo thrust toward him, flicking the point of his sword against his attacker's hand, jabbing it in about a half inch. His attacker let out a sharp yelp of pain and dropped his weapon.

The other attacker lunged forward. With the grace of a superior swordsman, Aldo turned toward his new assailant, then thrust his saber into the man's heart. The man dropped without a word.

"You've killed him!" the first attacker said, holding his bleeding hand. "You've killed my brother!"

Thinking perhaps that the man would launch a second attack, Aldo spun to face him again. However, the man turned and ran as fast as he could.

The repeated calls and insistent shaking of his father awoke Aldo from a fast sleep. "What? What is it?" he asked, sitting up in bed.

His father was holding the bed curtain open, a candle in his hand. His mother, Catalina, stood beside her husband, tears in her eyes.

"You must flee, Aldo. Tonight!" Sandro said in an urgent voice.

"Flee? Why on earth—"

"I have just been informed that the Council of Ten wants you arrested."

"The Council of Ten? Why? What do they want of me?"

"You are to be arrested for the murder of Antonio Sarducci."

"Is that the name of the man I killed tonight?" Aldo asked simply.

"My God!" Catalina gasped. "You mean you *did* do it?"

Aldo quickly explained what had happened, concluding, "It was clear that they meant to rob me."

"No, not rob you. Murder you," a female voice said from the darkness just outside Aldo's room.

Aldo recognized the voice as Francesca's.

"Francesca!" he gasped. "What are you doing here?"

"It was Francesca who brought word of the Council's plan," Sandro said. He turned toward her. "But what do you mean, the men wanted to *murder* Aldo? How do you know this?"

"It was Vitale Borgo's doing. He wanted Aldo murdered, but when Aldo fought back and killed one of his would-be assassins, Vitale and his hired killer instead went to the Council of Ten to report that Aldo is guilty of the crime of murder."

"That is preposterous," Aldo said. "Surely the Council will take my word over that of a wharf rat. What reason would I have to murder a common sailor?"

"They are going to testify that you approached them, offering to pay them if they would kill Vitale," Francesca said. "They will say that when they refused, you got angry and attacked them. Vitale is going to testify that he knows you wanted him dead, and that will give weight to the sailor's story."

"But they can't possibly believe such a ridiculous tale!" Aldo said. "I'm certain I can—"

"No!" Sandro said sharply. "If the Council rules against you, you have no appeal. They will execute you, and your body will hang for the crows to pick on. I won't allow you to take that chance." Sandro sighed. "As much as it pains me to say so, you must leave. Go back to Portugal."

"I won't leave Francesca," Aldo said.

Sandro gave a sad smile. "You don't mind leaving your father and mother, eh, but not this courageous young woman? Well, apparently you won't have to."

"What do you mean?"

"That is why I came personally, instead of sending word to you," Francesca explained. "I will not stay and be forced to marry Vitale. And never seeing you again would be too much for me to bear. I brought some of my things with me, Aldo. When you leave, I will leave with you. That is, if you will have me."

"Have you? Of course I will have you. I love you, Francesca."

Francesca gave a small cry of joy. "Oh, Aldo, how long I have waited to hear you say those words!"

Catalina took charge, steering Francesca out of the room. "Come, child. There will be plenty of time for pretty words once you are safely away from Venice. Aldo must not be distracted from what he must swiftly do, which is to dress and pack some valuables so that the two of you may pay for your journey." She looked back at her only son and smiled ruefully. "It would seem that the Cavalli men have more than just their heritage in common. Unlike your father, however, you, at least, will not be leaving Venice in chains—that is, not as long as there is a breath left in my body."

CHAPTER 16

FUNCHAL, MADEIRA

As was the custom, no priest was present at the actual ceremony that wedded Aldo Cavalli and Francesca Viviani, when the couple stood before a notary for the exchange of rings, but there were numerous witnesses. The fact that so many people came to the celebration, though neither Aldo nor Francesca was a resident of the island, was a testimony to the immense popularity enjoyed by the Da Costa family, who had taken Francesca in, treating her as their own daughter. For the marriage banquet, honoring the beginning of the couple's new life together, invitations went out to what seemed like every person on the island, and all of the guests contributed to the sumptuous feast. The wine, of course, came from the Da Costa vineyards.

The bride wore a gown made personally by Inês da Costa, who since childhood could sew with extraordinary skill. The dress consisted of a pale pink silk *gamurra*, whose open sides allowed the bloused sleeves to peek through, over which was worn a *guarnacca* of cobalt blue silk woven with gold threads and embroidered with gold flowers. A pearled wimple was draped over Francesca's blue-black hair, which was gathered into an elaborate knot.

When Inês had helped Francesca dress earlier, the younger woman had marveled at her dress and laughingly said, "It is as well that Aldo and I are being married here on Madeira and not back home. Surely such finery would violate the Venetian sumptuary law."

Though the Cavallis were not normally a showy family, Aldo was no less opulently garbed than his bride. His tight-fitting doublet was of a rich burgundy velvet, the hem embroidered with patterns of gold and the sleeves slashed to show the deep-blue silk blouse underneath. As the tight tunic displayed his narrow waist, so did the striped silk tights display his lean though muscular legs.

It was agreed by all that the couple were splendidly suited for each other.

Diogo da Costa, who gave Aldo the traditional slap on the back following the exchange of rings, laughed and told his friend, "Isn't this wonderful? Today we celebrate your marriage, and next week in Sagres we will celebrate mine."

"I am very happy for you," Francesca told her new husband's friend. "I do wish Luisa could have been here. I would have liked to meet her."

"You'll meet her soon enough," Diogo said. "And when you do, you'll love her as much as I. I know she'll love you, too."

"I'm sure we will be great intimates," Francesca said.

Diogo excused himself, leaving the bride and groom to greet others offering their congratulations. Aldo spotted an old friend and, taking Francesca by the arm, went over to speak with him.

"Giovanni Ruggi," Aldo said, smiling broadly. "What are you doing here?"

"I heard you were getting married," Giovanni replied. "But I didn't believe it. I asked myself, 'Who would have anything to do with Aldo Cavalli?' I mean, you *are* a Venetian, and everyone knows you can't trust a Venetian."

"Spoken like a true Genoese," Aldo laughed. "Giovanni, I would like you to meet my bride."

"The honor is mine, *Signóra,*" Giovanni said, making a leg.

" '*Signóra*,' " Francesca repeated. "That will take some getting used to." Staring at Giovanni with unabashed curiosity, she then asked, "Did Aldo say that you—you are Genoese?"

Aldo patted his bride's hand and told her, "Contrary to what you may have heard as a young girl growing up in Venice, not *all* Genoese have horns and a tail." He looked at Giovanni and laughed, adding, "Though a significant number of them do."

"Whereas everyone knows that all Venetians are born with a forked tongue so that they can speak from both sides of their mouth at the same time," Giovanni rebutted.

The two men clasped hands, and Giovanni noted, "I am told by Tome and Diogo that you will be expanding your fleet."

"Yes," Aldo replied. "Having been forced to leave home, I must now go into business for myself. Therefore I'll be adding another ship. Would you like to captain it for me?"

Giovanni's eyes grew wide with enthusiasm. "You would give me command of one of your ships?"

"Yes, my friend. I have been watching you for some time now. You are exactly the kind of man I would like to have in charge of my ship."

"Thank you, Aldo!" Giovanni said. "You will not be sorry for this. I promise you. I will be a worthy captain."

Aldo clapped his friend on the back. "Oh, I have no doubt of that. That's why I asked you."

SAGRES

Francesca Cavalli sat at a writing table in the bedchamber of her house—the one she had shared with Aldo for two months now—composing a poem. The hectic social schedule of a young woman coming of age in Venice had allowed her scant time to engage in such endeavors.

But she had all the time she needed now, for Aldo was away on another voyage, and she was left at home, alone, with a great deal of time on her hands.

I await your return, my sweet,
The sound of your voice so pleasing.
The touch of your lips will complete
A prelude to love's gentle teasing.

Just a short distance away, in their own house, Diogo and Luisa da Costa were undressing in their bedchamber, having just returned from a banquet. Luisa's handmaiden stood silently in the corner, waiting to attend her mistress.

"I wonder why Francesca has attended none of the festivities given of late," Diogo mused. "I would think that with Aldo away, such amusements would make the time pass more easily for her."

Luisa was removing a jewel-encrusted medallion, the latest expensive piece of finery she had purchased since she and Diogo were wed. "I should think that would be easy enough for even you to understand," Luisa replied tartly. "She hasn't attended because she hasn't been invited."

Diogo was sitting on the edge of the bed, struggling to pull off a boot. He stopped and, ignoring the barb, looked up in surprise and asked, "She hasn't been invited? Do you mean to tell me she hasn't been invited to *any* of them?"

"That's right," Luisa said. She tossed her necklace casually, almost carelessly, onto a jumble of jewelry lying on the table.

"I wish you would be more careful with your things, Luisa," Diogo scolded. "They are terribly expensive, yet you seem to have such little regard for them."

Luisa turned to glare at her husband. "Is that all you care about?" she asked. "How much something cost?"

"No, that's not all I care about," Diogo retorted. "But it wouldn't hurt for *you* to consider how much something costs before you treat it so irresponsibly."

"Really, Diogo. You carry on about money like a peasant. Money is of no concern to me."

"For someone who has no concern about money, you manage to spend a great deal of it."

"Do you intend to deny me the privileges of our rank?" Luisa asked, her tone acerbic.

"No, no, nothing like that," Diogo replied quickly. "I don't want to deny you anything, you know that. I just— Oh, forget that I said anything."

"I certainly shall forget it," Luisa said, stepping out of her gown. The young handmaiden immediately snatched it up—before Luisa could launch into a tongue-lashing—and put it away in the armoire.

Clad only in her chemise, Luisa sat down and began combing her hair with a bejewelled tortoiseshell comb. The chemise was loose fitting, and as Luisa combed her hair, her arm movement had the effect of bringing her breast almost entirely out of the garment, then covering it again. The unintentional action titillated Diogo to the point that he could no longer pursue the question of spending, even though, in less than two months' time, Luisa's extravagant ways were beginning to tell on his considerable fortune.

He returned to the earlier subject. "Why hasn't Francesca been invited to any of the banquets?"

Luisa put down the comb and looked straight at her husband. "Diogo, I know that Aldo Cavalli is one of your friends, but, really, friendship can only be stretched so far. I do what I can for Francesca, poor dear, but I'm afraid it is hopeless."

"But you still haven't answered my question. Why has she not been invited?"

"Well, that should be obvious, shouldn't it?" Luisa replied. She picked up a brush and returned to her hair. "Her family disowned her."

"But how did such information get out?" Diogo asked, puzzled. "I know that Aldo told very few people the story of their elopement."

Luisa quickly turned away from her husband, hoping he didn't notice her reddening face. "I truly don't know," she lied. "It got out, that's all. And decent ladies and gentlemen will have nothing to do with her."

"Then we must do something," Diogo insisted.

"Do something? What do you have in mind?"

Diogo smiled. "A great banquet," he said. "A huge banquet—bigger than anything Sagres has ever seen."

"And who is to give such a feast?" Luisa asked.

"Why, you, of course."

"I? Diogo, I can't possibly—"

"Of course you can. Luisa, my darling, you are expert at such festivities. I want you to stage a huge celebration."

"Such things cost money," Luisa said, her interest stirring.

"Spend all the money you need," Diogo replied. "Just make it magnificent."

The thought of staging a celebration grander than all others, even if it was for someone else, held tremendous appeal for Luisa, and now her eyes were sparkling with excitement.

"I will, Diogo. Oh, I will!" she replied enthusiastically. "This will be the finest banquet ever held in Sagres!"

"And Francesca will be the guest of honor," Diogo said.

"Yes, yes, of course," Luisa replied. Her mind was already racing ahead to the event itself, and she was so caught up in it that Francesca, though she was to be the guest of honor, was already being pushed aside.

Not since Prince Henry had built his city had there been a celebration of such magnitude in Sagres. The events held in the court paled before the extravagance brought forth by Luisa's ambition and vanity—and Diogo's rapidly dwindling fortune.

Luisa had a huge platform erected, the expanse covered by a canopy—elaborately festooned with flowers and garlands of greens—to protect the celebrants should the weather turn foul. Its wooden planking covered with fine tapestries, the platform was filled with tables and hung with rich draperies. There hundreds could dine, waited upon by a small army of servants.

Whereas one or two strolling musicians would serve at a function in Prince Henry's court, Luisa had a dozen. In addition to the musicians, guests were entertained by dancers, acrobats, and jesters. The tables were laden with huge platters of pork, lamb, fowl, and beef. Showing off the fact that her husband was a very successful trader, Luisa added several exotic dishes to the array: roasted haunch of zebra, glazed hippopotamus tongue, and curried ostrich eggs. Seeing that the display was met with the appropriate awed delight by her guests, Luisa felt that she had achieved her goal.

Or almost. Far from intending to honor Francesca Cavalli, as Diogo believed, Luisa intended to embarrass Francesca in front of the nobility of Sagres. Luisa was certain such elegance would be intimidating to Francesca, who, like a quiet little mouse, would go hide in a corner, meeting no one and saying nothing, thus ensuring complete social ostracism.

To Luisa's surprise and consternation, however, it soon became clear that far from being intimidated, Francesca was effervescent, completely in her element, gracious to all the important personages and never once giving any indication that she had been excluded by them from their celebrations. Joining a group of guests dancing to tunes played by the musicians, she performed many a fine turn, and her grace was lauded by the others.

By evening's end Francesca had received more invitations than she could possibly accept, many of them to intimate private gatherings—so exclusive that even Luisa, despite her rank, was not included. And by evening's end the young woman sulking in the corner was Luisa, eaten up with envy and jealousy and anger as she watched Francesca charm even the most aloof member of the court. *She*, not Francesca, was responsible for this gala banquet—a banquet that was, by everyone's account, the most sumptuous ever given in Sagres. But did so much as one person congratulate her for her efforts?

Answering her own question, Luisa was propelled into a deeper gloom.

For the remainder of the evening her mood did not improve, which went unnoticed by Diogo, who was pleased and excited at how well the event had gone for his good friend's wife. At the conclusion of the revelry he was certain that an inequity had been rectified, giving him a profound sense of well-being.

As Diogo and Luisa retired to their bedchamber, he exclaimed, "What a magnificent celebration! My love, you outdid yourself! Sagres will long speak of this event."

Luisa, sitting at her dressing table, had barely spoken a word since witnessing her plans going awry—though Diogo was too excited to notice her silence.

"And wasn't Francesca delightful?" he continued. "She won't be sitting at home alone anymore. Why, she has gone from being an outcast to the most popular woman in Sagres. Isn't that wonderful?"

Luisa turned to glare at him. "Really, Diogo, you don't know when to speak and when to keep quiet, do you?"

Diogo smiled. "Oh, I understand," he said. He walked over to stand behind her and, reaching down, cupped her firm young breasts. "After a success like tonight's, it's better to keep silent and celebrate some other way."

"Get away from me, you dolt!" Luisa screamed. Twisting out of his grasp, she pushed him away. Grabbing the first thing she could get her hands on—a rare porcelain vase—she threw it at him. It hit the wall and shattered, the bright blue pieces scattering about the room.

At first too shocked to speak, Diogo finally sputtered, "Luisa, what has gotten into you?"

"Get out!" Luisa shrieked. "Get out, get out, get out!"

Holding his arms in front of him to fend off any other missiles, Diogo made it to the door of the bedroom.

"My darling, I don't understand! Won't you at least tell me what is wrong?"

"No!" Luisa shouted, throwing her hand mirror at him. The mirror hit the floor and shattered in its frame. Lying propped against the wall, the fragments reflected Luisa's face—wild-eyed, nostrils flaring, lips in an angry snarl—in every jagged piece.

"I'll sleep in the chamber next door," Diogo muttered to his manservant, who stood ready to do his bidding, at a loss as to what had set his wife off—this time.

*   *   *

Francesca Cavalli was doing needlework when a rose suddenly landed on her lap. Startled and surprised, she looked around. Her young husband, smiling broadly, was standing just inside the doorway.

"Aldo!" she exclaimed, jumping up. Her needlework frame fell from her hands and clattered to the floor. She ran to his open arms, and he embraced her, picking her up and swinging her around.

"Are you pleased to see me?" he asked, though unnecessarily.

"I am happy beyond words," Francesca replied. "You've no idea how long I have looked forward to this reunion. I have been counting the days, hours, and minutes."

"I don't like reunions," Aldo said.

Francesca leaned away from his embrace so she could look into his face. "What? You don't like reunions?"

"No," Aldo said, smiling. "And we shall have no more."

Francesca's face fell. "But, Aldo, what are you saying? That you don't want to come home to me anymore?"

"I don't want to come home to you anymore . . . because I don't want to leave you anymore. Francesca, I have purchased a house for us—a very beautiful house much larger than this place—in Arguim."

"Arguim? The trading factory in Africa?"

"Yes. Oh, you will love it there, Francesca! It is the most exciting place in the world, filled with all manner of strange and wonderful things and visited by sailors from all the known lands and Negroes of every African tribe. You will come, won't you?"

Francesca laughed. "Of course I will come. I love you, Aldo. Don't you know that I would follow you to the ends of the earth?"

Aldo grinned. "Some people believe that Arguim *is* the end of the earth. Oh, Francesca, you'll be happy there, I promise you. It's quite primitive as yet, to be sure—

nothing at all like Sagres, much less Venice—but I will make you happy."

Francesca touched her husband's cheek. "Just being with you makes me happy."

"Are you *crazy*?" Luisa da Costa asked Diogo coldly. "Do you actually expect me to go to some—some Godforsaken heathen place to live in a straw hut with Negroes and wild animals?"

"You won't be living in a straw hut," Diogo replied. "Aldo told me there are several conventional homes there now, built by traders who have since left the region."

"Aldo told you."

"Yes. He and Francesca are going. Please say that you will go, Luisa. You like Francesca. You'll have a wonderful time there."

Luisa looked at him scornfully. "Oh, I'm sure I would," she replied. "We can sew together."

"Sew? Well, yes, I suppose you could if you wanted to," Diogo said, ignoring the sarcasm. "But the servants would most likely do that. You would be much too busy arranging entertainments."

"For the Negroes, I suppose," Luisa said dryly.

"Some Negroes would come to such entertainments, yes. They are tall, magnificent-looking fellows who are kings of their own people. But there will also be visitors from many other nations, for no matter who comes to Arguim to trade, they do so only with the permission of Prince Henry. Arguim is, after all, under the control of us Portuguese; therefore, those of us who are Portuguese bear a certain responsibility."

"And high station?" Luisa asked, beginning to show interest.

"High station? Yes, I suppose so," Diogo said.

"You say Aldo and Francesca are going. But they are Venetian. What would their station be?"

Diogo, blinded by love, replied, "What a true friend you are to Francesca, concerned for her privilege. Which is all the more reason you should be going. We will be of high enough standing to ensure that Francesca is well received."

"And just what would our standing be?" Francesca asked. "Who would be above us?"

"Well, the governor and his wife would be, of course," Diogo said.

"Who else?"

"I don't know, really. There are few dignitaries in the governor's court."

"Husband, would anyone there be from a higher social rank than my own?"

Diogo chuckled. "Now I see what you're getting at." He reached out to stroke Luisa's hair. "No, my dear. I am sure you would be second only to the governor's wife."

"I see," Luisa said, her eyes lighting up at the possibilities. "Diogo?"

"Yes, my dear."

"You do agree, don't you, that such a position would require new clothes and jewelry?"

"Luisa, be reasonable! You are spending all that we have on clothes and jewelry now!" Diogo sputtered.

"But if I go to Arguim with you, then I must have the appropriate wardrobe. You *do* want me to go with you, don't you?"

"If I didn't, we would not be having this conversation," Diogo replied testily.

"Correct me if I am wrong, but in Arguim you will make more money, will you not?"

Diogo sighed, then smiled and curled a ringlet of Luisa's hair around his forefinger. "Yes," he said. "I will make more money in Arguim."

Luisa smiled coyly. "And what is the money for if not to keep your wife happy?"

Diogo laughed aloud. "Very well, my dear, you win," he said. "Lord knows, I do want to keep you happy. Buy all the silks you need for new dresses, and I will have the jeweler's guild send around their finest pieces. Fill the ship with your wardrobe. I don't care what it costs, as long as it means you will go to Arguim with me."

ON BOARD THE *GOLDEN HAWK*

"Captain, sails!" Nigel Cooper called down through the hatchway.

Robert Denbigh, who had been at the chartboard in his cabin, put aside the dividers and stepped out of the door of his cabin into the dark shadows of the after-bay.

"Where away?" he called.

"Two points off the starboard bow, sir. It looks like there are at least three ships. Moorish corsairs, by the cut of the sails."

"I'll be right up," Robert said.

"Robert, is there a problem?" Lady Diane asked. She stood in the doorway of her cabin, which was next to Robert's, but a whisper away.

"It's nothing we can't handle," Robert replied with a smile. "But just to be safe, I'd better go topside and have a look."

Even as Robert sought to calm Diane's fears, however, he was having his own doubts. If all three ships decided to attack, there would be little he could do to fend them off, for they would have the advantage in numbers, firepower, and maneuverability.

The first mate was standing by the rail when Robert reached the deck. He handed Robert the spyglass he had been using.

"Over there, Captain," Cooper pointed out.

Robert peered at the distant ships through the glass; then he snapped it shut and handed it back. "Damn!"

"Which will we do, Captain? Fight or run?" Cooper asked.

"How much longer until sundown?"

"Just over an hour, sir."

"If I had my choice, Mr. Cooper, I would run," Robert admitted. "But as they have the angle on the wind, they will easily overtake us."

"Then we'll fight," Cooper said.

"Aye, Mr. Cooper. We'll fight," Robert replied. He sighed and looked back toward the hatch that led belowdecks. "Though with Diane aboard it is not the option of choice."

"Shall I run out the guns?" Cooper asked.

"Yes. And put musketmen in the shrouds and cross-bowmen at the rails. I want the pirates to see that they have not happened upon an unarmed merchantman. We won't make it easy for them. If they want to loot our hold, they'll have to pay the price."

"Aye, Captain," Cooper said, grinning broadly. "We'll send more than one of the heathens to meet their Allah before this is all said and done."

"What can I do to help, Robert?" Diane asked from behind him.

Robert spun around, surprised that she had come up on deck. "You heard?"

"Yes."

Robert took her in his arms. "Are you frightened?"

"Yes," she said quietly.

He lifted up her chin with his finger. "Good," he said. "If you're frightened it means you will stay out of harm's way."

"But I want to help."

Robert studied her face. "Very well," he finally said. "Do you think you're strong enough to help with the wounded?"

"Yes."

"Good. Then go to my cabin and assist the ship's surgeon, for that is where we'll set up to receive the aggrieved."

Diane gave him a quick kiss on his cheek. "God be with you, my love."

"God be with all of us," he murmured.

Diane hurried below to Robert's cabin and found that his door had been removed. One end rested on the small table where she and Robert took their meals; the other end was supported by a narrow desk that protruded from the wall. She saw also that a series of pegs and holes secured the door in place and realized that it had been designed to become an operating table.

The surgeon's sea chest sat beside the table, and he

now removed its tray. Closing the lid, he placed the tray on top of the chest so that all the tools were readily accessible—the saws, blades, and bone snips of his profession.

"Pardon me, miss, but you won't want to be here once the fighting gets started," the ship's surgeon told Diane.

"Captain Denbigh sent me here to assist you, Mr. Prouty," Diane said.

Matthew Prouty was a white-haired, kind-looking old man. He was unsure of his actual age but knew that he must be "over sixty." He had no surgical training and had been appointed to his present position solely because it was conceded that he had seen more arms and legs removed than anyone else on the ship. And as he had already removed a few himself—with no fatal results—he had won the confidence of the crew.

Prouty stroked the gray stubble on his chin and stared at Diane. The glint in his steel-gray eyes softened. "All right," he said. "If you've the stomach for it, I suspect you'll come in useful. We'll be needing the slops bucket."

"The slops bucket?"

"Aye, lass, the slops bucket. We'll need something for the arms and legs."

"Oh," Diane said, suddenly feeling a queasiness in her stomach.

"Are you all right?" the surgeon asked, peering at her face.

"Yes, yes, I'm fine. I'll get the bucket right away."

"Good girl."

Climbing back up the ladder, Diane crossed the deck, watching the crew getting ready for the upcoming battle. Ropes and grappling hooks had been brought on deck and laid out for easy access. Everyone had removed their shoes to keep the best possible footing on planks soon bound to be slick with blood, and those who had long hair had it tied back out of the way. The men were all in position, looking silently out toward the three approaching ships. The distance between the ships was much smaller now, and Diane knew that soon they would be close enough together for the battle to begin.

Locating the slops bucket, she took it belowdecks to

the surgeon. He put it in position under the table, then went over to a nearby chair and sat down.

"What do we do now?" Diane asked.

"Now, miss? Why, we wait."

Following Prouty's example, Diane found a chair. However, she was too anxious to just sit quietly and wait, so she left and went back up on deck to see what was happening.

What she saw horrified her.

"Oh, my Lord!" she gasped. The three Moorish ships were so close now that Diane could see the pirates standing along the rails and climbing in the shrouds.

The corsairs kept up a steady maneuvering, and the *Golden Hawk* answered the maneuvers turn for turn. Robert's men laughed and cheered at the tactics.

Diane asked what was going on, and Cooper explained, "The pirates are trying to get into position to fire a broadside at us, miss, but Captain Denbigh isn't allowing that. He's matching them tit for tat, keeping them always at the disadvantage."

Suddenly one of the Moorish ships fired off a cannon. A large stone crashed through the rail on one side of the *Golden Hawk*, passed cleanly across the deck, then smashed through the rail on the other side. It splashed in the water a hundred yards away, leaving behind broken timbers to mark its passage.

"Return fire!" Robert shouted, and all five guns of the *Golden Hawk* boomed loudly. The ship rolled back from the volley, and smoke billowed out so thickly that, for a moment at least, nothing could be seen of the pirate ships. When the smoke finally cleared away, Diane saw that their own broadside had done tremendous damage to one of the Moorish corsairs. Shattered spars and dangling rigging appeared in the hull, just under the bowsprit.

"We raked her, Captain!" Nigel Cooper shouted excitedly.

"Reload and fire again!" Robert ordered.

"Aye, Captain!"

One of the other pirate ships had taken advantage of the situation to get into position, and now it answered fire.

Several stone balls arced across between the ships, the distance rendering them into mere specks. Watching them speed toward the *Golden Hawk,* Diane was terrified. She momentarily had the irrational idea that they were all coming right for her, that they were going to converge on her chest, and she froze in fear and grabbed hold of a stanchion.

One of the stones curved downward, and then Diane heard the crash of timber as it smashed through the hull.

"Mr. Cooper, send a damage party to find the impact of the stone," Robert ordered. "If it hulled us at the waterline, we must make rapid repairs to keep the sea out."

"Aye, Captain."

The third corsair fired now, and four more stones crashed into the *Golden Hawk.* One hit a cannon and knocked it off its mounts. It fell on one of the gunners, instantly crushing him dead. Another ball hit the deck, sending up a dangerous shower of splintered wood, including a large, sharp fragment virtually the size of a stake that stabbed through one sailor's leg just below the knee, and he fell to the deck screaming in agony. The other balls crashed through the rigging, cutting rope and poking holes in sail.

Almost immediately after that volley came a second fusillade, this one from small cannon loaded with grapeshot and taken into the shrouds of the enemy ships. A cloud of grapeshot hit the deck of the *Golden Hawk* like a sudden hailstorm of iron pellets, and still another sailor screamed in agony.

"Miss, the surgeon's asking about you," one of the sailors said, and Diane, shaking herself out of her fearful stupor, went below, reaching the surgeon's side just as the first wounded man—the sailor with the chunk of wood protruding from his leg—was carried in.

The surgeon didn't even glance at the stake. Instead he began sawing through the leg just below the fragment, slowly, methodically, oblivious to the sailor's screams of agony. Suddenly Diane felt an overwhelming queasiness, then a giddy light-headedness, then nothing.

*   *   *

"How are you?"

Diane opened her eyes. It was dark—so dark that she could barely see Robert, who was sitting on the edge of the cot in her cabin. She tried to sit up, but he put his hand on her shoulder and gently but firmly pushed her back down.

"What happened?" she asked.

Robert squeezed her hand. "You fainted."

"Oh, I remember now. That poor man, he was in such terrible pain."

"He'll be all right," Robert said. "In a matter of weeks he'll be wearing a wooden peg, getting on almost as well as any of us."

They were silent for a few moments, and Diane remarked, "I don't hear anything. Is the battle over?"

"Fighting stopped when night fell," Robert explained. "My hope is that we can slip away from them in the dark."

"Will we be able to?"

"We can try," Robert said.

"I'd like to go up on deck," Diane said, sitting up again. This time Robert didn't protest.

"Are you sure you're up to it?" he asked.

"Yes, positive."

"All right. Fresh air might do you good at that," Robert agreed. "I'll go with you."

They climbed the ladder to the deck and stood there for a moment. There was no moon, but its absence seemed more than compensated for by the stars. They were spread across the sky in splendid glory, like thousands upon thousands of sparkling diamonds, scattered on the black tapestry of the heavens.

The first mate was standing near the rail, looking out into the darkness, and Robert asked, "How are we doing, Mr. Cooper?"

"They're still with us, Captain. Look."

Robert followed his first mate's finger and saw lights bobbing just above the sea.

"They're so confident that they haven't even doused their lanterns," Robert said.

"The heathen bastards," Cooper swore. "I'd like to run into them one ship at a time."

Robert stroked his chin as he stared at the lights on the pirate ships. "What I don't understand," he said, "is how they're able to follow us. I mean, there's no moon tonight, how are they doing it? If it weren't for the lanterns, we wouldn't see them at all." He shook his head. "Tell the helmsman to come due south."

"Aye, aye, sir," Cooper replied, leaving to transmit the order.

Diane shivered, and Robert put his arm around her. "Don't be frightened," he said.

"I'm not frightened now," Diane replied. She smiled at him. "Not as long as I'm with you."

"Diane, if we get out of this—" Robert amended his statement. "I mean *when* we get out of this, I'm going to put in at Madeira. I have friends there who can make all the necessary arrangements for us. I want you to be my wife."

"Why, Robert, I'm already your wife," Diane said, smiling up at him.

"You are in all the ways that count," Robert said, pulling her closer. "But you deserve to have it made legal, and if we can't get anyone in England to perform the ceremony, we'll get it elsewhere. That is, if you'll do me the honor."

"Nothing would make me happier," Diane said, pressing against him to kiss him.

"Captain, we're showing a light!" one of the sailors suddenly shouted.

"*What?*" Robert yelped, breaking off the kiss.

"There, sir, do you see it? The reflection is on the water."

Robert leaned out over the rail and looked where the sailor was pointing. At first he didn't see a thing because of the foam of the ship's wake. Then a change in the wave pattern moved the foam away, and there, shining brightly in the water, Robert clearly saw the reflection of a lantern.

"Damn!" Robert said, angrily. "Where the hell is that coming from?"

The sailor who had first noticed the reflection rigged a line to the rail. Then he climbed onto the rail and, holding on to the rope, leaned away to examine the ship.

"Captain, it's coming from your cabin," the sailor said.

"My cabin?" Robert replied. Suddenly he groaned. He remembered that the surgeon had asked permission to use a lantern and he had granted it, provided the windows be tightly sealed. But he hadn't said anything about the air scuppers, and the light was getting out.

"It's that fool surgeon!" Cooper said angrily. "I'll take care of him."

"No!" Robert called. He sighed. "It isn't all his fault. I gave him permission to use the lantern, but I forgot about the scuppers."

"Well, the least we can do now is put it out," Cooper said. "We've got better than an hour till light. Maybe we can still lose our escort."

"We've got to try, anyway," Robert said. "Tell the surgeon to douse the light."

"No, wait!" Diane suddenly called. "Don't put the light out!"

"Diane, I know you're worried about the wounded," Robert said. "But we don't have any choice, we must douse the light if we're to get away."

Diane grinned slyly. "No," she said. "Leave the light burning and it will *help* us get away."

"What do you mean?"

"We'll need one of the small boats," Diane said.

"What?" Cooper asked, confused.

A slow smile spread over Robert's face, and he nodded. "Get the boat," he ordered.

"This is the craziest idea I've ever heard, sir," Nigel Cooper said a short while later as they stood near the after-rail. "You think it'll work?"

Robert and Diane stood with Cooper and the rest of the crew, watching the glow of light behind them growing fainter as the distance between grew greater. A lantern had been tied to a pole affixed to the small boat, which had then been set adrift—a lure to hold the pirates at bay while they scooted off under cover of darkness. Robert had thought Diane's suggestion was a good one.

"We'll know soon enough," he said, answering Cooper's question. "If the Moors are still on our tail when the sun comes up, we'll know we didn't fool them."

By now, nearly every man of the *Golden Hawk* was on deck, anxiously watching the tiny, bobbing light. When it finally dropped below the horizon and disappeared from view, they let out a cheer.

"Hold your cheer, lads," Robert said. "We'll see if there's anything to celebrate when dawn breaks."

Robert walked back to the quarterdeck, and Diane came to join him.

"Do you think it will work?" she asked.

"I think we've got a good chance," Robert said. He smiled at her. "Putting the lamp in the boat was a brilliant trick, my girl. If we have escaped, it's because of you."

They stood at the rail, side by side and hand in hand, looking toward the northern horizon. To the east the sky gradually began to grow lighter.

"Captain! No sails on the horizon!" a lookout shouted down from the crow's nest. "It worked! We've outfoxed them!"

Cooper, admiration on his face, stepped over to Diane and looked around at his seamen. "Fellows, I'd say there's no doubt we've something to celebrate now. Three cheers for Lady Diane!"

CHAPTER 17

FUNCHAL, MADEIRA

The *Golden Hawk* was tied up at the wharf, its masts bare and its rigging hanging from the crossarms. It rocked gently back and forth as heavy barrels of wine were rolled up the gangplank, then across the deck to be stowed.

English ships like the *Golden Hawk* could call on Portuguese ports with trade goods such as wool and dye from their own country, and they could take aboard a cargo of Portuguese goods in exchange. But they were not allowed in the "Guinea trade," so there was little opportunity for them to make tremendous profits on the goods they did carry.

Robert said nothing to his Portuguese hosts, but he intended to ignore those restrictions when he again set sail and to carry on illicit trade where possible. Though he had in the past augmented his trading with selective piracy against the Moors—his one attack against a Christian ship had been an exception, for Usedimare's Genoese galley had set up a blockade and had been lying in wait for him— with Diane aboard ship he would carry out no piracy at all, contenting himself with trading. Even that enterprise carried an element of risk, however, as evidenced by the attack launched against him by the three corsairs just a few days before.

Although Robert had been a pirate, he had nothing in common with the Moorish corsairs. During the time he had been engaged in the profession of the "Gentlemen of the Sea," he always strictly adhered to a rule he had drawn up: Ships that asked for quarter were spared—once they were relieved of their cargo.

However, most pirates didn't follow such a rule, and with great frequency ships went out never to return. The cost of covering the shipment of goods was growing so high that shippers were beginning to complain that the only people able to get rich in trading were the insurance brokers.

When Pedro da Costa learned that Robert Denbigh had landed, he dispatched a messenger with a note inviting him to stay at his home while the *Golden Hawk* was in port. Robert sent back his thanks, saying that he would come if he could bring along "a friend." Pedro communicated back at once that of course Robert's friend was welcome.

When Robert and his "friend" arrived, Pedro and Inês, as well as their son and daughter-in-law Tome and Soledade, came out into the courtyard to greet them. At first Robert's friend appeared to be a slender youth. However, it quickly became obvious that it wasn't a boy at all, but a young woman dressed as a boy.

"Why, you're the one everyone is talking about!" Inês said.

Diane grimaced with embarrassment. "Everyone is talking about *me*?"

"Oh, my, yes," Inês said. "Everyone has heard of the English woman who has chosen to live on a ship disguised as a boy and about her clever ploy to escape from pirates. How is it you come to be dressed this way? And how did you devise such a plan?"

Diane laughed self-consciously. "As to your first question"—she glanced at Robert—"well, I fear the reason behind it is a long story; however, clothing myself in this way makes living aboard ship far easier. And as to your second question, I'm not sure how I came up with such an idea," she admitted. "I was so frightened that I could hardly think of my own name."

"Well, however you did, it was a good one," Pedro put in. "And such cleverness deserves reward. You must let us extend our hospitality to you for as long as you are on Madeira."

Diane's face fell. She looked at Inês's and Soledade's beautiful garb, then at her own shabby men's clothing, and shook her head.

"What is it, my dear? What's wrong?" Inês asked.

"Please," Diane said, "I cannot possibly impose myself on you dressed this way—and yet I have no other clothes."

"You have *no* other clothes?"

"I'm afraid not. Under the circumstances, I feel lucky to have even these."

"Exactly what circumstances are you talking about?" Pedro asked.

"It's a long story," Robert said. "Perhaps best told with food and drink."

"You can tell your story over the evening meal, if you wish," Inês said. "But in the meantime, I will find something for this poor child to wear. She certainly can't continue going around dressed like this."

Inês suggested that Soledade help select a wardrobe for Diane—which gained imperative when they learned of the marriage that was to take place between the English couple. Robert offered to help, but Inês wouldn't hear of it and, in fact, waved him away, insisting that what was going on now was "for women only."

Robert left the three women bustling about and went to the veranda, sipping wine and talking with Pedro and his older son.

"Diogo has gone to Arguim," Pedro replied in answer to Robert's inquiry.

"Ah, yes, Prince Henry's trading factory," Robert said. His face lit up eagerly. "Would that he would grant me a license to participate in the Guinea trade as he has done with so many Venetians and Genoese."

Tome shook his head. "I am afraid that that is absolutely out of the question," he said. "Even though the *Infante* is himself half English, he will never grant trading privileges to the English."

"I know," Robert said. He smiled. "But that won't keep me from trying to find a way to get in there. Diogo is there, you say?"

"Yes. He and his . . . wife," Tome said, unable to keep from scowling.

"His wife? I didn't know he was married."

"Sometimes, neither does his wife," Tome muttered.

"Tome!" Pedro scolded. "That is no way to speak of your sister-in-law."

"I'm sorry, Father," Tome said. "It's just that I can't stand to see my brother used by that woman he married. And that's just what she's doing to him."

"Perhaps things aren't as bad as you think," Pedro suggested. "After all, she did agree to go to Arguim with him. And Arguim is a far cry from Sagres. I can't imagine that she has a fine life there."

ARGUIM

The governor's residence was well attended for the banquet being held that evening. Emissaries from all the nations represented at Arguim were on hand for the festivities and food. Music, laughter, and multilingual conversation filled the brightly lighted hall.

Standing beside a wall, watching the revelers, were Diogo da Costa and his friends Aldo and Francesca Cavalli. Both young men had made very successful moves by coming to Arguim; where they had once attempted to outdo each other by the audacity of their explorations, now they were in an intense but friendly competition for trade—a competition that had been economically beneficial for both.

"Oh, Diogo, thank you for inviting us," Francesca Cavalli said, her eyes sparkling with excitement. "Why, this almost reminds me of—" The words trailed off, and her eyes grew misty. She turned away quickly.

"Reminds you of what?" Diogo asked, his own exhilaration rendering him insensitive to her dismay.

Aldo placed his hand on his wife's arm. "Venice," he said, answering the question for his wife. Then to Francesca he said softly, "I'm sorry. I know you want to go home."

"No!" Francesca exclaimed. "I *am* home. Wherever you are, my love, is my home."

"But you do miss Venice, don't you?"

"I miss the things that were," Francesca admitted. "I miss growing up in such splendor and I miss my once-loving family—though I have not yet recovered from the terrible wound of being turned out by them." She threw back her head and smiled. "But I do *not* miss being a cloistered maiden, nor do I miss Venice as it would be for me now. Besides," she said, taking in the tapestried and garlanded banquet hall with a sweep of her hand, "do we not have places just as splendid here? And I have your love, so what more could I want? No, worry not about me, Aldo. I am happy here—happier than I have ever been in my life."

"And speaking of happy, where is your bride, Diogo?" Aldo asked.

"I don't know where Luisa is," Diogo answered. "The last time I saw her, she was talking to Duarte d'Afonso."

"Who?" Aldo asked.

"Duarte d'Afonso. You remember him, don't you? He was one of the toadies in the court at Sagres. He's the great-great-nephew of King Afonso the Fifth."

"Oh, yes, I remember him now." Aldo smiled. "As I recall, he was one of your rivals, wasn't he?"

"I suppose he was," Diogo said. He grinned, gesturing at his chest. "But you see who won."

"What is he doing here?"

"Haven't you heard? Since my father-in-law has done so well with his ship, every nobleman in Prince Henry's court has decided to go into the business. Duarte is here on one of his father's ships."

"And how is he doing? As well as Filippo Strozzi?"

"No one is doing as well as Strozzi," Diogo laughed. "I only wish that I knew his secret."

"Don't we all," Aldo said. "He makes more in one voyage than any of the rest of us do in three. I have never known anyone who was as brilliant a trader as he."

"All this talk of business is beyond me, I fear," Francesca said. "If you gentlemen will excuse me, I think I will see if I can find Luisa."

"Yes, do," Diogo said. "You are her dearest friend. I am sure she will be happy to have your company."

"You are her dearest friend." Diogo's words echoed in Francesca's head. She wondered if he had just said that to be polite, or if he really didn't know the truth. Perhaps he *didn't* know. He was so slavishly devoted to Luisa that he saw none of her faults.

Ordinarily, Francesca thought, it was good for a husband to be so in love with his wife that he could see no failing in her. But Luisa's behavior in Arguim was so abominable that she was alienating everyone. Because of Aldo and Diogo's friendship, however, Francesca worked hard to maintain a relationship with the difficult young woman.

It was not easy. Contrary to what Diogo thought, Francesca Cavalli was probably the person Luisa Canto da Costa hated most. The irony was that Francesca was virtually the only woman left in Arguim who still tried to remain on friendly terms with her. Yet neither Aldo nor Diogo noticed the strain between the women. They were so blind in their friendship with each other that they didn't see the difficulty that existed between their wives.

Earlier, Francesca had seen Luisa climb the staircase that led to the bedchambers; though she had been watching for her, she had not seen her come back down. Perhaps Luisa had overheard the occasional unkind remark aimed at her and had gone off to sulk. If that was the case, she felt obligated to go to the wife of her husband's best friend and comfort her.

She went up the stairs and momentarily stood on the landing. It was eerily quiet, especially when compared to the gaiety that floated up from below. Throwing off her hesitation, Francesca turned right and walked down the long, shadowed hallway. She hadn't gone but twenty feet when she heard noises.

The sounds—moaning, or perhaps groaning—at first frightened her. She thought perhaps someone was in pain. But the groans were followed by murmured words in a woman's voice that sounded somewhat like Luisa's.

Curious, Francesca quietly opened the door to the room from which the sounds were coming, then gasped at what she saw. There on the bed, the bedcovers cast aside, lay the writhing, naked bodies of Luisa and Duarte d'Afonso.

"Duarte, oh, Duarte!" Luisa cried out. "Oh, yes, it is wonderful!"

Oblivious to their unexpected visitor, the couple grew more and more frenzied in their movements, their moans, and gasps. Then everything ceased. They lay spent in each other's arms, breathing heavily.

Francesca wished she could work a spell like those of the wizards she had heard of, one that would render her invisible. But of course that was impossible.

Then she had an inspiration. Taking a deep breath, she said loudly, "Luisa, everyone is asking about you."

Her voice filled the room. Luisa and Duarte froze for a brief moment, then scrambled apart. Francesca nearly laughed in spite of herself as Duarte grabbed desperately for the bedclothes, trying to cover his own nakedness as well as Luisa's.

"Francesca! My Lord, what are you doing here?" Luisa asked.

"I was looking for you—oddly enough, I was concerned about you. I heard noises and came to investigate. I did not mean to spy."

"And so now you cannot wait to run to my husband with the tale, I suppose?" Luisa said bitterly.

Francesca shook her head. "Have no fear. I will not tell."

"Oh, bless you, *senhora*," Duarte said.

"I must get back to the others," Francesca said. "I will tell them only that I found you and that you are about to rejoin the party." She looked sternly at Duarte. "I believe it would be best for you to leave now," she added.

Duarte chuckled. "Don't worry, I shall. This banquet has been quite . . . satiating," he said insolently. "I'll just slip out one of the side doors." He gave Luisa a quick kiss. "I'll see you on the morrow, my love."

"No!" Francesca exclaimed fiercely.

Eyebrows rising quizzically, Duarte stared at her. "No?" he repeated. "What do you mean, no?"

"I am not counseling you to leave only this . . . revelry, *signóre*. I am counseling you to leave Arguim. Immediately."

"I can't do that," Duarte said. "My cargo holds are hardly loaded. Are you suggesting that I sail with but a half-full ship?"

"Empty, half-full, or full, it makes no difference to me," Francesca said. "I strongly urge, *signóre*, that you sail at first light."

"Don't be foolish," Duarte said. "I have no intention of leaving now."

"If you do not, I shall be forced to tell Signóre da Costa of your dalliances with his wife," Francesca said with quiet determination.

"That will not be necessary," Luisa said quickly. "Duarte will leave on the morrow."

"But I can't—"

"You *will* leave," Luisa said.

Duarte sighed. "Very well. I will set sail with the morning tide."

Francesca nodded. "Excellent." Turning to leave, she paused and eyed Luisa. "I shall be waiting for *you* downstairs. I would counsel *you* not to keep me waiting long."

Giovanni Ruggi's caravel was a painted ship on a painted sea, its bright white, glaring yellow, and brilliant gold contrasting with the deep blue. As had happened when he had sailed with Antoniotto Usedimare, Giovanni was again becalmed in a vast, oppressive stillness.

For a full day now they had been deserted by the winds, and the sun that blasted overhead was pitiless in its intensity. The canvas hung lifeless, as if the ship were some living thing and the sails were its lungs, unable to take a breath. The sailors no longer feared that the sun would boil away the water, leaving them stranded on the bottom of the ocean; instead, they were utterly lethargic, ambling listlessly about the deck like sleepwalkers. They stared up at the sky, then the sails, trying to remember the sound of the wind in the canvas and the ropes at strain. It was a sound that no one heard when the wind was right but that everyone missed when the wind had died. Its absence left a hollow spot in their very souls, and they ached for it and tried to will it back.

Giovanni licked his finger and held it up, turning it slowly all the way around.

"Do you feel a wind, Captain?" Hector Ruis, the ship-master, asked.

"Not a whisper," Giovanni answered. He smiled. "But it'll be back before morning, I'm certain of it."

"If you're certain, Captain, then it will be so," Ruis replied.

"I'm glad to know you have such confidence in me. But perhaps you should remember that I'm not God."

"Maybe not, but you have His ear."

Giovanni laughed loudly. Still chuckling, he picked up his telescope and opened it to look at the ship that had been following them until the winds failed and then it, too, was becalmed.

"Who do you think it might be, Captain?"

Giovanni snapped his telescope shut. "I don't know," he said. "But from the shape of the sails she is definitely Portuguese."

"Good. These waters are full of pirates. It will be an advantage to have one of our own sailing with us. A lone pirate won't set upon two ships—and if there is more than one pirate, they might have second thoughts."

A sudden ripple of canvas made everyone look up in surprise to see the sails puffing out.

"The wind is back!" Giovanni said, grinning. "And we've someone to share the voyage with. It looks as if our luck is changing. And now, Signóre Ruis, I shall leave things in your hand while I take a nap. I haven't slept a wink since we were becalmed, and that was twenty-four hours ago."

"*Sim,* Capitão Ruggi," Ruis said. "Enjoy your nap. I will look after things."

Giovanni glanced again at the distant ship and saw that it was now under way and closing the distance between them. Suddenly, and for no explicable reason, he had an uneasy feeling about it.

"Signóre Ruis," he said, turning back to his shipmaster.

"*Sim, Capitão?*"

"Wake me when that ship is close enough to hail."

"*Sim, Capitão.*"

It being much too hot to go into his cabin, Giovanni found a small patch of shade on the poop deck. Lying down, within moments he was fast asleep.

Hector Ruis stood at the wheel, holding back, allowing the other ship to close on them. As the other caravel drew nearer, Ruis could confirm Giovanni's judgment that it was a Portuguese vessel.

"Senhor Ruis, it is nearly close enough to hail," one of the sailors said. "Shall I awaken the captain?"

Ruis looked over at Giovanni, whose slow, rhythmic breathing attested to how deeply he was sleeping. "No," he said. "Let him sleep. There is no need to bother him."

"*Sim, senhor.*"

The other ship drew closer, then closer still, until it was right alongside. Ruis waved at the helmsman of the other ship and his wave was returned.

Suddenly the sailors on the other ship threw back canvas covers to disclose five cannon. Ruis watched in horror as the cannon were touched off. A thunderous boom was followed by a billowing cloud of smoke. Chain and grape shot raked the deck of Giovanni's ship, shattering spars, cutting rigging, and ripping sails to shreds. A heavy stone shot crashed through the hull, just under the bowsprit.

Ruis looked over at Giovanni, who had been awakened by the tumult. Giovanni immediately started to stand, but a collapsing spar knocked him down again, and he lay sprawled—dead or unconscious, Ruis couldn't tell—on the deck.

Suddenly the pirate captain ordered his boarders across, and they swung over from the yardarms of their ship. Ruis stood on the poop deck, sword in hand, ready to fight. He noticed that one of the few crewmen to survive the fusillade was struggling to his feet.

"Here, *moco!*" Ruis called. "Up here with me!"

"Sim, senhor!" the young man replied, climbing the steps up to the poop deck, which was normally reserved for officers.

The young sailor stood back-to-back with the shipmaster as they attempted to fight off the boarders. The fighting was furious, and three of the pirates went down under the desperate slashes of the two defenders. Finally, however, a broadsword swung by a muscular pirate neatly severed Ruis's head from his neck.

The young sailor cringed in horror as his officer's head rolled across the deck in front of him. With his defenses down, three pirates easily thrust their blades into the youth at the same time. He collapsed, fatally wounded.

Giovanni regained consciousness at about that time and immediately realized that it would be unwise to make his presence known. Almost completely hidden by the sail and the spar, he wasn't obvious to the pirates and seemed to be the only one of his crew left alive. The pirates were prowling the deck, giving the coup de grace to anyone they suspected had any life left in him. Giovanni played dead.

One of the pirates standing nearby turned toward his ship, now tied alongside Giovanni's vessel. Putting a hand to his mouth, he called, "No one left alive over here, Captain!"

"Good job, men," the pirate captain said, climbing over the railing.

Giovanni's head was pounding from his wound, and he was fighting to stay conscious while at the same time remaining perfectly motionless. He opened one eye to a slit and saw the pirate captain standing less than three feet away from him. The man had his hands on his hips and was looking back toward the bow, which meant that his back was to Giovanni. Still, there was something about him, something dark and deep and painful. . . .

"Empty the holds," the pirate captain ordered. "Then set the ship afire and stave in the hull just under the waterline. That way we'll be sure she's destroyed even if the fire should go out."

It had been a successful voyage for Giovanni, and his hold was full of gold and pepper and nutmeg. The pirates were equally pleased with his success, laughing appreciatively as they transferred the hijacked booty. Giovanni wanted, with every fiber in his being, to get up and hack them to pieces, then throw them individually into the sea. But there was nothing he could do.

"That's it, Captain. We've cleaned out the holds."

"Good. Let's take care of the ship."

Thoroughly enjoying their work, the pirates set several fires; then three of them went down into the hold and knocked a hole in the hull. Moments later they came scurrying back up to the deck.

"We had best get off," one of the men said. "This vessel won't be afloat much longer."

The pirate captain was the last man to climb over the railing to his ship. Just before he did, he turned to have another long look around the ship he had just defeated— and Giovanni got his first good view of him.

The man was a little older, a little grayer, and a little heavier than Giovanni remembered. But the face, with its jagged purple scar like a lightning bolt, was the same evil face that had haunted his dreams for seven years. And he still wore the gold chain that Giovanni had given to his beloved, Iole Zarous—the chain he had watched this same man rip from her body.

Giovanni felt himself screaming with rage. He felt himself disentangling from the mangled sails and broken spars. He felt himself charging across the deck and putting his hands around the pirate captain's neck, squeezing, squeezing, squeezing, the ghastly countenance turning blue and the eyes bulging out. And finally he felt the pirate's windpipe crush under his grip. . . .

But he felt all that in his imagination only, for try though he did, he was unable to move. With a silent groan, he passed out again as the pirate captain abandoned the burning, sinking ship.

The *Golden Hawk* was heeled over under full press of sail as she approached the listing ship from the southwest.

"Mr. Cooper, what does she look like now?" Captain Robert Denbigh asked his first mate.

Nigel Cooper cupped his hands around his mouth to call up to one of the sailors high in the shrouds. "How is she doing?" he shouted.

"She's down by the bow," the sailor called back from the crow's nest. "Only the stern is above water."

"What about the fire?" Cooper called.

"No fire, sir," the lookout reported.

"I suspect the fire was forward and has been put out by the sea," Robert said.

"Aye, sir, I suspect so," Cooper replied. "What I don't understand is why she didn't go all the way under."

"There must be enough air trapped in the stern to maintain buoyancy," Robert suggested. He walked over to the rail and looked out toward the crippled ship, to which they had been drawn by the smoke.

"Hang on, lads," he said quietly, eyeing the caravel. "That is, hang on if any of you are left alive. We'll be there as quickly as we can."

Diane came over to stand at her husband's side. The

wind blew her hair across the front of her face, and she brushed it aside, bracing herself against the roll of the ship by grabbing one of the shroud lines, doing it as naturally if she had been going to sea all her life.

"Oh, Robert, do you think we'll find anyone alive?" she asked.

"I don't know, my dearest," Robert said, putting his arm around her. "But we'll know soon enough."

"Captain, if she's carrying any cargo . . . ?" Cooper asked hopefully.

"Aye, Mr. Cooper," Robert replied, turning back to his first mate and smiling. "If she's carrying anything, we'll transfer it to our own hold. 'Twould only be our due, don't you agree?"

"Aye, Captain, that it would be."

It took another half hour of tight sailing and maneuvering to close the distance. As they neared the caravel, the damage it had sustained was evident. The forward half was awash, while the after half was cluttered with wreckage. Bodies littered the deck, though some were already covered by the sea that washed over the deck, and it would be just a matter of time before they floated away.

"I guess it's all too obvious what happened, isn't it?" Robert said in clipped tones. "The bastard Moors who missed us were luckier with these poor souls."

"Aye, sir," Cooper replied, "I would say they were. 'Tis for certain then there'll be no cargo left."

"No, I wouldn't think so," Robert agreed. "Nor survivors, from the look of things." He sighed. "Come about, Mr. Cooper. We can do no good here."

"Aye, aye, sir."

"Robert, wait!" Diane called. "Look! Someone *is* alive!"

Robert looked where Diane was pointing and saw that, indeed, someone was moving.

"Belay that order to come about, Mr. Cooper!" Robert shouted. "Lady Diane is right. There *is* someone alive. Lower a boat!"

"Aye, aye, sir," Cooper replied, relaying the command. As the men lowered a skiff, Robert strapped on a sword and started amidships. "Are you going across, Captain?" Cooper asked in surprise.

"Yes."

"What if it's some sort of trap? You'd be safer here."

Robert laughed. "Mr. Cooper, if I wanted to live the safe life, I would never have put to sea. Lower the boat, lads," he called.

A couple of crewmen swung the small boat away from its davits, then lowered it to the water fifteen feet below.

"Robert, please, do be careful!" Diane called.

Robert smiled, then threw his bride a kiss as he grabbed a line and lowered himself into the small boat. The two sailors waiting there immediately began rowing over to the stricken ship.

When Giovanni Ruggi regained consciousness and saw the ship coming alongside, he first thought that it was the returning pirate. Then he saw the rows of shields grouped four across, decorated alternately with the Cross of Saint George on a silver background, a golden fleur-de-lis on a blue background, the Tudor rose on a green-and-white background, and the golden portcullis on a red background. Long forked pennants flew gaily from the mastheads, yardarms, and other parts of the vessel, and they, like the sails, were marked with the Cross of Saint George.

Giovanni suddenly realized that he had seen this very ship before. It was the English pirate, the same man who had spared him so many years before—the same man, in fact, who had steered Antoniotto Usedimare into the venture with Prince Henry.

But what was he doing here? Was he with the Genoese pirate who was sailing the Portuguese ship?

No, he couldn't have been. There had been only one ship before, and it certainly wasn't this one.

With a great effort Giovanni managed to get out from under the sail and spar and drag himself over to the railing.

He couldn't stand and walk, but then he probably wouldn't have been able to even if he hadn't been wounded, the angle of the deck was so severe.

He hung on to the railing, watching. As the skiff closed the distance, he recognized the man riding in the bow of the boat, the man with whom he had fought so many years before.

"Ahoy there," the Englishman shouted, speaking Portuguese. "Are you the only survivor?"

"Yes," Giovanni replied. "Have you come to finish the job?"

"Finish the job?"

"Have you come to kill me?" Giovanni clarified.

The Englishman shook his head. "No, my friend. If we wanted you dead, we would let the sea do the job for us. This ship hasn't long left."

"It was a good ship and a brave crew," Giovanni said sadly.

"Sir, I know you, don't I?" the Englishman said as the boat drew alongside. He narrowed his eyes as he studied Giovanni. "But you were much younger then."

"We've met," Giovanni acknowledged. "Under circumstances strikingly similar to these."

The Englishman shook his head again. "No, my friend. Not at all like this. As I recall, I left your ship undamaged and your crew unharmed. The man who did this obviously had no such compassion. Come with us. We'll see to your wounds and put you ashore in a friendly place. If you trust me, that is."

Giovanni felt his head beginning to spin and knew he was about to pass out. Nevertheless, he managed to force a weak grin.

"I trust you," he said. "I don't have much choice." He barely got the words out before everything went black again.

When Giovanni opened his eyes he knew he was on board a ship—but what ship? The pitch and roll of any vessel at sea had a particular feel; the smells of tar and teak and salt sea air were familiar; the sound of creaking wood, stretching rope, and air spilling from sails was the customary one. But everything else was unfamiliar. Where was he?

For a moment Giovanni thought he had been captured, and he sat up quickly. Too quickly, in fact, and his head started spinning and he nearly passed out again.

"Easy, easy; hold on there," a woman's voice said, speaking English.

"You—you are a woman!"

"You are correct," she said with an easy laugh. "My name is Diane Denbigh. I am the wife of the captain of this ship."

Confused, Giovanni looked around. "What ship is this?" he asked. "And how did I get here?"

"This is the *Golden Hawk,* and my husband and his men brought you here from your own ship."

"Do you not remember what happened to you, lad?" a male voice asked.

Giovanni put his hand to his head and felt the bandage. "I was—we were attacked," he said. "By pirates."

The sailor nodded. "Aye, that you were, lad, that you were. Captain Denbigh pulled you off the sinking ship, and Lady Diane has been treating your wounds like you was one of our own. But then, that's the way of it with our chief. I don't reckon you Portuguese fellas have run across many like our captain," Nigel Cooper remarked.

"I am Genoese," Giovanni corrected, remembering now the Englishman who had rescued him. "Where *is* your captain?"

"He's aft, where he should be," the first mate said. "He asked to be told when you was awake good enough to talk. Not ramble, mind you, like you been doin' for the last two days—but actually talk."

"Would you please go fetch the captain, Mr. Cooper?" Diane asked.

"Aye, ma'am. I'll have him here directly."

"Did he say two days?" Giovanni asked after the first mate had left. "Have I been here for two days?"

Diane smiled. "Actually, Mr. Ruggi, you have been with us for *three* days."

"How did you know my name?"

"You've talked a good deal. You haven't always made sense, but you have talked. If it isn't too painful, Mr. Ruggi, who is Iole?"

Giovanni sighed. "Iole Zarous," he replied. "She—she was the one I was to marry."

"Was?"

"She is dead. Killed by the same man who slaughtered my crew."

"Oh, you poor, poor man! To bring your love to sea, only to see her lost to pirates. How painful that must be."

"No!" Giovanni said sharply, so sharply that it startled Diane. "She was killed by the pirate, but he was not a pirate."

"Good sir, your delirium has made you irrational once again," Diane said with concern. "Your words make no sense."

Robert entered the cabin just then, asking, "So, how is our friend doing?"

"He is awake," Diane said. "But I fear that he is fevered anew, for he is speaking in riddles."

"Well, I must say he certainly looks better," Robert said. "How do you feel, my friend?"

"I'm somewhat groggy," Giovanni admitted. "Dizzy, too."

"It's no wonder that you are dizzy, after the blow you took on your head. And you haven't eaten in three days."

Giovanni smiled self-consciously. "That's it," he said. "I'm hungry."

"I'll have the cook bring you some porridge."

Giovanni grimaced. "Porridge? I'd rather eat paste than English porridge."

Robert chuckled. "Now you know our secret. English porridge *is* paste."

"Robert, hasn't the poor man suffered enough?" Diane asked, laughing. "Don't make him eat porridge. I'll prepare a soup for him."

"*Ah, grazie, signóra!*"

* * *

Giovanni sat on the edge of the bed, being spoon-fed the soup Diane had prepared for him.

"Do you feel well enough now to clear up the riddle?" Robert asked.

"What riddle?"

"You said your betrothed was killed by a pirate who was not a pirate. What does that mean?"

"Today he is a pirate," Giovanni answered. "But once he was a soldier, at Constantinople. It was there that he killed my beloved."

"Ah, yes," Robert said, clucking sympathetically. "We all heard of the butchery by the Moslems at that terrible battle."

"No!" Giovanni said sharply. "He was *not* a Moslem!"

"What? Not a Moslem, you say? Surely you don't mean he was a Christian!"

"Yes, a Christian, in Constantinople on a holy mission to defend the faith and the people of the city." Giovanni was quiet for a moment. "But he betrayed that faith. And those who sought assistance from him were instead killed by him."

Giovanni told his chronicle then, relaying the terrible events with such vividness that his listeners could almost hear the bloodthirsty cries of the triumphant Turks as they looted and plundered the defeated city and the screams of terror and piteous pleas for mercy of the hapless citizens.

And then came the part that was most terrible of all, of how Giovanni had gone to the home of Iole and her family to lead them away from the slaughter, only to face the unspeakable horror of finding their spitted bodies lying in the street. He saw his beloved, his Iole, her throat cut, flies crawling through the ghastly wound and in and out of her gaping mouth and across her half-open, unblinking, unseeing eyes. And there in the courtyard, covered with the blood of his victims and wearing around his neck a gold chain that Giovanni had given Iole, was her murderer.

"And he wasn't a Turk, he was Venetian!"

Giovanni spat the last words in hate and anger; then he hung his head, spent from the effort of having to relive by the telling of it such a calamitous part of his life.

Diane wiped tears from her eyes; Robert kept a stony silence.

Finally Robert said, "And now the Venetian has gone over to the Moslems to become a pirate for them. What unspeakable treachery that is."

"No," Giovanni corrected, "he does not serve the Moslems. He serves no one but himself."

"I don't understand. I thought you were attacked by pirates."

"He *is* a pirate," Giovanni explained. "But he is operating from a Portuguese ship."

Robert stepped over to the porthole and looked out at the sea. "Well, now, that explains much. In these treacherous waters the sight of another Christian ship is always an agreeable one. I can see how this Portuguese pirate—"

"He is Venetian," Giovanni interjected. "He is sailing a Portuguese ship, but he is Venetian."

"Venetian, yes," Robert said. "Well, I can see how this Venetian can close on his victims with such ease. He is welcomed as one of our own. But we'll be able to put a stop to his deception. As soon as we reach port, we'll report him to the authorities, and they'll be able to obstruct him soon enough. What is the blackguard's name?"

"I don't know," Giovanni replied.

"You don't know? But I thought you said you knew him."

"I didn't say I knew him; I said I recognized him."

"And you would know him if you saw him again?" Robert asked.

"Know him? Oh, yes, I would know him. I have his face burned into my memory. I'll never forget that face, never! Worse, he still wears the chain he stole from the neck of my beloved, my Iole."

"We will avenge your Iole for you, lad. And your crew," Robert said. He rubbed his hands together almost gleefully. "Prince Henry has not been as open to granting

licenses to us English as he has to you Genoese and Venetians. But if I bring him information as to who is doing the
piracy, I just might get one of those licenses. Lad, when I
found you, it was a lucky day for both of us. You shall be
my passage to Prince Henry's trading factory at Arguim."

CHAPTER 18

ARGUIM

In the two weeks since Francesca Cavalli had happened upon Luisa da Costa's indiscretion, Luisa, fearful that Francesca might yet betray her, had sought to counter any damage such tales would cause by being especially attentive to her husband. As well, she went to great lengths to be solicitous of the Cavallis, which pleased Diogo greatly.

"It gladdens me that you and Francesca have become even more congenial companions than ever," Diogo said one evening as they awaited the arrival of Francesca and Aldo.

"Yes," Luisa replied, "well, she is a gracious woman, and, of course, this remote place unites us even more in a common bond."

"That's what I've been saying all along," Diogo said.

After the meal that Luisa took special pains to oversee, Diogo and Aldo retired to Diogo's study to discuss mutual business arrangements, leaving Francesca and Luisa alone. With a wave of her hand, Luisa dismissed the hovering servants.

"Shall we go out on the veranda and look at the sea?" she invited. "It is so beautiful under the moonlight."

"Yes, thank you," Francesca replied. "I think that would be lovely."

Draping cloaks about them, the two young women went out onto the stone terrace to look at the moon's silver glow on the dark sea. They stood in silence for several moments before Luisa, unable to hold her tongue any longer, blurted out the question that had been plaguing her.

"When are you going to tell? I can't take this much longer!"

Francesca looked at her with an expression of surprise on her face. "Tell? Tell what?"

"You know what," Luisa said in an anguished voice. "When are you going to tell Diogo that you discovered Duarte and me in a—a compromising situation?"

Francesca looked back at the sea. "Please," she said quietly. "Put your mind at ease. I have no intention of telling anyone. Most of all Diogo."

"But surely you aren't serious," Luisa said. "This is your opportunity to ruin me. I know how much you hate me. Why don't you do it?"

"I have no desire to ruin you, Luisa," Francesca said softly.

"But you hate me," Luisa said. "Surely you hate me as much as I hate you. Believe me, if the situation were reversed, I would have told immediately. By now you would be gone, disgraced forever by your action."

Francesca sighed. "Yes, I've no doubt you would tell." She smiled. "Fortunately, you will never discover me in such a situation, because I will never *be* in such a situation. But you need not worry about me, Luisa, for my lips shall remain sealed."

Luisa's small, brittle laugh was totally without mirth. "Oh, I understand now," she said. "I understand perfectly. You just want me to worry. Yes, that's it. You'll keep quiet while I torment myself with worry until one day, when I least expect it, you will tell everything. Is that it?"

"I will never tell."

"Am I supposed to believe that your silence is due to your great love for me?"

Francesca smiled sweetly. "Oh, no. I have no great love for you. I don't hate you as you seem to think, but I have no love for you. I do, however, love my husband. And my husband's affection for Diogo is so great that he would be affected by Diogo's pain."

"Of course, that's true, isn't it?" Luisa mused. "Diogo would be shattered by such news, and that would, as you say, hurt Aldo as well."

"Yes."

"And you, ever the loving wife, would do anything to spare your husband such hurt," Luisa continued.

"That's right. Now you understand why your secret is safe with me."

Luisa suddenly smiled triumphantly. "Yes, I understand it all quite perfectly now. Which makes for a very interesting situation. Because, you see, like it or not, Francesca, you have just become my accomplice."

The young Venetian woman was confused. "Your accomplice? I don't understand."

"Oh, but you should," Luisa said. "Thanks to you, I can now see anyone I please, take as much pleasure as I please where I please, and not worry one whit about Diogo discovering my infidelity. And, my dear Francesca, it is forever incumbent upon you to do all in your power to keep my indiscretions secret from him."

Francesca gasped. "That is not at all what I intended! And if you are serious about pursuing this path, there is every possibility that Diogo will learn of your unfaithfulness."

"Well, then it is up to you to see that he doesn't find out, isn't it?" Luisa said, too sweetly. "Now, if you will excuse me—I think I shall go see if Diogo and Aldo are finished with their business discussion. After all, I must show Diogo that I am his devoted wife."

She turned and walked back inside, leaving her companion standing alone on the veranda.

Francesca felt like weeping at the injustice of it all.

But Luisa was right. She would do everything she could in order to keep Diogo from being hurt. She had no choice.

Across town, Captain Filippo Strozzi was sitting at a table in a waterfront tavern. He was drinking wine and ogling the three winsome young black women the proprietor was parading before him. All three were naked, their skin glistening from the palm oil that coated their well-formed bodies.

The young women were prostitutes, a trade they had been forced into by their master, the shop owner, who sold their services just as he sold wine and food. Two of the girls had accepted their fate, and they preened and posed for Strozzi, hoping to be the one he chose, for their master always gave them some slight reward if they pleased their customer. The third young woman was still a newcomer, and she was bitterly unhappy with her lot. While the other two twisted and turned provocatively, she remained perfectly still and stared at the ground, as if such inaction would render her invisible.

In truth it had just the opposite effect; while the other two faded into the obscurity of sameness, she, by her indifference, became conspicuous. His interest piqued, Strozzi smiled and pointed at her. The two girls who were not chosen pouted and quickly walked away. The third young woman began to weep, and her nude body shook with silent sobs.

Ignoring her sorrow, Strozzi hustled the girl into a small, dreary room the innkeeper provided for just such a purpose. When the Venetian took her a few moments later, he took her savagely, hoping to intensify his pleasure through her cries of pain. He was denied that gratification, however, because the girl suffered his attack in complete silence. Angered by her lack of response, Strozzi was even more brutal.

When at last he had satisfied his lust, he fell across her, spent from his efforts, his foul breath hissing into her ear. She lay quietly, listening until his ragged breathing smoothed into the rhythm of sleep.

As soon as the girl was sure Strozzi was asleep, she quietly and carefully moved out from beneath him. The sounds of revelry from the main room of the tavern filtered into the room as the girl snatched an ill-fitting coarse dress that hung from a hook on the back of the door and threw it on. Then she padded across the room, which was illuminated only vaguely by light coming in from outside, climbed through the open window, and dropped to the ground outside. She waited for a second, expecting to be challenged, but when no challenge was issued, she skulked away from the tavern, then ran quickly through the night, choosing the back streets and alleys that led to the distant palisade.

The wall had been built by the Portuguese to protect the trading factory from the encroaching jungle as well as from any warrior tribes that might be lurking therein. The girl belonged to one of those selfsame tribes, and once outside the walls of the trading fort she knew that she would have to run for only an hour or so before she would be safely back in her own village.

Suddenly she heard voices, and she stifled a gasp. She was too far away from any structure that would offer concealment, so she did what she had frequently observed animals doing: She froze. Despite the terror-driven pounding of her heart, she remained absolutely motionless as two armed guards came walking by, passing no more than thirty feet in front of her. They abruptly stopped, and the girl, certain that she had been seen, expected them to come rushing over to her and drag her away. Then she realized that they had stopped only so that one of the guards could relieve himself. He did so, the other guard made some guttural comment, both laughed, and then they continued on their way, oblivious to her presence.

Only when the guards were out of sight and beyond hearing did the young girl dash to the palisade. Through an almost superhuman effort she managed to scramble up the wooden stakes and clear the top, landing in the soft ground on the other side. She then forged across the river and into the trees, heading toward her village, feeling the wind in her hair and the cool grass beneath her bare feet.

The pain and humiliation she had suffered were gone now. She was free.

"Capitano! Capitano! Wake up! Wake up!"

The sailor's shouts and the banging on the door finally got through and, like a cork surfacing from beneath the water, Strozzi regained consciousness. He threw his arm across the bed to reach for the young woman he thought was still with him. When his arm found nothing, he woke up fully oked around in anger.

Where the hell was she? He had paid for the entire night—and the night wasn't over until he was out of bed. He would be taking this up with the tavern owner. Suddenly he smiled. Perhaps he could use this as an excuse for another night with the young girl, this time without having to pay for her services.

"Capitano! Capitano Strozzi!"

With a groggy head and a tongue fuzzy from the amount of drink he had consumed the night before, Strozzi got out of bed and padded over to the door. Jerking it open, he found his first mate standing there.

"What is it, Remilio?" Strozzi asked irritably. "Why are you banging on my door at this hour of the morning?"

"We have trouble, *Capitano,*" Remilio said. "Very great trouble."

Grunting, Strozzi walked back from the door and, by that action, invited his first mate in. Remilio followed him over to the bed and stood by, obviously very nervous, as Strozzi began putting on his clothes.

"What sort of trouble are you talking about?" Strozzi asked as he reached for his breeches.

"Do you remember the ship we saw?" Remilio asked.

"Hell, man, be more specific. What ship? We were at sea for weeks. We saw *many* ships."

"Not many like this one, *Capitano.* It was the one we spotted as we were sailing away from our last, uh, engagement."

Strozzi's foggy brain instantly cleared. He recalled that as they were leaving their last victim sinking and in flames, the sails of another ship had appeared on the distant horizon. He glared at his first mate.

"Are you certain?" he asked.

"I'm positive," Remilio said. "You recall how I climbed to the top of the mast to more clearly observe the other ship through the spyglass and saw that it was an English ship."

"Yes, I remember."

"That ship is coming in to port now. *Capitano,* you must know that if we saw them, they saw us. And that means they will know that we are the—"

"Watch your tongue, man!" Strozzi barked. Then he lowered his voice. "We are in a public place here. Suppose someone overheard your words? Would you have us all drawn and quartered?"

"*Scusa, signóre,*" Remilio said, shuddering at the thought. "But what are we to do?"

"I don't know yet," Strozzi said. "Hold your tongue and let me think."

"*Sì, signóre.*"

Suddenly Strozzi got an idea. "Remilio, has the English ship dropped anchor?"

"Not yet, *Capitano.*"

Strozzi smiled. "Good, good. When it does, we'll be waiting for it."

"We?"

"Yes," Strozzi said. "You and I—and the local authorities. Remilio, we are about to do our duty. We are going to the authorities with the news that the pirate who has been terrorizing the Guinea trade is none other than the English captain."

"But do you think the authorities will believe us?" Remilio asked.

Strozzi laughed. "Why shouldn't they? You were certain that they would accept the Englishman's accusation against us, weren't you?"

"Yes."

"And you are right, they *would* believe it. For they are looking for someone—anyone—to blame for the high losses. Such people will believe whoever makes the first accusation. Therefore, it is incumbent upon us to carry the tale to the authorities before the English ship even arrives. That way no matter what the Englishman might say, he will be disbelieved simply because everyone will think he is merely trying to wriggle out of trouble."

"Yes," Remilio said, grinning now, "we will be the accuser rather than the accused."

"Precisely. And now come along, Remilio. It is time we did our civic duty, you and I."

Robert and Diane Denbigh stood on the quarterdeck of the *Golden Hawk* as it slipped into the bay at Arguim. More than two dozen ships were riding at anchor there, and though their masts were free of sail, colorful pennants and flags flew from every line and staff. Glancing to the shore, the couple saw a number of buildings—houses, government buildings, and warehouses—fighting for space along the harbor, while the docks and the shoreline teemed with activity. Beyond the trading city lay the lush green jungle, so filled with birds that their cries and squawks could be heard even at this distance.

"Oh, Robert, isn't this the most exciting place you have ever seen?" Diane asked.

"It certainly is," Robert said. He put his arm around Diane's shoulders and pulled her to him. "And it will be even more so when we're granted a license to trade here."

"What if Prince Henry won't grant us the license?" Diane asked.

"And why wouldn't he, I ask? After all, we did save one of his own captains, albeit a Genoese, not a Portuguese. Besides, we come armed with the information the Portuguese need to stop the pirate who's been preying on their ships. I think they'll be particularly interested to learn that he is a Christian, not a Moor. No, I'm certain, Diane, that we'll have no problem getting a license to trade. It is only our just reward." He laughed. "In fact, the only problem I foresee is that they will be treating us like such heroes that we'll have a difficult time getting away to carry on our business."

"I hope you're right," Diane said.

"Of course I'm right," Robert replied. He pointed then to a skiff being rowed across the bay, filled with a number of armed men wearing the brightly colored uniform of the constabulary. "Look there. Unless I miss my guess, that's an official escort, coming to bring us greetings from the authorities. Mr. Cooper?"

"Aye, Captain?"

"See to our visitors."

"Aye, Captain," Cooper said, stepping to the railing.

The boat pulled alongside the *Golden Hawk*, and as the first mate issued instructions to his crewmen, the visitors scaled the ladder and came aboard.

"Who is the captain of this vessel?" one of the uniformed men asked.

"I am," Robert answered, stepping forward. "Robert Denbigh at your service, sir. This is my wife, Lady Diane, and my first mate, Nigel Cooper. Do you represent the governor?"

"I do. Is the entire ship's complement on deck, Captain Denbigh?"

"Aye," Robert answered, somewhat puzzled.

The governor's representative nodded at his men, who quickly drew their arms, stepping into position to cover all the crew.

"Here!" Robert shouted loudly. "What is this? What are you doing?"

"Captain Denbigh, as representative of His Excellency the Governor, who holds his appointment by the sufferance of His Majesty, Prince Henry, I hereby place you and your entire crew under arrest. Under that same authority, I hereby take possession of this ship and all cargo and equipment aboard her."

Robert let out a long, slow sigh. "All right, gentlemen, I understand now. I know what this is all about. You are arresting me for sailing into Portuguese waters without proper papers." He smiled engagingly. "But, I pray thee, wait until you learn why I'm here before you pass your final judgment. I rescued one of your own captains from a sinking ship, and I am merely returning him to you. And, if

His Majesty sees fit to present me with trading papers as a small reward, well, I could be persuaded to accept them."

"Captain Denbigh, you and your entire crew are under arrest for piracy on the high seas."

"*What? Piracy?*" Robert shouted. "Are you mad?"

"Place him in manacles," the governor's representative said.

"Wait a minute!" Robert said. "I'm no pirate. I rescued one of your men from—"

"Silence him," the official ordered, and someone near Robert hit him over the head with a club. Robert dropped to the deck, unconscious.

"Robert!" Diane screamed and started toward him, only to be restrained by one of the soldiers.

"Round up the others and take them ashore," the official commanded, and before the sailors could even begin to react, they were all prisoners.

Held fast by one of the soldiers, Diane could do nothing except stand in shocked silence as she witnessed what was going on around her. Looking at her husband's crumpled form, she feared that he was dead, but she took heart when he moved and began to groan.

"What about the woman, sir?" the soldier who was restraining Diane asked.

The official eyed her at length. "Stay on board with her," he finally ordered. "I'll be back to tend to her personally."

"Yes, sir," the soldier said, grinning. "Over there, *senhora,*" he ordered, pointing to a box where he wanted her to sit.

Too frightened to do anything but follow the soldier's orders, Diane complied. The other soldiers took Robert and his hapless crew with them as they began rowing ashore. When Diane looked down at the small boat, she saw that it was loaded with so many of her husband's crew that she feared it might capsize. Their captors had the complete advantage. Were the crewmen to try anything, the boat would be swamped, and as they were all in chains, they would surely lose their lives. As a result, they sat very quietly as the boat was rowed across the water.

Like Diane, the guard watched the boat as it worked its way toward the shore. When it was nearly halfway there, he turned from the rail to look at Diane, giving her a leering smile.

"Well, now," he said, tugging at the codpiece over his leggings. "It seems you and me are here all alone."

"There has been a terrible mistake made," Diane said, her heart beginning to pound. "As soon as the governor learns the truth, my husband and his men will be released."

"Do you think so?" the guard asked.

"Yes, of course."

"Well, no matter," the guard replied, coming up to her. "Even if they are released, it'll take long enough, I wager." He grabbed for her breast.

"No!" Diane said, jerking away from him. "Get away from me!"

"Scream if you want," the guard said. He grinned evilly. "I like it when the women scream."

"Please," Diane whimpered.

"And I like it just as much when they cry." He chuckled. "Do whatever you wish. There's no one to hear you."

"*Wrong*," a voice suddenly said.

Startled, the guard spun around. A man was standing at the hatch.

"Giovanni!" Diane said. "Oh, thank the Lord!"

"Who are you?" the guard asked, puzzled by the unexpected appearance of another man. "I thought all the crew went ashore."

"I'm not one of the crew," Giovanni Ruggi said. "I was captain of my own ship—a ship that was attacked and destroyed by pirates. This ship rescued me."

"Do you expect me to believe that? Do you expect anyone to believe that?" the guard snorted. "You are but one of the crew who escaped arrest, that's all. And now you are trying to pass off the same story as the others."

"Look at this wound, sir," Giovanni said, pointing to his bandage. "Do I look like I am making up a story?"

"You look like a fool to me," the guard rejoined.

"Get off this ship," Giovanni ordered. He started

toward the guard, but dizziness overcame him, and he staggered, then reached out a hand to keep himself from falling.

"Giovanni, you are still weak," Diane said. "You shouldn't be walking around!"

The guard chuckled. "She's right. Here. These will help you stay put." He removed a pair of manacles from his belt and tossed them at Giovanni. They fell to the deck at Giovanni's feet with a loud clank. "Put those on," the guard ordered.

Giovanni shook his head as if ridding himself of the dizziness, then started toward the guard again.

The guard's smile broadened, and he pulled a large knife from its sheath. "*Senhor*, you don't listen as you should. Now I shall have to teach you a lesson."

Though weak and unarmed, Giovanni nevertheless took a fighting stance.

"Giovanni!" Diane shouted, and she pulled a knife from the folds of her dress and threw it toward him. It stuck in the planking of the deck, quivering and twanging.

The guard looked at her, surprised. "Were you saving that for me?" he asked.

"I was," she replied.

He sneered. "You should have kept it. For after I cut this fool's heart out, I'll be coming for you."

Giovanni pulled the knife from the boards, then crouched slightly, holding out the blade in his right hand, the point moving menacingly back and forth, slowly, like a cobra about to strike.

The guard slid in, raised his left hand, feinting with his knife. When Giovanni instinctively raised his left hand to block, the guard's arm slashed down with incredible speed, and his knife went in under Giovanni's arm. The blade burned like a hot iron along Giovanni's ribs, opening a long gash that spilled blood down his tunic and over his leggings.

Summoning up his soldier's training, Giovanni fought back the pain. He brought his left hand up sharply, and the knife that the guard was holding loosely—so confident was he that he was victorious—was knocked away from the man's grasp. Giovanni jabbed quickly with his right hand, sending his blade into the guard's diaphragm, just under the ribs.

They stood that way for a few seconds, Giovanni twisting and gouging, making sure his thrust was fatal, trying to stay on his feet against the pain burning across his ribs. The guard's eyes began to dim. Then slowly he crumpled, expelling a long, life-surrendering sigh as he did.

When Giovanni felt him falling, he turned the blade edge up, letting the guard's body disembowel itself by its own weight. When the guard hit the deck, he flopped twice, like a large fish gaffed from the sea. Then he lay still, his blood and bile staining the deck bright red and brackish green.

Giovanni stood over at him, holding his hand over his own wound, trying to stem the flow of blood that continued to spill.

"We have to get out of here," he said.

"Giovanni, you are badly hurt!" Diane said, starting toward him. "Let me tend to your wound."

Giovanni waved her away. "No time now," he said. "We must get away before they come back. Help me launch the boat."

They began the task of launching the skiff. It was a heavy boat and normally required at least two able-bodied men to get it swung down and into the water. Now the task was being done by one badly wounded man and a woman who had never attempted such a thing. Remarkably, they quickly—albeit awkwardly—succeeded. Equally remarkably, Giovanni managed to scramble down the rope ladder and situate himself in the skiff, after which Diane followed. Giovanni began to row, though each stroke seemed to make the blood flow all the more.

"Where are you going?" Diane asked, noticing that the boat wasn't approaching by the shortest route.

"To the house of my friend Aldo Cavalli."

"He can help us?"

"I certainly hope so. For one thing, Aldo owned the ship I lost to the pirates. But even were that not so, Aldo Cavalli would be the person I would most want to see now." He smiled. "It is so ironic. In my greatest peril, I seek the aide of a Venetian, a people long the enemy of the Genoese. However, I have learned not to judge the worth of a man by his nationality, but rather by the character of his soul."

Aldo Cavalli was sitting in his garden, working on his books. He couldn't help but chuckle as he worked with the several columns of numbers. How he had rebelled against this task in his youth. How he had longed to be strutting upon the quarterdeck of a ship at sea, rather than bent over a table of figures. And yet he was now thankful for those early years of instruction, for he had learned by experience that a great deal of business was, indeed, keeping the books.

At least these were his books, he thought, and not his father's. And that meant that when they showed a profit, it was a result of his own enterprise. And when he showed losses, he need feel no guilt for letting his father down. The losses were his and his alone to sustain.

"Senhor Cavalli?" The man who summoned Aldo from the gate of his garden was a black man who spoke the Portuguese of his original captors. The man was Aldo's servant, however, not a slave. Virtually all of Aldo's peers owned slaves as household staff, and many of them scorned Aldo for his insistence on having freemen. Aldo had persisted, however, and now few people made mention of it.

"Yes?" Aldo asked, looking up from his ledger.

"Capitão Strozzi is here to see you," the servant said.

Aldo sighed. He disliked Strozzi so much that he seldom saw the man, even during Strozzi's frequent and lengthy stays in Arguim. The wonder of it all was that once there was a time when Aldo had actually found Strozzi and his stories amusing.

"Did he say what he wanted?" Aldo asked.

"No, *senhor*. Only that he needed to speak with you on a matter of the greatest urgency."

Aldo chuckled. "Everything Strozzi does is of the greatest urgency. Very well, show him in."

When Strozzi came into the garden a few moments later, he was waving his arms around in great agitation.

"Have you heard the news?" he asked.

"The news? What news?"

"The pirates," Strozzi said. "We have captured the pirates! Would you believe it? They are English!"

Aldo shook his head. "The pirates who attacked me weren't English. They were Moors."

"Yes, yes, I'm sure there are Moorish corsairs out there," Strozzi said dismissively. "But haven't you thought that Moors couldn't account for the high losses our shipping has been sustaining?"

Aldo nodded. "The thought has occurred to me," he admitted. "And you say they are English? Where were they captured? What happened?"

"Why, they sailed into the bay, just as pretty as you please," Strozzi said. He beamed proudly and pointed to his chest with his thumb. "*I* am the one who went to the authorities and pointed them out."

"Oh? And how did you know who they were?"

"Because I saw them," Strozzi said. "On my last voyage we saw the English ship attack a Christian vessel. We tried to get there in time to help, but it was too late. The pirates had already sunk the Christian vessel and sailed away before we could do anything about it."

"You did rescue the men of the sinking vessel, did you not?" Aldo asked.

"We tried to," Strozzi said. "Unfortunately they were all gone by the time we arrived. Not one soul survived. And, of course, by then the English ship was too far away for us to pursue. But when it came into the bay this morning, I recognized it soon enough. Remilio recognized it as well and went with me to inform the proper authorities."

"Strozzi, I am curious. Why is it that you have just now spoken of this?" Aldo asked.

"I was ashamed," Strozzi replied. "I didn't arrive on the scene in time to help the poor sailors of the sinking ship, and when I gave chase to the pirate, he eluded me.

Since I had not managed to change the outcome of events, I saw no purpose in discussing it."

"But you changed your mind this morning?"

"Yes. When I saw the English ship sailing into the bay just as bold as you please, I felt I had to do my duty."

"Do you know who the Englishman is?"

"He has said his name is Robert Denbigh," Strozzi said.

"Robert Denbigh? Isn't he the man who is sailing for Tom Giles of Bristol?"

"Yes, I believe he is," Strozzi replied.

"But no, he can't be the guilty party," Aldo said. "I could never believe that of him—certainly not that he would attack other Christian ships."

"Perhaps it's time you did believe, Aldo," Strozzi said. "The last ship he attacked was one of your own."

"Mine?"

"Do you not have a ship due?"

"Yes," Aldo replied. "But as you well know, it isn't unusual for a ship to be many days—even many weeks— beyond its intended schedule."

Strozzi put his hand out on Aldo's shoulder and looked him squarely in the eyes. "I'm sorry to have to tell you this, my friend. But your ship will not be arriving in a few days, a few weeks, or even months. For the ship I saw sinking was one of your own."

"But you've said nothing before now," Aldo said, puzzled by Strozzi's late information.

"I'm sorry," Strozzi said. "But as there were no survivors, I sought to spare you the pain."

"No survivors," Aldo repeated. He sighed. "Poor Giovanni. How proud he was to have command of a ship. And now he is gone?"

"They are all gone," Strozzi said. "But we have the guilty ones imprisoned now. The governor intends to send them back to Portugal, but there is some question as to whether they will ever leave Arguim alive. There are many who want to see that justice is done right here."

"And I suppose you are among that number?" Aldo asked.

"Yes, I am," Strozzi admitted. "Why send them back to Portugal for punishment when we traders are the aggrieved parties? I say we should execute them right here in a public display. And as it was your ship they attacked and sunk, I would think you'd agree with me."

"I don't know—"

Aldo's reply was interrupted by his servant's sudden shout.

"Here! This is a private garden! How did you get in here? You can't go back there!"

"But I must!" a woman's voice said. "I must see Mr. Cavalli."

Puzzled, Aldo stood up and started toward the source of the commotion. "Let her in," he called to his servant.

"*Sim, senhor,*" the servant replied, and when he stepped aside, a beautiful, obviously distraught woman came running up to him.

"Please, Mr. Cavalli, you must help us," she said.

"Who are you?"

"I am Lady Diane, wife of Robert Denbigh."

"The pirate," Strozzi said.

"No! He is not a pirate!" Diane said sharply. "He is not a pirate, and I have proof."

Strozzi chuckled. "You have proof? What sort of proof?"

"I have a survivor from the ship that was attacked," Diane said. "He will swear that my husband was not the pirate, but rather the man who rescued him."

"You have a survivor?" Aldo asked. "Where is he?"

"He is here, with me," Diane said. She looked back over her shoulder. "By the gate. He has been badly wounded and has lost a great deal of blood. He is weak—so weak now that he can barely stand, and I fear that he may soon die. Please, come talk to him, listen to his story so that someone can witness for my husband."

"All right," Aldo said. "If he is a survivor from my ship, I *would* like to talk to him."

"It is a trick, Cavalli," Strozzi warned. "You are wasting your time. The woman is obviously lying. There were no survivors. The ship burned."

Diane looked at Strozzi in surprise. "How did you know the ship burned?" she asked.

"Because I was there."

"You?" Diane said. "You were there? Then you must be . . ."

"The pirate?" Strozzi asked, with an evil laugh. "Do you really think anyone will believe you if you call me the pirate? I was there looking for survivors, but there were none. I saw only a burning ship and your husband's ship, sailing away after having committed the foul deed."

"Well, we can clear the matter of survivors up soon enough," Aldo said. "Come, let us talk to the man you have brought."

"Believe me, he is no one," Strozzi said. "An imposter. There were no survivors."

Aldo and Strozzi followed Diane back through the garden, around the high, sculptured hedgerow. There, sitting on a stone bench just inside the gate, holding his hand to his stomach, was Giovanni Ruggi. Aldo was at first delighted to see him; then he saw that Giovanni had bled profusely and was probably near death, and his joy changed to despair.

"Giovanni, my dear friend!" Aldo shouted, running to the wounded man.

Giovanni weakly reached his hand up and rested it on Aldo's shoulder. When he looked into Aldo's face, Aldo saw that his eyes were clouded with pain. His face was drenched with sweat, and he appeared to be hanging on to life by sheer effort of will. He smiled at Aldo.

"I knew I could live until I saw you again," he said.

"What has happened, my good friend?"

"You must go to the authorities," Giovanni said. "They are making a mistake. The Englishman is *not* the pirate."

"Don't listen to him. He is crazy from the pain and the fever," Strozzi said.

Giovanni looked at Strozzi then, seeing him for the first time.

"*You!*" Giovanni screamed.

An incredible transformation took place. The eyes

that had been clouded with pain suddenly cleared—shining with recognition—then burned with hate. This same hate gave him the strength to stand up when, but seconds before, he could barely sit up.

"Giovanni, what is it?"

"The scar! The chain!" Giovanni said, pointing at the gold chain Strozzi wore around his neck. *"Assassino!"* He pulled his knife from his belt and started toward Strozzi, but Aldo reached out to stop him.

"Wait!" Aldo said. "You're in no condition to—"

Suddenly there was the flash of a sword blade as Strozzi lunged forward, plunging his sword into Giovanni's heart. Giovanni died in Aldo's arms.

"Strozzi! What have you done?" Aldo screamed. "You have murdered my friend!"

"It wasn't murder," Strozzi countered. "You saw him. He was a madman. He came after me with a knife. I had no choice. I had to defend myself."

"No, I don't think so," Aldo said. "I think you killed him to keep him from saying more. It *was* you, wasn't it? You were the one who attacked my ship. That's how you've been so successful. You aren't a brilliant trader—you're a pirate!"

A look of resignation, then challenge, washed across Strozzi's face. "So what if I am?" he asked. "No one is ever going to find out. They'll draw and quarter the Englishman and his crew in the public square, and everyone will be happy that the pirates have been taken care of—and I'll go my own way."

"What makes you think *I* won't reveal the truth?" Aldo asked, incredulous that Strozzi was so open with his admission.

Strozzi chuckled. "Because you won't be alive," he said simply. He was still holding the sword in his hand, its blade red with Giovanni's blood. "I'm going to kill you."

"What do you say, Aldo?" another man's voice suddenly asked. "Do you want me to kill him for you? Or would you like to borrow my sword?"

Aldo looked around and saw Diogo da Costa coming toward them. "Diogo!"

"I came to tell you about Robert Denbigh, to see if there was anything we could do about it," Diogo said. "I was lucky enough to get here in time to hear Strozzi's confession."

The expression of confidence left Strozzi's face, and he took a couple of hesitant steps backward, still holding his sword in front of him.

"What about it, Aldo? Who gets to kill this bastard? Me or you?"

"If you don't mind," Aldo said, "I would like the privilege."

"My pleasure," Diogo said, and, smiling, he tossed over the sword.

"Why, you insolent little pup," Strozzi said, regaining some of his confidence. "I was killing my first man when you were still peeing in your swaddling clothes. Do you truly believe you're a match for me?"

Strozzi lunged for Aldo, but Aldo parried his thrust easily, then counterthrust. For the next several moments the garden rang with the clang of steel upon steel as the blades crossed and clashed, thrust and parried.

Strozzi was the bigger and stronger of the two, and he took advantage of his size. He could press forward and, with pure power, force Aldo to abandon his position so that Aldo was unable to use his superior grace and finesse. The intensity of the exchanges was also beginning to tell on Aldo, and with each clash of the blade he could feel the ferocity all the way to his shoulder. The sword seemed to weigh more and more so that it was getting difficult to even hold it up, let alone use it to parry Strozzi's slashes and thrusts.

"Ask for quarter," Strozzi shouted over an evil laugh. "Ask for quarter; I might give it to you."

"Like you did the men on the ships you pirated?" Aldo replied, his words now coming in gasps.

"Yes," Strozzi said.

"Like the girl you killed to get the golden chain?" Diane shouted.

Strozzi laughed. "Ah, so he actually knew about that, did he? I wondered what he was talking about. You know the story I used to tell of the man holding a girl's severed head in one hand and her golden chain in the other?" he asked Aldo. He laughed. "Well, in fact, I wasn't being completely truthful. Actually, her head wasn't removed from her shoulders, and it wasn't a Turk who killed her. It was me," he bragged, all caution gone now.

Whether Strozzi was distracted by talking or just got careless, Aldo didn't know. However, suddenly there was an opening where none had been before, and, summoning all his strength, he lunged. Strozzi reacted too late to block. Aldo's blade penetrated flesh, and he shoved it all the way in. Strozzi's eyes reflected surprise, then pain, then nothing, clouding over with death even before he fell.

Pulling out his blade, Aldo stood panting, the sword hanging at his side. Diogo came rushing up to him, as did Francesca, who had been drawn out of the house by the sound of clanging blades. She flung her arms around her husband, tears of relief streaming down her face.

"Please!" Diane begged. "Now you must go and help my husband!"

"What say you, Diogo?" Aldo said, reluctantly pulling himself from Francesca's embrace.

"Were you wounded at all?"

"No," Aldo replied.

Diogo smiled. "Then let's go save an Englishman."

ONE YEAR LATER

Answering the wind, the caravel tacked eastward. To the north of their course was the verdant coast of Africa. Diogo da Costa, the shipmaster of the vessel, stood at the larboard rail, watching the coastline slide slowly by.

Of the three young men who had set out to expand the limits of the known world, only Diogo was still true to his ambition. His brother, Tome, was back on Madeira with his wife and their young child, already staking his place, independent of his father, as one of the leading citizens of Madeira.

Diogo missed his brother's companionship, but he

could find no fault with the path Tome had chosen. After all, Tome was happily married to a wonderful woman whose support had made his success possible. Perhaps if Diogo's own marriage had been more successful, if Luisa had been a little more . . . Diogo let the thought die.

Luisa, still the most beautiful woman Diogo had ever known, had returned to Sagres, which was, he supposed, unfortunate in one way. The younger Diogo had been so blinded by her beauty that he had closed his eyes to the fact that in choosing a wife, there were far more important things to be considered than physical beauty. Now he was trapped forever in a loveless marriage. Still, he decided philosophically, it was this loveless marriage that allowed him the freedom to follow his dream. Tome, had his beloved Soledade. Aldo Cavalli, *his* love at his side, had returned to Venice to take his place beside his father in the House of Cavalli and forced Francesca's family to accept her marriage. Diogo, on the other hand, had only the shell of a union. And now circumstances had made that shell far more important to Luisa than it was to him.

The conditions under which Luisa had returned to Portugal were much different from those under which she had left. Then her father had been a man of rank in Prince Henry's Court. Now Gonzalo Canto was in disgrace. Though he hadn't been found guilty of collusion with Filippo Strozzi, the suspicion that he had been somehow involved in Strozzi's piracy was still so strong that he was forced to vacate his position in the court. He was a broken man, living quietly on the subsistence provided him by his son-in-law. It was ironic that Diogo, once ostracized by Luisa's family as being beneath them, was now their sole means of support.

As a result of her precarious position, Luisa had become, at last, the ever-faithful wife. She was well aware that whatever standing in society she had was gained only by the wealth and prominence of Diogo da Costa. She had once lamented that she had ever consented to marry him, the son of a peasant father and a stained, though well-bred, mother. Now she had no intention of giving up her status as Diogo's wife. When he informed her that he would be sailing again, this time with Pedro de Sintra, a new explorer who was taking up where such men as Gomes and Usedimare and Cadamosto had left off, Luisa had no choice but to acquiesce meekly. On the day the ship had left, she even dutifully came down to the shore to see him off.

And now, with Tome back in Madeira and Aldo in Venice, Diogo, alone of the three intrepid young explorers, was still pushing at the outer boundaries of the known world. However, rather than feeling triumphant over the others, he felt more as if he had the obligation to carry on their collective dream, and he intended to record every sight, sound, and impression of this voyage, the better to share it with his brother and his friend.

"Well, my young colleague, what do you think now?" Captain Pedro de Sintra asked, coming up to stand alongside his second-in-command. "Have we found the passageway to the riches of the Orient?"

"I don't know," Diogo replied.

"You don't know? Why, we are sailing east, aren't we?"

"Yes."

"We haven't been able to sail east before because the continent of Africa has been in the way. Am I correct?"

"Yes."

"And is the Orient, and all the riches and spices it offers, not east of Portugal?"

"That is correct as well," Diogo agreed.

"Then how can you say that we are not sailing under the bottom of this great obstacle?"

"I have a friend," Diogo said, "an Englishman—"

"The man they thought was a pirate? The one you saved from execution?"

"Yes, the same. He has told me a story that was told to him by *his* friend, Tom Giles of Bristol."

"Yes, Tom of Bristol, I know of him as well. And what tale did this Englishman tell?"

Diogo pointed to the coastline. "According to Tom Giles, we are not sailing around Africa. We are sailing beneath a great projection. After we go so far, the coast of

Africa will start south again. Then we must sail around that, before we can truly start for the East."

"How does he know such a thing?" Sintra asked.

"He claims to have made the journey."

De Sintra smirked. "Does he, now? And upon what ship would he have made such a cruise?"

"No ship," Diogo replied.

"No ship? Then how was this journey made?"

"By foot. He walked it."

Sintra laughed uproariously. "And you believe him?"

"I don't know. I do believe that he took a journey of some magnitude. He was a friend of my parents, and they believe him. But that was a long time ago. He was young, afoot, and, perhaps, bewildered. It could be that we are indeed now at the southernmost tip of Africa. And if so, we really are on our way."

"And if not?" Sintra asked.

"If not?" Diogo turned and looked up at the sails of the caravel. "Then we have the satisfaction of knowing that we have sailed farther than any ship before us. And we have the dream of new horizons ahead."